OSCAR FROM ELSEWHERE

To my godsons, Connor and Louis, and
their lovely families, and to my Charlie

This is an Arthur A. Levine book

Published by Levine Querido

www.levinequerido.com • info@levinequerido.com

Levine Querido is distributed by Chronicle Books, LLC

Library of Congress Control Number: 2021952614

ISBN: 978-1-64614-202-6

Printed and bound in China

Published November 2022

First Printing

OSCAR
from
ELSEWHERE

by

JACLYN MORIARTY

LEVINE QUERIDO

MONTCLAIR · AMSTERDAM · HOBOKEN

THE MONDAY AFTER

OSCAR

MONDAY MORNING, I was sent to Mrs. Kugelhopf's office.

She's the deputy principal.

"Write a report," Mrs. Kugelhopf commanded, "accounting for every day you were not at school last week."

"Monday, Tuesday, Wednesday, Thursday, Friday," I replied, counting on my fingers. "Five days."

Mrs. Kugelhopf nodded.

I nodded back.

Mrs. Kugelhopf's office has a view of the wheelie bins. Her walls are the color of green grapes that have gone slightly moldy.

Hunching her shoulders, she shuffled her chair closer to her desk. She didn't look well, to be honest, but that was her emotions. She lets them get the better of her. "You will sit outside my office today," she informed me, "and you will write that report."

"What report?" I said.

"The report accounting for the days you were not at school last week!"

I gave her a careful look. With teachers, you never know how much education they have.

"*Monday, Tuesday, Wednesday, Thursday, Friday,*" I repeated slowly. "*Five days.*"

She nodded. I nodded.

"Five days *altogether*," I added, to be helpful.

We were stuck then. She looked at me.

Put her elbows on her desk, clasped her fingers together, and rested her chin on the thumbs. A little shelf made of thumbs.

"Do you understand what you are going to do?" she asked.

Big question, but I gave it my best shot.

"For my career? Play rugby league for Australia. For lunch today? Bolognese from the canteen. Next weekend? Well, I'm thinking—"

"*Oscar*," Mrs. Kugelhopf interrupted.

Her chair is a big leather palace of a chair. Mine was a spindly little wooden one. Two other wooden chairs were lined up beside me, ready for other kids to get busted.

Right now, those chairs looked nervous. Sitting there, trying to be quiet.

"I meant *now*!" Mrs. Kugelhopf cried. "What are you going to do *now*?"

"I'm on an in-school suspension," I reminded her kindly.

Mrs. Kugelhopf sighed. "How old are you, Oscar?"

Surprising twist in the conversation.

"Twelve," I replied.

"Exactly. You are twelve."

"If you already knew, why did you ask?"

"And Oscar"—she ignored my laser-sharp question—"do you remember the Friday *before* you decided to take an entire week off school?"

It seemed like a lifetime ago, that Friday. This is because my mind had been effectively shut down and restarted since then. Still, I remembered it perfectly.

"Yes."

"You were sitting right there." She pointed at my chair.

Actually, I'd been sitting in the middle chair, but I let it go.

"You had been sent here for snoring loudly in class. Hilarious, I'm sure. Do you remember I spoke to you about the value you contribute to the world? Do you remember I mentioned my own son, Eddie, who is four years old?"

We both looked at the photo on her desk. Cute.

I nodded.

"And remember how I said—"

I decided to change the subject.

"What does 'accounting' mean?" I asked, making myself a bit more comfortable.

"Get your feet off the chair," she replied.

I did what she asked.

"Get your feet off my desk!" Anger vibrated her voice then, like an electric guitar.

"So where *can* I put my feet?"

"On the floor! Put them on the floor!"

She did some deep breathing. Then remembered my question.

"Accounting," she said, and rubbed at her forehead quickly. "Accounting is to do with financial records. Why do you—?" Her face grew wide like a balloon into which someone had just blown a huge gust of air. "When I say 'account,' I do not mean I want you to *count up* the days you were not at school! I want you to describe what you were *doing* on those days. We *know* that your father dropped you at the school gate before the bell rang each morning last week, Oscar, but then what? You didn't come *through* that gate, did you? So kindly explain why the valuable time your father spent driving you here—and he is so concerned about you, Oscar, what a lovely man he is—"

"The loveliest." I nodded. "And he's my stepdad."

"All right, so, Oscar, explain to me *why* the valuable time of your stepfather in bringing you here, and the valuable time of your teacher in preparing lessons, have been *wasted*? Because *instead* of coming *into* the school, you chose to spend your time . . . doing *what*, Oscar? Tell me what!"

All those words came flying out of Mrs. Kugelhopf's mouth in a rush, as if the gust of air was screaming back out of the balloon.

"You should have just said that," I suggested.

I'd known what she meant all along, to be honest.

Just messing with her.

Also, listen, my teacher was fine without me last week. She had other kids to teach. I was not wasting her valuable time being gone. In fact, I waste a lot more of her valuable time when I'm there.

I told Mrs. Kugelhopf that it was going to take a bit of time to write this "account of Monday to Friday last week," and also that I'd need the help of a new friend of mine named Imogen Mettlestone-Staranise.

And that's how I came to write this. (Or half of it, anyway.)

Anyhow, here it is.

MONDAY

CHAPTER 1

OSCAR

MONDAY MORNING, 9:45 A.M., I went to Cam.

That's the skate park at Cammeray.

It's always quiet midmorning.

When I skated in, there was a dad with a little kid. Kid had a scooter; dad had a skateboard. The dad skated around a bit, showing off for his kid. The kid scootered, ignoring the dad. The dad attempted a trick right when the kid happened to glance at him. Trick failed. Kid stared at the dad kind of blankly.

"Right," the dad said. "Time to go home for a snack."

And off they went.

That was when I realized there were two other people in the skate park. *Murmur, murmur.* Skated over to see.

They were sitting close together on the ground up the back. On the tufty grass that runs between the skate park and the soccer field.

Two guys. Older than me. About fifteen maybe. T-shirts, hairy arms. Their boards were lying in the grass and they were hunched over something.

It was a hot day.

Hazy air. Cicadas.

I coughed. They looked up at me.

One of the boys was holding a little round mirror in his

palm. He closed his fingers over it, but not before it caught the sunlight.

I frowned.

"What ya doing?" I asked. "Killing ants?"

"You do that with a magnifying glass," mirror-boy told me. "Got a magnifying glass?"

"I don't want to kill ants," I said.

"Well then why did you just *mention* it?" he pounced.

That was unfair, and made no sense.

"What ya doing?" I asked again.

The other boy turned and looked at me more closely. He had a long, thin nose with flaring nostrils, like a jet plane. "You're Oscar," he said.

"Yeah."

Mirror-boy glanced up again. "Yeah?"

"Yeah."

"You've had a haircut," he told me. "Didn't recognize you. I've seen you skate here before. You're good."

"Cheers."

I didn't tell him he was good. I'd seen both of them skate here before and, to be honest, they're pretty average.

They were both studying me now. They glanced at each other, superswift, and mirror-boy raised an eyebrow.

The other one nodded.

"Thing is," he said, and his eyes went shiny. "There's meant to be another skate park. Size of a football field."

"Okay," I said. "Where?"

"Right here." He thudded his fist on the grass.

"Yeah, good on ya." Dropped my board, ready to skate away.

"No, Oscar, wait."

"We're serious."

"Trust us."

"It's real. It's right *here*."

Both of them were talking at once.

"There's a secret way to get there," jet-plane-nose boy explained.

"You hold a mirror in *just* the right place—" The other boy's hand darted around like a little bird, fingers still closed over the mirror.

"Only," his friend put in, scratching his jaw, "we can't find the right place. And we've gotta go."

They both stood up slowly, kind of groaning like old men.

"Keep trying if you want." Nose-boy looked over at mirror-boy.

"What?"

"Give him the mirror."

"Why?"

"So he can try!"

They carried on arguing a while. Turned out mirror-boy had bought the little mirror at the discount store for two dollars, so he wanted to keep it. He was pretty sure I could use anything reflective, he said. It didn't have to be this mirror. Switch my phone to selfie mode? Or did I have one of those foil bags of chips?

The other boy kept urging him to give me the mirror, explaining that if *they* couldn't go to the "killer skate park," *I* should be able to go.

In the end, he tried to grapple the mirror out of his friend's hand, and next thing, they were wrestling.

I started laughing. "It's all right," I said, holding up my hands. "You can keep your mirror."

They looked back at me from their wrestling hold. Mirror-boy sighed and tossed the mirror onto the grass at my feet.

"Try it," he said.

"Trust us," his friend added.

The two of them grabbed their boards and skated away.

"Good luck," they called over their shoulders, heading out of the skate park, onto the path, and off down the road.

A car droned by. Another one.

Helicopter someplace in the sky.

Nobody around.

I went and got my backpack.

Brought it with me to the patch of grass again, sat down, and unzipped my bag.

Nope. No food.

Stood up, picked up my board and my bag, ready to go. Looked down at the mirror, still lying on the grass, facedown. Of course, I didn't believe them. A skate park you could reach with a mirror? Lost the plot, the pair of them.

All I did was, I turned over the mirror with my foot, caught a glimpse of my eyes staring back—

My eyes?

Wait, *were* they my—

And then, there I was.

Standing at the foot of the best skate park I ever saw.

CHAPTER 2

IMOGEN

ONLY, IT WASN'T a skate park, was it, Oscar? It was the Elven city of Dun-sorey-lo-vay-lo-hey.

But you didn't know that at the time.

Hello, my name is Imogen Mettlestone-Staranise, and I am thirteen years old. I have been asked by Oscar Banetti to help him write this account.

At first, I said: "No thank you Oscar, I have no wish for additional homework."

I was only joking. Of course I would help him. (Although, to be clear, I definitely have no wish for additional homework. In case any overexcited teachers are about to jump in.) The fact is, Oscar is quite clueless. This is not his fault, but it would cause him difficulty in describing Monday to Friday of last week.

And so would the fact that Oscar himself was dead for most of Monday.

Before I begin, you should know that I don't really believe in "descriptive language." My teachers are always saying things like "Well, *start* believing, Imogen!" I take no notice. A thing is a thing. Who cares what it's like or how shiny it is?

As long as we're clear on that, I'll get on with it.

Monday morning, 6:35 A.M., I woke to a loud knocking on the front door.

I was home from boarding school for the holidays, along with my younger sisters, Esther and Astrid. We live in the mountain village of Blue Chalet. It's said to be picturesque. Our cousins, Bronte and Alejandro, were staying with us at the time. We planned to spend three weeks together swimming in lakes and climbing mulberry trees. (Alejandro is not *technically* a cousin, by the way, in case somebody is about to jump in and correct me. But he went to live with Bronte's family after escaping life as a pirate. So he's practically a cousin. Even if he *has* recently discovered that he's a prince and returned to live with his own royal parents.)

All five of us had been sleeping on mattresses on the living room floor, so we could chat through the night and have midnight feasts. When the loud knocking sounded early Monday morning, I stepped over the others' snoring bodies to reach the front door.

It was the postmaster. "Urgent letter!" he said and handed it over. "It arrived last night and I've just discovered it, so I rushed it up here."

He waited then, clearly wanting to watch me open the letter, but I said, "Thank you," and closed the door on him.

The letter was addressed to my sister Esther anyway. I turned it over to see the return address:

King Maddox HRH, Elven city of Dun-sorey-lo-vay-lo-hey

"Esther," I said. "Wake up."

My sister Esther is a Rain Weaver. This means she can cure people who've been affected by shadow magic. She only discovered she's a Rain Weaver quite recently and she's been in pretty high demand ever since.

However, this was the first time, as far as I knew, that she'd had a request from an Elf. Certainly the first time she'd heard from an Elven king.

The letter was a bit hysterical.

"*Please, please, please, Esther,*" it begged. "*Come urgently, at once, to the Elven city of Dun-sorey-lo-vay-lo-hey and perform a cure! It's vital that you get here before 10:00 A.M. on Monday!*"

It already *was* Monday.

The letter suggested Esther take a coach to the northeast, perform the cure, and then take another coach home.

"*Nothing could be simpler,*" the letter declared, and then it spent several pages describing the beautiful countryside surrounding the Elven city. Esther skipped that bit, of course, when she was reading the letter out to us.

"I'll go ask Mother and Father if it's all right," she said sleepily—she always takes a while to wake up properly in the morning.

Except Mother and Father had already gone out. There was a note from them on the kitchen table:

Gone to the markets to get fresh pastries for breakfast! Back soon!

"The morning coach leaves at seven," I said, consulting the schedule on the refrigerator. "It should get us to the Elven city just before ten. If we're going to catch it, we need to leave now."

I looked at the others. Their bright or sleepy eyes looked back at me.

"Are you fully recovered, Astrid?" I asked my youngest sister. She'd had an ear infection the week before.

"Completely," she agreed. "The antibiotics are finished."

I thought for a moment.

"Let's go," I decided. We scrambled into our clothes, grabbed a handful of silver and copper coins from the "emergency saucer" on the kitchen counter, and scribbled a note to our parents (*Back later!*).

Esther put the Elven king's letter in her pocket, and we sprinted down the road to the coach stop.

* * *

At 9:45 A.M., we stepped off the coach. (It was a horse-drawn coach, by the way. We have very few motorized vehicles in our region, although they are popular in some other Kingdoms.)

We were now in the middle of the countryside.

We set out along a laneway.

I was leading, as I'm the eldest.

I was followed by my sisters, Esther and Astrid, and my cousins, Bronte and Alejandro. (I say that to remind you who was there.)

The weather was warm. There were fields and meadows. Also: cows.

At 9:49 A.M., we arrived at the Elven city of Dun-sorey-lo-vay-lo-hey.

Only, it wasn't there.

All we could see was a welcome sign—

WELCOME TO DUN-SOREY-LO-VAY-LO-HEY!

TAKE CARE WHERE YOU STEP.

—and a huge blanket of silver.

The silver blanket was bright in the sun and made us squint.

It was the size of a football field—which is also the average size of a large Elven city—and it was lumpy. The lumps were in the shapes of tiny houses.

It seemed pretty clear that the Elven city of Dun-sorey-lo-vay-lo-hey was *underneath* that lumpy silver blanket.

"Now why have they gone and done that?" my cousin Bronte murmured.

We all giggled. It was the way she said it.

I cleared my throat. "HELLO?" I called. "ELVES?"

Silence.

"*HELLO?* WE HAVE BROUGHT ESTHER, THE RAIN WEAVER, TO SEE YOU, AS YOU REQUESTED!"

Here Esther added a call of her own: "THEY DIDN'T *BRING* ME HERE! THEY CAME ALONG TO KEEP ME COMPANY!"

True, but just a technicality. "COULD YOU PLEASE COME OUT FROM UNDERNEATH THIS BLANKET?" I bellowed. "AND BRING THE ELF WHO NEEDS CURING! SO ESTHER, THE RAIN WEAVER, CAN PROVIDE THE CURE!"

Elves are about the size of teaspoons and I was very interested to see what sort of shadow affliction this one might be suffering. I have seen Esther cure old men who can't stop dancing, young girls who can't stop crying, and children who've forgotten how to eat. Those are all examples of shadow spells.

"HELLO?" I tried again. "ESTHER, THE RAIN WEAVER, IS HERE!"

More silence.

"You don't need to keep referring to me as the Rain Weaver," Esther muttered, a bit embarrassed.

But I like doing that. I'm very proud that my little sister is a Rain Weaver. She's the only one in all the Kingdoms and Empires. Not to be sneezed at. My other little sister can read people's moods and tell you if they're lying. I'm proud of her too.

We stood in a row along the laneway, glanced at each other and then at the silver blanket again. Our eyes followed the lumps, the bumps, the contours, and the hillocks.

"Do you know what this is like?" my cousin Bronte asked suddenly. "It's like children have been asked to tidy their toys and have flung the silver living room carpet over the top of the toys instead."

Alejandro spoke up. "Yes," he said. "Or no, it is more like a silver ocean." His voice had become distant and dreamy, his accent pronounced. This always happens when Alejandro, the former pirate, gets near the sea.

Or near a big silver blanket that very slightly resembles the sea.

Bronte knelt at the edge of the silver and touched it with her fingertips.

"It's solid!" she said, surprised.

We all crouched then, and did the same, and she was right. It was not a blanket at all. It was a strange silver substance, as smooth and hard as glass.

That was the moment when uneasiness hit me.

If I were a descriptive sort of person, I'd say it was as if a deep shadow suddenly crossed my heart, the way a cloud crosses the sun.

"ELVES?" I shouted, sharply. My voice became commanding: *"ELVES! ARE YOU UNDER THERE? ELVES! ANSWER ME!"*

The others seemed to catch my uneasiness. Alejandro tried

getting his fingers beneath the edge where the silver met the laneway and lifting. It did not budge. He strained and strained—and he is very strong for his age, Alejandro—but nothing. We all began wrenching at the silver, groaning, using all our muscles.

"ELVES! ELVES! CAN YOU HEAR US!" The others were yelling along with me now, banging on the surface, at times trying to wrench it up again.

I caught sight of my reflection in the silver, and my eyes looked back at me—

Wait, I thought. *Those are not my—*

Then a hand touched my shoulder and I jumped in fright. It was only Astrid, my littlest sister. Her face was peculiar. She was staring.

"A boy," she said and pointed.

I looked across the silver.

A boy was standing perfectly still at the far end of the city. He carried a satchel on his shoulder and a short plank of wood beneath his arm.

"Where did *he* come from?" I exclaimed.

And that's when it happened.

CHAPTER 3

OSCAR

IT STARTED AS a kind of soft rumbling, low and deep.

I was still staring in total shock at the skate park at this point. It was silver, which was pretty unexpected, and huge. Completely empty except for a few kids down the other end. None of them had a board, as far as I could see.

Then the rumbling got my attention. I thought it was my stomach, because I was hungry. Right away, though, the sound grew into something else.

A howling wind, it was like—a wind that has picked up thousands and thousands of dead leaves and twigs, and is rattling them all together. Then it changed *again*, the pitch stepped up a notch, and it was more like a thousand screaming chain saws.

Jammed my hands over my ears and spun in a circle, trying to see where it was coming from.

Behind me there was just a bunch of countryside—fields and meadows as far as the horizon, but the horizon had a strange gray haze. Pollution?

No.

The haze was moving. The haze *was* the sound. The haze was rushing along, growing as it did into a great gray wave— as high as a house, as wide as the skate park itself.

And it was hurtling straight toward me.

CHAPTER 4

IMOGEN

MY MOUTH FELL open in astonishment. I looked sideways and saw the same thing had happened to the others. All our mouths were wide open—we were like a row of gum-dispenser machines.

In the distance, the boy began running toward us.

His satchel bounced on his shoulder. The plank of wood was clutched in his hand now and it pumped back and forth through the air as he ran.

Twice he checked behind him, and both times, seeing that fierce wave hurtling at him, he sprinted even faster.

He leapt over little hillocks and stumbled into crevices, up one mound, down the next.

The wave reached the far side of the Elven city.

"What *is* it?" Alejandro shouted. "Shadow magic?"

Of course. It must be.

I swung around to Bronte—she is a Spellbinder and can bind shadow magic—but her eyes were already closed tight, hands weaving the air with rapid twists and twirls.

"*Hurry,*" I whispered. "*Hurry.*"

Alejandro, on Bronte's other side, was also watching her closely, urgently. *It's all right,* I thought. *She'll make it stop. She'll make it stop.* Still, I pushed Esther and Astrid behind me.

Then Bronte's eyes flew open.

Her hands dropped to her sides.

"It's *not* shadow magic!" she shouted over the noise, her face bewildered. "I can't stop it!"

Still the boy sped toward us, tripping and swerving. Still, the wave rushed inexorably after him, closing in all the time.

We could see his face now, his eyes wild and wide. The wave was only a pace or two behind him, thundering ever louder—closing in, not just on the boy, but also on—

Behind us, a wooden fence bordered a field. "The fence!" I roared. "Climb the fence and *run*!"

We scrambled up the rails, grabbing one another's hands to drag each other up, kicking each other's faces (by accident), and swinging over the top. The others dropped to the grass and began to sprint across the field, but I stopped, clinging to a rail, and turned back.

The boy ran. He staggered—he was tiring. The wave was a horrifying shadow behind him. It loomed over him, it touched his shoulder blades.

"RUN!" I screamed. "FASTER!"

Another burst and he was almost at the edge of the city, almost at the laneway, almost at the fence.

A final lunge, his arms outstretched—I reached out to him, he leapt for me—

The wave gnashed the air behind him, bellowed like a beast—

And then it stopped.

Frozen. Silent.

The boy, however, hit the top rail of the fence and crashed to the laneway, dead.

CHAPTER 5

STILL IMOGEN

(AS OSCAR WAS DEAD)

OR ANYWAY, THAT'S how he looked.

Lying in the laneway, satchel flung in one direction, plank of wood in the other. Dark hair, bare brown arms, and face the ice-blue color of a winter lake.

I stumbled down from the fence, fell to my knees beside him, and shook him. Nothing. His eyes were closed. *Thunk* went his head against the ground as I shook.

"Wake up!" I ordered, shaking again.

Still nothing.

While I was splashing water from my canteen onto his face (no effect) and shaking him some more (his head just wobbled around), the others returned from the field. Slowly, cautiously, they climbed over the fence, and stared up at the frozen wave. It had a glossy metallic texture like a sculpture and it loomed right over us, perfectly still. With glances of mild trepidation, the others joined me around the boy.

I stepped back to let Esther take over the important work of shaking and splashing the boy—as a Rain Weaver who can cure shadow ailments, she has also developed an interest in general health.

She didn't shake or splash though. She listened to his chest, checked his pulse, and even prized open his eyelids. That's the sort of thing that comes with being interested in health.

But then she looked up at me and shook her head.

"He's not breathing and I can't hear a heartbeat."

I felt dizzy for a moment. I had to push the toes of my shoes hard into the path.

A breeze rustled the trees.

The boy lay on the ground, dead.

"We have to take him to a doctor," I decided. "We need to carry him to a doctor."

The others nodded. Alejandro said, "Wait," and swung himself over the fence again. He strode across the field, toward a copse of trees. The cows watched him. So did we. He began testing the strength and flexibility of branches.

He can build anything, Alejandro. That's from his pirating. Always carries strings, tape, and so on in his pocket, and keeps a travel toolbox in his satchel. After a moment, Esther followed—she likes to assist Alejandro and is fairly good with building things herself—while the rest of us stood staring at the frozen wave.

As we stared, we realized something. The wave was not frozen at all. It had only stopped its violent race forward and now was very, very slowly *oozing* itself back in the direction from which it had come. It was spreading itself over the silver substance that was already there, lumping and glooping over the shapes of houses, dipping into the roads between. It split into currents and rivulets that met again. As it settled into place, its glossy charcoal color paled and paled—until, as the oozing finally stopped and held still—it was silver.

"It's the same as the silver that was already there," Bronte observed. She knelt and knocked on the surface. "It's an extra layer."

"So another, wave must have come *before* this one," I said.

"The Elves," whispered Astrid. Her eyes were huge as she looked up at me.

"The Elves are not under there," I promised. "Think about how loud that wave was. When the earlier one came, the Elves would have heard it. They'd have rushed out of their houses and into the fields. Right at this moment, they're probably checking into Elven hotels. Getting themselves drinks from mini mini-bars and working out how to stop waves covering their city."

"Are you sure?" Astrid is ten and sensitive.

I put my arm around her shoulder. "Positive," I replied.

Bronte sent a swift sideways glance in my direction.

My eyes roamed along the laneway. The boy's satchel was lying in the middle of the path. It looked as crumpled and sorrowful as the boy himself. I picked it up and slung it over my shoulder.

The small plank of wood he'd been carrying lay on its side just beyond the fence. It had wheels, I realized. Four of them.

I reached under the fence and pulled it out.

It was a long narrow shape, curved at both ends. The top was as black as night, and the underside—the side with the wheels—was colored vividly like a sunset. The wheels were made of a rubbery material. Rubber, perhaps.

Alejandro and Esther returned while I was still studying the wooden plank. Between them, they lifted the boy onto a makeshift stretcher.

He flopped into place and lay still.

"Right," I said, tucking the plank of wood beneath my arm and taking one end of the stretcher. "Let's go."

CHAPTER 6

STILL IMOGEN

 **THE TROUBLE WAS** that we were in the middle of nowhere.

The morning coach had brought us down from the mountains and into a rural Kingdom that was nothing but farmland and fields.

(I realize farmers don't see the countryside as "nowhere," so I apologize to them. Really though, it is.)

I did remember seeing a roadside inn from the coach window not long before we'd reached our stop, so that's where we headed.

By the time we pushed open the doors of the inn—the Apple Blossom Bed and Breakfast, it was called—carrying the boy between us, it was around eleven. We were hot and breathless, our arms aching, foreheads sweating.

We set the boy on the lobby floor. The innkeeper came out from behind her counter. She gasped when she saw the boy— his eyes still closed, face still bluish white.

"This doesn't look good," she said gravely, kneeling by his side. "What happened here?"

We told her the story and she nodded along with our words, taking one of the boy's hands into her own. She had lots of white hair that fell forward in long curls, and lots of lines, some running across her forehead, others around her cheeks. These deepened as she studied the boy's face. The white hair, the wrinkles, the thoughtful nodding—all of this suggested to me that the innkeeper was a wise and helpful old woman.

I felt relieved.

"So the boy needs a doctor," the innkeeper concluded, looking up at us once we'd finished explaining, "and you're also worried about the Elves. You're hoping they fled from the city before it was first covered in silver?"

"Exactly," we chorused.

She gestured for me to help her stand again—she was elderly; such people have trouble getting themselves back up. It's not their fault.

"I will telephone the doctor," she announced, "and have her come at once. Then I will telephone the local police station. They have a True Mage liaison officer who will help you to locate the Elves."

Elves are True Mages. So a True Mage liaison officer sounded appropriate to me.

"Meanwhile," the innkeeper continued, "perhaps you children could carry this boy up to Room . . . hmm, to Room Seven . . . and place him on a bed?"

She smiled. "You've had a real fright," she added gently.

My relief became strong gratitude. I was very pleased with this innkeeper.

Still, it's one thing to carry a stretcher along country lanes; it's another to get it up a flight of stairs. It tips. The person on the lower stair suddenly has all the weight, and the boy on the stretcher begins to slide right off.

In the end, we managed it without too much thumping and bumping, and we placed the boy on a bed at the far side of Room Seven. There was a long row of single beds in the room, which was interesting.

We covered the boy with a blanket and Astrid set his plank of wood (the one with the wheels) alongside him, tenderly tucking that in too. It had seemed special to him. His satchel we placed on the floor.

Then we returned to the lobby.

CHAPTER 7

IMOGEN

(OF COURSE—JUST ASSUME IT'S ME UNTIL WE SWITCH AGAIN)

THE INNKEEPER WAS leaning on her counter in a patch of sunlight. Her white curls glowed.

"Hello," she said as we approached. "How can I help? I am Marion-Louise, the innkeeper. You're the children staying in Room Seven, aren't you?"

We stared at her.

"No," I said, uncertainly. "We just took that boy upstairs to Room Seven. Remember? Have you telephoned the doctor? And the police station about the Elves?"

Her smile faded. "Not possible," she said. "Telephone's off the hook."

"Put it back on the hook," Astrid advised, standing on tippy-toes so she could see over the counter.

Marion-Louise-the-innkeeper barked with laughter. "That's a good one! You're a clever little one!" she told Astrid. "No, no, I mean it's disconnected. Can't use it. Won't be fixed for another few days, apparently." She smiled. "What are your plans for today, children?"

Now, one thing I have not yet mentioned is this: I have a temper. My parents and teachers are always telling me to "control" it, but that only shows that they don't know what a temper is.

It's a lion that sleeps in your throat and occasionally leaps up, roaring and gnashing its teeth. It frightens me as much as anybody else. I didn't put it in my throat. I didn't go to an animal shelter and say, "I'll take that wild-looking lion over there, thanks, need it for my throat." Did I? No. It has nothing to do with me.

Control it, they say. Complete nonsense.

Anyway, at this point, I felt the lion stirring.

"So you've sent a *message* to the doctor and the police station instead?" I demanded. "As your telephone does not work?"

Marion-Louise shook her head. "No."

The lion rose on its haunches.

At this point, my cousin Bronte spoke up. Bronte is generally quieter than my sisters and me, and she has excellent manners. She can also be very firm when she wishes. She dresses up her firmness in her manners.

"We would be grateful if you could arrange to *have* messages sent to the doctor and police at once," Bronte said. "We are worried about the boy, and we need to find the Elves so that my cousin Esther can cure one of them. We don't have long, as we have to get the two o'clock coach back to the mountains."

Marion-Louise gave a start. "The coach back to the mountains?" she repeated. "But that's been canceled. There's a rockfall blocking the Pensill Pass. It won't be cleared until tomorrow morning."

I stared at her.

"We *need* to get home to Blue Chalet today," I told her. My sisters and cousins pressed close to the counter, all of them saying, "Yes, yes, we do," which strengthened my argument.

It made no difference.

"There's no way to get to Blue Chalet today," Marion-Louise said. "It's quite blocked." At least she sounded apologetic. That was something.

But not enough.

I took a deep breath. "In that case," I said, "we will send a message to our parents, please, to tell them where we are."

"No way to do that," Marion-Louise said. She seemed really sorrowful now. "The phone line is down, as I mentioned. I have no messengers. And there's no post office to send telegrams."

The lion started climbing to its feet, but I told it to lie down. None of this was Marion-Louise's fault.

Maybe so, the lion rumbled, *but this is* not *a wise and helpful woman.*

I agreed.

I looked at the others. We held each other's gaze and then we all shrugged. There was nothing we could do.

"Could we stay here for the night then?" Bronte asked quietly.

"Of course," Marion-Louise replied promptly. "You're in Room Seven."

It was clear we would have to solve our problems ourselves.

Alejandro asked if we could borrow horses, please, and Marion-Louise seemed charmed by this idea—or perhaps by Alejandro. He is a beautiful boy with the excellent accent of a former pirate. She directed us to the stables behind the inn.

Also, at my request, she took out a map and marked the locations of the doctor and the police station for us.

The hostler saddled up horses for us and we split into two groups, riding away in two different directions. Bronte and Alejandro went to fetch the doctor, and my sisters and I went to the police station.

I was feeling uneasy about those Elves, to be honest. I'd promised Astrid that they'd escaped in time, yet how could I know that? What if they were trapped beneath the silver substance? Or worse, what if the silver had—

I pressed my knees into my horse's flanks and leaned forward, urging him into a rapid trot.

I would not think about it.

My sisters trotted along behind me, both chatting noisily to their horses as they rode. They love animals.

The police station was closed.

It was in the middle of an overgrown meadow and it was locked up, shutters down, and a sign on the front door:

CLOSED FOR RENOVATIONS.
COME AGAIN SOON!

There was no indication of any building work under way, not so much as a wheelbarrow.

We turned around and rode back toward the inn, meeting Bronte and Alejandro on the way. They'd had no luck with the doctor either. She was attending a conference on stomachache and its treatment in the Sayer Empire, apparently.

The doctor's wife had told them that there was not a single other medical professional—not even anybody with know-how about health—in the entire region.

"This is ridiculous," Esther said sharply. She's not often sharp, my sister Esther, being more likely to be dreamy or quirky. (She loves writing stories and is always dreaming of the next one.) I understood her sharpness now.

This *was* ridiculous.

We spent the rest of the day riding around the countryside visiting every farmhouse we could see, knocking on doors, and asking the same questions.

Can you help an injured boy, possibly dead? Do you know who he might be? Is anyone missing a boy? Around twelve years old, dark brown hair, face currently blue?

Have you seen a crowd of Elves wandering around, complaining about their city being buried under silver?

May we borrow a telephone to call our parents?

The farmers were friendly. "How grim!" they all said. "The poor boy! The poor Elves! Poor you!"

They offered us apples, a jar of honey, the opportunity to bottle-feed their baby lambs, a chance to help them fill their pillows with feathers—but they could not offer any help.

The sun sank, the sky paled into orange and then into deep blue and finally black. Stars appeared.

We returned the horses to the stables, and we trudged, weary and dejected, back into the inn.

CHAPTER 8

IMOGEN

"OH, YOU'RE ALIVE!" exclaimed Marion-Louise.

She was polishing her counter with a dustrag.

"So we are," I replied coldly, not turning my head to look at her. I was walking toward the stairs. I was not in the mood for her.

"It's not safe for you to be out at night!" she called. "I was saying to Reuben just now, I said, 'Reuben? Those children from Room Seven are out there in the dark!' I said, 'We'll never see *them* again, will we? Who's going to pay their bill?' Didn't I, Reuben? Didn't I say that?"

She was half-shouting, peering across the lobby, which was softly lit by lamps. "REUBEN? DIDN'T I SAY THAT THE CHILDREN FROM ROOM SEVEN WERE AS GOOD AS DEAD?"

I stopped and squinted in the direction she was shouting. The others did the same.

In the shadows, we spotted a bearded man. He was seated in an armchair on the far side of the lobby, reading a newspaper.

He lowered the paper and replied in a low, steady voice: "Indeed you did, Marion-Louise."

"And how did you answer me, Reuben?"

Reuben raised his newspaper, covering his face again, and spoke from behind it: "I agreed with you entirely, Marion-Louise. Surprised to see the children back, that's certain."

There was a silence.

Reuben coughed and turned the page of his newspaper.

Marion-Louise nodded at us. "Yes, the Doom Lantern Witches roam this area at night," she told us. "There are twelve of them. Very powerful Witches. During the day, they cast vicious shadow spells everywhere they go. During the night, they kill any children that they catch outside."

Now I *did* look at Marion-Louise. I swung my head and stared. We had Bronte with us, and she can spellbind Shadow Mages—up to two or three at a time even—but *twelve* powerful Witches?

Bronte was looking at me in horror.

Astrid, fortunately, was falling asleep where she stood, and both Alejandro and Esther were busy holding her up.

"I'm *all right*," Astrid grumbled, her eyelids closed.

"Certainly you are," Alejandro agreed, getting a firmer grip as she slipped toward the floor.

I fixed my gaze on Marion-Louise. "If there are Witches roaming this region at night," I said, my voice like a low lion's roar, "you *might* have mentioned that earlier."

We all marched up the stairs then, Alejandro and Esther carrying Astrid between them.

CHAPTER 9

IMOGEN

THERE WAS A boy on a bed in our room.

Well, of course there was. We'd put him there.

It still gave us a fright.

We'd been so caught up with trying to find a doctor for him, we'd forgotten about the boy himself. If you see what I mean.

Still, there he was, eyes closed, face blue. Most of us gasped, which woke Astrid. Then we all gathered around the boy. We were loving and apologetic in our gaze. Astrid even stroked his hair. He looked peaceful, despite the blue.

Esther picked up the boy's satchel from the floor. "We should look through it," she suggested. "And see if it has any clues about who he is."

Sensible.

"He might be connected with the wave in some way," I realized. "He appeared right before it did. Maybe he somehow *created* it?"

"And then lost control of it." Bronte nodded. "There could be clues about that in his bag too."

The boy's satchel had two straps attached to one side and a zipper that ran all around the top. I tipped the contents onto the bed, and we studied them.

Here is what we found:

- Three or four pencils, all of which required sharpening
- An ink-filled pen, leaking
- A handful of papers, half-covered in scribbled, largely illegible, and often-crossed-out words or numbers. One of the papers had the marking of a muddy boot print. We decided it was schoolwork. At the bottom of one scribbled sheet, a tidier hand had written in red ink: *Not a bad effort, Oscar. Next time ask me if you're having trouble.*
- An open foil package marked with bright letters (ORIGINAL SALT & VINEGAR FLAVORED) and pictures. This package contained the crumbs of a snack, possibly crisps. Unexpectedly, a damp sweet had got itself glued to the outside of the package.
- A metal object with three curved arms, not much larger than the palm of my hand. None of us recognized this object, and Alejandro said it appeared to be a sort of a tool. As it was silver in color, like the wave that had covered the Elven city, I suddenly worried that *it* was what had created the wave, and that it might be about to create another. I flung it into the corner of the room.
- A small container, which clicked open to reveal a transparent object. Shaped like a small set of jaws, it was indented with the imprint of teeth—I flung that aside too.
- Another small container, which *also* contained a jaw-shaped object, again with teeth imprints—this time in a blue color—again, flung it aside in alarm.
- A soft black change purse, which clinked as I lifted it. When I tried to open it, it emitted such a sharp crackling noise that I flung it aside. At this point, I was tiring of flinging things.
- An orange. This had rotted so much its skin was patched with lurid greeny whites. Alejandro accidentally put his thumb right through the peel and into the pith when he picked it up. I'd have flung it aside, but Alejandro laughed,

tossed the orange in the bin, and wiped his hand on his trouser leg.

- And finally, a sheet of paper in an envelope. I took out the paper. It was a letter.

"Dear Oscar," I read aloud.

"I am so, so, so, so, so, so upset that I can't be with you for your birthday. I would give _ANYTHING_ not to be stuck here in Byron Bay at such a special time! Will you have a birthday cake? Send me pictures!!

I really hope you know how much I love you, Oscar. More than any other mother has ever loved their child. Seriously. More than the moon and the stars, the comets, the rainbows, the ocean waves, sugarcane fields. Everything nature has to offer, basically. It is just agony not to be with you, my little Oscar. My darling boy. Each day, I think of you and it's like a burning rock in the pit of my stomach. Honestly.

Love, love, love, love, love, love, love,

Your

Forever-loving

Mother."

I folded the letter carefully and placed it back in the envelope.

We looked at each other quietly. The room seemed filled with sadness.

"Well," I began—and then a voice said, "Hello?" and we turned to see the dead boy sitting up in bed.

CHAPTER 10

OSCAR

YEAH, THAT WAS me.

I woke up.

I was in a bed. My skateboard was in the bed too. Weird.

I looked around. The room was like a picture-book illustration of the cottage where the Three Bears lived—before Goldilocks trashed the place.

Flowerpots on the window ledge, flouncy curtains, wooden beams.

There was also a row of single beds and a crowd of kids going through my stuff.

The moment I spoke they all started screaming, crying, shouting, and clapping.

Loudly.

A couple of the girls even tore across the room like stampeding gazelles, jumped on the bed, and tried to hug me. Still carrying on with the screaming and crying, only now it was that much closer to my ears.

"YOU'RE ALIVE! YOU'RE ALIVE!" they were shrieking.

In the end, I grabbed a pillow, curled it around my head with one hand, and gestured in the air with the other for them to lower the volume.

For some reason, this made them shriek even louder. They seemed to find it funny.

"WE'RE BEING TOO LOUD FOR HIM!"

"HA-HA! LOOK AT HIM WITH THE PILLOW AROUND HIS EARS!"

"BECAUSE WE'RE TOO LOUD!"

"HE'S FUNNY! HE'S *ALIVE* AND HE'S FUNNY!"

I decided to wait it out, and eventually they calmed down to sobbing and laughing at a level that did not split my eardrums. They kept patting me though, and touching my head, like I was a toy, and a couple of the girls kept saying, "Oh, darling Oscar, are you all right?" which was mildly disturbing. How did they know my name?

"Sorry!" one of them said. "We've been going through your things! From your satchel! Your name *is* Oscar, isn't it? We thought you might be dead!"

Yes, I agreed. Oscar is my name. And no, I added, just to be clear. I am not dead.

I was going to point out that it was not a *satchel*, it was a *backpack*, except that reminding them that I was not dead had been a mistake. They were shrieking again.

There were four girls and one boy. Three of the girls looked so similar they had to be sisters—each was fair-skinned with braids. The other girl wore a yellow dress, had darker skin, and was slightly more aloof, a bit cooler. But she still seemed pleased to see me. The boy had a gleam in his eyes, brown skin, and a face with structure. You know those faces? Like you get on TV.

The girls all spoke as correctly as a great-aunt at a wedding and the boy had a wicked accent—dramatic.

"What happened?" I asked eventually.

I honestly don't know who said what in the conversation that came next. They all talked at the same time, and the girls with braids kept hugging me, which muffled the sound of whoever was speaking, while the boy jumped up and down on another bed, as if it was a trampoline. That was distracting.

"You were standing on an Elf's roof and a wave chased you!" they exclaimed.

An Elf's roof.

I decided to skip that bit.

"What *was* that wave?" I remembered that, that's for sure. So noisy. So brutal. Wild.

"You didn't create it?" someone asked.

I chuckled.

But they seemed sincere.

No, I said. I didn't create it.

"We thought it must be shadow magic at first, only it wasn't!"

I gave them all a steady look.

They looked back in an excitable way.

A braid-girl patted my shoulder. "Poor darling," she said. "Your face was so blue, we really did think you might be dead. Lucky we didn't bury you."

"Lucky," I echoed, but they didn't notice my tone.

Once they'd settled down again, I shot them all another steady look. "Shadow magic," I said. "Elves."

I meant to make a point here—my voice was loaded, the way my stepdad's is when he gets home late and I'm playing video games. He looks around the living room and points things out in a slow, heavy way: "Pizza boxes. On the floor. Spilled Coke. On the couch."

Except these kids didn't say, "Yeah, yeah, sorry." They just stared at me as if to say: "Yes? What's your point?"

Then one of them let her mouth fall open like a jar of mayonnaise. "He must be from the Northern Climes!" she said.

More frenetic excitement. They'd always wanted to meet somebody from the Northern Climes!

The good-looking boy, it turned out, had *been* to the Northern Climes, on *the ship* and there were *such beautiful* Kingdoms and Empires up there (he told the others) and the magic up there? "It is a whole different story!"

The others said they knew perfectly well that magic is different up there. Everybody knows that.

Still, it was "remarkable" that I was from the Northern Climes!

And so on.

"Is it true?" they demanded eventually. "Are you from the Northern Climes, Oscar?"

I scratched my head. "You mean the Northern Hemisphere?"

"Oh well, if you want to call it that. We call it the Northern Climes. The region up north."

"No. I'm from the Southern Hemisphere."

"You mean the Southern Climes?"

I breathed in deeply. "If you like."

"So he's not from the Northern Climes."

Disappointment all around.

Then confusion.

"Wait, so you *do* know about magic in the Southern Climes?"

"No," I said, carefully. "I do not know about magic in the Southern Climes."

That was maybe a mistake, because it meant a group lecture on "magic."

It went for quite a while, but the gist was this: True Mages are good and do bright magic, Shadow Mages are bad and do shadow magic, and Spellbinders are very nice people who can stop shadow magic by "binding" it.

"Handy to have around," I suggested.

Yes! They were pleased with me for picking up on the handiness of Spellbinders.

"Wait," I said, thinking aloud. "Shadow Mages do shadow magic, you said? So why don't *True* Mages do *true* magic? Why 'bright' magic?"

They all looked a bit blank. That's just how it is, they said, and the tallest braid-girl announced that she herself is "not really a fan of bright magic." The others all went, "Imogen!" and babbled at her a bit (I couldn't follow), so I guess that was a controversial take. Then they carried on with their lecture.

"In the ancient times—"

The ancient times.

This was getting out of hand.

"Right then," I said. "Thanks for that. I should be getting home now. Where am I exactly?"

"In the Apple Blossom Bed and Breakfast," one of the girls told me. "Do you live around here? On one of the farms?"

I shook my head. "City."

Sorrowful faces again. "We're in the countryside, I'm afraid, Oscar, and you can't leave the inn. There are dangerous Witches out there at night. Also, the telephone is not connected. We won't be able to help you get home until tomorrow."

Their faces became even more sorrowful.

I skipped the bit about Witches.

"No worries," I said. "I'll call my stepdad and ask for a ride."

Got my phone out of my pocket.

"Ah," I said, looking at the screen. "It's dead."

"Oh, I'm so sorry," they all murmured, moving closer to me. "What is it?"

I blinked at them. Held up my phone. "Battery's dead."

"Battery? Oh, it's just a toy! We thought it must be a friend of yours."

"Can I charge it?" I asked.

There was a confused pause, then they said, all at once:

"To the room?"

"Have you an account?"

"Don't you already own it?"

I decided to change the subject.

"What's your story?" I asked. "What are you all doing in a hotel? Is this a school excursion or something? Where are the adults?"

More shrieks, this time along the lines of "Oh!"

"We haven't introduced ourselves!"

"Where are our manners?"

"He must think us so rude!"

To be honest, "rude" was not the first word that came to mind about this lot.

They carried on laughing at having forgotten to introduce themselves, and at how "baffled" I must be.

"Mmm," I said. "It's okay." Checking the distance between myself and the door.

The tallest of the three braid-sisters did the introductions.

"My name is Imogen, and these are my sisters, Esther and Astrid," she said, pointing to the other two braid-girls. "Esther

is an expert on magic, writes great stories and, most important, is a Rain Weaver."

A pause. She clearly expected me to react. I looked around.
They were *all* waiting for me to react, their eyes wide and
shiny. They were fidgety with grins. Esther, the middle sister,
was blushing and studying her fingernails.

"A Rain Weaver!" I managed to repeat, as excitedly as I could.
They relaxed.

"Astrid can read people," Imogen continued, pointing to the
littlest braid-girl. "By that I mean, she always knows if somebody is lying and generally knows how people feel. Astrid,
how is Oscar feeling at the moment?"

"Confused," Astrid said at once.

That was an understatement.

"Annoyed," she added, smiling.

I thought I'd been doing a good job hiding that.

"Not surprising," the girl in the yellow dress put in, "considering he's been dead most of the day."

Everyone giggled.

"This is Alejandro." Imogen was relentless. The boy bowed
as if I was the Queen. "Alejandro was formerly a pirate—"

"Of course he was," I murmured.

They all seemed surprised by this. Imogen glided on.
"—Although he never did any actual pirating—"

"Shame," I joked.

Her eyes widened, but she didn't miss a beat: "—And he has
recently discovered his true identity as a prince. He lived with
our cousin Bronte's family for a while, and he's recently
returned to his long-lost royal parents."

"He's a prince?" I checked.

"It's all right, it hasn't gone to his head at all," the littlest
braid-girl, Astrid, told me.

"That was my main concern," I said.

"Most people are born as princes, so they are accustomed
to it," middle-braid-girl explained, "whereas it's all new to
Alejandro."

Again, they paused, only I had nothing whatsoever to say about the difficulties of adjusting to life as a prince—and so Imogen completed her job.

"Finally," she said, waving at the girl in the yellow dress, "this is my cousin Bronte. An experienced adventurer."

"Delighted to meet you, Oscar," Bronte said, "and even more delighted that you are alive."

And she stepped forward and shook my hand.

CHAPTER 11

IMOGEN

YES, BRONTE HAS very good manners, as I mentioned earlier. I didn't even think of shaking Oscar's hand.

(Before I continue: you make us sound like giddy flibbertigibbets in your chapter, Oscar. That is inaccurate. If we were glad to see you alive, that's because we're decent people. And if my sisters and I happen to wear our hair in braids, well, it keeps it tidy.)

Anyway, at this point, we were hungry.

We realized this when Bronte, in her politeness, asked Oscar if *he* was hungry. Before he had a chance to answer, Bronte added, as if surprised by this herself: "We haven't eaten since breakfast! I could *literally* eat that plank of wood and all its wheels."

Oscar put a protective arm around his plank of wood and Bronte laughed. So Oscar realized she was joking and he laughed too.

He struck me as very relaxed, leaning against the headboard, arm around the plank of wood, gazing around at us as we spoke. Now and then a dimple appeared in his right cheek. (I was surprised when Astrid said he felt confused and annoyed, as he seemed neither. But she's always correct, Astrid.)

I ran downstairs and ordered room service and, a short time later, Marion-Louise wheeled in our supper on a trolley. She wanted to know what we'd done with our "friend with the blue face." We pointed to Oscar.

"That's not him," she said with a chuckle. "*He* doesn't have a blue face." Then she left.

Everyone fell silent as we ate. We had to be silent, to concentrate on the food. It was fishcakes, beans, beetroot, and potato wedges, stacked up to form a sort of castle on each of our plates. Precarious. It took focus to eat without capsizing the castle.

Oscar, I noticed, simply tapped at the structure with his fork, sending the pieces scattering all over his plate before he began.

He finished first.

After supper, we decided there was nothing we could do other than go to sleep.

We didn't have any pajamas, of course, so we had to sleep in our clothes.

In the lamplight, we asked Oscar more questions about himself. He told us that he was from a city called Sydney in a place called Australia.

There was an uncomfortable pause. Nobody had heard of either, and we are all quite good at geography.

"The Kingdom of Australia," Bronte repeated carefully. "Where's that?"

"It's not a Kingdom," Oscar said mildly.

"An Empire then." We all nodded.

"Not an empire either." He smiled. "A country."

Nobody spoke, but we glanced swiftly at one another: in the Kingdoms and Empires, everything is either Kingdom or Empire.

"Right then!" I switched off the lamp, using a pretend-cheerful voice. "Let's get some sleep!"

There was no point carrying on a conversation with Oscar. He was clearly still suffering from the effects of a severe blow to his head.

* * *

I was just drifting to sleep when a low voice spoke.

"Imogen?"

I opened my eyes.

The voice had come from Oscar's bed. It was beside mine.

"Yes?" I whispered.

His eyes were bright in the darkness.

"What's really going on here?" he murmured.

I blinked at him.

"Seriously," he said. "What *was* that giant wave that came for me in the skate park?"

"I don't know," I replied. "What's a skate park?"

A pause. "Where are we really?" he asked.

I considered him.

"Tomorrow," I said, "we *must* find a doctor for you. You clearly have a serious concussion."

There was a creaking sound.

It was Oscar turning over in bed and settling down again.

There was quiet from him—and then, after a moment, a very deep sigh.

I couldn't sleep then.

I lay in the bed for hours, listening to the sounds of the others breathing more and more deeply as they slept. My mind darted between questions.

What would our parents be thinking right now? Exactly how angry would they be when we got home?

I didn't enjoy those questions so I moved on.

Where was Oscar *really* from? Why had he invented those place names and why was he pretending not to know about magic? Why had he been standing on the Elven city?

Speaking of Elves, *had* they escaped in time?

I sat up.

The letter from the Elven king. Had it said anything helpful that we'd missed?

I slipped out of bed and crept across the dark room. My hand felt around on the little table by Esther. Her hair ribbons were there—and so was the fat envelope. Good. She had taken it out of her pocket before she went to sleep.

I picked it up, then froze as Esther made a sudden snuffling noise. But she turned over and breathed quietly again.

I crept out of the room.

The corridor was dark, so I went down into the lobby. It was empty and dimly lit. There was nobody behind the counter and the grandfather clock in the corner said that it was 11:30 P.M.

I sat on one of the armchairs, in a circle of lamplight, and opened the letter.

CHAPTER 12

IMOGEN

(AS YOU PROBABLY WANT TO KNOW
WHAT'S IN THE LETTER)

To Dear and Most Illustrious Rain Weaver Esther (it said),

Please, please, please, please come urgently, at once, to the Elven city of Dun-sorey-lo-vay-lo-hey and perform a cure! It is vital that you get here before 10:00 a.m., Monday morning! Catch the morning coach to the northeast from Blue Chalet! Perform the cure and take the afternoon coach back home!

Nothing could be simpler!

I looked up.
Hmm, I thought.
I read on.

Our Elven city is set amongst the pastoral dreams, the bucolic splendor, the fields and furloughs, meadows and farms, orchards and creeks, rivers and roads, oh, see the sparkly—

Then there were the four pages of descriptive language about geographical features. As I mentioned earlier, we'd skipped those pages that morning.

I read them now.

They were insufferable, and a good example of why descriptive language is unnecessary.

At last I reached the final page.

. . . Yea! Here, we live in merriment and joy . . . or such we lived until noon on Friday.

For that was when the Doom Lantern Witches struck.

Our protective borders were down, of course, in preparation, and thus, using their powerful broomstick crochet, they cast a shadow spell upon us all—

I looked up sharply.

All?

Witches had cast a spell on *all* the Elves? The opening of the letter had asked Esther to perform "a cure." We'd thought that meant *one* Elf needed curing! We'd imagined a poor little Elf who couldn't stop shivering, or couldn't stop doing headstands! Or something. The usual shadow spell afflictions.

But *all* the Elves had been afflicted?

And it was the Doom Lantern Witches who had cast the shadow spell? Marion-Louise had said that they cast "vicious" shadow spells.

Poor Elves.

Only, what did the King mean when he said, "Our protective borders were down, of course, in preparation"?

My heart thumping quickly, I read on.

—and we beg that you, illustrious Esther, may please come here and cure us of this spell?

It is a spell that is sending us to sleep.

It is a sleep from which NOTHING can wake us. My fellow Elves are already slumbering where they fell in their homes. I cannot wake them no matter how I shout and ring bells and pinch their noses. It is only my kingly power that has kept me awake this long—yet soon the spell will overwhelm me. I feel such tiredness in my eyelids, I hear it in my yawns.

The spell will keep us locked in this sleep for a century.

This seems a dreadful waste of our time. Also, we really have to wake by Monday morning.

So please! Please! Visit us! And cure us, Esther! Quickly?

Thank you! I'll just pop this into the express post and then I'll crawl into bed.

Best wishes and thanks I send you,

King Maddox

The lobby turned slow circles around me. That's how it seemed.

Noises fell sideways through my mind like capsizing towers.

Asleep.

Asleep.

The Elves had been deep in sleep in their beds.

Nothing could wake them. Not a shout, not a bell, not a pinch of their noses—

Not the roar of a giant silver wave.

They were not safe in Elven hotels.

They were still there. Under the silver.

CHAPTER 13

IMOGEN

(STILL)

RIGHT AT THAT moment, footsteps sounded on the staircase.

A figure came hurrying into the lobby.

It was Oscar.

He was looking around furtively as he walked. His hair was sticking up all over the place. He had his satchel over one shoulder, his plank of wood beneath his arm.

I blinked.

"Oscar?" I said.

Oscar's eyes slid over to me in the armchair.

He paused. Then he ran to the front door of the inn, grabbed the handle, and turned it.

The letter fell to the floor. I was on my feet and sprinting.

I skidded the last few feet, kicked the door closed, caught Oscar around the waist, and tackled him. *Crash.*

We slid across the floorboards.

I let go.

Oscar sat up and blinked, bewildered. "Dude," he said.

"Sorry," I said, catching my breath. "I didn't know what else to do."

After a moment, I stood up, offered my hand to Oscar, and pulled him to his feet. "I didn't want you dead again," I explained. "I was just getting used to you being alive."

Sometimes I joke to lighten the mood.

Oscar stared at me.

"Oscar," I said. "There are Doom Lantern Witches out there. The innkeeper told us that they kill children at night."

A great, slow sigh from Oscar. "Look," he said. "It was good to meet you all, Imogen, and this game of yours is . . . interesting. But I want to go home. This is . . . I mean. I was in my local skate park. Couple of guys told me to use a mirror to reach *another* skate park. A giant wave comes for me. And now this game of yours? Magic and Witches and whatever? You have great imaginations, sure, but I'm good, thanks. Don't want to play. I'm out of here."

He reached down to pick up his satchel from the lobby floor—and stopped.

The satchel's zip was slowly sliding open.

An Elf wriggled out.

CHAPTER 14

OSCAR

LIKE A LIZARD squirming out of a drainpipe it was.

"What the—?" I said and dropped my backpack.

Don't judge me. You'd have dropped your backpack too, if a little critter crawled out of it.

Imogen went, "Oh!" and her hand sprang out and caught the Elf just before it hit the floor.

She opened her palm. I moved closer and looked.

Tiny little person standing there. Size of my pinkie finger.

Tiny face.

Tiny little hands on tiny little hips.

Tiny shorts. Teeny little head with teeny little bits of hair on top of it.

Teeny-tiny nose. *Teeny-tiny*—

And so on.

You get the picture.

Next thing, the little figure spoke.

"I thank you, O great Imogen," it began, and I lost it.

Couldn't help it.

Squeaky little high-pitched, high-speed voice. Like when people suck helium from balloons. Or like the chipmunks in those movies.

Laughed my head off until I picked up that Imogen was staring at me. She seemed annoyed, and pretty judgmental.

"Sorry," I said. "It's just . . ."

"Just what?"

I shrugged. "Sorry."

The Elf gave me a look too. Teeny, tiny, itty-bitty look. Started up again.

"I thank you, O great Imogen! You have plucked me from the air, saving me from certain doom upon the shiny boards below! And here I stand upon your palm!"

I held it together, but only just.

"Don't mention it," Imogen said. "Wait a moment. How do you know my name? And what are you doing in Oscar's bag?" She glanced at me. "We emptied it out earlier."

"Allow me to answer both questions in one fell swoop!" the Elf squeaked. It was extra funny because it was speaking in such a fancy way. I had to bite my lip. "I clung to the inner seam of the bag while you emptied it out upon the bed earlier, and then I listened as you spoke amongst yourselves of the items therein! As you spoke, you referred to one another by name! Soon I knew which of you was which! This"—it waved a hand, a teeny-tiny hand, in my direction— "is Oscar! Once dead, now alive! And you"—another hand— "my fine and courteous rescuer, to whom I owe my life, my joy, my very future! . . . are Imogen. Imogen, the mighty and brave!"

Imogen laughed.

"Enough," she said. "*Why* are you in Oscar's bag?"

The Elf did the funniest thing then. It sat down, crossed its legs, and kind of slumped forward. Fists on its cheeks, elbows on its knees. I can't explain why I found that funny, but I guess it's like when a baby does something grown-up? Like pretends to make a phone call? And it's cute because it's so *little* yet doing a perfect imitation of a real person.

That's what it was like. Teeny Elf sitting itself down in the way anyone might if they were feeling depressed.

Little Elf's body rose up and down, as if it was sighing.

"My name is Gruffudd," it said. "I am a child of the city of Dun-sorey-lo-vay-lo-hey. A mere boy of six years old."

Six! And talks like he's forty-six! Plus, I'd better stop calling him "it."

Imogen made a sound like "Ohhh."

"It is a truth that my parents find this wicked in me; however here is the fact. Await and I will tell you the fact. It is this. I like to play in the meadows when I ought to be at school. Very often, I do not wish to be at school. I wish to be in the freshness of the air, the brightness of the sun! And so I skip school! This is a crime?"

"Uh, yeah," I said. "Technically, skipping school is against the—"

Imogen and the Elf ignored me.

Gruffudd carried on. "When the Witches attacked my city on Friday, I was playing in the meadows. Thus, I missed it! I did not fall victim to the shadow spell! And so? I did not fall into a deep sleep like the others! What further proof could one need that skipping school ca*nnot* be a crime?" he cried.

I let that go.

"Upon returning to my city, I discovered that all were sleeping!" he continued. "They could not be woken! How sorrowful I was! How I wept! Well, that is not true." He paused. "My honesty flees on occasion. I did not weep at all. In fact, I was filled with joy. I ran from house to house, played with strangers' toys and ate treats of all kinds, from kitchens and from shops. That reminds me. I am hungry." He gazed up.

Imogen said, "Wait a moment," and disappeared around a corner with the Elf.

A moment later, she was back and there was half a slice of cake on her palm, alongside Gruffudd. He was eating. I guess she'd raided the hotel fridge.

"I enjoyed my time immensely," Gruffudd continued, wiping his mouth, "roaming amongst the houses, exploring offices and parlors. Of course, I knew that the silver waves were due this morning. Everybody knows that. So I made sure to *leave* the city before dawn, and I frolicked in the meadow then—"

"The waves were *due* this morning?" Imogen demanded.

Cough, cough—from the shadows.

We turned around to look.

CHAPTER 15

IMOGEN

 **IT TURNED OUT** that Reuben, the bearded man, was sitting in his armchair in the shadows.

He no longer had a newspaper and was holding a heavy-bottomed glass. He sipped from this as we stared at him.

"Have you been *there* all this time?" I demanded. "I didn't see you there! I was sitting directly—"

"I am everywhere and nowhere at once," Reuben replied, which I found irritating. "Come. Please. Sit with me. I wish to speak to you."

He dragged some other armchairs into a circle—they made terrible shrieking sounds as they scraped across the floorboards—and gestured for us to sit, so we did.

Gruffudd perched on the arm of my chair and Reuben leaned forward slightly and addressed him.

"Is it the quest for a new Elven king?" he asked.

"Exactly!" Little Gruffudd nodded.

Reuben smiled, his eyes shining. His beard was very thick. If I were descriptive, I would say it was the color of winter bracken, freshly dusted in snow. His skin was veiny and ridged, the way old men's skin gets.

He turned to Oscar and me and explained. "Once every hundred years or so," he said, placing his glass on a low table, so he could wave his hands as he spoke, "this particular Elven city holds a quest for a new king. Here's how it works. First, a bright magic spell buries the city beneath layers of silver. The Elves, of course, are perfectly safe when the silver comes, and—"

"They're safe!" I interrupted. "So the silver wouldn't have . . . suffocated . . . or crushed them?"

"Now why would it do that?" Reuben looked at me severely, as if I were a student who'd asked a very foolish question as a result of not listening in class. Gruffudd fixed me with the same expression.

I didn't care. I felt very relieved. Specifically, I felt as if gentle musical notes were swirling around me.

I smiled. Oscar smiled too, but I think that was just a general, friendly smile, and did not contain much understanding.

Reuben continued: "Yes, the city is buried under wave after wave of silver. These waves will keep coming regularly over the next few days until there's a positive *mountain* of silver. Any Elf who wishes to be king becomes a "quester." The Elves all know when the spell is due to begin, and questers make sure they're outside the city before the first wave. All other Elves must remain in their homes and wait. Questers then have five days to track down the key, unlock the spell, and set the city free. Whoever unlocks the spell becomes the new Elven king."

I breathed deeply. "So everything is all right," I said.

Reuben nodded, stroking his beard and added: "Of course, if *none* of the questers find the key in time, the city is doomed."

My swirling musical notes paused midair.

"Doomed?" I repeated.

"Yes," Reuben agreed, sounding oddly relaxed. "If the city is not unlocked by ten A.M. on Friday, one final wave will come—the biggest wave of all—and that wave *will* destroy the city. All the Elves will be crushed to death."

The musical notes fell to the floor with a clatter.

"That's ridiculous," I said.

Reuben shrugged.

"It's a *ridiculous* way for the Elves to find a new king," I persisted. "What if none of them finds the key?"

"All the Elves in the city will die," Reuben said irritably. "I just told you that."

"But!" I spluttered. "But . . ."

Reuben shook his head. "Don't upset yourself. It's bright magic. It's how it works. The questers are *motivated*, you see. And there are always at least a hundred Elves competing as questers. One of them is *sure* to find the key."

I looked down at little Gruffudd on the arm of the chair. "How many Elves are competing?"

Gruffudd peered up at me. "None," he said. "The Witches put them all to sleep, remember?"

CHAPTER 16

OSCAR

EVEN REUBEN LOOKED a bit shocked about that.

"*None?*" he said, his voice going deep and growly. "That's quite serious." He peered up at the ceiling, tugging on his beard. "I suppose they had all their protective borders down ready for the quest to begin and those Doom Lantern Witches took advantage and attacked. This really is . . . well, it's a disaster."

Gruffudd started to cry, his teeny shoulders going up and down. "I know! *I'm* going to have to do it! I have to save my city! I'm only six years old and I'm the only Elf who can do it!"

Harsh.

"Not to worry," Reuben decided. "These two children will help you in your quest."

"We will?" Imogen asked. "I'd have thought somebody more qualified might help. And we really need to get back to—"

"None more qualified to help this little Elf-child than you two, accompanied by your friends upstairs," Reuben interrupted, sounding more confident as he went along.

You two.

He was including me.

"Sorry," I said. "Going to have to give it a miss. I've gotta get home and—"

Reuben was shaking his head. "As for you, Oscar. Tell me, where are you from? Tell me all about you."

I gave him a look, then I told him that my mother's family was Italian and Scottish, my dad had been Chilean—Mum had met him on a holiday to California. He died in a motorcycle accident before I was born though. My stepdad was—

"Interesting," Reuben said, "but irrelevant for the moment. I mean—how did you get here?"

So I told him about the skate park and the mirror and the wave. Imogen added that I'd been dead all day.

Reuben chuckled. The craggy bits on his face got craggier. "You are from another world," he told me, "and you've come through a crack into ours for a reason. The Elves' bright magic will have put you into that death-like state for the day—it likely has inbuilt mechanisms to prevent people interfering with it. You won't be able to get home until the Elves are set free. Their bright magic will be blocking the crack between worlds. If it's not unlocked, you will be stuck here." He was very casual about this and went right back to addressing the Elf. "What can you tell us about the key?" he asked.

Gruffudd's voice started off confident, then slowed down as he carried on. "We learned in school that the key is kept in nine separate pieces. These are held by nine different people. The key keepers. They're all in this region . . . and we know who they are . . . because we learn songs that tell us who . . . they are. I think . . . Or give us . . . clues anyway . . . So. I do know . . . I *think* I know . . . *three* of the songs . . . but . . ."

A long, long pause.

"You skipped school the days your class did the *other* songs?" I guessed.

Reuben chuckled again. "Little Gruffudd," he said. "This is why you ought to go to school. You never know what you might learn . . . Imogen and Oscar, you will need your sleep for the quest that begins tomorrow. Meanwhile, I am going to have to help you without actually *helping* you. Hmm."

He paused and sat back into his chair. He was deep in shadow now and it was hard to see him. I squinted, trying.

Suddenly he was in the light again, hunched forward. His eyes had an excited, sparkly look.

"Gruffudd has three songs somewhere in his memory," he told us. "And each song contains clues to a key keeper."

"As to that . . ." Gruffudd began uncertainly.

"You do," Reuben insisted. "The songs will come back to you at just the right time, Gruffudd. Do not worry."

Gruffudd still looked doubtful, but Reuben continued.

"Imogen and Oscar, I am going to give each of *you* clues about three other key keepers. That will make up the remaining six."

"Righto," I said, ready to hear the clues.

Reuben shook his head. "I can't give them to you directly. I am going to hide each clue inside a . . . not a song. No. Inside a *memory*. Now, where should I put these memories?"

Back into the shadows he went, making muttering sounds.

And here he was, pressed forward again, even more excited. This time he had a small bottle in his hand. Looked like a fancy mineral water bottle, only with a cork in the top. It was that cobalt blue color that my mother likes—she collects jars and candleholders and things and lines them up on window ledges all over her house.

Reuben handed the bottle to Imogen.

"First thing tomorrow," he said, "take one memory from this bottle. You begin, Imogen, and then you and Oscar take turns. Only one memory at a time. Don't break the bottle."

Imogen was frowning. Probably thinking that if he didn't want us to break the bottle, plastic would have made more sense.

"The memory you take tomorrow morning will contain clues to the first key keeper, Imogen. Find that key keeper and claim their piece of the key. When I say "claim" I mean take it however you can—with some key keepers, you might ask politely; with others, apart from avoiding outright violence if you can, it's a free-for-all . . . You'll know the difference. Thus, the quest will begin. Once the quest begins, you cannot return to this inn until it's over. You must carry on to the next key keeper. Bring all that you need for a journey of three days and three nights. Collect all nine pieces and take the final key to the Elven city by ten A.M. on Friday. If you fail, a thousand Elves will die and Oscar will never return home. Do you understand what you must do?"

Imogen looked from the bottle in her hand to Reuben and back again.

"You're a *Genie*," she said suddenly.

Not sure how Reuben giving us an old mineral water bottle and detailed instructions about key keepers made him a Genie. Still, next thing you know, he'd vanished.

Nothing there at all this time except for shadows. I even touched the chair to be sure.

Imogen and I spent a bit of time staring at the empty chair and then at each other. Gruffudd seemed to have curled up and fallen asleep on the arm of the chair, and Imogen put him in her pocket.

"I'm very sorry," she said to me abruptly. "I didn't realize you were from another world. No wonder you don't know . . ."

"Anything?" I suggested.

Imogen laughed. "No, no, I mean . . . Still, you probably have very different magic in your world, so it's not your fault."

"No magic," I told her.

She stared.

"A completely magic-free world," I confirmed.

She was shocked but she held it together.

"Anyway, I fear the Genie is probably right," Imogen said, "and—"

"Of course I'm right," said a voice. Reuben was back in his chair. Pretty disconcerting, that. "Genies are always right," he added, and disappeared again.

Imogen raised an eyebrow and continued. "Genies do know things," she explained. "So I mean, can you cope with staying around and—"

"No worries," I said.

By now, see, I'd stopped being annoyed and confused. The switch in my mood had happened the moment an Elf squiggled out of my backpack.

If Elves were real, then all the other stuff about magic and former-pirates-turned-princes et cetera was probably real as well.

Genies too, I guessed. Although nobody was mentioning three wishes, which was annoying.

Anyhow, what I was thinking was this:

Who knows where this is or what it is, or why? Ah well, might as well enjoy myself.

CHAPTER 17

IMOGEN

THE CLOCK STRUCK midnight then—

BONG

BONG

BONG

BONG

(and so on, right up until twelve bongs)—
which meant, of course, that it was . . .

TUESDAY

CHAPTER 18

IMOGEN

TUESDAY MORNING, I woke early. Sunlight glowed at the edges of the curtain and lay in stripes across the beds. The others were still asleep.

This was lucky as it gave me time to organize my thoughts.

Right. Here was the problem.

An Elven city, and all its little Elves, would be destroyed on Friday morning if we didn't find a key.

The key was broken into nine pieces.

The nine pieces were held by nine different people: key keepers. To find the key keepers, we had to follow clues.

Typical bright magic, I thought, and my throat made a growling sound.

I'll tell you a secret. I despise magic.

Despise is a strong word. Sorry about that. I can't think of a better one just now.

Everyone despises *shadow* magic, of course. That's allowed. But most people are delighted by bright magic. They can't get enough of it. (My sister Esther has been obsessed with it for years.) Bright magic is the glistening, sparkling sort. Along the lines of butterflies and rainbows. It's performed by True Mages, such as Elves, Faeries, and Water Sprites, and it's all about love, healing, fortune, flight, problem solving, and so on. How could anybody not like it?

Well, I don't.

Here's why: it's too tricksy.

Everything's a game in bright magic, and the rules skitter away from you, turning themselves inside out. Prizes one moment, penalties the next.

I like people to look me in the eye, speak the truth, and be themselves. Don't sweet-talk or butter me up, don't swerve to the right at the very last moment, and *do not compel me to do something with a threat!*

If you want to find a new Elven king, *do NOT put a whole city of Elves—including tiny little child Elves!—in mortal peril!*

(Here, I looked beside me at Gruffudd. He was curled up in an open drawer in the chest by my bed, his thumb in his mouth, fast asleep. I'd placed him there in the dark last night, lining it first with my pillowcase. How many other Elf children were curled up in their own beds *deep beneath layers of silver?*)

Ridiculous! It was—

I realized I was breathing extremely noisily. I made myself calm down so that I wouldn't wake the others.

I hadn't finished organizing my thoughts.

All right, so that was the problem. What was the solution?

Obviously we would have to help Gruffudd find the nine key keepers.

I looked around at the others.

My cousin Bronte slept at the far side of the room, her head in the center of her pillow, chin pointing at the ceiling, as if she meant to raise a few issues with it. She, of course, was a Spellbinder. I hadn't mentioned that to Oscar as the identities of Spellbinders are always secret. Still, he would probably find out if we traveled together. Bronte would protect us from shadow magic while demonstrating excellent manners.

Alejandro, in the bed beside her, had his arms wrapped around his pillow as he slept: either hugging it affectionately or wrestling it to the ground. As a former pirate, he would build and repair things as required, sail a ship if called upon to do so, and—well, I didn't think his current princeliness gave him any special talents, but it added to his panache.

My sister Esther was hidden beneath her blanket, only her

hair slipping out, and my other sister, Astrid, was facedown, snoring softly. Esther, as a Rain Weaver, would be able to cure us if we were affected by shadow magic. She should also be able to sense magic of any kind and, if necessary, weave water. At some point later in life, she will be able to spellbind too—she's done a little training on that. There's a lot to being a Rain Weaver.

Astrid would be able to tell us exactly what people were thinking and feeling.

Finally, I looked at Oscar, in the bed beside mine. He slept fitfully. This way and that he turned, emitting gasps or growls.

No wonder, I thought. *Imagine discovering you were trapped in another world, far from your own life.*

He would not be helpful, of course, as he had no clue about this world. This was not his fault. I would have to keep an eye on him.

All right. That was our team. A very good team.

How would we find the nine key keepers?

Gruffudd had clues for three key keepers inside songs, and Oscar and I had clues for the other six. Our clues were inside memories in a Genie bottle. While that was strange, I would cope with it.

I'd have preferred to solve *all* the clues right now, make a list of the key keepers, and map out a route between them, except Reuben had said we had to figure out the key keepers one at a time.

I wasn't sure how I felt about Reuben.

I *hadn't* liked it when he said, "I am everywhere and nowhere at once," because I'd thought he was teasing me. Yet it turned out he was telling the truth. Genies *are* everywhere and nowhere at once. They're the reverse of the rest of us. They live outside time and space—they live outside *everything,* including magic—and they work inside dreams and memories.

Three of my memories were in a blue bottle.

That made my stomach go flip-flop.

I sat up in bed, reached a hand toward the bottle—it was on the chest of drawers beside me—and picked it up. It felt light and empty. Did memories have no weight?

How did we get a memory out of the bottle anyway? I peered through the glass but couldn't see anything in there. I pulled out the cork with a *pop!* and squinted, pressing one eye to the opening and—

There I was inside a memory.

I was six years old. I was following my mother around the markets at home. My two little sisters, Esther and Astrid, trailed behind me. Astrid was a toddler and walked unsteadily. They rock from side to side, small toddlers. We passed a stall crowded with trays of raspberries, strawberries, blueberries, and boysenberries. I stopped. I wanted a strawberry—they're my favorite. I reached out, but Mother said, "Imogen!" and I pulled back my hand. Next, there were pumpkins and gourds. I did not want a pumpkin, thank you. Then pots of honey set out in rows, then elegant bottles of olive oil, and so on. It was strange because I was small so my eyes were level with the produce. I did not have to look down to see things.

That thought made me look down. I was wearing my polished red shoes with the buckles. They'd been my favorite. I'd forgotten about them. I stopped to admire them and noticed, when I did so, a single red hair lying alongside my right shoe. It was on a yellow paving stone. The yellow paving stone was part of a path, I realized, with tufts of grass in between. Where did that path lead?

"Imogen?" said my mother.

I looked up. She had crouched down to speak to me. She handed me a silver coin. "Here," she said—

And I blinked.

I was back in the room at the inn. The memory was over.

Maybe Reuben wasn't a very experienced Genie. There was no clue inside that memory. All that it had done was remind me of my parents' note on the kitchen table the previous day: *Gone to the markets to get fresh pastries for breakfast! Back soon!*

I felt terrible thinking of them returning to an empty house, their arms filled with fresh pastries. Mother had been making a serious effort lately to focus on her children (us) and to remember things. For example, these days she remembered that Esther's favorite is blueberry tarts and that neither Astrid nor I can abide raisins. Father, also, had been spending less time reading his history books.

We should have been rewarding them for this change in their behavior by being there when they returned from the markets.

The memory hadn't even been accurate. There were no yellow paving stones at the markets. It was all cobblestone. I couldn't remember ever seeing a single red hair lying—

Oh. Wait. Was that the clue?

A yellow paving stone? A single red hair.

At that moment, a door slammed somewhere in the inn and the room around me stirred into wakefulness. Gruffudd jumped up and called in his squeaky voice: "Shall we have breakfast?"

The others sort of screamed in fright at that.

I explained everything to them—with interjections from Gruffudd, who leapt out of his drawer and sprang about the room introducing himself to everyone.

The story was a lot to take it in, especially considering they'd just woken up. But they listened carefully, only asking a few questions, and only staring in amazement at Oscar—whom they now knew to be a boy from another world—for four to five minutes.

Oscar himself, meanwhile, listened along in silence with sleepy eyes, the dimple flashing in his cheek.

"So," I said, once I'd finished explaining. "What do you think? Should we help Gruffudd save his city?"

"Of course!" the others all agreed, as I'd known they would.

CHAPTER 19

OSCAR

BREAKFAST WAS IN the dining room downstairs, and it was crowded and noisy.

It turned out that the inn had a whole lot of new guests, most of them as hyped up as ants that have found the sugar bowl.

A bunch of people wearing tuxedos walked around carrying brass instruments—trumpets and saxophones, that kind of thing.

A whole family were all wearing clown suits and makeup. They kept grabbing cutlery and glassware et cetera from other people's tables and juggling it. The other guests were pretty good sports about this and just said, "Oh!" quietly when a plate they'd been eating from was taken and tossed into the air.

Some people were in their pajamas and dressing gowns, and some came clumping along in muddy boots, brushing bits of straw off their clothes.

I was looking around at all this thinking, *Okay, so this is a different world. Don't judge.* But then I noticed the others had pretty judging faces of their own.

The innkeeper, Marion-Louise, was in a great mood. She pranced around handing out plates of eggs, sweeping up broken glass, and chattering with everyone.

"We're full to the brim today!" she told our table as she laid out pancakes and syrup for us. Her hand jumped back in fright when she accidentally brushed against Gruffudd. He was leaning against the pepper shaker.

Then she smiled and patted his head. "Oh, hello little Elf! Didn't see you there, sorry. Part of the quest, are you? That's why all the new guests are here, children, did you know? They've come to see Dun-sorey-lo-vay-lo-hey! It will be a true spectacle watching waves roar in and cover the city, over and over! Hundreds will be out there watching, waiting to see if the city is unlocked in time! It'll be like a carnival! That's why the performers are here—for entertainment."

She poured hot chocolate into our mugs and pranced away again.

We started eating. The others were talking about how to get a message to their parents and how to pack for a journey when we didn't know where the journey would take us and when nobody had anything to pack. I didn't pay much attention. I was watching Gruffudd. He was zipping around, from plate to plate, taking bits of everyone's pancakes. Now and then he sat down and scooped up some syrup with his hands.

He was superfast, that Gruffudd. Remember I said he was like a lizard when he jumped out of my bag? I kept thinking of lizards whenever I saw him running around. You know how lizards are tiny but they seem weirdly speedy, considering their size? Like they suddenly go *zip* across a footpath and *zip* up a fence and next thing they're over in somebody's yard, hiding from a magpie? Gruffudd was like that on the breakfast table.

And at many other points during our time together.

Anyway, so I was distracted and didn't really tune back in until I realized that Imogen was saying she'd already taken a memory from the bottle—something about going to buy fruit at the markets with her mum when she was little—and that she now had the clues to the first key keeper.

I looked over then.

Imogen, surprisingly, seemed embarrassed.

CHAPTER 20

IMOGEN

I *WAS* EMBARRASSED.

"A single red hair," I said, "lying on a yellow paving stone."

It didn't seem a very strong clue. That's why I was embarrassed. I felt as if my memory had failed. I mean—as if *I* had failed in my memory.

"What?" Esther asked, staring at me.

I repeated the clue. "At least," I said, "I *think* that's the clue."

Bronte leaned forward on folded arms. "What can you tell us about the paving stones?"

"They were shaped like apostrophes," I said, "and they all joined together to form a path, a path that led . . . somewhere."

"Yes, this is the nature of paths," Alejandro said encouragingly. He waited to see if I had more to add, and then he swung around and called, "Marion-Louise?"

Marion-Louise was whisking by our table, and she skidded to a stop at her name.

"Is there a person around who might know about paving stones? A builder? A contractor? A—how do you say this? A *paver*?"

Marion-Louise smiled at him. She was holding a tray of dirty glasses she'd just collected. She put the tray on her head. That is honestly what she did. Balanced a tray on her head, stood steady for a few moments—while the glasses trembled and swayed—then swept the tray back down into her hands.

A few people nearby applauded.

"Adequate," said the clown family, clearly annoyed that she was angling in on their territory.

"Hold up," Marion-Louise said, and she disappeared into the kitchen.

A moment later she was back, accompanied by a man in a chef's hat. He was holding a spatula.

"My sister has a construction company," he told us aggressively, as if we were planning to fight him for possession of his sister's construction company.

Alejandro asked if the man could introduce us to his sister, please, so we could ask her whether she ever used yellow paving stones shaped like apostrophes.

"No need," the chef said, still sounding fierce.

A moment went by.

"Well, but there *is* a need," Astrid put in.

"There's not," he bit back, "because *I* know the answer to your question. I help my sister out with paving sometimes. Also her bricklaying and tiling. You're talking about the golden curl paver."

"Curls!" I half-shouted, then quietened, embarrassed again. "Yes! They were shaped like big curls."

The chef crinkled his nose. "They're not very popular," he said.

At this point, Bronte smiled at him. "That's perfect!" she told him.

His anger diminished slightly.

"Cheers. Mind if I get back to the kitchen?"

"Just one more thing," Bronte persisted. "Can you think of any places where those paving stones have been used in this region?"

The chef gave his face a good rub to help him think (I assume), and tapped himself on the nose with his spatula (for the same reason, presumably, although was that hygienic?)

"The Hawthorne family," he said. "Waverley East Nature School. And the Very Funny Yolks Poultry Farm. They all have paths with golden curl paving stones."

"Does anybody with red hair live at those places?" I asked.

The chef glanced back toward the kitchen door. Smoke was drifting out of it.

"That I do not know," he said. "And, meantime . . ." He gestured at the smoke.

"Thank you for your help," Bronte offered.

The chef smiled and returned to the kitchen.

"I can answer that," said a boy in a dressing gown at the table next to ours. "Not the Hawthornes. Mr. H is bald as a rock, and Mrs. H has hair as black as a crow. Not the Very Funny Yolks Poultry Farm. They're a bunch of chickens. Ha-ha. But the teacher at Waverley East Nature School? She's got the most wonderful head of red hair! Teaches all the local farm kids— Grades One through Six. Taught me couple of years back. Mrs. Chakrabarti. She's your man."

That is how we decided that Mrs. Chakrabarti was the first key keeper.

CHAPTER 21

OSCAR

SEEMED TO ME that wasn't enough. What if the chef's sister had laid the pavers in *other* places, without the chef knowing? What if people could get them from a different construction company, or a wholesale place, and put them down themselves? What if the Hawthornes or the Very Funny Yolks Poultry Farm got *visited* by people with red hair? And so on.

The whole region could be filled with golden curl paths, red hairs lying all over them.

I kept my mouth shut though.

I was just along for the ride.

There was a fair bit more messing around then.

Marion-Louise seemed superexcited about helping us pack for the quest when Imogen asked her, and she made the chef prepare "food hampers" for us. She tracked down tents, sleeping bags, clothes from the lost property box, a map, a hatbox for Gruffudd to sleep in, a small velvet pouch where she said they could keep the fragments of key (optimistic), and so on.

She suggested we start our journey by borrowing the bicycles in the shed at the back of the inn.

"It's a pleasant bike ride from here to the Waverley East Nature School," she promised. "You'll find a pump and a few bike tools back there—take along whatever you like. And you can leave the bikes in any old shed or barn by the road when you're done with them."

"She's a *lot* more helpful than she was yesterday," Bronte murmured to me.

I stayed fairly quiet through all the preparations. Kept out of the way. All I thought of doing was putting that blue Genie bottle in the pocket on the side of my backpack. That's for water bottles, so it seemed pretty safe.

I gave the bottle a bit of a once-over before I jammed it in, and I couldn't see anything special about it. It was an empty bottle. A *pretty* bottle, sure, but did it have three of my memories inside it? Doubtful. And if it did, and Reuben had messed around with my memories, hiding clues inside them, wasn't that a bit . . . rude?

Ah, well.

In the end, I sat down in the lobby.

Gruffudd sat on the table beside me. We didn't have much to say to each other, but there was plenty to watch. So many strangely dressed people, finished with breakfast now, were heading through the lobby and out the front door.

Once the people had all left, Gruffudd did his teeny little sigh, which made me laugh, and he asked me for food, except I didn't have any.

"In your bag," he said.

"There's chip crumbs in here," I said, after I'd rummaged around in my backpack. "That's it."

He ate the crumbs anyway, and then he played a game where he kept climbing into the chip bag and then jumping back out of it and going, "Boo!"

I pretended to be scared each time he did that, which made him pretty happy—except it got old fast.

One time, Alejandro zoomed by, looked over, and asked if he could borrow my backpack for a minute.

"Go for your life," I said.

"My life?" He frowned.

"Just—I mean you can take it if you want."

"Thank you!"

And off he went with my backpack.

After a bit, he came back and said, "I hope you do not mind. I have gathered you some provisions from Marion-Louise for the days ahead."

I looked in the bag. Little stack of neatly folded shirts, balled-up socks, a pair of pj's, a bar of soap.

"Cheers," I said.

He bowed. "And I have attached straps on the reverse side," he said, "to hold your plank of wood."

"My what?"

"This plank you like so much? With the wheels?" He pointed at my skateboard. "I suppose that is the way in your world—you have planks of wood that you carry about with you. So. You will wish to have it with you on the quest? Difficult to carry on a bicycle, so may I suggest these straps as the solution?"

Then he disappeared again.

Alejandro was right. My skateboard fit perfectly in the straps he'd added—he'd remembered the size of my board. You held it flat to the bag, wheels facing out, wrapped the straps around, and buckled them up.

"Sweet," I said.

Gruffudd popped out of the chip bag. "Where?" he said.

"Where what?"

"The sweet. These crumbs are salty. Now I wish for a sweet. And not this worn-out one stuck to the packaging here."

I explained to him about the straps that Alejandro had made, and he climbed all over my backpack, checking it out.

"Excellent," he said in that squeaky little voice. "Yes. Superb craftsmanship. He is an artist, that Alejandro. Truly, a god."

He made me laugh so much.

One other thing I noticed, sitting in the lobby, was that Imogen and the others kept asking Marion-Louise how they could send a message to their parents. Telegrams, telephone calls, letter deliveries.

Marion-Louise kept telling them it was no use, that all the systems were still down or broken. No more postal delivery.

No telegram or telephone. No more coaches. No transport. A rockfall still blocking the pass through to the mountains.

Each time Marion-Louise shook her head like this, Imogen and her friends would make that wincing face you make when you're worried. They'd walk away, still looking worried.

It was Esther, the middle sister with the braids, who had just pulled that face after asking another question about sending messages when something occurred to me. "How did all these new guests get here then?" I called.

Marion-Louise and Esther turned to look at me. They were standing by the reception desk.

"Your hotel is full of people who weren't here yesterday," I pointed out. "So how'd they get here if there isn't any transport?"

Esther did a humorous double take at that and swung back around to face Marion-Louise. "*Yes!*" she said. "*How?*"

Marion-Louise bit her lip. "Oh, children," she said. "These guests arrived at dawn, in motorcars, with drivers, and the drivers have all driven away now!"

"Oh," said Esther, disappointed, but she shot me a smile, as if to say, "Thanks for the thought." Then she rushed off again.

Eventually, we were all standing on the driveway at the front of the hotel, holding our bikes, ready to go. There were packs on everyone's backs, more equipment tied to the sides of bikes, and some stacked in bike baskets.

Gruffudd was sitting on my shoulder, his teeny heels drumming. It felt like someone was gently tapping me with fingertips.

It didn't seem like a safe place for him to stay once we got going, though, so there was a bit of discussion about whose basket he should ride in. Eventually somebody asked for his preference.

"Of what do you speak?" he demanded, squeakily. (It felt tickly in my ear.) "I fail to understand!"

Turned out, he'd been thinking he'd get a teeny bicycle all of his own. When he realized this was not going to happen, he threw himself on his stomach and started crying. It felt like little drops of rain were falling on my T-shirt.

Anyway, they were still trying to comfort Gruffudd when Marion-Louise flew out of the door of the hotel shouting, "Hey!"

Two lace doilies were missing from our room.

"Here I've been helping you get ready for your journey, and you repay me this way! One of you has stolen my favorite doilies!"

Everyone stared at her.

"Why would we even want one lace doily?" Alejandro asked, genuinely confused. "Let alone two?"

This offended the innkeeper. "They were the most beautiful crocheted doilies you ever saw! Stitched with rosebuds! Why would you want them, indeed? Why would you *not* want them?"

Everyone started talking at once then, either trying to assure Marion-Louise that no offence was meant to her doilies or promising that they had not stolen her doilies. Astrid asked what a doily was.

I told her I thought it was a piece of material, like a mat, that you put on the furniture. Then you could put, like, a hot pot on top of it without leaving a mark.

"Don't you go putting hot pots on my precious doilies!" Marion-Louise cried, overhearing this.

I promised her that I would never even think of putting a hot pot on her doilies, which led to her pouncing: "Ha! So you *do* have the doilies!"

It took a while to convince her that, quite honestly, I had not come to another world to steal its doilies.

Eventually, Bronte made a very nice speech about how grateful we were for Marion-Louise's assistance in preparing for our quest, and how we had been doing much running about in the last hour, the door to our room often standing open, the room itself often empty . . .

"Oh, you're *right*," Marion-Louise said then, and tears filled her eyes. "So many new guests! Any of them could have slipped into your room and taken my doilies! I'll search their rooms while they're out, and their pockets when they return this evening. Quick! You'd best set off on your quest!"

Then we got ourselves and Gruffudd sorted, hopped on our bikes, and took off—in a slow, wobbly sort of way at first— while she stood there calling, "Farewell! Farewell! Good luck! Keep an eye out for my doilies!"

CHAPTER 22

IMOGEN

IT WAS A good day for a bicycle ride. The country road was long and straight, flat and smooth, and we rode beneath a big, blue sky.

This is going to be a great quest, I decided, *and probably nothing will go wrong.* That was a mistake, because next moment Astrid hit a bump in the road, shouted, "Ah!" and fell off her bike.

Esther, who had been riding behind Astrid, tried to veer around her and turned too sharply, so she fell too and toppled on top of Astrid. They were as tangled as a constrictor knot.

The rest of us waited, our toes to the road to keep our bikes steady, while my sisters giggled hysterically, disentangled themselves, gathered and repacked all the equipment, dusted themselves down, checked themselves and each other for grazes, assured us, and each other, that they were all right, apologized for the delay, got back aboard, and carried on.

Just as we had started riding again, a roaring sounded in the distance, and all six of us skidded to a stop in fright. There was something vicious in the sound. It was like a tornado carrying a thousand needles. It was also familiar.

"That's the noise that wave made, isn't it?" Oscar asked.

We looked at him in surprise. He'd been mostly quiet so far that day, and we'd avoided speaking to him ourselves, being shy of him now that we knew he was from another world. But he was right about the noise. (Actually, it was surprising every time Oscar was right. It seemed unexpected that a boy from another world could know anything, if you see what I mean.)

We all said, "Oh, yes, that's what it is!" in surprised and congratulatory voices, then we carried on riding, slowly, while the horrible noise continued. It was like a distant, ominous thunderstorm, only more ominous than that, because we knew it meant that an Elven city was being buried, and would continue to be buried until *we* found the pieces of the key.

We also knew that if we didn't find the pieces by Friday—if our quest failed—all the Elves would be crushed.

These were sobering thoughts. I looked around for Gruffudd, to see how sober he might be feeling, but I couldn't remember whose basket he'd ended up in. And I couldn't see him peeking over the edge of anybody's.

He was probably napping again. He often napped.

He struck me as very young to be a potential king.

Eventually, the noise faded and we rode more cheerfully again. We rode by fields with horses, cows, sheep, alpacas, or goats; by farmhouses and barns painted reds, blues, violets, and greens; by apple, peach, plum, and cherry orchards. I say this so you know what we rode by, rather than to be descriptive.

Friendly farmers waved to us from their porches or their fields, or from up in trees, or from ladders that leaned against barns. One of them shouted, "Get indoors! It's too hot to be riding!"

We waved back, calling, "Thanks!"

This is pleasant, I thought to myself. *I suppose the sun is getting warm on my shoulders, but otherwise*—and then the road turned a curve, and we were riding through forest.

Tall trees cast dappled shadows. These cooled us at once. Their branches stretched right across the road, meeting in the middle to form a sort of tunnel.

That's better, I thought. *I truly think that my sisters falling from their bicycles will be the only thing that goes wrong on this quest, and that otherwise—*

And then I found myself shouting, "Stop! Everyone stop!" and we skidded to a halt as—

pop!

pop!

pop!

pop!

—our bike tires were punctured by thorns.

"These are honey locust trees," I said sadly, pointing out the trees lining the road. "Also known as thorny locust."

We gazed at the trees and, in particular, at their thorny trunks and branches, and then we looked at the road. It appeared that the trees had given themselves a good shake in order to scatter a generous serving of long, spindly, and extremely sharp thorns in every direction.

"I did a school project last year on thorny trees," I told the others. "But I recognized them too late. It was like a slap in the face when I realized. I'm very sorry, everyone. The realizing should have slapped me sooner."

"It's not your fault," Bronte told me. "It's mine. Just that moment, I was thinking that this was going to be a perfectly pleasant adventure."

"I was thinking a similar thing," I admitted, at the same time as Esther piped up: "Me too! So it's my fault too. Apologies to everyone from me."

"Well, you won't believe it," Astrid began. "*I'm* sorry too, because—" I didn't hear what she said next because I caught sight of Alejandro and Oscar swinging their heads toward each other. Their eyes were very wide. Both of their faces suddenly contorted into bursts of laughter.

I supposed that, actually, it *was* funny, and I felt embarrassed.

Alejandro and Oscar finally stopped laughing for long enough for Alejandro to say, "Enough with the apologizing. It is nobody's fault except the trees." He looked around at them. "Ah, I am sure you have thorns for a reason, trees, I must apologize if I have caused you offense . . ." And then he and Oscar shouted with laughter for a while again. They kept saying, "Sorry,

sorry to laugh," to us, meaning it, and then realizing what they were saying, and laughing more, until eventually we were all laughing—us not quite so loudly as the boys.

Finally, Alejandro gave a happy sigh, said, "Let me take a look at the punctures," and dropped his own bike to the road— at which there was a high-pitched squeal and Gruffudd tumbled out of Alejandro's bike basket.

Gruffudd was bruised and grazed. He wailed for ages. Luckily, he hadn't hit any of the thorns, although he could have easily, which could have injured him seriously. I suppose it was the shock of that, along with the sound of his wailing (which honestly, went on and on, at a high pitch) that made us all suddenly snappy.

"Why did you drop the bike like that when Gruffudd was in your basket!" somebody demanded. (That might have been me.)

"I did not know he was *in* my basket!" Alejandro replied. He looked pale with guilt, and had picked up Gruffudd and was trying to comfort him.

Gruffudd kept pausing in his wails to say, "Mighty and lofty Alejandro! I thought you were a marvel! Yet you have flung me to the road! Why did you do that? Why? Oh, my heart is broken! Why? Why?" before continuing the wail.

"I thought you were in *Astrid's* basket," Alejandro told him. "I would never have flung you to the road!"

"*My* basket?" Astrid said. "I *wanted* him in my basket, but he said he'd go in yours!"

"I'm sure he told me he'd travel in your basket!" Alejandro argued.

"Well, Astrid fell off her bike earlier," Bronte put in. "So, he'd have fallen out at that point if he'd been in *her* basket. Didn't it occur to you that he must therefore *not* be in her basket, Alejandro?"

"I do not understand you," Alejandro told her, irritably.

The argument carried on, everyone blaming somebody, Gruffudd wailing, and Oscar quietly examining all our tires.

"Every single one is punctured," he said mildly, in a pause in our argument.

Even Gruffudd stopped wailing at that and looked surprised.

"I will fix them," Alejandro said, setting Gruffudd down on the side of the road and taking out the repair kit he'd found in the shed at the inn.

With Esther's assistance, Alejandro removed all the inner tubes, patched them, replaced them, and pumped them up again. Meanwhile, Astrid consoled Gruffudd with a piece of chocolate, whispering to him that *she'd* never have let him fall out of *her* basket (apparently forgetting that she'd fallen off her bike earlier). Bronte and I studied the map.

"It's not far," we told the others. "About half an hour down the road."

We wheeled our bikes slowly and carefully through the thorny patch, and then, when the trees gave way to fields again, we rode in silence until we turned a bend. There was a small country school. Its name was affixed alongside the open door of a weatherboard cottage with peeling paint:

WAVERLEY EAST NATURE SCHOOL

And there *she* was, standing on the veranda.

Mrs. Chakrabarti.

Schoolteacher, Grades 1 through 6.

Our first key keeper.

CHAPTER 23

OSCAR

IT HAD TAKEN about an hour to ride to the school from the hotel, including the break to fix punctures, so it was around 10:30 A.M. at this point.

It was recess time. The yard was full of kids. Some were sitting on the grass peeling mandarins, some were playing handball on the path (yellow paving stones shaped like apostrophes). A few girls had a skipping rope and were doing a jumping game with a chant:

"You find it in the morning

You find it in the night

You find it when you're snoring

You find it when you're quiet

You find it if it's sunny

You find it in the rain

And if you don't find it

I'll push you down the drain."

Harsh.

The teacher was standing on the veranda, leaning against a post, smiling down at a tiny ceramic frog. The frog was a gold-green froggy color and it sat on the far left of the top veranda step.

The teacher had hair that was a bright orange color—I don't get why people call that red. It's orange, not red, right? But they do—and it was wound on top of her head in a bun.

We left our bikes and packs out front and stepped between kids toward her.

Imogen explained the situation as we approached— schoolkids staring at us, or ignoring us and getting on with their games—and before she'd even finished talking—

"Why yes," Mrs. Chakrabarti said. "I *am* the Keeper of the Key."

Everyone seemed fairly amazed to hear this, so I guess it wasn't just me who'd had doubts.

There was an awkward pause for a moment and then some-body—I think it was Esther—said: "Um. In that case, may we please have your piece of the key?"

Mrs. Chakrabarti laughed like a drinking fountain. Bits of laughter splashing up and out of her mouth, I mean.

"You think it's as simple as *that*?" she said. "Ah, children." And she shook her head like an extremely annoying person.

CHAPTER 24

IMOGEN

EXACTLY.

"Why *shouldn't* it be that simple?" I demanded.

Keeping in mind that we had *nine* pieces to collect, and that anything could go wrong in our journey, and that we only had until Friday.

Astrid, who'd been distracted watching the children play, swung around. "You do know that Elves will be crushed to death if we don't get the key in time?" she snapped, sounding ferocious.

"Of course I know that!" Mrs. Chakrabarti laughed again. "Everyone knows. I *also* know that this is a competition amongst Elves to find their new king! The winner must prove themself fit to be a king! You are the first to arrive and, I mean to say, you're not even *Elves*!"

We all tried to locate Gruffudd, who had disappeared again, so that we could demonstrate that we did, in fact, have an Elf.

We needed to do a better job at keeping track of him.

Eventually, he squirmed out of Oscar's pocket—Oscar jumped in alarm to find him there—clambered up Oscar's arm, and perched on his shoulder.

"I am Gruffudd! The only Elf on the quest for the key! These fine and wondrous children are here at my beck and call, they are here at my command, here at my service! Bow before me, Mrs. Chakrabarti, Keeper of the Key, and *hand it over*!"

We giggled, although our giggles were also frown-laced. On the one hand, Gruffudd was a sweet child being playful. On the other hand, we were *not* here at his beck and call or his command. We were independent people, doing a large favor.

"Young scallywag," the teacher said, gazing at Gruffudd fondly. Then she raised her eyebrows. "The only Elf on the quest, eh? So *that* city is doomed. Anyhow"—she smiled over at us—"you still have to pass my tests before I give you the key. Ate-elevens."

There was a pause.

What did *ate-elevens* mean? Was it a game played in these parts? Who ate their elevens and how did elevens taste?

"Come on, come on, you're about to lose already!" Mrs. Chakrabarti urged. "Quick sticks! Ate-elevens!"

We looked at each other, mystified, and then a small schoolgirl, turning somersaults on the grass nearby, called, "Eighty-eight!"

"Ohhhhhh," we all cried. "*Eight times eleven!* Eighty-eight! It's eighty-eight!"

"You only know that because Sharmilla told you. Don't answer any more, Sharmilla! You're helping these children cheat!"

Sharmilla paid no attention, as she was somersaulting again.

We all argued passionately that it was *not* cheating, that we had simply not understood the question, and that, if we *had* understood, we would have answered correctly. Anything times eleven is easy. You just double the number. It's just eleven, twenty-two, thirty-three, forty-four, fifty-five, and so on.

"Well," said Mrs. Chakrabarti doubtfully. "Seven sevens."

"Forty-nine!" we all cried at once, keen to prove ourselves.

"Nine twelves?" she asked next, archly.

There was a brief pause.

"One hundred and eight," Bronte replied (while the rest of us were trying to recall—I always find that one tricky).

"All right, how about seven times four divided by two?"

A pause. "Fourteen!" Esther answered. "Unless there are

brackets? Are there brackets? This is an order of operation thing, isn't it? Or wait. Is it the same even if there *are* brackets?"

Mrs. Chakrabarti ignored her and asked another question.

This went on for some time. At least fifty mathematical questions were asked, and we answered as rapidly as we could. Some of the children in the yard stopped their games to watch, although they quickly grew bored and returned to playing. Our brains began to ache, or mine did anyway. Once or twice, one of us called a wrong answer, but another of us would, fortunately, correct them in time.

At last, Mrs. Chakrabarti nodded. "Not bad," she said.

"Excellent, my servants!" Gruffudd called squeakily from Oscar's shoulder. "You have answered well! Onward with our quest! The key, if you please, Mrs. Chakrabarti!"

This "servant" game of his could become tiresome.

"That's merely the beginning." Mrs. Chakrabarti smiled. "Next, you must clean my schoolhouse. We'll start with mopping the veranda—taking care not to knock over Ferdinand the frog on the step there—then we'll move to the windows, sweeping out the . . ." Her voice became inaudible as she moved into the classroom. We could hear her babbling away in there, opening cupboards, clanging and banging, a tap running, and occasional words floating out, "Dust the . . . empty the . . . sort through . . . polish the . . ."

"Oh, and sprinkle some fish food into the aquarium!" she finished, springing back into the doorway, a sloshing bucket of water in one hand, mop in the other. "Enjoy!" she concluded.

We looked at one another in horror.

My temper stirred and growled. Bronte looked sideways at me and spoke up in her most polite voice.

"Mrs. Chakrabarti," she said. "Although we would be glad to assist, that would take hours. We still have several key keepers to visit before Friday."

"Think of the Elves!" Esther pleaded.

Mrs. Chakrabarti shrugged. "That's exactly what I'm doing," she said. "I'm ensuring that the new Elven king is sufficiently committed to the quest."

"I am!" little Gruffudd called. "I am thoroughly committed! I order my servants to carry out every single task Mrs. Chakrabarti requires! And perhaps a few more, for good measure? At once!"

Oscar tilted his head and gazed at the Elf on his shoulder.

"Don't look at me like that," Gruffudd complained.

"As Keeper of the Key," Mrs. Chakrabarti declared, "I require—"

Chuckle.

That was Astrid chuckling. A low, quiet chuckle, unexpected, so we all turned to look at her.

She was smiling at Mrs. Chakrabarti.

"Can you say that again?" she asked. "What you just said?"

The teacher frowned. "As Keeper of the Key," she repeated obligingly, "I require—"

But Astrid was turning to the rest of us: "She's not a Keeper of the Key at all. She's lying."

CHAPTER 25

OSCAR

"OH BLAST," SAID Mrs. Chakrabarti, setting down the bucket of water. "I should have got you to do the cleaning first. Before the sums."

She leaned against the post again and shrugged.

What?

Excuse me, *what?*

What?

That's what my brain was doing.

The others said, *"Oh, for goodness' sake!"* and *"Are you serious?"* and Bronte put a calm-down hand on Imogen's back and told her to breathe. (She *was* breathing. Noisily.) Next thing, they were heading back toward the front gate. "Should we try the Very Funny Yolks Poultry Farm instead?" one of them asked.

They processed a lot faster than me, I guess, because I was still standing on the veranda thinking:

What?

Mrs. Chakrabarti had *lied?*

She'd wasted our time pretending to be a key keeper? But—

"Why would you *do* that?" I demanded.

In reply, Mrs. Chakrabarti smiled. The weird sort of smile that teachers give that means: *Well, I just KNOW more than you do!*

It didn't help me find forgiveness in my heart, I can tell you now.

"Come on, Oscar," Bronte called from her bicycle. "We'd best get moving."

"Onward and upward," Gruffudd urged from my shoulder, kicking his little heels against me in a way that could start to bruise. "It is fortunate that Astrid can read people so well."

Fortunate, sure, but why had she not *read* Mrs. Chakrabarti earlier, before we'd answered all the math questions? (To be fair, I'd let the others answer, math not being my best subject. Still.)

"I was looking away when she first said she was Keeper of the Key," Astrid called from the gate (as if she'd read my mind). "Sorry."

"Don't blame yourself," Imogen told her. "It didn't even *occur* to me to doubt her. It's lucky you realized before we'd cleaned her blasted school and fed her blasted fish." (Bronte did the calming hand thing again.) "Hurry up, Oscar. We have to try one of the other places."

They were all loaded onto their bicycles, waiting for me. I glanced back at Mrs. Chakrabarti.

She smiled her infuriating smile again and then, right as I stepped down from the porch, she whispered, "But I can *tell* you who the key keeper is."

"Hold up," I called to the others. "She knows who it is."

* * *

Turned out, she wanted us to play a game before she'd tell.

"You six questers will compete with the students in my school." She gestured at the kids in the yard. They were getting a bit restless—their games had turned wild—some hair pulling, some shoving, a fair bit of outraged shouting for the teacher's help.

I guess recess had been going for a while.

"If one of you, just *one* of you, is the winner of this game?" Mrs. C went on, ignoring the violence and screams for assistance, "I will tell you the actual identity of the key keeper."

Astrid studied her face closely.

"She's telling the truth this time," she announced.

So we played the game.

It was a bit like a game I used to play at after-school care.

Markers labeled NORTH, SOUTH, EAST, and WEST were set up in four separate corners of the school yard. Competitors gathered in the middle. Mrs. Chakrabarti stood on the veranda, facing the wall, and shouted instructions like "Skip!" or "Dance!" or "Hop on the spot!" Now and then, she'd spin around, and you had to freeze. Anyone who didn't freeze in time was out.

The wild-card element was this: occasionally she'd say, "Home is . . ." and then, as she spun around to face us, she'd shout a direction. The moment she said, "Home is . . . !" you had to sprint to the north, south, east, or west marker. Anyone still in the middle was out. And if you weren't in the corner she'd chosen? You were out.

So it was a game of reflex (being able to freeze instantly), a game of speed (getting yourself to one of the corners as soon as she said, "Home is . . ."), and a guessing game (guessing the right corner).

There were about forty schoolkids, and six of us "questers."

Gruffudd sat on the top step watching the game while nibbling on a piece of banana.

About this game.

It moves pretty fast.

Each time she spun around, Mrs. Chakrabarti would catch a handful of kids who hadn't frozen in time. They'd be out. Another couple of kids would try to freeze in an awkward pose, like on one leg, so they'd topple over onto the grass and be out.

Alejandro was eliminated because he got too focused on his dance moves. They were pretty funny—we were laughing at him and had trouble freezing in time ourselves.

But it was when Mrs. C did her "Home is . . ." thing that the numbers fell drastically. Basically, kids would rush to all four corners, spreading out fairly evenly, which meant that, when she declared the "home" direction, three-quarters of the kids would be eliminated.

Bronte and Imogen were eliminated the first time she did it. It was just luck that Esther, Astrid, and I happened to be in the west corner, her choice.

Another lucky thing:

Because I used to play this game at after-school care, I knew to keep a close eye on Mrs. Chakrabarti. You get a sense, from a sudden tension in a person's shoulder, or a twitch in their foot, say, of when a person is about to spin around. That way, you can be ready to freeze—or to sprint to a corner.

This is why I noticed something weird the first time she did her "Home is . . ." bit.

She looked up and to the left before she did it.

Up and to the left was the school sign:

WAVERLEY EAST NATURE SCHOOL

It was printed in a slightly fancy way, and the first letter of each word was big and bold and curly. Like this:

*W*AVERLEY *E*AST *N*ATURE *S*CHOOL.

This funny feeling, like *zoop!*, went sideways through me.

I ran west.

West was what she chose.

A few minutes later, it happened again—her head went up so she was looking directly at the sign and she said, "Home is . . ."

People rushed to the four corners. Everyone squawking, changing their minds, zipping around.

I went east.

". . . east," she said.

Esther and Astrid had also ended up east, so all three of us were still safe.

A bunch of other kids got out, of course, and there was a lot of groaning. All the eliminated players became spectators. They stood on the path cheering and shouting advice.

Imogen was shouting something. I couldn't understand the words at first, in all the noise, then I made it out: "Next time she says 'home,' *go to different corners!*"

That made sense.

There were ten or twelve kids left in the game, including us three.

The best probability of one of us getting it right would be if we went in separate directions.

The game went on for a while, Mrs. C having us jump up and down, turn circles, do push-ups, and then freeze, freeze, freeze. We were down to the experts though, kids determined to win. It was going to be the "home" turn that got us.

Mrs. C stood up there facing the wall.

She was perfectly still.

A tiny shift in her right knee, and *spin*, she was back around. I froze.

We all did.

She turned back. "Choose a partner and waltz with each other!" she instructed. Kids partnered up, giggling. Astrid was grabbed by a smaller girl from the school and they started half-waltzing, mostly tripping over and laughing.

Esther happened to be beside me, and we shrugged and joined hands.

I wasn't sure exactly how to waltz—I knew it was some kind of 1, 2, 3 thing, but Esther seemed to know. She was good at it too, which was surprising, since she seemed like a dreamy one. She was leading me in the moves so smoothly that it was easy. Her eyes stayed on Mrs. C though, and I could tell she was using my tactic.

When Mrs. C did it again—head turning toward the school sign—I felt a sudden tightening in Esther's right hand. I looked at her face. She was biting her lip, watching.

"Home is . . ." Mrs. C cried, and even as Imogen shrieked, "*Go to different corners!*" Esther and I both flung ourselves to the north.

"North!"

Esther and I were safe.

Astrid had gone west. She joined the others, looking sad.

Only three players left.

Esther, me, and a small kid, maybe eight years old.

He wanted to win fiercely, that kid, you could see it in his face and the way his shoulders hunched. His whole school wanted him to win too, and they were all screaming their heads off. "Go, Raoul! Go, Raoul!" So I guess his name was Raoul. He got even fiercer at the sound of them screaming. Also, he blushed a little bit, which was cute.

The three of us were hopping in little circles, Mrs. C's latest instruction.

She spun around.

We froze.

I was on one foot.

Mrs. C studied us. Long, drawn-out moment. I could feel a tremble somewhere deep within me.

I was going to fall.

Caught my balance.

Held it.

Stayed frozen.

"Okay," Mrs. C said. "This has gone on long enough. The next time I send you home, that's where the game ends. Winner—or winners—will be chosen at that point. Keep hopping in circles."

She turned back around to face the wall.

Murmurs ran through the crowd. She'd allowed for a tie. There could be a tie. Or *nobody* could win.

"Go, Raoul! Go, Raoul!" the crowd chanted in a low murmur that grew and grew.

Bronte and the others tried calling, "Go, Oscar! Come on, Esther!" but their voices were pretty comprehensively buried by the chanting.

"*Next time, go to different corners!*" Imogen bellowed, cutting through. She was cranky at Esther and me for disobeying the last time we went "home," except she couldn't be *that* cranky since it had actually worked out.

I was getting dizzy.

Hop, hop, hop, around, around, around.

It hurt my neck, trying to keep an eye on Mrs. C while I hopped.

"*Go, Raoul! Go, Raoul!*"

I wondered if Raoul had the right idea. He wasn't watching Mrs. C, or anyone at all. Actually, his eyes were *closed*. That was how he concentrated. Not a bad technique. Should I try—

And then I saw Mrs. C's head turn toward the sign.

I looked at Esther. She'd seen it too.

"Home is . . ."

"*Different corners!*" Imogen shrieked.

It was going to be south.

I sprang toward south. Esther did too.

A split second.

Raoul threw himself to the west.

I understood why. It had been a while since she'd said 'west.'

But it was going to be south.

"*Different corners!*" Imogen blasted.

I knew it would be south.

Then—and this is all happening inside a split second, by the way—I caught sight of Mrs. C's profile, and she was smiling that smile. That *superior* smile.

Lightning fast, it came to me.

Mrs. C's voice earlier: *If one of you, just one of you, is the winner of this game?* she'd said, *I will tell you the actual identity of the key keeper.*

If one of you, just one . . .

Did that mean . . . ?

Last second, very last second, I sprang away from south.

Mrs. C spoke a word and spun around.

CHAPTER 26

IMOGEN

"SOUTH."

That's the word that Mrs. C spoke: "South."

A frozen moment.

Raoul was west.

Oscar was in the middle.

Esther was south.

She had won.

Every kid in the school shouted *"NO!"* heartbroken, then abruptly every child noticed Oscar, still stuck in the middle. This improved their moods considerably. They erupted into laughter.

Oscar grinned crookedly and bowed, so they laughed even harder. Next, he turned and shook Raoul's hand.

"You played well," he said.

Raoul nodded, very serious: "Thank you. You too."

To Esther, Oscar said, "Nice one," while trying to bump fists, which confused her.

We rushed over to congratulate Esther. It was tricky to do this audibly, as the schoolchildren were still in hysterics about Oscar.

"He couldn't make up his mind!"

"So he ended up stuck in the MIDDLE!"

"He'd have WON if he'd just STAYED in the south!"

And similarly obvious things.

I felt terrible. "Sorry," I said to Oscar. "That was my fault for telling you to go to different corners. You and Esther could have tied for first place."

Oscar shook his head. "Your strategy made sense," he said. "Anyway, Esther won and that's what matters."

Esther herself had lapsed into a daydream.

Mrs. Chakrabarti blew a whistle.

When she blew it, loud and sharp, her students fell completely silent and lined up in pairs at the foot of the stairs.

"Right then," Mrs. Chakrabarti pronounced. "One, and *only* one, of the questers has won the game. If two had tied for victory, you would *not* have succeeded."

That was a confusing moment for me because my temper surged at her for being tricky. However, we had won. Therefore there was no point in its surging.

"I will now reveal the identity of the key keeper!" Mrs. Chakrabarti continued. She paused with unnecessary drama.

We were on the grass just beneath the veranda. The schoolchildren, still in neat lines, stared at us.

We held our breath.

Would it be the Hawthornes or the Very Funny Yolk Poultry Farm?

"It's *her*," said Mrs. Chakrabarti.

And she pointed to a small girl at the back of the line.

Sharmilla. The girl who'd told us the answer to the first math question. Long dark hair, large dark eyes, holding a coiled-up skipping rope.

This child stepped forward.

"I am the Keeper of the Key!" she said.

"Oh, for goodness' sake and badness' sake and moderately fine's sake too," little Gruffudd called from his place at the top of the stairs. "Are you serious?"

The girl frowned. "Sometimes?" she replied. "Sometimes I am serious. Other times," she confessed, "I'm quite lighthearted."

"Do you really have a piece of the key?" Astrid demanded.

"Why yes," the little girl replied. "It's in my pocket." And she reached into her pocket and drew out a small metal rod, knobs at both ends, shiny silver.

"That's not a key!" a nearby schoolchild scoffed. "It's a stick!"

"It's a *piece* of a key," Mrs. Chakrabarti corrected him. "Now, Sharmilla, was your pocket the safest place to keep your piece of key?"

"It's where my mother told me to put it!" Sharmilla argued. "She always kept it in her pocket, and so did my grandmother, and my great-grandmother, all the way back to when the Elves first gave it to our family to keep for this day!"

Mrs. Chakrabarti nodded. "Very well. Don't get in a state, dear. And tell us, Sharmilla, is there any task you'd like these questers to perform before handing over the key?"

All six of us questers sighed.

Sharmilla looked at us shyly and said, "Perhaps one of you might get down the ball I accidentally kicked onto the roof of the schoolhouse yesterday?"

Esther said she would do it, as she likes climbing, but Alejandro, who used to do a lot of shimmying up the mast of a pirate ship, had clambered to the roof before Sharmilla had stopped talking.

We all looked up at him. There was a brief silence.

"You're so high!" Sharmilla called. "Touch the sky!"

Around her, the children laughed and chanted: "You're so high! Touch the sky!"

Alejandro reached his hands into the air, as if trying to touch the sky. The children cheered. He grabbed the ball, tossed it to Sharmilla, and scrambled down again.

"Thank you." Sharmilla smiled, and she held out the metal rod and placed it on my palm.

We had the first piece of the key.

CHAPTER 27

OSCAR

YOU MIGHT BE wondering what I was thinking about all this—the new world, I mean, and running around with a bunch of strangers looking for bits of a key.

Mostly I was thinking it was better than school.

As we rode our bikes away from Waverley East Nature School—heading for a meadow down the road which had a bunch of shady trees and which Imogen said looked like a good place to stop to sort out the next key keeper—that was the loudest thought in my brain. Those kids were lining up to start learning stuff again and here I was on a bike, riding on a country road.

It was also more relaxing than skipping school usually is, because there was no chance somebody could bust me. (It had never once occurred to me before this that the solution to getting busted is to head to another world.)

So to summarize, I was pretty happy. There *had* been a tiny moment, after the game, when the schoolkids were laughing about how I forgot to go home, when I suddenly thought: *Wait, I will be ABLE to go home, right?*

That was a wild moment. I stepped out of it fast and moved back to being happy.

I had plenty of questions, of course. Like, what exactly was a Shadow Mage? Plus, why did a bunch of Elves sit down a hundred years ago and think to themselves: *How do we choose a new king? Make it hereditary? Hold elections? No, tell you what, let's break a key into nine pieces, hand them around, and bury ourselves under gooey silver stuff. Yes. Genius. That's the one.*

Another question: how were we going to weld the pieces of key back together once we had them all?

I didn't ask anything though. If I started, it could be like turning on a tap that you can't turn off. I'd be the water running down the drain and disappearing into the pipes.

Still, there was one question I did ask as we dropped our bikes on the grass and settled under a tree close to the road: "What year is it?"

Why did I ask that question?

Well, as we left the school, Imogen and the girls turned back and went to speak to Mrs. Chakrabarti for a moment. That left Alejandro and me on the road on our bikes. We talked a bit about the game, and how lucky it was that Astrid had realized Mrs. Chakrabarti wasn't the key keeper before we cleaned the school.

"How does she do that?" I asked.

"Ah, it is a skill of hers," Alejandro replied. "To read people? A magnificent skill. She developed it playing poker, and she is a champion player—so are her sisters. It is surely a true skill within her and yet also? She has a nature like sunshine."

Then he did an impressive wheelie on his bike, so I tried it too.

The girls joined us then. Turned out they'd been asking the teacher if she could please get a message to their parents. Same as back at the hotel, though, the teacher had apparently told them she couldn't help.

So the girls were depressed, which got me thinking.

This world clearly didn't have mobile phones or email. Horses and carriages seemed the main way to get around, and "automobiles" and even "telephones" were special and rare. All this, along with the clothes, the decor, and the language, gave the place a 1920s vibe to me. (My stepdad likes to play this video game that's set in the 1920s. The graphics are excellent, or anyway that's what he tells me each time he plays it.)

Had I traveled not just to another world, but also to another time?

That's why I asked the question.

And: nope.

Turned out I hadn't.

The others flashed each other the look they often shared when I spoke, and they told me what year it was. Same as at home.

So it was only that my world was way ahead of theirs in terms of technology.

I felt a bit proud then. We had so many inventions that they didn't! I could make a fortune introducing computers and the internet here! I could make their lives *way* more convenient!

If I knew how to build computers and the internet, of course, which I did not.

Still. I was proud.

CHAPTER 28

IMOGEN

WELL, I WAS exhausted.

I hadn't slept much the night before, but it was more than that. It was this: I'd been thinking that the tricky part of this quest would be finding out *who* the key keepers were.

Not getting the key from them.

The idea that *eight* other key keepers might all be as tricky and challenging as Mrs. Chakrabarti exhausted me.

Of course, Mrs. Chakrabarti was not the key keeper. It was the little girl, Sharmilla, and she only needed us to get a ball down from the roof.

However, that was just a technicality.

There were too many twists and turns, and we'd barely even begun.

I decided we should take a proper break and eat lunch before we solved the clue of the second key keeper. It was Oscar's turn to take a memory from the Genie bottle. That made me uneasy. Would a boy from another world know how to have a memory? Or how to spot a clue inside a memory? Did they even have memories in his world? Or clues?

The others were still chatting excitedly about how annoying Mrs. Chakrabarti had been, and how lucky it was that Esther had gone north—or whatever direction it was that she'd gone; I think it was south, actually—and that also made me listless. I'd given Oscar the wrong advice about going in different directions, which had turned out to be the *right* advice, for the wrong reason. Confusing.

They had spread out some towels on the grass and were looking for lunch in our packs. Gruffudd grew bored of waiting and began munching on a dandelion but quickly spat that out.

I roused myself and found the sandwiches that the chef had prepared. I handed them around. Tomato. Soggy.

I felt even more weary.

After we'd eaten, I was about to ask Oscar if he was ready to take a memory from the bottle when Bronte spoke.

"Can you tell us why you have that plank of wood?" she asked, sounding a bit shy. "I think I heard you call it a "boardskate"? What's it for?"

I was pleased with her for asking, as I'd been wondering the same thing. I think the others had too, because I noticed them fall quiet and turn to Oscar.

Oscar smiled at the question.

"You ride it," he explained, and he unstrapped it from his backpack, carried it over to the road, and placed it on the ground. Then he stood up and stepped onto it. Keeping one foot on the board part, he set his other foot on the ground and pushed. The device ran along noisily for a short distance while he held his balance, then it hit a dip in the road and he stumbled, stepped off it, and picked up the board.

"Oh," Bronte called politely. "I see."

"And you can do tricks," Oscar added. He dropped the board again, rode it for a short distance, then jumped in the air, lifting the board with his feet somehow and tapping it so that it spun around—twice, I think—very quickly before landing again with a *thud*.

"Oh, it's a *magic* object!" most of us exclaimed in a chorus.

Oscar frowned. "No. It's a skateboard."

"With bright magic in it?" Esther suggested.

He shook his head.

"Then how did you do that? Make it spin like that? If it doesn't have bright magic?"

"Practice." He shrugged, standing half on and half off the board. "It's just a trick."

Astrid wanted to know what other "tricks" people did on their boards in his world, and Oscar began speaking a peculiar language, saying things like *pop shove, 360 kickflip,* and *50–50 grind.*

After he'd finished his list I asked, "And what's the point of it exactly?"

"Yes, why do you do it?" Esther wondered.

Very briefly, a blank expression fell over Oscar's face. He walked back toward us and began re-strapping his skateboard to his satchel.

I felt as if I'd made a mistake but didn't know what it was.

"Oscar," I began, at which there was a yelp from Gruffudd. He had been lying on his back on one of the towels, and now he leapt to his feet.

"I remember!" he said. "A key keeper song! I remember one of the songs we learned at school! Listen as I sing!"

And then he sang. Twirling in circles, little jumps left and right, this is what he sang:

"In the Curlicue Forest,

Across the Old Putty Bridge,

There's a dark, hidden cave

Where some Radish Gnomes live.

Good luck getting in!

They'll not answer the door,

They'll not answer your shouts,

They'll not answer your calls!

But if somehow you manage

(We don't hold much hope!)

Be wary and cautious

(Who knows if you'll cope?)

They won't offer coffee,

They won't give you tea,

But if you are lucky?

You might grab some key!"

When he stopped, he bowed deeply, then straightened up and frowned.

"Why do you all look so *serious*?" he asked.

Of course we looked serious.

The second key keeper was a Shadow Mage.

CHAPTER 29

OSCAR

I DOUBT I was looking serious. I still hadn't figured out what a Shadow Mage was.

The others got into a huddle and started an intense conference. I can only remember bits of what they said. Imogen was doing the most talking, at the same time as breathing exactly like my stepdad did that time he tried to run a half-marathon without any training (they had to call the paramedics in for him). *"Why* would they have made a *Shadow Mage* one of the key keepers!" was the gist of what Imogen was saying, but there was a lot of *ridiculous* and *preposterous* mixed up with that.

Esther explained that True Mages sometimes make deals with Shadow Mages, to "complicate" their spells. "The Elves must have given the Radish Gnomes a reward in exchange for their becoming one of the key keepers," she suggested. "They would have to follow certain rules to keep their reward."

"Including a rule that says they can't use their shadow magic against us?" Imogen asked, suddenly hopeful.

"Well, no," Esther said. "I doubt it. They'd have included a Shadow Mage as a key keeper to make the quest more challenging and dangerous. The shadow magic would be *part* of the challenge."

"It's all right," Bronte put in. "I should be able to spellbind two or three Radish Gnomes—"

"And if there's more than two or three?"

"Hmm . . ."

More *ridiculous!* and *preposterous!* from Imogen.

There was talk of Bronte constructing a Spellbinding ring of protection—whatever that was—around all of us, which would "hold against several Radish Gnomes"—then more talk about how you had to "stay inside the Spellbinding ring" and you couldn't "move around with it."

Also, making a Spellbinding ring near the Radish Gnomes' cave would *alert* them to our being there, apparently, since they'd be able to sense the Spellbinding, so we'd lose the element of surprise?

That's all I can remember, and I might have some of it wrong.

I know they all kept talking for a while, and Imogen looked at the map and figured out the route to the Curlicue Forest and the Old Putty Bridge. She mixed things up by saying *ludicrous!* and *absurd.*

Astrid and Alejandro mostly just tried to be calming, and Gruffudd sang his song and did his dance, over and over and over—which was the opposite of calming.

That's how they should teach everything at school, by the way. Through song and dance. It still wouldn't stick in my mind, but it'd be funny, watching the teachers try to carry it off with their croaky old voices and bodies.

I didn't really get all the hysteria. Based on Gruffudd's song, it might be tricky to get a Radish Gnome's attention, and they wouldn't give us a cuppa—I was pretty sure I'd cope without one. The others kept saying *Radish Gnome* in voices like you might use for *shark attack* or *math exam.* A Radish Gnome sounded cute to me. Little guys probably (I thought), the size and shape of radishes.

Anyhow, we packed up and got back on our bikes.

Imogen was still in a fierce mood.

She started telling us to get a move on. She kept looking at her wristwatch (not having phones means they have to wear watches to tell the time) and speeding ahead of us on the long, flat road. The rest of us pedaled slowly at first, and then sped up to make her happy.

Not long after this, we turned down a country lane—rougher terrain, wildflowers and weeds, bumpier riding, but pretty. A few more turns down smaller lanes, more and more trees as we approached a forest, and then we reached a shed. It had a rusty old tractor standing alongside it.

"Here will do," Imogen decided, opening the shed door and wheeling in her bike. We all did the same. Inside the shed there were cobwebs and more rusty farming equipment. We managed to fit our bikes in, leaning up against each other, and Imogen pushed the door closed behind us.

"Come on, it's this way." She was frowning at the map.

I looked back at the shed. "There's no lock," I said.

The others did that lightning-quick look at each other, and then shook their heads politely. "No, Oscar," they agreed. "There is no lock."

"We're dumping the bikes there? Without locking them up?"

All their eyes crinkled, and Alejandro grinned. "In your world, your bicycles escape unless you lock them? Your bicycles are living?"

They all had shining eyes, so happy to hear about the living bicycles in my world.

"No, in my world bikes are not alive. People steal them."

Their faces fell.

"Why would anybody take a bicycle that didn't belong to them?" Imogen demanded, after a moment. "Your world sounds very odd, Oscar. Come on, let's move fast. Everyone got their packs? Who has Gruffudd? You do, don't you, Esther? Oh, he's with Bronte? He moves very quickly. We must keep a closer eye on him. Okay. Let's go." And she headed off down an overgrown track into the woods.

I felt bad for disappointing them about living bicycles, and also pretty defensive of my world. I mean, sure, my world might be "odd," but if we were *there*, we could have googled the locations of the key keepers, got an Uber between them, using GPS to find them, and texted ahead to let the key keepers know we were on our way.

We could be finished up and chilling by a pool somewhere.

I didn't say anything though, I only had some irritable thoughts.

Alejandro fell into step beside me. "People steal things in this world too," he told me, low-voiced. "We have crime, do not worry. Remember the innkeeper, Marion-Louise, complained that her lace doilies were stolen not a few hours ago? In fact, I used to be a pirate. This is what pirates do! They steal things! There are no pirates in the countryside though, as there is no call for them here, being no ocean. Do not let Imogen bother you. She is in a mood."

That cheered me up. I liked Alejandro.

We walked along the track through the woods. Gruffudd went to sleep in Bronte's pocket. Gnarly old trees cast shadows, lime-green leaves swayed in the breeze, birds sang.

The track was narrow, so we had to walk single file, plus we were carrying all the packs that had been tied onto the bikes. They were heavy. Nobody was talking, they were just breathing. Everyone breathing.

Bronte was at the front of the line, ahead of Imogen, and Esther at the back, behind me. After a while, Imogen slowed down again and said in a soft voice: "It's not far. Everyone, stay close together and stay very quiet."

As the woods grew darker, the path even narrower, there was a strange mood growing in the others. Their pace slowed right down. When I looked at anybody, they'd be biting their lip, or glancing at the others, miserable. It was a bit like they'd decided to head to a police station to confess to murder and get themselves locked away for life, and were really starting to question that decision.

Not long after this, the line stopped again.

Imogen gestured for us all to gather close to her.

"Around the next corner," she whispered. "There should be

a bridge over a gully—the Old Putty Bridge. The Radish Gnome cave is on the other side. Is everyone ready?"

There was a long pause, then the others nodded.

"Sure," I said.

"SHHHHHH!" they all hissed.

(Their *shhhh*s were louder than my *sure,* by the way.)

"Sorry," I whispered.

"All right," Imogen murmured. "Bronte first." Another pause and then: "Let's go."

CHAPTER 30

IMOGEN

LOOK, I DON'T think I was as cranky as all that. It's true I was a *little* cranky, but who can blame me? They'd included a *Shadow Mage* as a key keeper! Which was—

All right, maybe I was as cranky as all that.

Poor Oscar. We should have explained things to him as we went along. He really didn't have a clue. To us, though, it *was* unimaginable that a person might not know about Radish Gnomes. Radish Gnomes, or at least the idea of them, had been stirred into our realities from early childhood, the way you might make the ridiculous decision to stir raisins into a cake mixture.

Yet Oscar had grown up in a whole different cake. Of course he didn't know.

Around the corner we slid, Bronte's hands raised, ready to bind.

The forest opened out to a deep gully here, rocky and overgrown with ferns and moss. A wooden suspension bridge spanned the gully, our end blocked by a locked gate. Across the bridge, low in the cliff face, was a hemisphere of darkness: a Radish Gnome cave.

"Can you sense the shadow magic?" Bronte whispered to Esther.

Esther seemed uncertain. Rain Weavers in ancient times

were able to sense good and evil, so Esther should be able to sense both types of magic. Experts also think that she should theoretically be able to spellbind when she's older, and Bronte has been teaching her the basics. I started to edge closer to Esther, to shield her while she tried to sense the shadow magic, but Bronte pressed me behind her.

Here's the truth about Radish Gnomes.

They are short and stocky, often bearded, with claws as long and sharp as daggers. These claws are infused with shadow magic and can be shot vast distances at dizzying speed. Hurled at victims' ankles, the claws slice through flesh, cracking bone, so that the victims fall to the ground, helpless and screaming.

By nature, Radish Gnomes are surly and grim. Their moods range from low-level grumpy to outright ferocious, and they go about their lives with scowls and hunched shoulders. My mother sometimes tells my father that he's behaving like a Radish Gnome—when he's trying to give up pipe smoking, say, or when he stays up late doing his research and drinking whiskey, and then is woken at dawn by noisy birds.

Generally speaking, though, my father is easy-tempered and he has never once tried to vent his anger by flinging a razor-sharp claw.

At this point, we were observing the cave, trying to work out if we could get in there and grab the piece of key.

"We could climb over that gate," Oscar suggested.

"SHHHH," we all hissed, and Bronte turned and whispered to him that there was a shadow spell on the gate that would prevent that.

Then a glimpse of color caught my eye.

What was that?

A bird? A flowering fruit tree, swaying in the wind?

Again. Deep crimson in the green.

"Should we—" Oscar began.

"Shhh," I told him.

A faint crack.

I squinted hard—a flash of light—

"Bronte!" I hissed.

And at once, her eyes closed, her hands rose, her fingers flew. Faster, faster. I saw her tremble, stumble in place. Her movements seemed stiff and clumsy at first, then grew faster, smoother. Her teeth were clenched, eyes squeezed shut—

"Done," she breathed.

Astrid screamed.

I spun around as the first claw hit.

CHAPTER 31

OSCAR

THEY WERE SHOOTING blades at us.

Actual blades.

Well, technically claws, only I didn't know that at the time, and they sure looked like hunting blades to me.

They'd crept up on us from behind, these Radish Gnomes, crouched low, and *whoosh, whoosh, whoosh,* curved slices of silver were zooming through the air, straight at our calves.

Not kidding.

Pfft, pfft, pfft. Like cracking whips.

You could *feel* them hitting you. Physics and logic told you they were slamming into your shinbone, so you *sensed* it happen. You shouted and clutched your knees as if it *was* happening.

But actually the blades stopped just short of hitting. Froze in the air and clattered to the ground.

It was like there was an invisible wall surrounding us and the knives kept smashing into it—silently—and then, disappointed, slipping down.

"Stay still," Bronte ordered, which was *hard* because every part of you wanted to run or to curl up in a ball.

Bronte herself was turning slow circles on the spot, around and around, squinting, concentrating hard. At one point she stopped suddenly, closed her eyes, and her hands started twirling in the air again. Not twirling really, more crisscrossing, criss-crossing, superfast. She opened her eyes again.

Pfft, pfft, pfft. The blades kept coming.

Coming and falling, coming and falling.

Eventually we all stopped panicking and watched, only flinching now and then. A few moments later, the blades stopped altogether. Two men and a woman, all shorter than I am, and hairier, more muscular, and angrier looking than pro-wrestling champions—all wearing skullcaps and dressed in sleeveless shirts, trousers, and boots, emerged from the trees.

So, yeah, turned out Radish Gnomes were not cute little roly-poly sweethearts after all.

They rounded on us, fury deep in their faces. Their expressions made me think of teachers who've just caught you trashing the science lab.

"*You* were the ones throwing knives!" I said.

I didn't mean to. The words jumped out. It's a habit I have, defending myself when teachers look at me like that.

It was also a very fair point.

"Shhh," the others told me softly.

"*Spellbinding.*" The woman coughed. I don't think she was actually coughing, it was more her voice was low, raspy, and biting, like a cough. She raised her hands and formed them into fists to emphasize her point, and that's when I understood that the blades were actually *claws.*

They were growing out of her knuckles, curved, silver, and glinting.

When I say *growing*, I mean literally growing. Right before my eyes. Replacing the ones she'd thrown, I realized. It made me feel a bit sick, but it was hard to look away.

Imogen cleared her throat. "Radish Gnomes," she said. "We are here with Gruffudd, an Elf from the city of Dun-sorey-lo-vay-lo-hey. We believe you have a piece of the key." She took a deep breath and added optimistically, "May we please have it?"

"*Elf?*" a Radish Gnome demanded. He sounded asthmatic with irritation. "I see no Elf!"

"Here's an Elf!" Gruffudd squealed. We all looked up. Gruffudd was sitting high in a nearby tree, waving.

"How did you get *there*?" Imogen scolded. Gruffudd gave a teeny Elf shrug in reply.

"A Spellbinder in our neighborhood," the female Radish Gnome growled. Then she spat onto the grass. A glob of green. That's how she felt about Spellbinders, I guess. "Key! Why do you speak of a key! We have no—"

One of the men grunted. "We do, actually," he muttered. "The Elven key? Remember? It's hanging on a hook in our entryway."

"—no key other than the Elven one that hangs from the hook in our entryway," the woman finished. Nice save. "To get *that* key you'd have to get into our cave! Which is a *minor* problem for you. It raises the *minor* issue that nobody gets into our cave unless we let them. Or not without suffering *minor* damage, anyway."

Then she ripped off her skullcap, threw it on the ground, and stamped on it. I guess to demonstrate what the minor damage would be? "*Get out of my sight,*" she snarled.

We got out of her sight. Ran into the forest.

I glanced over my shoulder as I ran, worried they might attack us from behind. All three Radish Gnomes had already turned and were facing the locked gate to the bridge. One of the men raised a fist. A claw shot out of it, flew across the bridge, and hit a small red diamond painted directly above the cave's opening. The padlock clicked and the gate swung open.

I turned back and caught up with the others.

* * *

After running between trees in a random way, tripping over and picking each other up, we finally found a clearing, collapsed, and panted for a while.

Then we said over and over that we couldn't *believe* how close we'd come to being sliced to pieces by the Radish Gnomes.

I stopped being quiet, because my heart was pumping so fast. It sort of pumped out my voice. I told the others that the claws had looked *exactly* like the blade of a karambit I'd once had. They started asking questions about what a karambit was though, and details of its weight and speed and so on, and I had to clarify that my karambit had not been a *real* Indonesian hunting knife. It was a virtual weapon in the game *CS: GO*.

That stopped the conversation in its tracks.

"*Counter-Strike: Global Offensive?*" I said. "A game? You play it on PC, PlayStation, Xbox?"

Their faces became more and more distressed with each word, which I should have predicted, so I changed the subject and asked why the claws hadn't actually hit us.

"It is because we have Bronte," Alejandro told me, and he grabbed Bronte in a slightly rough hug. "The best Spellbinder in all the Kingdoms and Empires! However, Spellbinders keep their identities secret," he added, as Bronte laughed and murmured that she was "a long way from being the best."

"No, seriously," Alejandro said in an aside to me, "this is a secret. Tell anybody and I will cut your throat."

I honestly couldn't tell if he was joking or not.

Anyhow, turned out that Bronte had "made" something called a "Spellbinding ring," which was like a force field that protected us from shadow magic. The Radish Gnome claws, being infused with shadow magic, fell to the ground when they hit the Spellbinding ring.

"She made the Spellbinding so fast," Alejandro added. He clicked his fingers. "Like this. Like lightning."

"Only because Imogen noticed the Radish Gnomes in time," Bronte said.

I started to realize that if Imogen hadn't caught sight of the Radish Gnomes when she did—and if Bronte had been a fraction slower in making the force field—the claws would have hit us.

This made me feel quiet again.

Next, everyone started giving an opinion on how to get into the Radish Gnome cave now that we'd had a chance to "observe" it. I personally did not have an opinion; except that I thought

"Radish Gnome" was much too cute a name for those people (the others agreed with me but didn't find this observation helpful).

Astrid said that Radish Gnomes tend to nap in the afternoon.

"They do?" Esther asked, doubtfully.

"We learned about the sleeping habits of various mages at school last year," Astrid explained.

"*I've* never heard that," Esther argued, "and I'm *always* reading about magic."

They bickered for a while, Astrid holding her ground.

"So they'll probably go to sleep soon," Imogen said. "If we could get through the gate without waking them, I could sneak in and take the key."

There was an argument then about *who* would do the sneaking in. Bronte said she should do it since she was a Spellbinder. So she could . . . you know, spellbind the Radish Gnomes if they woke up.

Imogen worried about how much "animosity" the Radish Gnomes had toward Spellbinders. "If they *do* wake up," she said, "there'll be too many of them for you to spellbind and they'll destroy you, Bronte."

Astrid said she would do it only everyone told her she was too little. She shrugged like she'd given it a try.

Then it was down to Imogen and Alejandro, and they both seemed keen and got into an argument about that. I didn't really understand why they were all so set on doing something so dangerous. I decided they were bluffing.

"I'm up for it," I said. That made them go silent for a bit. They changed the subject. Could we even cross the bridge anyway? Could Bronte use her Spellbinding skills to unlock the shadow magic on the gate? Those were the questions.

Bronte said she'd noticed that the magic there was "strong and tangled."

"I'm pretty sure it has a sort of inbuilt alarm," she said. "It would alert the Radish Gnomes that someone was trying to unlock it."

"Even if you spellbind *very* softly?" Alejandro asked.

"Even then," Bronte replied, and then catching his eye she realized he was teasing, and kicked him.

"All right, another approach," Imogen decided. "We need to entice them out of the cave and slip in ourselves while the gate is open. Any ideas, Esther?"

Immediately, Esther started listing facts about Radish Gnomes. She'd read a book called *The Astonishing Truth About Radish Gnomes,* she explained. ("As you do," I said, for a joke—they all frowned.)

"It was for a speech assignment at school," she told me gently.

Radish Gnomes have phobias of small green apples, refrigerators, and tortoises, she said.

"So we throw these things at their cave and then we run in?" Imogen asked doubtfully.

We had red apples, not green, and nobody had a refrigerator or tortoise on them. Astrid became upset at the idea of throwing tortoises.

"It is the throwing of refrigerators that bothers me," Alejandro said. We laughed and moved on.

"They *like* earthquakes, volcanoes, and explosions," Esther said.

"Check your pockets," Gruffudd suggested. He was sitting on Bronte's shoulder. "You might have put an earthquake in there earlier. We can *tempt* them out of the cave with an earthquake."

He seemed serious.

Everyone smiled at him, and he complained that he was hungry. Astrid peeled a banana for him, and he complained that it wasn't chocolate.

Eventually, there was a depressed silence.

"It's a shame we don't have claws of our own," I said, "that we could shoot at the red diamond."

They looked at me with their usual confused expressions. This seemed unfair. I was talking about *their* weird world now, not mine.

"The red diamond above the opening to the cave?" When

they still seemed baffled, I told them what I'd seen the Radish Gnomes do, and how the gate had opened when the claw hit.

They looked at each other, and then back at me.

"Why did you not tell us that *sooner*?" they all breathed.

"I didn't know . . . that you didn't know."

Imogen smiled at me suddenly. "Of course you didn't," she said. "Don't blame yourself."

To be honest, I hadn't planned to.

CHAPTER 32

IMOGEN

I'M GLAD TO hear it, Oscar. My mother often says that time spent blaming oneself is time that could be better spent blaming somebody else.

At this, my father usually chuckles and says, "I'm not sure that's the expression, Nancy. I believe it's actually time better spent *solving the problem.*"

That afternoon in the forest, it took only a few minutes for Alejandro to solve the problem. He found a suitable tree, cut down a branch, and carved it into the shape of a bow, adding notches for the string. He had twine in his pack, and he wound this together to form the string. Next, he carved some arrows from a fallen log, and Esther located birds' feathers to fix to the arrows' ends.

We had another short argument about who should sneak into the cave, which I won because it was obvious that Alejandro would be more useful as an archer.

Finally, we all crept back to the gully's edge. There was the locked bridge and there, across the way, was the mouth of the Radish Gnome cave. It was black and silent. We waited a few moments, watching, but could hear nothing except occasional birdsong, and the sound of distant gurgling in the gully deep below.

We began to creep about then, collecting the claws that had

fallen to the ground when they hit Bronte's Spellbinding ring earlier. Alejandro bound a few of these to his arrows.

He checked that I was ready, stepped closer to the gate, silently set an arrow in his bow, raised this to his shoulder, aimed across the bridge to the cave, peered down the sight line, located the red diamond on the rock face, drew back the twine, and shot.

The arrow struck the red diamond.

Honestly, it happened as swiftly as that. No hesitation, just one smooth, flowing motion, and *thwunk,* it had hit its target.

After the *thwunk* we all froze, tensing, watching the cave. Bronte kept her hands raised, ready to Spellbind if necessary. The others pressed close to her.

Nothing.

Darkness and silence.

We looked at the bridge gate.

Also nothing. The padlock hung in place, stolidly locked.

It hadn't worked! Oscar had been wrong! Of course, we should never have trusted a boy from another world. Not that it was his *fault,* he'd simply misunderstood what—

A faint *clank,* and the padlock clicked open, a soft *creak,* and the gate swung wide.

It had worked.

(Sorry for doubting you, Oscar.)

"You all right?" I whispered to Bronte. She nodded, hands still in formation.

I glanced at Alejandro. His eyes met mine. He had set another arrow into his bow and was holding it aloft, pointed toward the cave, ready to shoot if necessary.

I turned and ran.

Through the open gate.

Onto the bridge.

I ran on my toes, fast and light as I could, but the bridge creaked, once, twice. The wind blew back my braids, made my eyes water.

The dark cave opening rushed toward me, growing ever larger.

I reached the other side.

Cold air wafted from within the cave, along with a dank, musty smell.

I paused. Crept slowly, slowly up the grassy embankment, edging closer to the opening. The coldness intensified.

I stopped.

Was Astrid right? Did Radish Gnomes sleep in the afternoon? Or were they crouched in there, silent, ready to attack?

From inside, the silence persisted.

My heart seemed to be scuttling right up my throat. It pattered like rapid rainfall.

I was at the entrance to a Radish Gnome cave, unprotected. Blinking in at pure darkness.

They were watching me! They could see me clearly out here in the light! They were smirking at me, their claws ready to—

I took a deep breath. Forced myself to be still, and listen.

More silence.

And then, faintly, strange sounds from within. Rattles, grunts, whistles. Deep, long inhalations followed by blasts of air like steam from the chimney of a train.

The sounds of Radish Gnomes sleeping.

I breathed out. Astrid had been right.

Hanging on a hook in our entryway, the Radish Gnome had said.

I took another slow, agonizing step. My foot hit a dry leaf with a *crunch.* I froze again. Almost yelped in fear.

Paused.

But the silence carried on.

I reached around the stone lip of the entryway and felt the cave wall. Cold and damp. I patted it gently. Nothing there. Nothing there.

I slid my hand all around. A squelchy softness made me gasp.

Moss, I realized.

The piece of key must be on the other side. I took my hand away, ready to try over there, and then, to be sure, slid my palm lower.

A sharp edge. Cold metal.

I ran my hand over the shape. It was a hook and . . . yes, hanging from the hook, a piece of solid metal.

Slowly, slowly, I unhooked it.

It made a soft clanging sound as I drew it away, and I held my breath once more. Again, nothing happened.

I drew it out.

A similar shape, although this time curved. A deep indentation, which must have been what held it to the hook.

I clutched it hard, swiveled, and ran. Down the grassy embankment.

Onto the bridge with a *thud*.

Across the bridge, I could see the others beckoning wildly. Their faces were vibrant with panic.

I swung around, terrified.

Nothing behind me.

So why were they . . . ?

Then I saw it. The gate was slowly, steadily, creaking closed.

I'd taken too long!

I sprinted. Pushed my feet hard against the boards of the bridge, pounded my arms, drove my legs, ran faster, faster, faster than I'd ever run before. Forgot about being quiet. Gasped for air.

The others surged forward, trying to push the gate. Their faces strained with the effort, yet the gate carried on steadily closing.

I skidded toward it.

It was all but closed. Hands reached out, dragged me through the gap and—

CLUNK.

It closed behind me.

I fell to the ground, gasping for breath, and then, after a moment, held it up so the others could see: the second piece of key.

CHAPTER 33

OSCAR

🌿

 **I STILL DON'T** know how Imogen did it.

She was only halfway across the bridge and the gap was the size of my hand. Seriously. We all started pulling, pushing, dragging at the gate to keep it open, but it carried right on shutting. Relentless. That's the word.

It was like she decided that *nothing* was going to stop her and that gave her jet propulsion power.

We didn't hang around at the Radish Gnome bridge, obviously. As soon as Imogen held up the piece of key, we slipped back into the forest, grabbed our packs from where we'd left them, and carried on running until we reached a muddy creek and Imogen decided we were far enough away from the cave.

Bronte made a Spellbinding ring around us anyway. I couldn't actually *see* anything, but now that I knew what Radish Gnomes were, I was happy to know it was there.

"I don't think we should stay long even with the Spellbinding ring," Imogen decided. "I think we should find out who the next key keeper is and head in that direction." She looked at me.

Ah. My turn to do the memory thing.

Well.

I wasn't really one for remembering things, and I kind of doubted it would work for me. Still, I took the bottle out of my backpack pocket and pulled out the cork.

"See, I don't think it's going to—" I began.

Then there I was, standing in the ocean up to my knees. I was about seven years old. A jingly feeling in my chest. My stepdad was in the water beside me.

Ha!

I remembered this!

It was Freshwater Beach. He wasn't my stepdad then, he was my mum's new boyfriend, Joel. He had promised to teach me to surf.

I looked down, and yep, there was a surfboard in my hands. I was actually pushing it along through the water. We were heading out to catch my first wave.

Joel was talking to me. "Thatta boy," he said. "Okay, once you feel the wave start to lift you, you paddle like your arms are turbocharged."

I nodded, and looked to my left. Another kid was pushing a surfboard not far from me.

Only on his surfboard was a violin.

Standing up straight, this violin.

"Crystal clear water here," Joel said, but I was watching that violin fall sideways—

I blinked around at the others. The memory was over.

That was fast.

They were all looking at me.

"Did you remember something?" Astrid asked.

I nodded.

"Was it a good memory?"

"Sure."

"And could you tell what the clue was in the memory?" Bronte wanted to know.

I laughed and said I knew exactly which bit was the clue.

"A violin fell over on a surfboard," I said. "I'm pretty sure that never happened that day."

The others looked at each other and frowned. *Falling violin, falling violin,* they said to each other, shrugging. Music? Gravity?

Something else occurred to me. "While the violin fell, my

stepdad was saying something about crystal clear waters." It might have been part of the true memory, only I didn't think so. It was sort of jarring. The surf had looked too rough to be "crystal clear."

Esther's eyes widened. "Can I see the map, Imogen?"

Imogen unfolded the map and passed it to Esther, who rustled it around, rustled it around, and then: "Ha!" She jabbed her finger at the map. Nobody could see what she was jabbing at.

"Crystal Faeries!" she said. "They often have their palaces behind waterfalls! And look! Here on the map! *Violin Falls!* I think the next key keeper is a True Mage! A Crystal Faery! And they're right *there*!"

Everyone laughed then. Probably more laughter than was called for. It was delayed shock from the Radish Gnomes, I guess. And it was a funny clue. A falling violin. Violin Falls.

Imogen took the map from Esther and asked if we were ready to go right away. She seemed happier too. "Good job, Oscar," she said to me, while I was sticking the blue bottle back in my backpack's side pocket.

That made me laugh again. "I didn't do anything," I said, but Gruffudd was shouting that he wanted to ride in Imogen's pocket as she was a "true and mighty hero with speedy legs upon a bridge."

"Alejandro's the true hero," Imogen replied as she scooped the Elf into her pocket and headed off. "He shot that arrow at the target on his first attempt."

I waited while Bronte followed Imogen, then went Alejandro, then Astrid. Esther and I joined the back of the line.

"Yeah, how *did* Alejandro do that?" I asked Esther.

The track was narrow here, almost not a track at all, and pretty quickly the forest was turning denser and darker. It was rainforesty—ferns and moss, mud and rocks, water gurgling, and trickling back and forth across the track. Birds flicked between trees and called in long, haunting notes. Frogs rasped at each other.

"How did who do what?" Esther replied.

She tripped over a root. Tree roots everywhere around here,

tangling and looping together, and Esther kept staring at puddles of water and missing them.

"Alejandro," I said. "Making the bow and hitting the target first go."

"Oh, Alejandro, yes," she repeated. She tripped again, and I reached to steady her.

"Thank you, Oscar," she said politely, and carried on walking.

Ah well. Not going to answer then.

"It's because he was a pirate," she said suddenly, a few minutes later. "Alejandro. He's marvelous, isn't he? As you know, he's actually a prince, only he was stolen away as a baby and raised by pirates. And you see . . ."

At this point, she had to hesitate so she could push aside a branch. The foliage was so thick we had to constantly hold branches aside to get through.

She carried on, slipping and sliding along, gazing around her at the streams of water, reaching to touch damp spots on trees.

"And you see," I prompted her.

"Oh yes!" She stumbled a little and saved herself by grabbing onto a branch. "The pirates taught Alejandro how to fight with swords and fire cannons and guns and how to shoot a bow and arrow. They would stop at deserted islands, and that's where he learned self-sufficiency—how to make things out of the landscape. But of course . . ."

She stopped again. The track was even trickier here, crisscrossing the creek. You had to step from rock to rock. *Splash.* Esther kept missing the rocks and landing a boot in the water.

"Oh dear," she murmured each time she did that, then she'd smile and reach down and swirl her hands in the water.

"But of course," I reminded her.

"But of course, I think he must have a natural affinity for crafting things. And for marksmanship. Practice alone cannot raise you to such a level. He's so talented, Alejandro, yet also modest. Enthusiastic about life too, which is a pleasure to see— While he lived with Bronte's family, he became quite passionate about the cinema, for instance, having never seen a film in his life at sea. I think he saw a film every other day with Aunt Isabelle and he still reads all the cinematograph magazines. He has a beautiful pirate accent—I hope he doesn't lose that now he's no longer a pirate." She paused to wrench her boot out of a muddy puddle it had hit. There was a good squelching sound. "The pirates who raised him were the most violent and ruthless on all the oceans. When he realized this, aged eleven, he ran away from them. Well, they caught him again, didn't they?"

"Did they?"

"Yes. And they . . ."

She paused and studied the dewdrops on the wildflowers and ferns.

"And they . . . ?"

"They beat him very badly, and locked him up. Once more, he escaped and nearly died doing it. That's when Bronte found him. She rescued him and brought him home to live with her family in Gainsleigh. They're best friends and like sister and brother. It's rather sad that they've found out about Alejandro being a stolen prince—I mean, it's *wonderful* they did, and so lovely for the King and Queen to have their son back. But—"

Esther stopped so suddenly I nearly bumped into her.

"Oscar," she said. "I've remembered. I'm supposed to be at the back of the line, trying to sense any Shadow Mages so I can warn you all. I *might* be able to spellbind too, except I'm still learning that, so I'll probably only shout a warning. Can you go ahead of me please?"

"Sure." I sidled around her.

She carried on behind me, murmuring to herself.

"Would you like me to cleanse your teeth?" she called suddenly.

"No thanks," I replied, pretty fast. I felt my eyes widen. They cleaned each other's *teeth* in this world? "I'll get myself a toothbrush somewhere, and I can . . . I can brush my teeth myself."

"Oh!" She giggled. It was an unexpected sound, and sweet. She'd been seeming so serious. "No, I mean cleanse them of shadow magic."

I carried on walking, thinking about that.

Eventually I turned back. "I'm pretty sure there's no shadow magic in my teeth."

"We looked through your satchel, remember? And there were two objects in there molded to the shape of teeth. I assumed you were using them to deal with a Witch spell on your teeth. I can't think what else they'd be for." Esther stopped again. "I keep forgetting to look around," she murmured.

"We don't have Shadow Mages in my world," I reminded her. "So no Witch has shadowed my teeth. You must be talking about my mouth guard," I realized. "I use it for footy. It protects my teeth."

"From Witches."

"No, Esther, from getting smashed in by other rugby players. Do you have footy in this world? Rugby league, I mean?"

"Oh yes, we do," she said, pleased. "I've heard about that on the wireless radio. Thank you!" I was holding back a branch for her to pass by. "And I have other cousins who play soccer," she added proudly. "They never stop kicking balls around their kitchen. I don't know if they wear . . . what did you call it? Mouth guards? I don't know if soccer players smash each other's teeth in or not. I'll ask them."

"And the other teeth thing in my bag was my plate," I said, deciding to steer the conversation away from soccer. I didn't want to get into an argument about violence in rugby league and how I should choose soccer instead. My mother calls up to lecture me on that enough.

"Your plate?" Esther repeated sounding perplexed. "It wasn't a plate."

I stopped to catch my breath. The path was running up the side of a hill at this point, and there was a fair bit of climbing.

"Yeah, it was."

"No, Oscar, a plate is a flat, round object from which you eat your—"

"A retainer then," I said. "To fix my teeth."

"So they *are* shadowed," Esther said. She sounded very patient. "Would you like me to—?"

This conversation was not the easiest I'd ever had.

"See," I said, stopping again and pointing to my teeth. "They're jumbled. The retainer is going to straighten them. If I actually wear it." I added this last bit to myself really. The retainer had been loose in my backpack for weeks. Probably wouldn't do much good to my teeth from there.

"After the plate I'll probably get braces next year to finish off the straightening."

"Braces? No. They hold up your trousers." Esther was very definite about this. She paused. "And why would you straighten your teeth?"

"Because they're crooked. See?"

"So what?"

"Well, so they should be straight."

"Hmm." Esther frowned, trying to understand. "Why would you want to straighten jumbled teeth? I like them. They're charming. We'd better walk faster; the others are a fair way ahead."

And she sidled around me and strode off, slipped once, hopped up, and said, "Oh, Oscar, I'm meant to be at the back. Can I walk behind you?"

CHAPTER 34

IMOGEN

 **MEANWHILE, I WAS** up the front with Bronte.

Gruffudd had curled up in my pocket and fallen asleep. It was pleasant, having that slight extra weight and warmth bumping gently against my right side.

It also made me uneasy about the possibility of tripping over and squashing him.

I tried to be careful.

Only, I was distracted. There was something wrong with the map.

I stopped once again to pull it out of my pocket, unfold it, squint at it, and swear at it. I folded it back away and kept walking. Now there was something wrong with the *landscape*. I swore at that instead.

I knew that I was being childish. It was not the *map's* fault, and not the *landscape's* fault. It must be *my* fault. That made me swear some more. (Under my breath, of course.)

"Imogen, are you all right?" Bronte asked.

"Look," I said, shaking out the map again. I pointed with a fingertip. "*This* is where we came from and *this* is where we're headed. You see?"

"Yes."

"No, you don't. You're just saying that. Look more closely."

I could tell Bronte hadn't looked properly. She's not really interested in maps.

"Show me again?" she asked contritely, and I did.

"All right," she said, once she'd focused for a while. "So that's where we left the bikes, that's where we came into the woods, that's the Radish Gnome cave and bridge. That's the creek where we stopped, that's the track we're following, so at the moment, we must be . . ."

"Here," I agreed, pointing. "Which means the path should *not* be climbing yet. Look, the terrain should be flat until *after* the grove, but this is steep! And the sounds of water are getting much louder than they should be! I'm sure we just passed this enormous rock but we shouldn't have passed it yet! Look, the sun is *there*." I pointed to the sky through the foliage. "Which means we're headed . . . Wait."

I pulled the map away again and the edge tore. I peered at it, frowning.

Then I blinked.

Had I imagined that?

"Did you see that?" I asked.

"What?"

"There! It did it again!"

I could feel a smile growing on my face.

"You have to look at it sideways and you can . . . Look! Look at it sideways!"

Bronte humored me by tilting her head a little.

"No, tilt it more!" I was laughing properly at this point, and a voice called, "What's so funny?"

It was Astrid, tramping along the track behind us, Alejandro with her.

"Come here!" I told them. "Look at the map! Watch! Watch!"

The way they were looking at me, I could tell they thought I'd got too much sun while we were cycling earlier.

"Yes," they all said kindly. "I see what you mean. Shall we carry on?"

But I was tilting the map this way and that, turning in a circle as I did.

"Oh!" Astrid said suddenly, grinning. "I saw it!"

Alejandro gasped. He had seen it too. "This," he said. "This is not how maps work."

Bronte stared at all of us, then at the map, and back at us again.

I tilted my head and caught it happen again. This is what was happening: the large letter *N*, signifying north, kept slipping right across the page. Then it would zip back to its original spot, slide to the bottom of the page, and spin around.

"This map is broken," Alejandro said gravely. "Throw it away."

There was the sound of footsteps and Oscar emerged up the track, followed by Esther. We beckoned them to come closer and study the map. There was a lot of "Look! It did it again!" and "Did you see it, Esther?" and "Unacceptable!" from Alejandro— to whom maps, charts, compasses, and so on, are very serious. This is to do with his history sailing the oceans, of course. Bronte was annoyed because she never seemed to catch it.

I was happy because I'd been right. There *was* something wrong with the map, and not with me.

A curious thing happened then. The more we exclaimed to each other at the letter *N* slipping and sliding all over the map, the louder our voices grew. We had started at the usual level and then we were crying out excitedly and soon we were practically shrieking at each other.

It was so loud that Gruffudd woke up.

"WHAT'S WITH ALL THE SHOUTING?" he called, squirming around until his head emerged from my pocket. He clung onto the edge with his tiny hands. "AND WHAT IS THAT NOISE?"

We all stopped and looked up in surprise.

He was right. The noise was immense. Unconsciously, we had begun shouting in order to make ourselves heard over it.

It was a sound like static on the wireless turned to full volume. A rush of sound, a constant blast.

"WHAT *IS* IT?" Bronte cried.

Then I smiled again. I swiveled the map carefully around

and around until the *N* locked into place. It stayed still. Then I looked more closely.

Violin Falls, I read.

I beckoned the others to follow me around the next bend and there they were: the falls themselves.

A huge waterfall plunged down a cliff face and into a ravine below. The water was the bright white of fresh snow, and it clattered and crashed, clattered and crashed, rushing down slick and shiny rocks. Speaking descriptively, it seemed to be laughing with joy at its own exuberance.

We had arrived.

CHAPTER 35

OSCAR

IMOGEN WAVED US around the corner from the falls to a sheltered spot in the rocks where we could hear each other better.

"You all stay here and I'll see if I can find an entry to their palace behind the waterfall," Imogen said. "It would be too dangerous for—"

"No!" Astrid exclaimed. "Don't go climbing behind waterfalls, Imogen! You'll fall and be killed!"

"Don't worry about me," Imogen assured her.

"I *will* worry about you if I want to!" Astrid half-shouted.

Esther, who had been chewing her fingernails, swung her head up like a ninja. "Careful," she told her sisters. "Don't squabble. Crystal Faeries can't stand any kind of discord. That means arguments," she added quickly, seeing Astrid looking annoyed. "To Crystal Faeries, beauty and harmony are everything."

"Regular Faeries think that's just an affectation," Bronte put in. "They find Crystal Faeries pretentious and self-satisfied."

Esther nodded. "The way to knock on a Crystal Faery's door—" she began, but Imogen interrupted: "Well, they don't have a door. It's a waterfall."

"Shhh," Esther begged. "If we start being irritated with each other, they'll sense it. Even our tone of voice has to be filled with love and joy now we're so close. They can't hear us but they can *sense* us." She was making her own voice sound like a teacher welcoming a "very special guest" to a class—that fake voice teachers get when they want to make visitors think that they're super nice people? At the same time as sort of subtly warning the class that they'd better behave.

It was both funny and a bit of a horror movie vibe, hearing Esther talk like this.

She carried on. "The way to knock on their *waterfall* door is to sing to it about something we find beautiful. All of us. Taking turns."

"Are you kidding?" That was me speaking. I hadn't meant to speak; I was enjoying being quiet.

But was she kidding?

Esther shook her head. "We should also start calling each other things like *honeypot* or *sweet pea*. All right, pumpkin?" She looked straight at me.

I laughed.

She nodded at that. "Perfect, sweetheart," she said. "Crystal Faeries like laughter too. They're basically the opposite of Radish Gnomes. You got that, honey?"

"You bet, gorgeous," I told her, and she did a cute little smile and gave me a thumbs-up.

Imogen swept into action. "In that case, my . . . young treasures, let's proceed to the waterfall and sing what we find beautiful."

"Good plan, sunshine."

"Lead the way, moonbeam."

"Right behind you, sugarplum."

The others were getting in on the act.

We left all our bags and backpacks in the sheltered corner and headed back to the cliff's edge. There, we could stand adjacent to the waterfall. It was superloud again, which was a good thing, I thought, as I wasn't keen on the singing bit.

The only person who's ever heard me sing is my mother. Back when I was taking guitar lessons I used to sing along when I practiced at home, and Mum was always on about how I had "perfect pitch" and "a voice to rival a nightingale."

Take no notice of that. It's the way my mother is. It took me a while to figure this out, but you can't trust a word she says.

"She's prone to exaggeration," my stepdad told me once. "Hyperbolic, she is. Ignore her."

So I stopped singing along when I played, and soon after that I quit playing.

Anyhow, we lined up, not too close to the edge—Imogen kept pushing us back a bit and calling, "Careful, honey bunnies!"

Esther started.

"*Beauty is Mount Opal under winter snow*," she sang, inventing the tune as she went along, "*a dragon swooping across its peak.*"

"I can see Mount Opal from my bedroom window at home," she explained to me in an aside—as if "Mount Opal" was the part that needed explaining.

Did·they actually have *dragons*?

I sighed. I wouldn't put it past them.

"*Beauty is the ocean*," Alejandro sang next, in a big sailor-style voice. He stopped. We all looked at him.

"That's it." He shrugged. "Beauty is the ocean."

Bronte took a turn next, only I couldn't hear her properly. She looked embarrassed to be singing. She started off saying something about family board games on rainy days with "Aunt Isabelle, the Butler, my parents, Alejandro, and various visiting aunts," and then her voice got lost in the waterfall and she turned around blushing.

Imogen must have been inspired by Bronte's rainy day because she sang about how beauty is sleeping late on a stormy morning, and Astrid sang about hanging with her dad. She didn't use the word *hanging* or *dad*, that's just how I interpreted it. I think it was "spending a pleasant afternoon of laughter with Father."

I tried to mix things up by shout-singing, "*Beauty is a sick frontside powerslide.*" The others gave me polite nods with their usual glances at each other that mean "What is *up* with this guy?"

I think I saw the waterfall give a kind of twitch when I was singing, but then it fell back into place again.

Everyone waited, watching it.

It carried on crashing down.

"Well?" Imogen said, frowning. "Haven't we all done our songs?"

"Patience, my frosted angel," Esther reminded her at the same time as little Gruffudd poked his head out of my pocket—I had *no* memory of him being there—and squeaked: "Do I not *exist!*"

Then he scrambled down my jeans—it pinched a bit—and went springing along the cliff's edge singing, "*Beauty is the city of Dun-sorey-lo-vay-lo-hey, a gem of a city, a marvel of magnificence, a dazzle of delightfulness, a—*"

And so on. I was distracted by fear that he was about to fall over the cliff, and amazement at how fast he could run, so I didn't concentrate on the words. He was zooming backward and forward, jumping over our boots, swinging from our boot-laces, twisting between our ankles. Everyone's head was swinging back and forth trying to keep up with him. It was like this:

"Where is he?"

"He's gone over!"

"No, he's here."

"Where? Oh, he's in my sock!"

He kept vanishing and then springing back into sight again still singing, "*. . . a willow tree of wondrousness, a teaspoon of terrifitude . . .*" before vanishing again.

And back again, "*. . . a fingernail of fantasticness, a gherkin of great-esquitude . . .*"

His voice grew screechier and faster all the time, his words more and more ridiculous: "*a chair leg of carrotcakewith-creamcheesiness—*"

At that point, the waterfall sort of flung itself sideways, like somebody throwing open your bedroom curtain in the morning when you've slept too long and are superlate for school.

The thundering sound fell to a quiet drizzle.

Where the waterfall had been there was a slick, dripping black rock wall. And then, as we watched, the wall started to . . . melt?

It really seemed to be melting.

And then it started to . . . molt?

Like when things fall off of something? Only, the bits falling weren't bits of rock. They were . . . I squinted.

Rose petals.

"This is *wild*," I said.

"No, no," Esther murmured. "No, my sugary pumpkin pie. It's Crystal Faeries. Come on, let's go in."

CHAPTER 36

IMOGEN

CRYSTAL FAERIES ARE True Mages. This means they practice bright magic.

I mentioned earlier how I feel about bright magic?

Keep that in mind as you read on.

First, we filed along the ledge of the waterfall and in through a gap in the rocks.

"The frowns!" exclaimed a voice. "Please, erase the frowns!"

The ledge was wet, of course, from the constant flow of the waterfall, but now it had also been made impossibly slick with rose petals. Filing along that ledge was terrifying. We took one slow step at a time, wobbled, gasped, and clung to the wall. No wonder we were frowning.

"Still frowning! Still frowning! Aaah, that is better. Come! Smile! You are in a place of bliss and harmony! Smile, my buttercups!"

We were standing under a trellis that was wreathed in flowers. The flowers brushed against our hair, caressing our earlobes and tickling our noses. We kept ducking away from them.

"My angelberries! Stand still! Embrace the touch of nature! Oh, you have much to learn!"

The person speaking was the first Crystal Faery I had ever met. Although I do know a few Faeries—the matron at my boarding school is part-Faery—Crystal Faeries are rare. As far as I know, regular and Crystal Faeries are the same species. Both are True Mages with the appearance of regular people, both enjoy beauty, music, and nature, and both specialize in healing, love, and communication spells.

The only difference is that Crystal Faeries take their own Faeryness far too seriously.

"Perhaps you have dreamed of meeting a Crystal Faery before?" the woman standing before us suggested. She was dressed like a flower. By that I mean she wore a long green skirt and a blouse formed of several overlaying pieces of material, like petals, all in shades of apricot. "My dears, your dream has come true. Here I am. You may call me Sapphire. Sapphire, the Crystal Faery." She smiled a soft and loving smile. I could only just see the smile as her face was hidden by the dangling flowers.

Astrid giggled and then coughed and said, "Sorry."

"Sorry?" Sapphire repeated. She crouched and picked up a xylophone that, we now realized, had been lying by her sandaled feet. *Ding!* She played a note. "You are sorry for *laughter*?" She dinged it again. *Ding!* "Imagine apologizing for one of our greatest gifts!" *Ding!* For her next sentence, she struck the xylophone at almost every word. "Laughter . . . *ding!* . . . is . . . *ding!* . . . the fruit . . . *ding!* . . . that feeds *ding!* the soul! *Ding! Ding! Ding!*"

Astrid pressed her mouth tight against a burst of laughter, but it escaped through her nose.

"Snorting, however," Sapphire said, her loving smile slipping a touch, "is not recommended."

She breathed in deeply, played a series of notes on her xylophone, breathed again, and smiled.

"There are Elves amongst you," she murmured, as if she was saying something terribly wise. *Ding! Ding!*

Gruffudd burst out of my boot, which made me jump in fright and knock my head on the trellis.

"There are indeed!" he hollered. "And here he is! The Elf! Greetings, Sapphire of the Crystal Faeries! It is I! Gruffudd of the Elves! A fellow True Mage! What a *relief* to see one of my own kind! As grand and entertaining as these children are, with their hopeless yet endearing efforts and their many bumblings and mistakes, one feels a sort of calm washing over one when one encounters another True Mage! You and I are one and the same, are we not?"

"*Hey,*" we all said to Gruffudd, and he shrugged. "What can I do?" his shrug implied. "It's the truth."

Sapphire's smile, meanwhile, became a little tight. "Certainly, we are both True Mages, Gruffudd," she agreed, accompanying this with a series of rapid *dingdingdingdingdings!* "Would we truly say that we are one and the same?" She chuckled sweetly and then, speaking loudly over Gruffudd's voice, "Yes! Yes, we would!" She asked: "Was it *you,* little Elf, who found your way to our palace, leading the children here?"

"Well, no," Gruffudd admitted. "That was Imogen." He gave my sock a pat.

"Imogen?" The Crystal Faery stepped forward and pressed her forehead against mine. I tried to behave as if this was perfectly normal. "You are remarkable, Imogen. Very few solve the puzzle of the skittery map. It only skitters when you try to reach our palace, by the way—the map will be a regular map again for your travels onward. And you also knew how to knock on our waterfall door?"

"No, that was my sister Esther," I told her, using the opportunity to pull my head away. I pointed to Esther.

"*You* are Esther the Rain Weaver!" Here Sapphire took Esther's hands in her own and drew her through the flowers to gaze at her. "Remarkable. An honor to meet you. Dear Esther, we have much to discuss. I must insist that you visit our Faery treatment center one of these days. You must share your wisdom and skills with us, and perhaps . . ." She smiled ever more lovingly. ". . . perhaps, *we* can teach you much that you do not know?"

Esther gave a little start. "Oh, definitely. I mean, sure. I mean, of course, I hardly know *anything* about healing. You obviously know . . ."

"Yes, dear. We will know more than you. Crystal Faeries have been healing for many generations. You must not cast shame upon yourself for what you do not know. Right then."

She released Esther, reached up through the gaps in the trellis, pushing aside flowers—very gently at first and then a *little* more roughly as they kept falling back onto her wrists—and felt around up there before drawing down a tiny velvet box.

This, she held out on the palm of her hand.

"The key," she said. "Our piece of the key is in this box."

A dramatic pause.

"And what must we do to get it?" Alejandro checked.

"You could start by taking the box," Sapphire replied briskly. She caught herself and laughed softly. "Dear ones, the challenge was *locating* our palace and getting yourselves in. Imogen and Esther—dear Rain Weaver"—here, she paused to rest her knuckles gently on Esther's cheek—"have succeeded. The key is yours."

We all glanced at each other, and I reached out, took the box and opened it.

The third piece of the key was inside it.

"Thank you, Sapphire," I said, feeling a bit breathless. "We are very grateful and won't take any more of your time. Come on, everybody." I turned toward the entryway, then thought of something and swung back again. "Although, one thing—do you think you might be able to send a message to our parents for us? Or tell us where we can send—"

"Oh!" Sapphire interrupted. "Oh, sweet children! You've forgotten your reward! For your achievement in acquiring this piece of the key, I invite you to tour our palace! Very few people see a Crystal Faery palace in their lifetime. We are so well concealed. It will truly be an honor to you. Come!"

I did not want to tour the palace at all.

Not even remotely. It was getting late, we were all hungry, and I had no idea where we would sleep that night.

Yet I couldn't see a way out of this. I looked sideways at the others.

"It *will* be an honor, Sapphire," Bronte said, giving me a slight, apologetic shrug. "Thank you."

And that is how we came to tour the Crystal Faery palace.

Sapphire, leading the way, moved as if she was taking a leisurely skate across a frozen pond. Mostly, though, she was walking on tiles, carpet, marble, and rose petals.

Rose petals were everywhere.

They spilled down walls and formed puddles or piles, like grass clippings after somebody has mown a lawn. Several Crystal Faeries wandered around scattering them. Others gathered up the piles of petals in their arms and then scattered them in another spot across the room—for no purpose whatsoever, as far as I could tell. Some Crystal Faeries leaned against the palace walls playing their xylophones, some lounged on cushions doing needlework, some blew softly into flutes, and some swirled around in soulful dances.

All the Crystal Faeries were dressed like flowers, and all smiled lovingly at us as we passed.

The palace itself consisted of a series of interlinked rooms and courtyards.

"Seven courtyards," Sapphire told us. "The cubic courtyard, the hexagonal, the tetragonal . . ." Her voice disappeared beneath the sound of her clanging away on her xylophone.

The rooms were furnished with long, low couches, the walls covered in tapestries, and the tables were sprinkled with—salt flakes?

"Yes, it's salt," Astrid whispered, tasting it.

"Don't *eat* anything!" I hissed at her.

The next room, however, was a banquet hall, and its tables were piled with fruit and cakes. Mangoes, cherries, strawberries, papayas, raspberries, blueberries, blackberries, coconut cakes, cinnamon cakes, frangipane cakes—and everything drizzled with honey.

"This we might eat," Alejandro murmured, while the Crystal Faeries seated at this table looked up and smiled, their teeth as dazzling as sunlight.

"Dear children," one said. "Allow us to introduce ourselves. I am Amethyst. This is Moonstone."

"And I am Tiger's Eye."

"Green Aventurine."

"Agate."

They recited their names, smiling tenderly, along one side of the table, and down the opposite. One of them gave a little shiver, and the others said, "There she goes, vibrating again. That's Rose Quartz. Like clockwork, she is," and they all laughed as if it at some private joke.

"Come along, children," Sapphire beckoned, and we left the room—even though I looked very pointedly at the food.

In the next room, peacocks scuffed through the rose petals. In the following, flamingos admired their own reflections in a fishpond. Giant silk and paper snowflakes had been attached to the walls, some of them fixed to form letters.

"AFEEBA," Alejandro read aloud. "This is a word I do not know. What does it mean?"

Because he was raised by pirates, Alejandro's vocabulary is not always complete. However, I did not know this word either.

"Afeeba?" I repeated and shook my head.

In the next three rooms, the same word was strung up, formed of paper stars, paper swans, and—simple paper.

"What does *afeeba* mean?" I asked.

Sapphire turned and smiled as if I was her lost teddy bear returned to her after a long absence. "Come," she murmured. "I will show you the exit."

The next room was lit with lanterns. A door stood open down the back.

"Take that door," Sapphire told us. "It leads to a slide, which will carry you gently to a perfect campsite for this night."

"Thank you," I replied, still remembering my manners, just. "Only, our packs are near the waterfall entryway. We'll go and get them."

Sapphire laughed gently. "Your luggage has been taken to the campsite for you. It awaits. The site is close to the Tumbling River, where you can rent boats for your onward journey in the morning. Come. Hurry."

She shepherded us toward the door and paused. "Oh, but Esther!" she exclaimed. "You will stay with us! You will visit our Faery treatment center and sleep on a golden bed of satin and silk!"

"Will I?" Esther asked, surprised. "I thought that you said I should visit one of these days . . . I didn't know you meant . . ."

"Today." Sapphire nodded. "Today is certainly *one of these days*. It is this day. You will join the others at their campsite at 7:00 A.M. tomorrow. Farewell, others. It's been a pleasure."

At that point, Oscar squirmed, probably because Gruffudd had been riding in the hooded part of his jacket and was clambering up the back of his neck.

"Ah, a perfect place for an Elf." Sapphire smiled. "And yet tremendously dangerous. Perhaps he should ride in somebody's pocket for now. The slide is rather steep and somewhat hasty. Gentle, of course. It's a *gentle* slide. Although it is also . . . Well . . . Enjoy!"

And then, while everyone was shooting Esther worried looks, and I was whispering to her that she did *not* need to stay if she didn't want to, and Esther herself was looking bewildered, Sapphire gave us all a great shove right through the door and onto a *huge* and *giddyingly fast* slide.

Nothing gentle about it.

CHAPTER 37

OSCAR

**TO BE HONEST,** I didn't take to the Crystal Faeries. I see Imogen's point about bright magic being too tricky—I couldn't figure out what was going on a lot of the time, and it was all about how *pretty* things were. It reminded me of the way some girls comment on other girls' Instagram posts—"OMG! So beautiful! Love you!" and you know they don't mean a word of it.

I mean, don't shower us with roses that only make us slip. Don't take a hungry bunch of kids into a room full of food and then whisk us right back out of there.

The slide part though?

That, I liked a lot.

Pitch-black, more twists and turns than a garden hose, and we were skidding along so fast we got friction burns.

The others liked it too. We tumbled out the bottom onto a patch of grass and everyone was laughing. I had thought the girls might complain about the bumps, but right away they tried climbing back up for another go. (Not possible. Too steep and slippery.) Even the smallest one, Astrid, who had a bruise on her leg the size of a pizza slice, was raving about it.

Still psyched from the slide, we looked around the campsite the Crystal Faeries had found for us. It was a perfect patch of soft green grass encircled by fir trees. Our packs had been placed in a line at the base of a tree, and it was good to see my skateboard, still looped onto my backpack. The blue bottle also looked fine peeking out of the pocket.

There was even a stack of firewood ready. You could hear the river nearby, birds calling to each other, rustles of little animals.

So then I thought: *Huh, maybe bright magic isn't so bad.*

Dusk was closing in, so Imogen decided we'd have dinner right away. She set Gruffudd up in a sort of chair made of bark, told Alejandro and Astrid to start pitching the tents, and asked Bronte to form a Spellbinding ring around the campsite to keep it safe, and then to head out with me to fetch water from the river, and kindling from the forest for the fire.

"Esther might be having a luxurious night in a golden bed of satin and silk," she finished, shifting packs around and unbuckling straps, "but we'll have a feast with toasted marshmallows for dessert."

* * *

"What's the story with Esther?" I asked Bronte as we walked into the darkening woods, squinting around for sticks and twigs. "Why did the Crystal Faeries want to keep her for the night?"

Bronte had crouched to gather kindling. She stopped and looked up at me. Her eyes went glinty in the falling light. "Esther is *amazing*," she said, straightening up. "It's strange to me that you don't know this, since it was in all the newspapers. However, it's not your fault you're from another world."

"Cheers," I said.

Bronte grinned. We walked slowly, scuffling through bark and fallen leaves as we talked. "She only discovered she was a Rain Weaver recently, when she had to battle an ancient Fiend. She was so strong. She saved all the Kingdoms and Empires."

"*Esther?*" I said, double-checking. No offense to Esther, but hadn't she been that dreamy, absentminded girl tripping over things in the forest?

Bronte nodded. "And as a Rain Weaver, she's the only person who can cure shadow magic spells. True Mages have always been able to *treat* them a little, taking the edge off their effect, but Esther can actually *cure* them. She can also sense both shadow magic and bright magic, and she's learning how to spellbind."

We'd reached the river now. "I'm so proud that she's my cousin," Bronte added, looking around. The riverbank was mostly overgrown, with a small sandy beach cut into the bank. A few battered, upturned rowboats lay on this beach, alongside a painted sign: RYAN CORDUROY'S ROWBOATS FOR RENT

No sign of Ryan himself though.

We returned to the campsite, bundles of kindling under our arms, tins full of sloshing water, feeling pretty chill.

Turned out, though, that the Crystal Faeries had forgotten to deliver the pack that contained our food—the only things to eat were some stale oatcakes—and, if that wasn't enough, the matches were in the food pack as well.

Then, at the exact moment Alejandro got the fire going—using some trick where he snapped rocks together—it started pouring.

The rain kept up all night. Gruffudd cried himself to sleep in his hatbox bed because he was so hungry. The tents leaked. We'd dragged everything under cover as soon as the rain started, which meant there was no room to lie down. My skateboard wheels were rammed into my side. Outside, birds made sudden screeching noises.

And I lay there, water dripping onto my nose and running down the side of my neck, thinking this: *Let me get this straight. I'm on a trip with the following people:*

1. *A former pirate/current prince who escaped from a pirate ship and can shoot arrows and make fire from stones*

2. *A smart ten-year-old girl who can read minds*

3. *A girl who makes "Spellbinding" rings*

4. *A girl who steals keys from the caves of Radish Gnomes, escapes using Olympic-speed sprints, and reads broken maps*

5. *A girl who saved her entire* world *from some ancient monster, and*

6. *An Elf.*

And who am I again?
A kid who skips school to ride a skateboard.
What did Mrs. Kugelhopf call me? A—

SCREECH! went another bird outside before I'd finished that thought and, for the third time in a row, I jumped and hit my head on the tent pole.

Eventually, I guess, I fell asleep.

When I woke up, of course, it was . . .

WEDNESDAY

CHAPTER 38

IMOGEN

ESTHER WAS MISSING.

I woke at 8:00 A.M. to the feeling of fingertips being pressed all over my face.

"STOP IT!" I said and opened my eyes, ready to blast whoever thought it was amusing to play my face like a piano.

It turned out to be Gruffudd. He was dancing on my face. "I remembered my next song and dance! For the next key keeper!"

"Stop it," I repeated, pushing him off my face. "All right, well done, but don't remember it on my face. What time is it? Is Esther here?"

I couldn't quite believe I'd just woken up. I'd have sworn on the backside of a seven-horned rhino (as my father likes to say) that I'd never fallen asleep. Screeching birds, dripping tent, snorts and snores, crowded packs, hunger cramps, worry about finding keys in time—they'd all kept me awake.

Now my first thought was: *We should never have left Esther with the Crystal Faeries.*

I don't know why that thought was so clear. Crystal Faeries are True Mages. They would keep my sister safe, wouldn't they? Even if bright magic can be frustrating, and sometimes dangerous, it wasn't *malicious*, was it?

I scrambled out of the tent anyway, calling, "Esther? Are you here?"

The others were all stretching and yawning. No sign of Esther.

"She was supposed to be here at *seven*," I said, and I rammed my head into the opening of the slide.

"HELLO?" I called. "ESTHER?"

Esther, Esther, Esther, the slide echoed back.

"Do not worry," Alejandro told me. "She will be here. I will go to the river for water while we wait."

Bronte followed to help him.

It had stopped raining, which seemed to have put the sun, trees, and birds into wildly good spirits. The sun blazed excitedly, the trees dripped splashily, and the birds exclaimed to each other in loud whistles. I found all three irritating.

"I suppose we should pack up the camp while we wait," I told Astrid and Oscar, and there was a cry of protest from Gruffudd.

"My song! My song!"

"All right, you sing and dance while we pack up," Astrid suggested, and so he did.

He seemed to like this song. It had an ominous tone, and a dramatic beat (provided by Gruffudd himself, stamping his feet), and he sang it several times. It went like this:

"Oh, Edward T. Vashing

He's so dashing

He's a driver crashing

A chef potato mashing

A banker cashing

Checks!

Oh, Edward T.

He's a honeybee

Works in biology

And in zoology

In psychology

Pharmacology

We'll have to wait and see

If he will agree

To give us the key

Who knows!"

When he reached "*Checks!*" and "*Who knows!*" Gruffudd emphasized the words by kicking something. Once, he kicked my ankle, and another time it was a tent peg. The tent peg sent him flying and he landed inside a boot.

"All right," I said, helping him out of the boot. "Thank you, Gruffudd. So the fourth key keeper is a fellow named Edward T. Vashing. Whoever *that* is. Wherever *he* is."

My mood had not improved. I squinted into the slide again— it continued not delivering Esther to me.

"He sounds a bit overworked," Oscar observed.

"Yes," Astrid agreed. "Too many jobs. Driver, chef, banker, biologist, and so on. He ought to choose just one."

That made me smile, although only for a moment.

Gruffudd carried on singing and dancing while Oscar, Astrid, and I stepped amongst the muddy, squelchy grass, peeling our shoes up and placing them back down, gathering our possessions and shaking them out—shaking our heads as we did at how waterlogged our things had become.

At one point I glanced sideways at Oscar, who was helping me to roll up the sleeping-bags. As usual, he was quiet and self-contained, but now I saw there were shadows beneath his eyes, and his face was pale. I shook off my worry about Esther for a moment and tried to imagine what all this might be like for him.

"I suppose this is not the best vacation you've ever been on," I suggested.

He chuckled. "It's not Disneyland," he said, the dimple appearing in his cheek. At once, though, it faded, and he squeezed the sleeping bag tight, stuffing it into its cover.

Disneyland. I suppose that's a territory in his world.

When Alejandro and Bronte returned from the river, Gruffudd was still singing.

"Edward T. Vashing," Alejandro breathed, emerging from the forest. "You are not saying that he is a key keeper? You are not! You are surely not!"

His eyes were lit up like fireworks.

CHAPTER 39

OSCAR

IT TURNED OUT that Edward T. Vashing was a movie star.

Alejandro could *not* get over the fact that Imogen, Astrid, and I hadn't recognized the name.

"You, I will maybe forgive, Oscar," he decided eventually, "because you are from another world, although even so . . ." Still a bit much for him. "As for *you*, Imogen and Astrid! You have no excuse! Edward T. Vashing! Writes, directs, and stars in some of the greatest films of our time! I cannot . . . I do not— Well, I have lost my respect for you."

Bronte raised an eyebrow and stage-whispered, "I hope he doesn't ask if *I* knew who Edward T. whatever is."

We all laughed, and Alejandro whirled around, spilling water everywhere.

It was pretty funny, which was good for Imogen. She was really fretting about Esther. She was pretending it was all good, so she wouldn't scare Astrid, but you could see it in her eyes. And in the fact that she kept ducking her head into that slide and shouting Esther's name.

Alejandro explained that Edward T. Vashing had played the *role* of driver, chef, banker, and so on, in various movies. That's what Gruffudd's song was referring to. He also told us he'd read in a movie magazine that Edward T. Vashing's latest film was being shot each morning this week in a village on the Tumbling River named . . .

He borrowed the map from Imogen, checked it closely, and then pointed.

"Glenhaven. There," he said. "It is maybe an hour's boat ride downriver from us. As soon as Esther arrives, we will rent boats from this man on the beach—Ryan Corduroy—he is there now. We have just seen him, Bronte and I. And we go. Yes?"

The excitement in Alejandro's eyes was at the exact same level as the worry in Imogen's.

We finished packing up and we waited.

And waited.

Staring at the slide.

Imogen's worry started to infect everyone. There was a sort of restless itchiness around. Where *was* Esther, anyway?

This was why they should have mobile phones.

(I kept that thought to myself, as I didn't think it would be helpful.)

"I hope the boat doesn't sink," Bronte said—I think she was just making conversation to fill the time. "It looked pretty old."

"Well, you're an excellent swimmer if it does," Imogen told her.

"*You're* a better swimmer than me," Bronte replied. "You win all kinds of races, Imogen!"

"No, no, you're better than me, Bronte, I'm sure," Imogen argued. "And Alejandro is also better, of course."

"Not at all," Alejandro replied.

Astrid sighed. "You're all lying."

Everyone looked at Astrid. "You *all* secretly think you're the better swimmer," she explained. "I can see it on your faces."

Everyone burst out laughing, and then Alejandro said, "I am certainly the best. I have grown up on a pirate ship and spent my days swimming in the ocean."

Imogen and Bronte didn't argue with that, although Imogen told her little sister that she didn't *always* have to point it out when people were lying. "Sometimes we just lie from politeness," she explained.

That broke the tension for a bit. Not long later, though, it slid back in.

Esther didn't slide back in though.

It got to be almost 10:00 A.M., and Alejandro was properly agitated. He kept that to himself too, but his knees kept bumping up and down. He'd said that the filming was happening in the mornings, I realized. He was thinking he was going to miss his chance to meet Edward T. Vashing.

"Imogen?" Gruffudd spoke up. He'd been surprisingly still and quiet for the last hour, but now he'd climbed onto Imogen's lap and was gazing up at her. "Imogen, may we go and get the key? Before it's too late? For my . . . city? We still have . . . many pieces of key to collect."

Imogen blinked and gazed back at him. "You're right," she said eventually. "We might have trouble finding Edward T. Vashing if we miss him this morning. We *should* go, only—"

Bronte spoke up. "I'll wait here for Esther," she offered, "and we'll join you in Glenhaven once she gets here."

"You can't wait alone," Imogen argued. He eyes roamed over Astrid (too young) and me (too otherworldly) and ended on Alejandro. "Do you mind waiting with Bronte, Alejandro?" She frowned. "No, wait. You want to meet the movie star. *I'll* stay. Will you be . . . ?"

Bronte shook her head. "You all go. We don't know how difficult it's going to be to get the key from Edward T. Vashing. You might all be needed. I'm sure Esther can't be much longer. Go. And I'll see you there."

There was more back-and-forth, and we ended up down at the river renting a boat.

Ryan Corduroy was a big guy with a shiny bald head who told us we could drop off the boat with his cousin, name of Jasper Kestrel, whose boat rental business was further along the river.

So the four of us—Imogen, Alejandro, Astrid, and I—stacked all our packs into a rickety little boat, climbed aboard, and pushed away from the shore. We were pretty low in the water, what with all the weight.

Bronte waved and headed back to wait for Esther.

The boat was your basic simple rowboat with a pair of oars. No rudder to steer—you had to use the oars to do that. Imogen took the oars first, and eventually we all took turns.

We rowed along, nobody saying much.

Imogen kept staring at the riverbank and at her fingernails when she wasn't rowing. Alejandro was sort of bouncy and wanting to talk, but he picked up that Imogen was not in the mood. There wasn't much to see. Just forest on both sides of the river.

Wind rustled leaves. Trees dripped rainwater.

Eventually, on the right riverbank, grassy areas began to appear between patches of forest.

A paved towpath turned up next, running along the edge. A man on a bicycle rode by and *brring*ed his bell at us.

More and more people walked or cycled on this path, meadows and gardens behind them.

Distant sounds began to crowd toward us too—people calling, a horse whinnying, a dog barking. Even a motor revving.

A riverside dock emerged, surrounded by bobbing boats.

"This must be Glenhaven," Imogen decided, heavily. "There's a boathouse up there. Let's stop and ask if anybody knows where Edward T. Vashing is filming."

We bumped against the dock, tied up the boat, woke Gruffudd and put him in Alejandro's pocket (his favorite place at this point, since Alejandro had solved the clue in the song), and climbed onto the bank.

The towpath had run into a village square now, crowded with well-dressed people. A few of them were carrying parasols, shading themselves from the hot sun.

There was a row of shops, each painted a different pastel color. Pink, orange, blue. POST OFFICE, said a neat sign on one shop. GROCERY STORE, the next. CONFECTIONERY. And so on.

We stood in a cluster, stretching our aching rowing arms and discussing who should stay with the boat and who should start knocking on doors, asking for—

"CUT!" shouted a voice. "SOMEONE GET THOSE CHIL-
DREN OUT OF HERE!"

Alejandro's eyebrows jumped. "I don't think we need to
knock on any doors," he said, and pointing, he whispered, "It's
him."

Cameras. Lights. We were standing in the middle of a film set.

Edward T. Vashing was heading our way, and even his mustache looked angry.

CHAPTER 40

IMOGEN

I'D NEVER SEEN a film set before. I was busy revolving in place, realizing that everything about this square *was* peculiarly bright and clean, and noticing the man on the ladder holding a huge light, the tangled cords running around behind the stores, the woman scurrying between faces with a makeup brush—when Edward T. Vashing stormed up.

He was dashing, even with his face crimson with temper. A boater hat was set at a rakish angle on his dark and wavy hair. The rolled-up sleeves of his white linen shirt revealed his muscular forearms. He had excellent cheekbones, striking eyes, a fine mustache, and a pleasing mouth, which he now opened in order to speak.

"Just *what*—" he began, but Alejandro was already speaking.

"You are directing this film?" Alejandro asked, his eyes asparkle. "And also starring in it? And you wrote it too? I must tell you. Your performance in *The Lost and Broken Lily Petal* surpassed all other performances in the cinema last year. You are a *genius.*"

"We're sorry to interrupt your filming," I remembered to say.

"We are here about the city of . . ." Astrid paused. "Dun-sorry? Dun-worry? I've forgotten! I'm so sorry, Gruffudd!"

"It is all right. He is asleep again," Alejandro said, checking his pocket. "And it was Dun-sorey-lo-vay-lo-hey."

"It's been buried under silver," I explained. "We only have until Friday, so it's *urgent*."

As we spoke, the crimson faded from Edward T. Vashing's face and a smile grew in its place. "Of course!" he said. "Of course! What is the matter with me? You are excellent! Perfect!" His voice was rich and warm, and seemed to carry right across the square and even down along the river. "Come, children! I know exactly what I wish you to do!"

We glanced at each other. I felt grim but relieved. Here was a key keeper who had planned our challenges in advance, which was efficient. We could get the key, then get back to figuring out where Esther was.

"The boys," Edward T. Vashing said, pointing at Alejandro and Oscar. "I would like you to climb the roof of the boatshed—"

More climbing. We'd done that at the schoolhouse. Possibly Edward T. Vashing had accidentally kicked a ball up there too, like the little girl, Sharmilla.

"—and jump from the roof into the river," Edward T. Vashing finished.

Most unexpected. However, the boys shrugged. The day was warm; their clothes would dry. Gruffudd would have to get out first, of course.

"We'll get bathing trunks for you," Edward T. Vashing added. "Right, you girls . . ."

My job was to dress up in a frock and bonnet, and wheel a hoop between the people on the square. Now and then he wanted me to stop wheeling the hoop, mop my brow with a handkerchief, and then carry on.

Astrid was handed a short skipping rope and told to skip. ("I'd prefer to jump into the water with the boys," she told me, and I agreed that I'd prefer that too. "Still, you had an ear infection just last week," I reminded her. "So maybe best not to swim." She sighed and nodded.) As she skipped, she was to chant a song, which Edward T. Vashing promised to teach her.

We stared at Edward T. Vashing as he handed out these

tasks, and then he snapped his fingers: "Wardrobe! Makeup! Hair!" He beckoned people over, issuing instructions.

"He wants us to be in his *film*," Alejandro murmured, and at last it made sense. We should have realized sooner. I'd been bedazzled by Edward T. Vashing's handsome mustache.

So that's what happened.

All shined up, in starchy clothes with powder on our noses and rouge on our cheeks, we were sent to our places. All the other actors stood in their positions, poised as if they were playing the statue game back at Mrs. Chakrabarti's school. Edward T. Vashing looked into the camera lens, called a few commands to the actors—move a little to the left; straighten your hat there—and then he stood back and cried in an impassioned voice, "Make me sigh! Make me cry!"

The actors all laughed and chanted back at him: "Make me sigh! Make me cry!"

I supposed that was the actors' rallying cry.

Edward T. Vashing nodded and called, "Action!"

The boys scrambled onto the boatshed roof and jumped into the water. Astrid skipped. I pushed a silver hoop between adults and mopped my brow with my handkerchief. The adults wandered about, chatting to each other and occasionally laughing.

Then Edward T. Vashing himself walked into the scene.

"Hey ho!" he said in a sonorous voice to a beautiful woman in white. The woman twirled her parasol, gave a cheeky smile, and replied, "Not if *I* can help it!"

Edward T. Vashing tossed back his head and laughed. There was a pause. Then: "Cut!" he called. "Great *job*, everyone! That was *perfect!*"

And everyone relaxed.

Astrid coiled up the skipping rope, and she and I went to the river's edge to where the boys were bobbing around in the water.

"That was easy," I said. I was in a slightly better mood. Being in the movie scene had been a distraction from worrying about Esther. Also, why was I worrying? She was just running late. She and Bronte would be along any moment.

Alejandro and Oscar were both still in the water, grinning and splashing each other.

"Come on," I called to them. "Hop out and let's all get changed. Hopefully, Edward T. Vashing will—"

"RIGHT!" called Edward T. Vashing from across the square. "Let's go again, people! Places!"

It turned out he wanted to film the scene again.

And then he wanted to do it again.

And again.

Over and over and over and over.

With completely empty stomachs.

Each time, the boys had to scramble back out of the river, towel themselves down, have their hair ruffled, and return to the boatshed ready to climb it again. Each time, Edward T. Vashing would shout, "Make me sigh! Make me cry!" and everyone would repeat the chant back at him. **ACTION!** And Astrid had to skip and chant the same rhyme. I had to spin that hoop between the chattering adults and mop my brow with a handkerchief.

"Hey ho!" Edward T. Vashing would call and the woman in the white dress would twirl her parasol and say, "Not if *I* can help it!"

Then Edward T. Vashing would laugh and shout, "Cut! *Perfect!* You people are marvels! You are doing this *just right!*"

Before making us do it again.

At first, it was fine. As I rolled the hoop, I admired the actors' clothes. The women wore drop-waist silk dresses in lime greens and daisy yellows, decorated with beadwork. Some had cloche hats set on sharp-edged bobs, others wore strings of pearls and velvet slippers. The men swaggered about in waistcoats and baggy trousers that tapered in at the ankles. The sun shone and the hoop rolled.

Soon, though, things began to annoy me. The crinoline dress they made me wear was childish. I felt embarrassed. It had a wide blue sash and a prickly collar. Every time I tried to adjust the collar, to stop it prickling my neck, the sash slipped. One of the actors I passed with my hoop said, *tch,* and frowned when-ever I swerved around him. I suppose he thought it added char-acter to the scene, but I began to want to shout, "I've been *told* to swerve my hoop past you like this! And *I* think I do it very well!" I could easily have bumped his leg with the hoop if I hadn't been concentrating, yet I never did, or only once or twice, when I was particularly annoyed with him.

After a while, I also became angry about the dialogue. It made no sense. "Not if *I* can help it!" the woman in white said.

If I can help what? What did she mean?

I suppose it had something to do with the plot of the film. On its own like this, however, it was nonsensical.

As the sun grew hotter, I could see Astrid beginning to wilt. The poor girl had to keep bouncing up and down, her legs scissoring back and forth over the rope. She grew weary of sing-ing the same chant too. I know this because at one point she switched to one of her own, then Edward T. Vashing bellowed, "Cut! Cut! Perfect work, everyone! Perfect work, skipping girl! Only please, you *must* use the chant that I taught you. Why switch?"

"I was weary of the other one," Astrid told him.

"Brilliant," he said (unexpectedly). "Still. Stick to the script."

So she had to go back to singing:

"You find it when you're happy

You find it when you're sad

You find it when you're snappy

You find it when you're glad

You find it on a bookshelf

You find it in the fridge

And if you don't *find it*

I'll throw you off the bridge."

Her voice faded, growing hoarse.

I was glad that Alejandro and Oscar were having fun at least, leaping into the river, but I soon realized that they were looking grim at the idea of having to pull themselves out of the water, get toweled down, and climb that boatshed again. Oscar cut his shin open on a nail in the shed wall, and filming was delayed while they mopped up the blood. He didn't even flinch, I noticed, as they washed his wound and bandaged it. He just went back to his mark and scrambled up onto the roof when it was time. It must have stung though.

Eventually, I began to believe that I would spend the rest of my days listening to Edward T. Vashing say, "Hey ho!" while I pushed a silver hoop, only ever stopping to mop my brow.

I had fallen into a sort of reverie about this new life of hoop pushing, I suppose, because I gasped aloud when Edward T. Vashing called, "Lunch!"

The *tch*ing man laughed at me. "That gave you a fright, eh?" he asked.

I fixed him with what Father calls my "death glare."

He blinked and hurried away.

CHAPTER 41

OSCAR

 **I KNEW RIGHT** away he wanted us to be extras in his movie. I was in no way "bedazzled by his mustache."

It did make me do a double take though, that mustache.

Anyhow, it wasn't so bad for Alejandro and me. We got worn out by climbing, and I was a bit worried about how rusty the nail was. Nobody mentioned getting a tetanus shot, so I didn't raise it. Generally, it was fun. I liked jumping into the river. We had contests on who could jump farthest, and we did bombs, pin jumps, belly flops, tumbles. Alejandro was good. He could do double backflips. I guess from his time as a pirate.

Edward T. Vashing didn't notice what we were doing for ages, and when he did, he said: "Perfect! *Magnificent* work, boys. But please. Only regular jumps."

He was pretty funny.

* * *

At lunchtime, trays of sandwiches were handed around. We were so hungry we didn't care that they were tomato again, like yesterday.

The other actors and film people wandered off behind the buildings, chatting, while Edward T. Vashing sat on a little stool by the river. He ate his sandwich and held a book on his knees, writing in it.

Imogen whispered to us that we should all get changed into our regular clothes, get the key, and leave.

"We need to go back," she said. "Esther and Bronte are taking much too long."

So we changed and headed over to Edward T. Vashing. Imogen led the way, head up straight, ready for a fight.

"Mr. Vashing," she said, stepping up to him. "I'm afraid we *must* leave."

He looked up at her surprised, chewed, swallowed, brushed his face, and said, "Of course! You've all done *sensational* work here today! We're packing up, anyway. I only like to film in the morning light. Thank you!"

Imogen blinked and frowned a bit, the way you might if you had your boxing gloves on and were dancing on your toes ready to pound a punching bag, then somebody picked up the punching bag and put it in the closet.

"*Superb!*" said a voice, and for a moment I thought Edward T. Vashing had turned extremely high-pitched and squeaky.

But it was Gruffudd. He'd been watching from the sidelines while the filming went on, and now somehow he'd scrambled onto Imogen's shoulder. She was surprised to see him there. We all were.

Edward T. Vashing stared. "You have an *Elf!*" he exclaimed. More bits of sandwich flew from his mouth.

"They don't *have* me," Gruffudd lectured. "*I* have them. They are my servants performing the quest for—"

"Yes, we have an Elf!" Imogen interrupted. She was pretty snappy. "Mr. Vashing, while we know you are a film star, we are *trying* to save an entire Elven city, and we *must* find—"

"Oh good gracious." Edward T. Vashing shook his head. "This is about that key, isn't it? The key to the Elven city? The silver waves have started? You need to collect my piece of key?"

"Yes!" Imogen cried. "We *told* you that the moment we arrived!"

He stood up, patting at his pockets, still shaking his head. "No, no," he said. "You didn't. I'm afraid you didn't tell me a thing."

He walked away from us, moving amongst the camera equipment, gazing up at lights and down at cords, kicking these around.

"WE DID!" everyone argued, although privately I was thinking: *Did* we? I remember they mentioned the name of the city, but did they actually mention the key?

Edward T. Vashing stopped abruptly and looked back at us, his eyes widening. "Oh, your *audition*! It *wasn't* an audition, was it? When you all got here and were chattering away? I thought you were doing a set piece for me! Excellent, it was! And no wonder." He chuckled. "You were serious. Come along, don't look so solemn. I know I have my piece of the key here *somewhere*. I'd have given it to you at once if I'd realized you wanted it. I thought you were the extras for my film, see? I wonder what became of *those* children? I mean to say, if they'd arrived in time, this would never . . . As it was . . ."

Mutter, mutter, mutter—and then, "Ah, here it is!"

He was studying his camera.

"Taped to the side of the camera," he called over his shoulder, carefully picking the edges of masking tape. "I remember now. I thought if I put it here, it would be easy to grab the moment an Elf turned up looking for it."

He hurried back to us, a glint of silver in his hand. "You were *magnificent* being the extras. Nevertheless, I expect that scene will be cut from the film. *Hey ho,* I say, and she says, *Not if I can help it,* and I laugh. Laugh? Honestly, none of it makes sense. Ah well, that's life in the movies. Here you go."

And he handed over the fourth piece of the key.

CHAPTER 42

IMOGEN

I DON'T KNOW what was going on in my head.

A lot of thumping. The lion was thumping its tail.

"Where *are* Esther and Bronte?" I demanded. I wasn't addressing anybody in particular. Just the air.

I'd gone into a trance being filmed. I should have focused. If Edward T. Vashing hadn't wasted our time, I could have.

"Come, Imogen," Alejandro said, guiding me toward the boatshed.

Oscar's expression had grown guarded. Astrid was staring at me.

I breathed deeply.

"We need to get back to them," I said. "Something is wrong."

Alejandro was firm. "They will be here," he said. "Come, we will sit on the jetty by the boatshed, see? And watch the river. While we wait, we can solve the next clue. It is your turn for the memory, no? Imogen? Oscar, could you . . . ?"

Oscar reached into the boat, drew out the bottle, and held it out toward me.

"Absolutely not," I said. "First, we need to figure out how to go back upriver and collect the girls." But Gruffudd had vaulted from my shoulder to Oscar's, and from there onto the side of the bottle itself. He curled his arm around the bottle's neck and, with the other hand, tugged at the cork.

"*Stop!*" I commanded, only it was too late.

I was in a memory.

I was nine years old and standing in the town square at home.

My little sisters, Esther and Astrid, were sitting on the edge of the fountain, gazing up at me.

"You will stay *right* here," I was saying. My voice was furious. "Esther, I want you to count to one hundred by twos. Astrid, I want you to—"

I paused. Astrid was six. Could she even count to one hundred yet?

"I want you to count as high as you can. Sit here, and *count.*"

As I glared at them, my eyes fell to Esther's knees. They were grazed and bloody.

There was a rattling sound, somewhere below my chin. I bent my head forward to see. Around my neck were several strings of beads in greens, oranges, and crimson. Surprising. I didn't own beads.

I strode away from my sisters, the beads still rattling, and almost collided with a thicket of bamboo. Also surprising. There was no bamboo in our town square. This thicket was dense, the slender trunks rich gold, planted amidst bristly gray weeds. They shot up to the height of tall men before tapering off into sharpened points. It was like looking at a thicket of spears.

I blinked. These were neither bamboo nor spears. They were brooms. Buried facedown. The prickly gray weeds were in fact the brooms' brushes. The broom handles, poking up in the air, had been sharpened, possibly with a carving knife.

Why were so many brooms buried in the town square? Who had carved their ends into sharp points and why?

The air around me grew suddenly cold and shadowy. Uneasiness in my chest sharpened like the broom ends themselves. I turned to check on my sisters, but the thicket of brooms extended behind me now. It blocked my view of the fountain. "Esther?" I shouted. "Astrid? Where are you?"

No reply. The sky was heavy with dark clouds. At my knees, a black cat stared up at me, its tail slowly undulating.

"Pilkington Town," the cat said, speaking in a gruff man's voice.

I jumped in fright at the sound of a cat speaking. Cats don't speak. But something strange was happening in the thicket of brooms. Each broom was twisting in place. Creakily, busily, twisting around and around, up and up—and then, one at a time, the brooms were plucking themselves from the earth with *pops*.

Each broom shook its brush loose of soil and then paused, hovering just above the ground.

As I watched, every broom pointed its sharp end directly at the fountain, directly at my little sisters—and then they began to fly.

I screamed.

CHAPTER 43

OSCAR

❦

 **THAT'S A BIT** of an understatement. Imogen screamed so loud I'm pretty sure she burst not only my eardrums but the eardrums of Alejandro, Astrid, Edward T. Vashing, all the actors, the film crew, and the fish swimming in the river.

"It's *Witches!*" Imogen was babbling. "The Witches have Esther and Bronte! Those Doom Lantern Witches! Why did I leave Esther with the Crystal Faeries? And then I left *Bronte* alone too? What is *wrong* with me? What was I thinking? Now I've lost a sister *and* a cousin!"

Alejandro frowned deeply. "Imogen," he said. "Esther is a Rain Weaver and Bronte is a Spellbinder. Of course they are all right to be left alone."

"They are *not* all right," Imogen insisted.

Astrid spoke cautiously. "What clues did you see in your memory, Imogen?"

"Broomsticks with sharpened ends. A black cat." She spat the words, pacing up and down the jetty.

Both Astrid and Alejandro nodded slowly. "Okay, that sounds like Witches."

"It does," I agreed.

"So you have Witches in your world?" Imogen pounced.

"Not *real* ones." I smiled. The others stared at me in their usual baffled way before getting back on topic.

"Beads too," Imogen was muttering. "That was part of the clue. I was wearing beads. And Witches wear beads."

"Not in our world they don't," I put in.

"Your Witches aren't *real*, Oscar," Astrid reminded me, sounding a bit testy.

Imogen had stopped pacing and her head was swinging back and forth between us without actually seeing us. "We need to rescue Esther and Bronte. Now. How do we get back to them? We need a boat with a motor to head back up the river."

"Imogen." Alejandro put his hand on her shoulder. "The clues you just saw were about the next key keeper. This is not ideal because it sounds like the next key keeper is a Witch. It does not mean, though, that Esther and Bronte are in danger of Witches *now*. It is not a . . . This is not how the clues work, is it?"

Imogen shook off his hand. "It's exactly what it means," she snapped. "They are."

She was peering at passing boats. Not a single one was motorized. They were all rowboats or punts, people gliding along, smiling in the sunshine.

"WE NEED TO GET HELP!" Imogen shrieked, and she balled up her fists like she was about to start pounding someone. "BEFORE IT'S TOO LATE! *HELP ME! CAN'T SOMEBODY HELP ME?*" Next thing she was on her knees, dragging all our packs out of our boat and dumping them—*Boom! Boom! Boom!*—onto the jetty. She sprang to her feet.

"Help you with what?" said a voice, and we turned to see Bronte and Esther strolling toward us.

Imogen burst into tears.

CHAPTER 44

IMOGEN

I COULDN'T STOP crying. It was very embarrassing.

You see, I'd been sure—absolutely convinced—that Esther and Bronte had been taken by Witches. (I realize that doesn't make sense, so if somebody's about to jump in and say that: hush up.)

I couldn't stop hugging them, then standing back and *looking* at them. My sister Esther with the smudge of dirt that always seems to be on the side of her nose. Her slightly muddled frown. The way she runs her hands down her braids, out of habit, accidentally loosening them. A ribbon was missing from one of her braids. A bootlace was untied. That is all typical of Esther.

My cousin Bronte in her stylish yellow dress with her quiet smile, her dark hair and dark eyes. Her eyes were shy but with a glimmer. Her hands were in her pockets, but then she drew them out and twisted her bangle. This is all typical of Bronte.

Esther was apologetic.

The night before, she told us, Sapphire had taken her directly to the treatment center the moment we slid away. The center was just a large room in their palace, she explained, and it had been crowded with patients who'd been attacked by the Doom Lantern Witches.

"There were probably around thirty patients," Esther said, "all lying on beds, frozen in the most uncomfortable positions.

It was paralysis magic. The Faeries had treated them with a thawing spell, which had only relaxed the muscle spasms in their necks. They were still trapped and *truly* in agony. You could see it in their eyes."

She had stayed up until all the patients were cured, then fallen asleep on the floor—so she hadn't slept in silk and satin sheets after all.

"And did Sapphire teach you some Faery healing spells like she promised?" Alejandro asked.

"Well, no," Esther said. "I fell asleep, as I said, and when I woke up, there were four new patients to treat—children, actually. They said they'd been on their way to a film set, to be extras in a movie with Edward T. Vashing, when the Doom Lantern Witches intercepted them. I cured them, but they needed to stay and rest for the day. They were so disappointed."

"They needn't have been," Astrid said dryly, and we told Esther and Bronte how we had spent the morning.

"Anyway," Esther continued. "More and more people kept arriving, needing to be cured—those Doom Lantern Witches are vicious!—and then I heard a clock chime and realized how late it was. Next thing Sapphire turned up and said, 'Are you still *here*, Esther! Why, you were meant to meet the others *hours* ago!' And she took me to the slide and I went down it—so fun—and Bronte was waiting for me at the bottom and we rented a boat. I'm so sorry," she finished. "I'm truly sorry."

I hugged her again. "It's all right, darling Esther," I said. "I'm just happy to see you alive. Although it's a shame you didn't think of sending a message to us, it's not your fault. I forgive you completely."

I felt light-headed with happiness.

At that moment, I didn't even care that the next key keeper was a Witch.

As long as we were together it would be fine.

"I think it must be a coven of Witches somewhere near a place called Pilkington Town," I told the others, "because that's what the cat said to me."

We found Pilkington Town on the map. It was on the right

bank of the Tumbling River. Perfect. We had two boats now and could simply carry on.

"We'll stop when we reach the town," I suggested, "and ask for advice on how to deal with the local Witches. At least they're not the Doom Lantern Witches—these ones will be known as the Pilkington Town Coven, I expect. They're probably moderate Witches—irritating but not dangerous. We should try to enjoy the boat ride."

We distributed the packs between boats and climbed aboard.

"What's happened to Gruffudd?" Bronte called as she stepped into a boat with me. It tipped precariously; she stumbled and grabbed the side.

Gruffudd, who had been sitting on my shoulder since Esther and Bronte returned, was no longer there. I double-checked.

"He's over there," Oscar called, pointing. The Elf was lying on his tummy on the river's edge, gazing down into the water.

"Esther, grab him, would you?" I shouted. She had wandered along the river and was closest to him. "Astrid, careful! Why don't you come in this boat with Bronte and me? No, stay where you are now. Alejandro can come in our boat."

So this is how it ended up: Bronte, Alejandro, and I in one boat, and Esther, Astrid, and Oscar in the other. There was a short argument over who would row first. I don't know why except that we were tired, and I've noticed that we do fight when we're tired, or have spent too much concentrated time together. Or for absolutely no reason at all. I think it's the nature of life. The sun shone hard, spangling the water.

In my boat, Bronte was rowing and her arms seemed to strain against the water.

"Has the current changed direction or something?" she asked. When we looked at the water though, leaves and twigs were skimming along in the same direction we were.

"It is because you are weary," Alejandro suggested. "We did not sleep much in the night. Would you like me to row?"

That started another mild argument—again, for no reason— which was interrupted by Astrid shouting, "What's *that*?" from the other boat.

She was pointing back toward the boatshed we had just left. A tiny shape was leaping up and down on the river's edge.

"Is it an animal?" Esther wondered. "A frog?"

"It's a toy," I suggested. "A clockwork toy."

Bronte frowned. "It looks like *Gruffudd*." She stopped rowing. So did Esther, who was rowing in the other boat. We drifted slowly, peering back at the distant little shape.

"It can't be Gruffudd," I said. "He's with us, isn't he? Which boat is he in? Gruffudd? Gruffudd?" I called his name several times, but there was no answer.

Our eyes ran over each other's shoulders. We checked nooks and crannies in the boats, inside our pockets, and under our packs.

Then we looked back toward the boatshed again.

The tiny figure still leapt up and down, tiny hands waving wildly. "*Help!*" carried faintly on the breeze. "*You forgot me!*"

"Esther, did you not *get* him?" I asked.

In the other boat, Esther stared at us wide-eyed. "I mean, I *think* I did. Didn't I?"

We rowed to the bank, tied the boats to bollards, and Bronte scrambled out. The rest of us sat silent, waiting, while the boats bobbed up and down. Bronte sprinted along the towpath.

When she reached the boatshed, she crouched, picked up the little figure, put it in her pocket, and sprinted back again.

"It's Gruffudd," she told us shortly, as she climbed aboard again.

Gruffudd himself popped his head out of her pocket: "It is!" he told us proudly. "And Bronte is my *favorite* person in all the Kingdoms and Empires! Although I was abandoned, she has saved me! Thank you to the beauteous and mightiful Bronte!"

"I'm the one who noticed you," Astrid pointed out.

"Thank you to beauteous Astrid too," Gruffudd agreed.

He slithered out of Bronte's pocket and made himself comfortable in the folds of a soft pack.

"Sorry, sorry, sorry," Esther was saying, covering her face with her hands. "I was *sure* I'd got him! I must have imagined it! I suppose I was distracted!"

"Do not blame yourself," Alejandro called to her. "You also must be weary after your night."

"It's all right, Esther," I told her. "It's not your fault."

We all fell silent. The two boats rowed side by side. The heat grew more powerful. Insects buzzed and bit at our elbows and the backs of our necks. The towpath disappeared from the riverbank, replaced by grass and weeds. Now and then we passed little cottages, or people fishing from the banks. Eventually both sides of the river grew thick with bush and trees, and there were neither houses nor people. We seemed to be the only boats on the river, and there were no sounds but the plashing of the oars and the smacks as people slapped at insects.

Alejandro swapped places with Bronte, and she sat back with a huge sigh, wiping sweat from her brow. In the other boat, Oscar took over the rowing from Esther.

"Oh!" Esther said suddenly. "I almost forgot. The Crystal Faeries gave us a gift! It's in my pocket. No, the other pocket, I suppose. Hmm. Oh, here it is. Yes."

We waited patiently.

"It's Faery dust," Esther explained, "spelled with communication. You sprinkle it on water, and you can talk to whoever you—"

She didn't finish as we were all exclaiming, "Esther! *Seriously?*" laughing with disbelief, for here, at last, was a way to send a message to our parents.

CHAPTER 45

OSCAR

**NEXT THING THEY** were practically falling out of the boat to get the magic dust sprinkled on the river water, so they could make their calls.

It was like Facetime or Zoom, I guess. Only you just had to say the name of the person you wanted to contact, and their face popped up, a bit rippled, on the surface of the water. Another difference was that the face popped up even without the person hitting answer or joining the meeting. No choice.

That seemed like a flaw in the system to me. You could easily catch someone in the bathroom.

First, they called the three sisters' parents. The parents looked hugely happy and relieved for a moment, but that pretty quickly switched to *WHERE HAVE YOU BEEN? WHAT WERE YOU THINKING? WE ARE SO DISAPPOINTED.* And so on.

It turned out those parents had been in touch with Bronte's and Alejandro's parents too, to tell them their kids were missing. So there were strict instructions to get in touch with that lot instantly.

"Why did you have to tell them?" Esther wondered.

That was a mistake.

"WHY DID WE HAVE TO *TELL* THEM? WE WERE *RESPONSIBLE* FOR THEIR *CHILDREN* AND WE HAD *LOST* THEIR CHILDREN! BECAUSE OF *OUR* IRRESPONSIBLE

CHILDREN! IMOGEN, I AM ESPECIALLY DISAPPOINTED IN *YOU*, AS THE ELDEST . . ." Et cetera, et cetera.

A lot of angry shouting like that came flying off the surface of the river water that day.

The only conversation without shouting was the one with Alejandro's parents, who I understand are a king and a queen. They seemed sad.

"We only just got you back," they said sadly, and gurgily— the river water affected voices. "We thought that we'd lost you again. We wanted you to have a relatively normal childhood, but now we're really regretting not sending palace guards with you on your visit to the mountains."

The others all defended themselves. They kept holding up Gruffudd and saying, "How could we resist helping this little Elf!"

"How *indeed*!" Gruffudd agreed each time.

But the parents kept going on about how the kids should never have gone off on a coach *in the first place* without parental permission.

Bronte seemed to have the best defense to that—she'd traveled the Kingdoms and Empires *completely alone* two years earlier, when she was *ten*, at the *command* of her parents (she said all this fairly loudly for her—she'd seemed like a quieter one before this—even frightening birds into silence).

Imogen's point was that she was thirteen, Esther's that she was a Rain Weaver, and Astrid's that she was in the company of her older sisters plus her cousin Bronte, who was a Spellbinder. "*Plus* a pirate," she added.

Alejandro, the pirate, seemed a bit bemused and kept pointing out his own pirating past in a slightly embarrassed way.

These all seemed like pretty solid arguments to me, but the grown-up faces in the river carried on gurgling in fury.

At some point in each conversation, I got introduced. I had to lean over the edge of the boat to show my face. I can't remember all the names. There were too many. (Bronte seemed to have *four* cranky adults to deal with, her parents, an aunt, and a butler.)

Alejandro's parents were a king and a queen, as I mentioned, only they looked like regular people. No crowns or capes.

The adults were all polite to me, saying things like "Oh, hello there, boy from another world," but they were distracted in the way adults get when their minds are on how angry they are with their own kids.

When it was over, and we were sliding along the river surface, with only the sounds of the oars splashing and birds calling, little critters scuttling about on the river's edge, the others were pretty quiet.

Occasionally they would glance at each other with an expression on their faces. I don't know what you call this—it's when your bottom lip curls down and your eyes open wide. Like you're saying "oops" with your face.

They did that to each other a bit and then, suddenly, they all started laughing.

Alejandro was laughing his head off along with the rest of them, but he shot me a sideways look between our boats and said, "I do not understand why I am laughing." Then carried on laughing.

They settled down eventually and stayed quiet for another while, some of them frowning to themselves again.

Splash, whir. Splash, whir went the oars, as we rowed along. The air had that fresh, green smell that it gets after rain, and the water was full and busy.

"Oh, Oscar!" Esther said suddenly. "*You* must want to contact your parents! While I don't know if the Faery dust works for communication between worlds, you could—"

"Nah," I said. "It's sweet."

Esther looked a bit startled. "Have you . . . *tasted* it?"

"No, I mean it's all good."

"Well, I hope so." Esther leaned over the boat and touched the water with her fingertips. "I hope none of it has gone bad. Like I said, I don't know if you can communicate with other worlds—"

"It's okay, Esther," I said. "Thanks, but I'm okay."

Esther fell silent.

We slid along the river. One of the boats would pull ahead and then the other. There seemed a low-level competition going on between the boats all the time, which nobody mentioned. Mostly we were evenly matched.

Around this time I noticed that Imogen's face had stopped being deliriously happy. She looked like she was closing in on herself—sort of hunched over, she was. Lost in thought.

CHAPTER 46

IMOGEN

YES, IT'S STRANGE how moods can swerve in unexpected directions, but that's exactly what happens to me.

At first, after we spoke to the parents, my mood was excellent. I was happy to have Esther and Bronte with us again, and relieved to have let our parents know where we were. Two great weights had lifted from my shoulders.

Then I looked over at Esther in the other boat and noticed that she was hanging over the side, running her hands through the water where our parents' faces had just been. She always does that. She loves water.

Careful, I thought. *Don't lean so far over.*

I think that's when my mood shifted. The words of my parents kept circling my mind. *So irresponsible! So disappointed in you!*

Although I had flicked those words aside earlier, they now began to crawl under my skin.

I mean to say (I thought, as my crankiness grew), *it's not as if you are* usually *around to notice when we go missing. We're usually at boarding school!* Father is often away for work. And it's true that Mother is getting to know our preferences in pastries, but *previously* she had no clue! She was always forgetting things about us. She once bought Astrid a pink coat for a birthday present even though the color pink makes Astrid get stomach cramps.

When you think of it like that (I told myself) how *dare* she criticize me for being irresponsible?

How *dare* she be disappointed in me?

I knew all this sudden righteous anger was to do with guilt. It *had* been my idea to run to get the early coach without asking our parents' permission. True, we'd have missed the coach if we'd waited for them to get back from the markets, but maybe they'd have come up with another way to help Esther get to the Elven city in time? Also, we should have left a more detailed note. *Back later!* had not been helpful.

Finally—and this was the part I had been setting to the far side of my mind—well, at this moment, we were on our way to see some Witches.

We hadn't mentioned that to our parents, of course. We had only explained that we had a few more key keepers to see and then we would be at Dun-sorey-lo-vay-lo-hey by Friday morning, and would take the afternoon coach straight home. We had begged them to leave us alone until then.

"I will keep the others safe!" I had promised. "I *swear* it! We'll see you at home on Friday!"

How could I make that promise?

This was the moment when Esther raised her hand from the water and called, "Oh! I forgot it!"

We looked across at her. The air was close and dank-smelling now, almost fetid.

"Forgot what?" Alejandro asked.

"The Crystal Faeries found our food pack," she explained. "They said it had been hidden in shadows when they collected our things, and they only realized they'd missed it this morning. They apologized for not putting it at the campsite—you must have been so hungry last night! Anyway, they gave it to me to bring, and I left it at the top of the slide."

There was a pause and then:

"*ESTHER!*" we all shouted. Even little Gruffudd jumped to

his feet and joined in with his high-pitched voice: "*Esther! Oh, ESTHER! What have you done this time, Esther!*"

My temper leapt into the boat out of nowhere. "What *is* going on with you, Esther? You have become *ridiculously* absentminded!"

"Have I?" Esther looked miserable.

"You *have!*" Astrid agreed. "You forget *everything!* You forgot to leave in time to meet us. You forget to send us a message that you were late. You even forgot Gruffudd! He could have been left behind on the riverbank!"

"He could have fallen into the river and drowned!" I cried. ("I'm quite a good swimmer though," Gruffudd said, but I was still shouting.) "He could have been mistaken for a worm by a crow!" ("I *am* a bit like a worm," Gruffudd agreed.) "He could have been trampled by boots!" ("Oh yes, boots." Gruffudd shuddered.)

"And you forgot to tell us about the Crystal Faery dust so we could call Mother and Father," Astrid added. "And now you've forgotten our *food?* I'm *hungry!*"

"Do you know what, Esther?" I asked. "You're becoming exactly like our mother."

"Yes!" Astrid agreed at once. "You are!"

There was a sudden absolute silence. Esther stared from me to Astrid and back. We held our heads high, meeting her gaze. Alejandro set his oars into their locks and sent me a troubled look. Even Oscar sensed that something significant had happened and stopped rowing.

An icy breeze seemed to touch the back of my neck.

It had been a terrible thing to say and I knew it. Our mother's forgetfulness has hurt all three of us girls deeply in the past. It's a big part of why we're so close. It has braided us together.

For a moment, Esther simply sat in stunned silence. Then her face flared with rage, her hands lifted, she twisted them rapidly in the air, and two plumes of water leapt out of the river and crashed onto my and Astrid's heads.

SPLASH!

We were instantly drenched.

Water poured down my face and soaked my clothes. It pooled around my feet in the base of the boat. Alejandro and Bronte threw themselves away from me, to avoid getting wet themselves. In Esther's boat, Oscar was openmouthed with confusion.

"ESTHER!!!" Astrid and I howled.

"You used your *Rain Weaver* skills to splash your sisters?" Alejandro asked, in wonder. "Your ancient, mystical Rain Weaver skills?"

"IT'S FREEZING!!!" Astrid wailed.

It was.

"Oh hush, all of you," Esther said, looking extremely guilty. "It's not *cold,* it's hot . . ." She frowned and looked up. Gray clouds had hidden the sun. The icy breeze that I'd imagined a moment before blew once again and I realized I *hadn't* imagined it. It was real.

Without us noticing, the weather had turned.

Furthermore, I realized, our boats were hurrying and bumping along with the current even though nobody was rowing.

"Up ahead," Bronte pointed, rising slightly. "Something is happening to the river. What is that? It looks like a forest in the middle of the river!"

"The river splits," Alejandro said, taking hold of the oars again. "It's dividing around that land. Which arm do we take? Does it matter?"

I was shivering violently, my teeth chattering. "I'll check the map," I said. I reached into my pocket. The map was going to be *sodden.* I tried the other pocket. I hoped I'd still be able to read it. I tried the first pocket again. Both pockets at once. I looked down at my feet, and kicked around in the puddle of water. "Where is it? Where's my map?"

The boats were rushing along ever faster, closing in on the split.

"Keep trying to find it," Alejandro said, his voice calm as he worked to steer the boat along the center of the river, ready to turn either left or right. The tall trees rushed toward us.

In the other boat, Oscar was attempting to do the same, his

face tense. His boat had been well over to the right side of the river though, and he was dragging hard at the oars, trying to center it.

Suddenly, I recalled that Pilkington Town was on the right bank of the river.

"Go right!" I said.

Oscar eased up on his steering and allowed his boat to veer back toward the right. Alejandro forced his way in that direction. We were almost at the split.

Then the map appeared, flapping open at my feet, and there on the page was the river itself, snaking along—cleaving in two along a long, thin island—and joining together further downriver, long before Pilkington Town. It didn't matter which arm we took. Except—

I grabbed the map from the boat floor and squinted it. There was something else printed there—

Along the right branch.

A long word in very pale ink.

DANGEROUS

"The right side is *dangerous*!" I was on my knees, gesturing wildly. "Take the left! Take the left!"

Alejandro wrenched our boat to the left. Oscar tried to do the same.

Too late.

Our boat surged to the left.

Oscar's surged right and disappeared.

CHAPTER 47

OSCAR

"THE RIGHT SIDE is *dangerous!*"

Great to have those words ringing in my ears as our boat went flying to the right.

She wasn't wrong either.

Instantly, the water got wild. It had already *seemed* kind of wild because we'd been moving at a pace, only now we were going full throttle.

I'd always thought waves belonged in the ocean, but here they were, frothy, white, and coming at us from every direction like a pack of frenzied dogs. Astrid was shivering from head to toe, Esther was waving her arms wildly, trying to do her water-controlling thing, only she couldn't get her balance—the pair of them were bouncing one minute, crashing sideways the next.

"Go back! Go back!" Astrid screamed at me.

Very likely, I'm sure.

Nowhere we could go but forward like a speeding Lamborghini. I tried to use the oars to slow us down and one got wrenched out of my hand and flung into the water. Disappeared.

Rocks started springing up above the surface of the water. How'd the water get so low? How'd the rocks get so high? At first, just a couple over near the bank, then more and more appeared.

This is white-water rafting, I realized, *in a rowboat.*

We were done for.

I faced front on my knees and tried to steer around the rocks. Shoved the oar against them.

WHACK. That's how it sounded and felt when we hit a wave. Boat bounced so high my stomach bounced along with it. I kept falling sideways with a *thud* and scrambling back up again.

The girls behind me were scrambling to hold down our packs while at the same time clinging to the sides of the boat to stop flying overboard themselves. All three of us were getting splattered. It was like someone *SLAPPING* your face one moment, *SLAPPING* your back the next. Water stinging your eyes, running down your neck, up your nose, into your ears. You could taste it down the back of your throat: ice-cold dirty river water.

Rocks coming at us from every direction. Rammed the oar into one rock to shove the boat sideways and it jarred right up into my shoulder blades. Here came another. Rammed the oar into that one and the oar split in two with a crack.

We belted into the next rock.

Boat flew high and tipped us out.

CHAPTER 48

STILL OSCAR

MOUTHFUL OF WATER. Under the surface. Ice-cold. White noise. Head up, gasping for air. Crashing sound sinks to low roar. *Crash . . . roar . . . crash . . . roar.* River had its elbow in my side. Under the surface. Pure panic. Head up. Roaring again. Mouthful of water. Clothes like weights. Hit a rock, tore my arm open, blood in the water. Head up, gasping for air. Water gets ahold of me and tosses me diagonal. Hit a rock, cut my head. Blood in my eyes.

And so on.

The rocks smashed me up but stopped me drowning.

Thanks, rocks.

Pure luck that I ended up thrown against the bank at one point. Grabbed at some weeds that were sprouting from the mud there and dragged myself up and over.

Lay flat on my stomach. Heavy breathing. A tickling of blood down my forehead. Closed my eyes a moment.

Dragged myself up to look for the girls.

"Esther?" I called. My voice came out strange. "Astrid?"

"We're here." Faint voices, further along the riverbank. "We're okay. Are you okay?"

"No," I said, and fell back down again.

So that was the three of us, lying on the riverbank for who knows how long, like a bunch of old rags.

We might have stayed there forever, but at some point I realized I was shivering all over.

Someone has put this old rag in a freezer, I decided, and I curled myself in amongst the frozen peas and ice cream, laughing a bit.

I was losing it.

I sat up suddenly and my head started spinning. I thought I might be sick. Then I *was* sick a bit.

Wiped my mouth. Wiped the blood out of my eyes.

"Esther?" I called again.

She and Astrid were sitting up now, holding on to each other, trembling. They both looked kind of battered.

"We have to get warm," Esther called, then she sat there doing nothing, and so did I. "I couldn't do my Rain Weaving," she added more softly, after a moment. "The boat kept flinging me around."

Wind gusted by. It had a low, shivery sound to it. The sky was purple. Behind us the forest looked thick and gray and prickly.

After a moment, Esther hauled herself up, and dragged Astrid to her feet. I saw all this through my peripheral vision but didn't turn my head. Too cold. The two of them limped toward me.

They were dirty, wet, grazed, and bruised. Leaves and dirt in their hair. Their braids had come loose and turned into straggly wet streaks over their shoulders.

The three of us stared at the river. It spat and splattered in there like an overheated frying pan.

No sign of the boat or our packs.

"You've lost your piece of wood," Astrid said sadly.

Piece of wood.

"My skateboard?" I felt a sudden terrible twisting in my gut. Tried to unknot it fast: *It's just a board. I can get another. It's not that—*

Then I remembered with a mighty rush of relief: "Nah, my board was in the other boat with my backpack. So was Gruffudd, right? In the other boat?"

They both nodded.

"Lucky." I felt my eyebrows go up. The Elf could never have survived that river.

"But you guys have lost your stuff," I added. "Some of it could have washed up on the bank or got stuck on a rock, maybe? Want to walk along and look?"

Right then, the wind blew a blast of cold air that actually shoved me sideways.

Esther shook her head. "We need to get to shelter," she said through chattering teeth. "And you're bleeding, Oscar. Come on, let's walk into the forest. Maybe there'll be a cave or something."

* * *

Better than a cave.

We found a track through the trees, which opened to a clearing, and right before our eyes: a log house, two stories high.

Chimney. Flower boxes in the windows. A shovel on a hook by the front door. Welcome mat with several pairs of rubber boots lined up beside it. A vegetable patch out the front with a rake lying across it.

Perfect.

I knocked on the front door. My knuckles were a sort of translucent blue color. Knocking turned them pink.

Nothing.

Knocked again.

Called out.

Astrid's face was the same white-blue as my knuckles, and she was doing this weird occasional shiver thing. Like perfectly still and then a full-body spasm. She was breathing in a similar way—no sound and then a rasping breath.

Esther looked from me to Astrid and back again. "Astrid needs to get warm," she said. "And you need to fix up that cut." She reached for the door handle and turned it.

It opened.

We walked inside.

CHAPTER 49

STILL OSCAR

BIG LIVING ROOM with comfy corduroy couches. A fireplace in the corner with a stack of wood beside it. Couple of empty vases on the mantelpiece, rugs on battered floorboards.

"Hello?" Esther called into the house.

But it had an empty feel. Kind of chilly and echoey.

"I don't think anybody's here," Astrid said, only she said it with chattering teeth so the words were spun out and vibrating.

Esther crouched by the fire and reached for a log. "Right," she said. "I'm going to build a fire to warm us up. It's a nice place, so I'm sure nice people live here, and they'll understand. Oscar, can you—"

"As long as we don't eat their porridge," I joked.

"Why would we do that?" Esther stacked more logs in the fire, shoving in some kindling.

"Or, you know, sit in their chairs. 'Goldilocks and the Three Bears.'"

"What's a Goldilocks? Hopefully there aren't any bears in these woods. Oscar, find the bathroom and wash that cut of yours. And can you take Astrid and see if there are towels to dry her off? And some clothes for her to borrow? Once I'm done lighting the fire, I'll try to bandage your cut for you."

She turned back to work.

Astrid and I went dripping past the staircase and down the hall. It was dark and cold, but there were open doors into a kitchen, a laundry, and then a bunch of bedrooms. Beige macramé decorations hung from nails on the wall.

"Here we go, Astrid," I said, finding a bathroom. It was small and painted a salmon pink. A shower in the corner with an off-white shower curtain. Bit of mold around its edges. The toilet had a fluffy cover on its seat, and there was a potted plant sitting on the window ledge.

I took a towel—a grass-green color it was, and a bit threadbare—from the railing, and handed it to Astrid. Only, she was shivering too much to do anything except stare at it in her hands.

I took the towel back, wrapped it around her, and gave her wet head a good rub, the way my mother used to do to me when I was small. Her face disappeared behind the towel.

When she reappeared, her hair was in a big tangle and she'd snapped out of her trance and was grinning at me.

"I'll see if I can find some dry clothes for us," she said, turning to the bedroom across the hall. "You wash off that blood."

While she rummaged around in the drawers in there, I looked at myself in the bathroom mirror. The blood had dried in a splatter pattern on my cheek, like the shadow of a winter tree. A network of branches, some thin, some just twigs. It was good, like a horror movie. I wished I had my phone so I could take a selfie, although if I'd had my phone it would have been destroyed when I fell in the river. Anyhow, I remembered, the battery was dead.

I found another towel, ran water over it, and was washing the blood away, dabbing at the cut—still bleeding a bit—when a door *slammed* and Astrid called out in a voice that made me stop cold.

All she said was, "Oscar? Can you come here?" But her voice was like that of someone who's just set the kitchen on fire.

She was standing in the middle of a bedroom.

She'd changed into an adult's knitted jumper, which was bright lemon yellow, had pockets, and was long enough on her to be a dress. She'd also taken out a couple of extra jumpers,

I guess ready for Esther and me, and these were draped across the bed.

Her face was white as printer paper. As soon as she saw me, she started pointing at things around the room.

A tangle of colored beads lying on the dressing table.

A black cat, curled up asleep in the corner.

A postcard tacked to a corkboard: VISIT SUNNY PILKINGTON TOWN, it said, with a picture of a beach umbrella.

"I don't get it," I said.

Now she pointed to the wardrobe. "Look in there," she whispered.

Whatever was in that wardrobe must have scared her enough she'd slammed its door. I reached out nervously. Didn't want to see a headless ghost.

Door *creaked* as I opened it, which made me laugh. At first, I couldn't see much in the darkness. A row of wire hangers, dresses on a few of them. A jumble of shoes on the floor. Seemed pretty normal. Then I peered harder at the shoes. Underneath them, lying across each other at diagonals, were a bunch of wooden poles.

Not wooden poles, but brooms, I realized, touching the soft bristles at the end of one.

Funny place to keep brooms. And why so many?

I pulled one out, making the others roll around noisily, and held it up. Its end had been carved into a knifepoint.

Behind me, Astrid started babbling. "The beads, the cat, Pilkington Town, the brooms! These are all Imogen's clues for the key keeper. Oscar, Witches live here! We're in a coven! And *look!*"

She had turned over a cushion on the bed. On the other side, it was cross-stitched with a picture of a lantern and beneath that the word

DOOM

"It's the Doom Lantern Coven," she whispered.

"Esther?" I called.

We headed straight back to the living room, me holding up the broom, Astrid the cushion. Esther turned from the fire, which was now roaring.

That's when we heard voices approaching the front porch. Adult voices talking and laughing, a group of them.

"Hey, why is there smoke coming from the chimney?" A man's voice sounded above the chatter.

"Peculiar," said another voice. "We're all *here*, aren't we?"

The voices paused, then carried on moving closer. "Did we leave the fire burning?"

Footsteps on the front stairs.

In the living room, all three of us had frozen in place Finally Astrid hissed, "They're Witches, Esther! They're Witches!"

Esther grinned, thinking it was a joke. "*Astrid,*" she said—and then she caught sight of the broom in my hand, the cushion in Astrid's.

"Go," she murmured, rising and pointing down the hall. "*Go, go, go.*" Herding us back down the hall and into the last bedroom.

The front door opened and the voices boomed now.

"The fire's been lit!"

"Someone's been *in* here!"

"What's going on with—"

I didn't hear what they said next. Esther had forced the window open, and we were scrambling outside.

We sprinted across the grass toward the woods, quiet as we could, and had almost reached the trees when there was a burst of laughter and a cheerful shout. "I *see* them! Let's *get* them! They're *there!*"

CHAPTER 50

STILL OSCAR

NEVER RAN SO fast. Into the woods, arms pumping, right behind the girls. Slipped on wet leaves and mud patches.

Behind us came the footsteps of a bunch of Witches, pounding along, laughing and shouting.

The woods were crowded. Trees huddled up together like they were chilly. You had to turn side-on and squeeze your way between. You kept getting caught by shrubs and tripped by roots.

The sounds of the Witches kept closing in on us.

They were worse than the Radish Gnomes. Scarier. Those Gnomes had been mean and angry. This lot were mean and they *loved* it. They kept hooting, as if chasing a few kids was a blast for them. As if our fear was their wine and cheese night.

No clear track between trees. It was more like a maze. Esther was ahead, and she kept slamming into dead ends—walls of trees, or murky ponds—yelping, and having to circle back.

Those footsteps kept pounding right behind us. It was surreal. I had this out-of-body sensation for a moment and almost stopped, turned, and demanded: "Are you *serious*?"

Then one of them screamed: "QUIT RUNNING! YOU KNOW WE'RE GOING TO CATCH YOU AND SNAP ALL YOUR BONES!"

And the others shrieked with laughter.

Right behind us they were. Bashing into trees. Laughing again. Calling to each other in these breathless, excited voices.

"Go that way and we'll trap them!"

"Helen, you go around here and cut them off!"

"Gary, climb that tree! See if you can spot them!"

I did glance back a couple of times and caught glimpses of them. They looked like ordinary, nerdy parents, in cardigans and baggy pants, except there were brooms clutched in their fists, sharpened ends like spears.

I was breathing so hard it was loud and raspy in my ears. Stitch in my side. Chest burning.

Then I slammed into Astrid.

She'd stopped.

Esther was ahead, also stopped. She was pointing at a tree. A big tree, reddish brown, with a gaping hole in its trunk. Hollow trunk.

Esther mouthed at us, "Get in there."

Not safe at all. I shook my head.

The Witches were right behind. They'd catch up any second. Find us easily in there.

"GET INSIDE!" If you can shout with your face, that's what Esther did.

Astrid and I obeyed. Squeezed into the tree, Esther right behind us.

It was wet and dank in there, just big enough for the three of us, pressed close together, trying to pant in silence.

Dark, but the sun through the opening lit up Esther's hands— they were raised and trembling.

She started moving them fast, up and around, up and around—still trembling, yet kind of graceful too. It was how Bronte's hands had moved at the Radish Gnome cave.

"She's making a Spellbinding ring," Astrid whispered, supersoftly. "But I don't know if she *can*." I looked at Astrid's face. Her eyes were red, her cheeks crisscrossed with tears. She'd been crying as we ran. I gave her shoulder a squeeze.

Esther's hands jolted to a stop. She started again. Her face was a wreck of frowns.

Crashing and thumping outside. A couple of the Witches surged right by the tree—we saw brooms swinging, cardigans flying—and then a voice called, "Hey!"

And another: "Oh yeah, I smell it too."

Crack of twigs breaking. Olive greens and tan browns flashed by.

We heard them gathering nearby.

"Spellbinding," a woman said, and the others grunted, irritated: "What a stink. You're right."

"They were kids, weren't they?"

"And only a couple of them? If it's just a child Spellbinder, we can take them easy."

"Yeah! Let's take them down!"

Esther's whole body was shaking. Her hands kept right on moving. The tears started up again on Astrid's face, rushing down her cheeks. She was biting her lip hard, trying to stay silent.

"Should we try it?" another voice pondered.

"We are VERY GOOD AT BROOMSTICK CROCHET!" one shouted, for our benefit. "We will *shatter* your Spellbinding! You may as well come out now!"

A pause.

(Later, Astrid told me that "broomstick crochet" is how Witches do shadow magic, but I got the gist at the time.)

"You know what?" That was a deep male voice. A shuffling sound. He was kicking leaves. "Those kids might be after that Elven key we have."

"That's happening now?"

"Apparently. Silver waves started Monday. I heard talk of it in town."

Suddenly they were all yelling their heads off. "OUR BROOMS ARE AS SHARP AS RAZORS!"

"AS SHARP AS THE VENOM OF A DEATH ADDER!"

"AS SHARP AS THE TEETH OF THE TIGER SHARK!"

They paused. I caught sight of Astrid's face, twisted up so that her eyes were squeezed shut, teeth biting hard into her lower lip.

They repeated those three lines several more times while Esther's hands kept on moving, and Astrid hid her face behind *her* hands, and my heartbeat got faster than a Formula 1 race car.

Then one of the Witches spoke again, this time in a much softer voice.

"What if they've already *found* the key?"

"I hid it," another replied. "In a special place. No way they found it."

Whisper, whisper, then a cackle of laughter.

"Genius! You're right. No way they looked there."

"Okay, but still, what if they're part of a group and *others* are in the house looking right now?"

"Ah, for—"

A lot of swearing then. The voices began to move away, speaking faster. "Let's get back there just in case" and "Hurry, come on!"

The last thing I heard, fading into the distance, was "That was fun anyway" and, "More fun if we'd cracked a few of their bones," followed by a burst of happy laughter.

And then quiet.

More quiet.

Esther's hands finally stopped moving, but she held one finger to her lip. Astrid nodded.

We waited.

Huddled together. Damp bark, wet moss. Esther and I still in our river-wet clothes. Astrid in a Witch's yellow jumper. The girls' eyes bright in the darkness.

For a long, long time, we waited.

Then Esther slowly, slowly leaned out of the gap and looked left, right, up, and down.

Slowly, slowly, she crept out of the tree and into the clearing. Her head darted this way and that.

"They're gone," she murmured.

Astrid and I climbed out too, and Esther grabbed Astrid and squeezed her in a sideways hug.

She took a deep, shaky breath. "No idea where we are," she said. "We need to contact the others."

"Bronte will know what to do," Astrid whispered. She glanced at me. "You might not realize this," she said, "but our cousin Bronte is both brilliant and kind. A skilled Spellbinder and an excellent adventurer."

Esther was nodding in agreement, her hand in her pocket. She drew out a little cloth pouch. "The pouch got wet in the river, but maybe . . ." She untied the knot, pulled it open, and reached in her fingertips. "It's damp." She frowned. "Still, we can try."

Ah, of course. That Faery dust that they'd used to call their parents.

Astrid pointed to a small puddle on the ground. Old rain caught between the roots of a tree. Brown and muddy.

"It *should* still work," Esther said, although she sounded like she was trying to convince herself.

She sprinkled some powder onto the water.

"*Bronte Mettlestone*," she said.

The powder sat there on the surface. The muddy puddle sat there being muddy.

Nothing.

"*Bronte Mettlestone*," she said again.

Still nothing.

"Try Imogen," Astrid told her. "Try Alejandro."

"Imogen Mettlestone-Staranise?" Esther said, desperation in her voice. She scooped out more of the Faery dust, sprinkled it again.

"Imogen?"

A long pause.

Nothing.

More dust.

"Alejandro, the Stolen Prince of Cloudburst?"

Nothing.

More dust, more dust.

She was half-crying now. "It must have been ruined in the river! You probably can't get it even a *little* bit wet!"

"Maybe it's because the puddle's too muddy?" Astrid suggested.

"Yes, try giving it a little stir," Esther told her.

Astrid stepped closer to the puddle, crouched down, reached out her hand and—

"STAY EXACTLY WHERE YOU ARE!" a man's voice boomed. "DO NOT MOVE A MUSCLE."

CHAPTER 51

IMOGEN

MEANWHILE . . .

. . . our boat, as you might recall, had traveled left.

I shouted in horror, begging Alejandro to go back, but of course that wasn't possible.

Our branch of the river carried on at a vigorous pace, the water dark and inscrutable. I sat there shivering, my thoughts darting in every direction, trying to find a solution. Moments before I'd been ready to strangle Esther, and now I was back to being frantic about her.

And I'd lost Astrid and Oscar too.

What was *wrong* with me? Why couldn't I keep control of these children? They were like marbles that kept skittering away.

The current was so strong that Alejandro settled the oars into the locks and let the boat coast. He spoke kindly to me: "Take a breath," he said. "Do not panic. Relax and check the map. Does the river join up again at some point?"

"It does," I answered, showing them the map. "Look, Pilkington Town is quite a way past the point where the branches meet—that's why I hadn't noticed the split. Or the word *dangerous* on the map!" My voice wobbled. "Why is it printed so faintly? And what do they mean, '*dangerous*'?"

Did the river water become poisonous? Were there Shadow

Mages floating on its surface? Did it become a series of waterfalls—sheer cliffs over which the others would plummet?

I took in a great breath ready to sob—and then I flung my shoulders back and straightened up. I grew fierce with concentration. I peered around at the passing banks.

The bank to our right—the long, thin island—was thick with bushy trees and overgrown with shrub. We could try to land there and force our way through to the other side. But they could be anywhere along the river.

"I think we should get past the island, to the point where the branches join," I said, "and see if they're there. Can I row?"

I took the oars from Alejandro and rowed.

On the left bank, things had become calm and cultivated. A paved path ran along the river's edge with short green lawn beyond it. We passed an oak tree with a swing attached to a branch. A woman walked a dog. Pleasant cottages appeared. Up ahead, a bearded man sat with his legs dangling over the river's edge, his feet bare, trousers rolled up.

"Imogen," said a voice.

I frowned.

Where had that come from?

A strange whizzing sounded from deep in the boat then, which made us *all* frown. It turned out to be Gruffudd spinning the wheels of Oscar's boardskate, which was still in our boat. We were quiet for a while, watching Gruffudd stretch out his little arms and give a mighty pull, setting the wheel rolling, before running around to the next wheel and doing the same.

"Imogen," the voice spoke again.

I must be imagining it.

We had almost reached the bearded man now, and I turned to look more closely at him.

"Imogen," he said, for the third time.

It was Reuben the Genie.

My stomach gave a leap like a startled rabbit. Still, I kept my expression steely. (I hope I did, anyway.)

"We can't stop," I told him, as I rowed by. "We have to find the others."

"Take another memory," Reuben called.

I stared at him over my shoulder.

"*No,*" I retorted. Why were people always trying to get me to "remember" when I was busy? "It's not even my turn to take a memory! It's Oscar's! We haven't even been to the fifth key keeper! We can't go looking for the sixth! And we have no *time!* We have to find the others!" My voice grew louder as we traveled quickly away from him, skimming along the river.

Reuben pushed himself to a standing position and cupped his hands around his mouth.

"YOU'VE GONE OFF COURSE!" he called.

"I *KNOW* THAT!" I bellowed back.

"So take another memory." His voice was quiet again now, yet somehow I could still hear it. "And get back on course."

I craned my neck behind me. He had turned from the river and was picking a path along the grass away from us, his feet still bare.

I carried on rowing. The others—Alejandro, Bronte, even Gruffudd—were all staring at me.

"He *is* a Genie," Bronte told me softly. "And you know that Genies are usually . . ."

Oh, for crying out loud.

"I know they're usually right, but we don't even have the bottle! It's in Oscar's bag, and that must be—"

Gruffudd made a loud huffing sound and *dragged* Oscar's bag sideways. Of course. Oscar's bag was in our boat. Gruffudd had been playing with the boardskate—skateboard?—wheels.

"Here," he said, trying to get both arms around the bottle to tug at it. Alejandro reached around him gently and slid the bottle out.

I set the oars in their rowlocks again. Our boat bobbed up and down, drifting slowly. The current had grown sluggish again.

Alejandro held out the bottle, eyebrows raised.

I took it from him. Once again, I pulled out the cork. And once again, I was in a memory.

The memory was from only a week ago.

I was shouting at a woman at a flower stall.

"THIS IS *RIDICULOUS!*" I shrieked.

The woman had just bought a bunch of tulips, which she held close to her chest, as if they might protect her from my shouting.

Behind her shoulder, I could see a covered bridge, freshly painted in red and black. Well, *that* made no sense, there was no—

I blinked and looked at the others.

"The clue is a covered bridge," I told them, taking up the oars again. "Red and black. That's all I know. So let's keep going and try to find the others and then we can—oh."

Up ahead, spanning the river, there it was.

The red and black covered bridge.

Again, I stopped rowing and let the boat drift toward it for a moment.

"Should we stop?" Bronte wondered.

I shook my head. "We'll come back to it," I decided. "First, we have to—"

A Water Sprite surged out of the river, grabbed the side of our boat, and hauled herself up so she could see us all.

"Hello," she said and smiled. "Looking for a key?"

CHAPTER 52

STILL IMOGEN

THE WATER SPRITE folded her arms over the edge of our boat, rocking it slightly, while her legs dangled in the water. She looked like an ordinary woman, although her shoulders were broad, arms very muscular, and fine tendrils of seaweed grew on her dark skin. Her hair was long, and it tangled with these tendrils.

"Indeed, I *do* seek a key!" chirruped a voice. It was Gruffudd—he had scrambled up my sleeve and was now perched on my shoulder. "Or at least, a piece of a key! Most noble Water Sprite, my name is Gruffudd, an Elf of the Elven city of Dun-sorey-lo-vay-lo-hey and these are my humble servants of the quest, here to—"

"Yes, yes." The Water Sprite smiled more broadly, so that her eyes crinkled. She was very beautiful. "I am Gabriella, Queen of the Water Sprites, Division 775, and I have heard tell of your quest, little Gruffudd. Forgive me a moment . . ."

Abruptly, she let go of our boat, slid down, and vanished beneath the water again. Water Sprites are True Mages. They cannot stay in dry air long: they need to replenish often.

While we waited, I noticed that several people on the riverbank were staring in our direction. "A Water Sprite," they called to each other. "I'm sure I just saw a Water Sprite. She was hanging off the side of that boat over there!"

They quietened, waiting, and when Gabriella leapt up again

there were gasps and hisses of "There! She's there!" and "Shhh, don't scare her away."

Gabriella ignored them. "I have my piece of the key right here," she said. "Would you like it?"

We nodded, all of us, and I said: "Yes, please."

"All right." One elbow clinging to the edge to hold herself in place, she pressed her other hand, closed in a fist, toward me. The hand opened. A glint of silver on her palm. I reached out and—

The hand snapped closed over the silver and the Water Sprite slid beneath the surface again.

"Oh, she's gone under again," voices informed each other on the riverbank. "Let's see if she comes back."

"I *hope* she comes back." Bronte sighed. "I knew that was too easy."

Again, we waited, the boat drifting on the current, while the crowd followed us along the bank, calling to each other, "She's back! Oh, sorry, that was a fish. My mistake."

At last, the Water Sprite burst up again, shaking her long hair and grabbing the side of the boat again. "One thing before I hand over the key," she said.

I tried not to sigh.

"Only," she continued, "I've been hearing about your quest— Mages gossip, you know—and things have been going missing."

"Missing?"

Gabriella nodded. "The innkeeper, Marion-Louise, lost her crocheted doilies."

"Oh, *that*," we all spluttered. "*We* didn't take her doilies! The door to our room was open, and we—"

Gabriella began counting on her fingers. "Yes, I agree it could have been anyone, but the schoolteacher, Mrs. Chakrabarti, says that a ceramic frog disappeared from her school steps while you were there. The Radish Gnomes claim you stole a skullcap. The Crystal Faeries think a silk snowflake vanished from their palace. And I've just now got word that Edward T. Vashing, the film star and director, was sad to find the shoelace missing from his left boot directly after your departure."

She released the side of the boat in order to raise both hands in a thoughtful shrug and sank beneath the water once again.

"*What have you been thinking?*" Gruffudd shouted, abruptly enraged. "You children would jeopardize my quest? I trusted you! I believed in you! Yet you've been *stealing* from the Keepers of the Key!" He was stamping his tiny feet on my shoulder.

"Ouch," I said, wriggling. "Stop it, Gruffudd. Of course we're not stealing! I remember that frog on the school steps! Its name was Ferdinand! Nobody would have taken Ferdinand! That Radish Gnome threw her skullcap on the ground and stamped on it! It's probably under some leaves or bark where she left it! The Crystal Faeries had snowflakes and stars and decorations *everywhere*! One probably just lost its glue and slipped off the wall! And as for Edward T. Vashing's *shoelace*! I mean to say—"

"This will be some kind of game or trick or challenge," Alejandro suggested.

"*You* would speak? But you are a *pirate*! Pirates steal! You did it!" Gruffudd scowled at Alejandro, who only chuckled in response.

"I was never a *practicing* pirate," he pointed out. "I escaped the ship especially to avoid becoming one."

"Oh stop it, Gruffudd," Bronte said. "None of us would steal. Alejandro's right, it's—"

"What about the other boat? Oscar is from another world!" Gruffudd reminded us.

That stopped us. We glanced at each other, troubled. What did we know of Oscar's world? Maybe stealing was common there? He *had* mentioned about bicycle thieves . . . Perhaps he was one? Maybe it was *polite* to take little bits and pieces that did not belong to you in that world?

I wriggled in frustration. I was sure Oscar wasn't involved. "Well, *I* want to find the other boat and rescue my sisters!" I said. "I don't want to waste time proving our innocence! If she won't give us the—"

The Water Sprite was back again, water dripping from her

hair into our boat, peppering our packs. "You don't need to prove your innocence," she said. "I see in your eyes that you did not take a thing. Rumors are dangerous things. A falsehood begins and it rolls from place to place, gathering mistakes and mishaps. These other items were probably lost in accidents, or lost long before, or borrowed innocently. Who knows? Here, children, take the key."

And once again she held out her fist and opened it. Once again, an oddly shaped chunk of silver metal glinted.

This time, I grabbed it.

"Another thing," Gabriella said, with a mild, reproving glance at me for snatching. (I bit my lip guiltily.) "I suggest you go *here* directly." Her hand opened again, and this time there was a gold card on her palm.

THE ROYAL GAYNOR HOTEL

it said, in elegant script.

Gabriella smiled. "This is my gift to you. Carry on until the broken arms of the river join again. Not long beyond that point, and well before Pilkington Town, you will reach Hannah's Jetty. There, a carriage awaits. This is for hotel guests who arrive by river. Take the card, Imogen."

I shook my head, trying to explain that we could not afford a hotel and that, in any case, we needed to rescue the *others*, but the Water Sprite smiled more gently and pushed the card into my hand.

"Take it," Gabriella insisted. "You will stay there tonight. Give this card to the carriage driver. Ask his advice on any issue. He's a marvel."

She dipped into the water for a moment, then surfaced again. "Children, be a cad," she said. "Be a cad. Be a cad. Be a cad."

Anyhow, that's how it sounded to me. *Be a cad. Be a cad. Be a cad.* Afterward, Alejandro and Bronte agreed that this *was* what it sounded like, but Alejandro thought she was telling us to be good, and Bronte that she wanted us to be *glad*.

Both of those interpretations made more sense.

Another dip into the water, another surge upward, a smile,

and one more soft "*Be a cad*," then the Water Sprite glanced at the crowd on the bank. She waved, shouted a musical "Good-bye, everyone!" dove into the river, and disappeared.

The crowd broke into delighted applause.

CHAPTER 53

STILL IMOGEN

IT TOOK ABOUT half an hour before the river met up with its lost arm and joined forces again, and then another ten minutes before we saw a jetty. Rickety and sun-worn, a few boards missing, the jetty jutted out from the right bank. HANNAH'S JETTY, said a sign.

By this point, my fingers were twisting together with impatience. We bumped against the boards, and Alejandro quickly tied up the boat, while I climbed ashore. I swayed for a moment, my legs having forgotten how to carry me on land. Bronte clambered out after me, Gruffudd now clinging to her shoulder.

The sky was blue but the air was crisp and chill. The jetty led to a patch of rough grass and then a dirt road winding away into forest. We had seen neither boats on the river nor dwellings on the shore for some time, and there was no sign of anybody here either.

"There," Bronte said, pointing.

Around a curve in the road, an elegant black carriage approached. Its door was embossed with the same curling script as on the gold card: THE ROYAL GAYNOR HOTEL. Four glossy horses trotted toward the jetty. The driver sat very still and erect, facing forward, elbows up, reins neat in his hands.

"Hold," he commanded, and the horses stopped. One flicked an ear, another kicked out at something on the road, then all four held themselves still, heads high.

The driver turned toward us. "The Royal Gaynor Hotel?" he inquired, raising his cap. He had a neat, pointy beard and sunken cheeks.

"Well, yes, we have this—we have this gold card—but we *must* find the other boat—before we do—the river split—and we don't know—we have this . . . can you recommend—can you advise . . ." I was babbling.

The driver arched an eyebrow and reached to take the card I was waving at him.

He studied it.

Then he smiled at us. "Welcome to the Royal Gaynor Hotel," he said. "My name is Octavius. The hotel invites you to make yourselves comfortable in the carriage. The hotel shall deal with your luggage and will—"

"Oh, the rowboat," I faltered. "We're supposed to return it to—a cousin, I think? I forget! There was a place where we . . . but we *have* to find my sisters first!"

"And Oscar," Gruffudd added from Bronte's shoulder. "We must find him too. Had you forgotten, Imogen? The boy from another world? I just now remembered him. Personally, I had forgotten."

Octavius glanced at our boat in the water. "That is one of Ryan Corduroy's rental boats," he informed us. "The hotel shall arrange to return it to his cousin, Jasper Kestrel. If I interpret you correctly, I understand that your friends were in a separate boat? They took the dangerous branch of the river, and you are concerned for their safety? The hotel will assist you to locate them."

I nodded vigorously. "Yes, yes! Exactly! So you know somebody who might be able to take us there? To see if we can—"

Octavius held a hand to the side of his mouth and whispered loudly: "When I say *the hotel*, I really mean *me*." Immediately, he dropped his hand and resumed his formal tone. "The hotel shall assist you to locate them. Please." He stepped down and opened the door of the carriage. "The hotel invites you to climb aboard."

I glanced back at our packs in the boat.

"The hotel will take care of them," Octavius assured me, so I stepped aboard the carriage, the others following.

The inside was plush, its seats cushioned. A shelf held a jug of iced water, wedges of lemon floating about in it, and several empty glasses.

Through the window, we watched as Octavius stepped swiftly along the jetty, leaned into our boat, and emerged with all of our packs. It was remarkable. He was a very skinny man in his suit, not much taller than Alejandro, yet he had gathered all the packs—some slung over his shoulders, some under his arms—his face maintaining its serene expression and, within a moment, had stowed them in the back.

We felt the *clunkety-clunk*s as he did this, and the shift in weight of the carriage, and then we watched as Octavius moved directly past the window and climbed up into the driver's seat again. The carriage set off at a trot.

* * *

It was probably an hour later that the carriage stopped again.

We had driven through forest along a dirt road, with only an occasional bump. Mostly, we'd been silent, watching through the windows. There seemed no reason to have stopped at this point—the forest was still thick and darkly shadowed. The sun was sliding toward the horizon.

We heard the soft *thud*s of Octavius climbing down, his footsteps on the road, and the carriage door opened.

"If a boat takes the right arm of the river, it is likely to capsize," he informed us. "Do not be alarmed. Your friends will no doubt have swum to shore. The hotel will now escort you through the forest to the riverbank."

He strode up to the horses, spoke to each of them quietly, stroking them, then returned to us.

"A point of note," he said. "There is a Witches' coven not far from here. A particularly cruel one: the Doom Lantern Witches."

My head emptied of every thought. It filled instead with a blaring sound like trumpets or train horns. I caught myself on the side of the carriage.

"Yes." Octavius nodded, grave yet still calm. "This is why the right bank of the river is considered dangerous. Not so much the wild waters, but the fact that those waters fling you close to the Witches. The hotel recommends that you stay close and quiet as we make our way." He glanced at Gruffudd. "You understand?"

Gruffudd squirmed and slid from Bronte's shoulder, dropping into her pocket.

"And if they're not on the shore?" I asked. I heard my voice trembling, which annoyed me. I straightened up. "If they've been taken by Witches?"

"Come," Octavius instructed. "The hotel will deal with issues as they arise. Kindly follow."

And he stepped into the trees.

We stared at each other in the gathering shadows, then set out after him.

Darkness intensified as we walked. So did a terrible feeling of dread.

Images crowded my mind: Esther, Astrid, and Oscar, thrown from a boat by wild waters. Dragging themselves to shore. Witches blazing toward them. Witches screaming their spiteful laughter.

Our silence as we tramped seemed to gather these images into it, pulling them into the shadows, into the wind that wound its bitter tendrils around us, into the scuffling of creatures in the undergrowth, the cracking of twigs, the pale *whoo-whoo*s of owls.

From the distance came the faint sound of voices.

"That sounded like Esther," Alejandro murmured.

We stepped more quickly, listening hard, but the voices faded.

The mood had grown so frightening, so overwrought, that the scene which appeared before us next felt almost inevitable.

There's a type of Shadow Mage called a Kwilligus. It takes a liquid form, the color of weak tea. It looks exactly like a puddle except that, from a distance, it can be seen to emit a faint rust-red glow.

If you touch it, it reacts instantly, like acid, and melts away your flesh.

Ahead of us, a Kwilligus lay like a puddle at the base of a tree.

Esther, Oscar, and Astrid were crouched in a ring around it, and Astrid's hand was reaching, reaching—a *breath* away from plunging deep into the Kwilligus's body.

"STAY EXACTLY WHERE YOU ARE!" Octavius boomed. "DO NOT MOVE A MUSCLE!"

CHAPTER 54

OSCAR

I GUESS ASTRID is more obedient than I am.

Pretty sure if someone had bellowed at me like that, I'd have finished what I was doing—stirring the puddle with my bare hand, to be exact—and *then* frozen.

But Astrid froze.

Imogen and the others came tearing up, Bronte doing that twirly Spellbinding thing, and the bellowing man whispered for us to "kindly follow with haste."

As if whispering at this point was going to fix the fact that he'd just bellowed.

We followed the others at a rush through the woods to the road, where a shiny carriage was waiting, as if we were all Cinderella. The road was dusk dark, and the horses were like inky shadows.

Before we got in, we stood in a huddle, breathing quickly while Bronte explained fast that the puddle had actually been a Shadow Mage that would have torn the skin and flesh from Astrid's hands.

Harsh.

Esther went dead white.

Imogen cried and hugged her little sisters, held them out so she could look at them, said, "You're okay! *Are* you okay? You're okay!" then grabbed them into a hug again before they had a chance to answer. She even reached her arms out to hug me, saying, "Oscar! You're—" And then she stopped. "You're *not* okay! There's blood all over your face!"

I'd forgotten about that.

There was a throat-clearing sound and Octavius introduced himself to us. Everything about him was very tidy, including his voice. He said, "The hotel advises that we board the carriage swiftly, and proceed to the hotel," before he looked at the forest, in a meaningful yet very tidy way. "The Doom Lantern Witches are not far from here. They no doubt heard my yell. They will be approaching."

I must have gone pale myself at that because he fixed me with a look and said seriously, "The blood is dry but you have clearly had a knock to your head. Do you have a headache? Blurred vision?"

"Yeah-nah, I'm all good," I said. "It's not a concussion. I've had a couple of those playing rugby league."

Octavius turned to the others, ignoring me, and said, "Please keep this young man awake during our journey. Engage him in conversation. Step aboard and we'll be on our way." He was scanning the forest as he spoke.

Astrid took a step up into the carriage and paused. "The Doom Lantern Witches have the key fragment," she told the others. "We heard them talk about it."

Gruffudd's head pushed its way out of Bronte's pocket. "If the Witches have the key, please, let us collect it *now*. Imogen?" His head craned up, trying to find Imogen in the dark. "Imogen? If the Witches are rushing through the forest toward us, why do we not double back to their home and find the key? Will you not consider my family, my friends, beneath a growing mountain of silver?"

At that exact moment there was a distant *crack!* like a car backfiring.

Or maybe a stick breaking as people moved through the forest.

There was a sort of horrified silence, and we all looked from Gruffudd to the forest to the open carriage door.

Octavius spoke up. "The hotel will, of course, assist in any venture you may undertake. However, the hotel would like to gently remind its honored guests that the Doom Lantern Coven is ruthless, and that night is falling fast. Night intensifies the Witches' already considerable power." His eyes ran over us before he finished: "The hotel would gently recommend that the guests, who seem rather tired, and somewhat injured, proceed at once to the Royal Gaynor Hotel for dinner and bed."

We looked back at the woods, pitch-black, and at the sky, a moody twilight gray.

Imogen took a deep breath and crouched down so she was face-to-face with Gruffudd. "We already have five pieces of the key," she told him quickly. "We got another from a Water Sprite this afternoon. And we still have tomorrow."

Gruffudd's lower lip trembled.

Another *crack!* from the forest.

"When you are doing an exam," Imogen said, speeding up even more, "you can be going along at a good pace and then you reach a very tricky question. It's often better to continue with the exam and come back to the tricky question at the end."

Exam advice. Unexpected.

Then I realized: "You mean we should keep going with the other key keepers and come back to the Witches at the end?"

Fairly reluctantly, Gruffudd agreed that this was a good idea, Octavius gave a subtle sigh of relief, and we clambered into the carriage and took off like a rocket.

* * *

The first thing that happened in the carriage ride was that we swapped stories of what we'd been getting up to. Imogen, Bronte, and Alejandro were great listeners, all three of them making a lot of shocked and impressed sounds as we talked about the rapids, getting thrown from the boat, finding the house, Astrid figuring out who lived there, the race through the forest, and Esther's Spellbinding. When you tell people you've been having a pretty intense time, you don't want them saying, "Ah well, whatever, you're all good now." You want their eyes wide and their heads shaking, mouths open and "*What?* Oh, you poor darlings!" That kind of thing is better, 'cause it means they get it.

They told us about how they'd seen the Genie, and the Water Sprite, which was a much shorter story.

After that I closed my eyes and rested my head against the carriage wall. Imogen yelped, "Oscar! We cannot let you fall asleep! Wake up!" and then I heard Bronte whisper, "What's he interested in? We have to keep him interested," and Alejandro said, "I know."

They tried to keep me awake by asking questions about my skateboard. Only they kept calling it a "boardskate."

Where had I acquired it? they wanted to know. And exactly how popular was this . . . toy . . . in my world? Offensive to call it a "toy," but I let that go.

Alejandro asked how all the pieces fit together, and I explained about the board, trucks, wheels, grip tape, and all that. "The grip tape is why I've got these holes in my shoes and socks," I said, pointing them out.

"You should stop using the grip tape then," Imogen advised. "Leave the boardskate—sorry, skateboard—blank."

I laughed. She seemed so definite.

Alejandro had been listening closely. "That heavy silver object we found in your satchel?" he asked. "This is a tool to be used on your boardskate?"

"Yeah, it's a skate tool."

"Oh!" Bronte said. "We thought you might have used that to create the wave."

I kept laughing at them. The more I did, the more intensely they asked their questions—I think they were worried that my laughing meant I *did* have a head injury. But they were just funny.

* * *

Esther didn't join in with the "boardskate" conversation.

She sat in the corner of the carriage and was silent. After about an hour of rolling along, she said very softly, "I should have known it was a Kwilligus and not water. I *know* water.

I'm a *Rain Weaver.* And I'm meant to be able to sense shadow magic."

Everyone looked at her.

"I did see darkness in the corner of my eye," she added. "I thought it was just that I was tired."

Then she turned her head so she was facing the carriage wall and I wouldn't have even known she was crying, except that her shoulders moved up and down.

Imogen took a break from quizzing me about my board to put an arm around her sister's shoulder. "It's all right, it all worked out," Imogen murmured. "You're nothing like our mother. It's all right, Esther, it's all right."

CHAPTER 55

IMOGEN

WHEN WE REACHED the hotel, Octavius opened the carriage door for us. It was suddenly freezing.

"What's going on with the weather?" Bronte asked as she climbed out. "It was hot this morning, yet it's been getting colder all afternoon."

"Indeed," Octavius agreed. "We are now on the outskirts of the city of Splendid. It has its own microclimate. Its weather systems sometimes creep out of the city and roll along the river and its banks. In Splendid, there has been snow lately. Here at the Royal Gaynor Hotel, our pond is frozen solid. At any rate, honored guests, welcome!" He gestured at the ornate white building. "The hotel will send your luggage to your suite while you—"

"Oh," Esther said softly. "The luggage from *our* boat is in the river. And so is the boat."

Octavius bowed at her courteously. "Thank you, Esther. The hotel is saddened by your loss. The hotel is also troubled by the nasty wound on Oscar's forehead and the hotel *does* suspect a concussion, despite Oscar's eloquent protestations. *Yeah-nah,* I believe he said. The hotel invites Oscar to come and see the hotel doctor. Meanwhile, the hotel invites the others to proceed to the private dining room. The hotel imagines you must be famished."

"I don't know what that means," Astrid told him, "but I am *very* hungry."

"Indeed," Octavius repeated, and he ushered us into the hotel.

After that, the night became like a dream.

If I become descriptive when I explain it, that is not my fault. It is the fault of the night itself.

The hotel lobby was extraordinary. Its walls were hung with paintings, mosaics, and tapestries, and they soared to a ceiling studded with chandeliers. These dipped and sparkled like icicles, their reflections glittering in the water of several fountains. Pale pink rose petals drifted, constantly falling from vents in the walls and being puffed about by heated air. The effect was subtler than the petals in the Crystal Faery palace had been—there were fewer of these petals and they were of a paler pink. They gave off an exquisite scent, and you felt as if you were seeing everybody through a lens of coral. People are prettier that way.

Behind a counter of marble and jade, a woman murmured, "Welcome to the Royal Gaynor Hotel," as we passed. Elegant adults in cocktail dresses and tuxedos drifted about amongst the petals or lounged before the roaring fireplace.

In the far corner of the lobby was a private dining room. Wood-paneled, with a long table set with polished silver, crystal glasses, and shiny candelabras. At the end of the room, a window overlooked a frozen pond. Outside, lit by golden lanterns, people in coats and scarves were skating in swooping circles.

"Please sit," Octavius told us. "Oscar, if you would be so kind as to follow me?"

He withdrew from the room, Oscar following, and we sat around the elegant dining table giggling now and then. I think it was a nervous giggling. Our clothes seemed too worn and crushed, our shoes too scuffed, for this hotel.

Soon, Oscar was back, his blood-splattered face cleaned and bandaged.

"Just a mild concussion," he told us. "No big deal."

He was accompanied by a waiter, who pulled out a chair for him and, with a flourish, set a cloth napkin on his lap. Oscar seemed startled by this.

The waiter regarded us all. "How hungry are you?" he inquired.

"Very," I said. "All we had for dinner last night was oatcakes, and all we've eaten today is a tomato sandwich for lunch." I realized something. "Bronte didn't even get a tomato sandwich because she was waiting for Esther at that time. What did the Crystal Faeries give you to eat, Esther?"

Esther blinked. "Oh. Nothing," she replied. "I suppose they forgot. I was so busy curing people last night, and then I fell asleep, and then I woke up and cured more and then I left."

There was a shocked silence around the table. "So you have not eaten anything since . . . lunchtime *yesterday*?" Alejandro checked.

"I suppose not," Esther agreed.

"Right then," said the waiter, and he turned and left the room.

"Esther," Bronte said slowly. "To be able to sense magic and Spellbind, you need to be eating well, sleeping well, and feeling as calm as possible. No *wonder* you didn't sense the shadow magic in the Kwilligus. The fact that you were able to Spellbind at all—when you've only just started training, and in those cir-cumstances—is astonishing."

Esther gave a very small smile.

A few moments later, a swarm of waiters arrived carrying trays laden with food. There was pork with crackling and apple-sauce, mint-and-rosemary lamb with gravy, crunchy potatoes, roasted carrots, and crusty bread. There were piles of steaming macaroni and cheese, stacks of mini-hamburgers and mini-pizzas, savory pastries and chicken drumsticks, salads of tomato and basil and candied walnuts, burnt butter pastas and smoked cauliflower, rich chocolate cake and delicate berry tarts, fizzy lemon drinks and watermelon juice.

As we ate, and watched the skaters on the pond, a great calm seemed to slide over us. Sleepily, we smiled at each other. We only spoke to say, "Would you pass the butter, please?" or "This lemonade is delicious" or "Gruffudd, you have your own plate of food, do you have to keep running around taking food from us? Oh, never mind. There's plenty."

Octavius returned just as we were setting cutlery down on empty plates.

"You may like to know that the hotel has retrieved and repaired the lost boat from the river," he announced, "and has delivered it to Jasper Kestrel. The hotel has also retrieved several items of luggage from the river and its banks, and has taken the liberty of drying these out and sending them to your suite. The hotel wonders if you would care for a moonlight skate before bed?" He gestured at the picture window.

After that, memories become even more mingled in my mind—coats and scarves and lace-up skates; the soft lantern light; the glow of the moon; Bronte and my sisters, all experienced skaters, graceful as dancers on the ice; Alejandro and Oscar, both beginners, wobbling and frowning, hands outstretched.

Cinnamon doughnuts; mugs of hot chocolate; holding hands with the other girls, speeding in circles; chocolate-dipped strawberries; skating backward; Oscar and Alejandro becoming reckless and racing, crashing and skidding, laughing, pulling each other back up—the crack of the blades.

A deep bubble bath; bare feet buried in soft, plush carpet; a tiny dollhouse bed on a window ledge and Gruffudd exclaiming, "I want that bed! I'll take that bed!" confused by our laughter; Bronte solemnly promising him that nobody else would take that bed; a window overlooking the city of Splendid—the banks of the skating pond merging now with the fat white pillows and feather-down quilts; sprinkling of stars in the cold night sky; sprinkling of city lights through windows; a confusion of lights, of waking and dreaming; our night murmurs slipping and blending into sleep—into the deepest, the most exquisite sleep, that I have ever slept.

THURSDAY

CHAPTER 56

OSCAR

THURSDAY WAS A funny one.

I mean funny-strange, not funny-ha-ha.

It sped out from under us like a pair of ice skates, everything going exactly right and also exactly wrong.

Most of the day seemed to happen in the morning, so I'll start with breakfast.

We had that in our suite, wearing plush white robes. There were matching slippers too, but we kept our feet bare to feel the carpet. That carpet! You wanted to squelch around in it. Soft and warm like a bathtub, it was. Only dry.

We ate while lying on the beds in our robes, stepping out now and then to feel the carpet. It was so brightly colored, the breakfast! The eggs, the fruit, the bacon. Everything! Everyone kept going on about how well they'd slept, and how soft the carpet was, and how brightly colored the breakfast was.

Imogen said the brightness meant it had nutritional value, and told us to "eat up"—we already were, it was delicious—then she asked how my head was (she'd asked that a few times the night before—they all had—it was cute)—then she remembered that she wanted to talk to Octavius about the best way to get back to the Witches.

She left her breakfast half-eaten and rushed off to find him.

While she was gone, I said something like, "She's pretty determined, isn't she?"

I was impressed she'd left her breakfast half-eaten.

The others all said things like "*So* determined! If she sees a problem, she solves it; that's Imogen. She's always been like that. She's great at swimming and kickboxing too."

That last part was unexpected. I'd seen no evidence of Imogen's kickboxing so far, which was probably for the best.

"Tell us about *your* world, Oscar," Esther said suddenly. She blushed a bit, as if she were suddenly embarrassed to have asked, so I said, "Sure," and started talking.

I couldn't help it: I told them that, in our world, there are cars, planes, computers, dishwashers, the internet, and mobiles, and that life is much easier as a result.

"Mobiles? Yes, we have them too. They hang above baby cradles. They *are* lovely," Esther said.

I explained what a mobile phone was, and they were all amazed—but then Alejandro said that, back when he was a pirate, he had visited some Kingdoms in the Northern Climes.

"Some have this technology that you describe," he said.

Astrid said, "Oh yes, Matron at our school went on a tour of the Northern Climes. She told us extraordinary stories about the province of Jagged Edge in the Kingdom of Cello, and its newfangled machinery."

I stared at them. They were crunching away at their food, sipping at their drinks, and did not seem to realize how bizarre this was.

"But," I said. "But, wait. You *have* those things in your world? So why would you not . . . why do you not . . ." Honestly, I couldn't believe it.

"We don't really want them," Bronte told me apologetically, and the others all nodded and started murmuring about how noisy such things were, or how complicated, and how letters and telegrams were so much "nicer."

"Motorcars *are* getting more popular in a lot of places," Astrid told me. "And we have steam-powered ships and trains, of course, and plenty of industrial regions. More and more people have telephones in their homes too. Our family has one in the kitchen. Our school principal has one in her office too."

"Except we're keeping it to a minimum," Esther explained.

This was all extremely confusing, and also annoying. Here's why: I'd been thinking that, even though these kids were better than me at basically everything, at least my *world* was superior. We'd invented all this stuff!

And now it turned out, they'd invented it too. They just didn't want it.

Alejandro seemed to realize I was getting depressed because he changed the subject and asked about animals in my Kingdom. (None of them ever got the hang of the word *country*.) I told them about koalas, kangaroos, red-bellied black snakes, and funnel-web spiders. Apart from Gruffudd, who was really bothered by the idea of funnel-web spiders, they all seemed happy to hear about the animals, and assured me they knew of "no such creatures."

Next, though, their questions turned to politics, agriculture, and "primary exports." I made all my answers up. Who listens in geography? I did keep sort of glancing around the suite, worrying that somebody else from my world might suddenly appear and catch me out.

Once they got onto the economy, though, the only thing I could think of to say was that our cash is brightly colored, whereas American notes are all one color. They stared at me, waiting for more, so I told them that my mother had once given me a few Fijian coins after she went on a holiday there with her boyfriend.

They seemed flummoxed.

"Wait a moment," Bronte said. "Are you suggesting that different Kingdoms in your world have different forms of money? However does *that* work?"

Luckily, before I could answer—I mean, before I could *not* answer—Esther said, "That reminds me, Oscar. Your change purse has been shadowed, hasn't it? Would you like me to cleanse it?"

My change purse?

Turned out, she meant my wallet. They all thought a Shadow Mage had cast a spell on it because it had made a "strange ripping noise" when they opened it.

That made me laugh.

I told them about Velcro. "Remember, we don't have any Shadow Mages in my world? No magic?"

They were pretty staggered by this information each time it came up. By now, we'd mostly finished breakfast, and were starting to pack up and get dressed.

"Not a *single* Shadow Mage?" Astrid asked, emerging from the bathroom, her toothbrush in her mouth. She took it out so we could hear her more clearly. "In that case, you must *never be afraid!*"

That was a bit extreme. "There *are* still scary things," I said.

"Like what?" Alejandro asked. "What frightens you?"

"Climate change, I guess."

"And what is this? This climate change?"

"Well, water levels are rising because—"

"You have an Ocean Fiend." They all nodded, wise expressions on their faces.

"No, it's global warming. From carbon emissions. We use a lot of power, see, because of—well, because of—"

Luckily, Imogen came back in at that point. I could see where the conversation was heading. My headache was starting to come back.

Imogen seemed happy. She said that Octavius had been "deeply sorry that the hotel would not be able to accompany us on our missions today, as the hotel would be looking after other guests." He had also "strongly advised that we stay very far away from the Doom Lantern Witches."

But once Imogen had "explained, cajoled, and begged," he'd sat down with her and worked on a schedule. If we could find the next three keys in the morning—so let's hope the next three key keepers weren't too far away, she said—we could take a 2:00 P.M. coach from central Splendid that would pass by the forest of the Doom Lantern Witches. Octavius had given her a bunch of firecrackers that we could use to scare them out of their house, then we could run in, collect their key fragment, and take a return coach to Splendid in time for a midnight train that would take us to a town called Yellowspot, which was three hours from Dun-sorey-lo-vay-lo-hey. From there, we could get another coach and arrive just in time to save the city.

Although it would be tight, Imogen believed we could do it.

"So come on!" she said, eyes sparkly. "Oscar? Do you want to take a memory?"

I'd forgotten about the memories.

(Ha-ha.)

This one was pretty short, like the last.

I was probably about ten years old and in a class at school. I was tearing strips off the bottom of my worksheet. If you put your palm down flat, and do a good, quick *rip*, it comes off straight.

"*Right*," said Ms. Dalmetti, spotting me. "I have *told you and told you*." She went marching up to the board to put my name in the sad-face column of the Behavior Chart.

Only, the Behavior Chart wasn't there. Instead, there was a sign hanging from a hook. Here's what it said:

SPLENDID CITY COURTHOUSE

COURTROOM 5B

THE HONORABLE JUSTICE DAABOUL

I blinked, the memory disappearing, and looked around at the others.

"I think this clue might be an easy one?" I said.

CHAPTER 57

IMOGEN

I KNOW WHAT Oscar means about Thursday speeding along going exactly right and exactly wrong.

Strangely, the right bits were mostly to do with collecting keys. The wrong bits had to do with us being—well, us.

After breakfast, we were all in warm and effusive moods. We seemed to spring along—like Oscar's kangaroos; the others told me about them when I got back to the room—laughing and chatting through the hotel lobby, blowing at the petals as they fell, sending them skittering through the air. Gruffudd was also cheerful, leaping from one shoulder to the next, popping out of somebody's pocket here and strapping himself to someone's bootlaces there.

The hotel carriage brought us into the city of Splendid. There, we climbed out, with all our packs, in front of the courthouse. It was a bright, blue-skied day, although rather cold. The city was a busy one, streets filled with automobiles and carriages, gentlemen in hats, ladies with swishy skirts.

Oscar seemed astonished by it all. "Now I *really* feel like I'm time traveling," he said, adding that it wasn't just the horses and cobblestones, the hats and the people smoking pipes. "It's the *toot! toot!*s of car horns," he said.

I think he would have stood staring and listening all day, but we hustled him in through the courthouse doors and into Courtroom 5B.

The courtroom was empty except for the judge, seated up at his bench. He wore a curly white wig, a black robe, and small round spectacles, and he was eating a muffin and writing something. A jug of water and an empty glass stood to the side, along with a gavel.

He did not seem at all pleased to see us gathering at his bench.

"What?" he demanded, frowning over his spectacles.

"That's not a very polite greeting," Astrid whispered.

"Nor particularly *legalistic* either," Esther added.

I trod on Astrid's foot and pinched Esther's arm while Bronte smiled up at the judge. "Your Honor," she said. "We apologize for disturbing your morning tea. We—"

"Well, you've got that wrong, haven't you?" the judge grumbled. "It's not my morning tea, it's my breakfast."

(*Very childish*, I thought, *for a judge*.)

"We apologize for disturbing your breakfast," Bronte said smoothly. "We are here on behalf of Gruffudd the Elf from the Elven City of Dun-sorey-lo-vay-lo-hey. The city has been buried beneath silver waves and—"

Gruffudd clambered on top of my head at this point and shouted, "It's true! Bronte speaks the truth," while getting thoroughly tangled in my hair. It hurt. Alejandro reached over and—very carefully—untangled the Elf.

"A pirate trial is about to start!" the judge snapped. "I can't have Elves getting tangled in people's hair! The dignity of the court is quite undermined by hair tangling!"

Alejandro looked at the judge curiously. He has an interest in pirates, for obvious reasons.

"A pirate trial?" he repeated.

"There's a small pirate village just outside Splendid," the judge explained irritably. "Pirates live there during breaks in pirating and take up regular land occupations. A strong honor code exists between pirates, so crime is low there; however, on occasion, a serious matter arises and they call on the Splendid law enforcement system. That's what's happening today. Which is why I cannot be convening with children and Elves! Besides,

I've not even finished my crossword! And you *know* I like to finish my crossword before the day's proceedings begin!"

"As a matter of fact, we did *not* know that," I told him, very firmly.

The judge looked startled. Then he gave a little nod. "Not from around here, I suppose," he said. "Everyone who lives in Splendid does know it, but I'll allow that you may not." He adjusted his spectacles and studied us. "Tell you what. Children sometimes have lively minds. If you can help me finish my crossword, I'll let you stay until morning tea. We can talk then, over chocolate éclairs. Not if you *can't* help, though. I cannot abide children who *don't* have lively minds. And don't go getting my meals mixed up again. I've just had *breakfast*, I say, and morning tea comes *next*."

We found him so peculiar that we simply stared.

"Well!" he barked. "Are you up for the challenge or not?"

CHAPTER 58

OSCAR

WE TOLD HIM we were up for it—but a crossword puzzle?

I'd be in trouble if there were geographical questions.

Or any other question that had anything whatsoever to do with this world.

The judge cleared his throat and read aloud: "*Liquid color concealed by stop ain't enough.*"

A long silence.

"Excuse me?" I said.

"*Liquid color concealed by stop ain't enough,*" he read again, sounding testy. "That's the clue. Five letters."

"It makes no *sense,*" Esther breathed.

"It's *absurd,*" Imogen stated.

But Alejandro was smiling. "It's a cryptic crossword," he said. "The Butler and I used to do them together at breakfast every day when I lived with Bronte."

"Breakfast," the judge grunted. "Yes. Precisely." He picked up his muffin and floated it around in our faces.

"It's an easy one," Alejandro added. "The answer is *paint.*"

The judge put his muffin down, looked back at the crossword, murmured, "Of course!" and began to write. The rest of us stared at Alejandro.

"*Liquid color concealed by stop ain't enough,*" Alejandro repeated the clue for us. "If a clue has a word like *concealed* in it, it's trying to tell you that the answer is hidden in the clue itself. If you put together the *p* from *stop* and the *aint* from *ain't*, you've got *paint*."

"Oh! Liquid color!" Bronte laughed. "Paint!"

Imogen cleared her throat. "Well," she said. "Now that we've helped, perhaps—" She was looking at the courtroom clock.

The judge rustled his paper. "Three down," he said. "*Rip sad consequences*. Four letters."

Rip sad consequences?

"You mean like *R.I.P. sad consequences*?" I suggested. "*Rest in peace, sad consequences?*"

The others ignored me, so I leaned up against the bar table. Based on TV shows, I think that's what it's called anyway. The judge was sitting at the *bench*, the little box off to the left was a *witness stand*, and the section where the jury sits is . . . the *jury box*? Not sure what you call the rows of seats where regular people watch.

"It's *tear*," Alejandro said. "T-e-a-r. *Tear* is another word for *rip*. You cry *tears* when you're sad. So a tear is a rip and it's also a consequence of being sad."

"Ho ho!" shouted the judge, which gave us a fright. He was writing furiously. "Okay, *one* more and we're done! Get this one and you can stay until morning tea."

"Or you could just give us the key right now?" Imogen suggested. The judge wasn't listening. He was peering at the crossword. He took a giant bite of his muffin, so crumbs spilled everywhere as he read the next clue.

"*Ve-ra roar mom o mud bump.*"

Even Alejandro looked worried about that one, but the judge chewed quickly, swallowed, and read it again: "*Vehicle found an ocean in love bond.*"

"Hmm," Alejandro said, while the rest of us carried on being confused.

Alejandro squinted, and repeated the clue slowly then quickly, slowly then quickly.

Vehicle found an ocean in love bond.

"Honestly," Imogen muttered. "How *anyone* is supposed to . . ." She tapped her foot crankily.

A door behind the judge's bench opened, and a woman with cat's-eye glasses leaned in. "Ready, Your Honor?"

"Of course!" the judge boomed, so loud that the water splashed in the water jug. The woman sort of bounced away, like a ball that had been thwacked by the judge's voice. The door closed behind her.

To us, the judge grumbled: "I have to leave. Haven't got my crossword done, though, have I? Which means you children will also have to leave. I said you could stay if you solved the clues. Did you solve them? No. Therefore, you cannot stay. Might seem cruel, but rules are rules, and rules are *particularly* rules in a courtroom."

He pushed himself to his feet, gathering papers and scraping away muffin crumbs.

We all looked urgently at Alejandro, whose eyes were closed.

"Just a moment," Esther pleaded with the judge. "Give him a bit longer!"

The judge was straightening his chair, dusting down his robe, turning around, reaching for the door handle behind him, when—

"*Carriage.*" That was Alejandro, his eyes suddenly opening.

The judge turned back. "Eh?"

"*Vehicle found an ocean in love bond,*" Alejandro recited the clue again. "A love bond is a marriage. An ocean can be a sea. So an ocean in a love bond is a sea—or the letter *c*—in a marriage. If you put a *c* in *marriage*, it becomes *carriage*. Which is a vehicle."

The judge flipped open his notebook, ran his hand along the page and cried, "You're right!" He grabbed a pen and filled it in.

"Sit in the gallery," he called over his shoulder, pushing open the door. "Front row. We'll chat again at morning tea."

Gallery. So that's the word, I guess, for where regular people sit.

CHAPTER 59

IMOGEN

THE PIRATE TRIAL took two hours. Here is what happened. First, two important-looking people in suits, one a man, the other a woman, hurried in. They were Splendid city lawyers, and not pirates. They sat at opposite sides of the bar table and began whispering to each other. Next, a small crowd of regular people, dressed more colorfully, settled themselves into the spectator seats around us. They were quiet, but their eyes seemed excited.

A huddle of reporters with notepads and a bearded photographer in an overcoat gathered at the back of the courtroom. *Click-*flash! *Click*-flash! went the photographer's camera—until one of the suited lawyers said, "Do you *mind*?" Her voice sounded loud and strange in the quiet courtroom. The *click*-flashing stopped.

A moment later, the woman with cat's-eye glasses was at the front. "All rise for the Honorable Justice Carim Daaboul," she commanded.

In came the judge. He sat at his bench looking dignified. However, when he glanced down, he suddenly frowned—his head swung back and forth, as if he was searching for something. *Perhaps he is missing his muffin and crossword,* I thought. All that was left there was the jug of water and glass.

The jury filed in next, a bit giggly—with nerves, I suppose—and sat in the jury box, straightening their clothes and their faces.

Finally, the accused, a man whose name turned out to be Killer Jack, was brought in by a police officer.

"With a name like that, no wonder he ended up as a pirate," Bronte whispered, straight-faced, and we all giggled.

He certainly looked like a pirate. He had spiky hair, a tattoo of a spiderweb on his left cheek, and a silver tooth, which glinted when he smiled. He only smiled once though, at the jury, in a hopeful way. The jury sent him stern frowns in response and his face fell.

The trial began.

Almost all the witnesses were pirates, but they had dressed in ordinary clothes and washed their faces for the trial. You could hear their pirate accents, though, and see glimpses of their pirateness—tattoos and hoop earrings, for instance; muscular forearms; and long, scruffy hair. Each witness was questioned by the two lawyers—first, in an ordinary, polite way by the man in the suit, and then in a more angry, dramatic way by the woman. The man, it turned out, was the prosecutor, and he wanted to prove that Killer Jack was guilty. The woman was Killer Jack's own lawyer, and she hoped to prove him innocent—a real uphill battle.

Killer Jack was accused of having murdered another pirate in the village, a man known as Plundering Pete.

"Pirates are always running around bumping each other off," I whispered to Oscar. His eyebrows leapt up at that. (By the way, if you find it odd that there was a lot of giggling in a pirate murder trial, that's only because you've never sat in on a pirate murder trial before. It jangles the nerves, and jangled nerves often lead to explosions of laughter. Happens at school all the time.)

The first witness, Bilge-Guzzling Becky, explained that she was a doctor both at sea and onshore.

Bilge-Guzzling Becky said that she had inspected the victim,

Plundering Pete, and concluded that he had been killed by a blow to the head with a cricket bat.

Killer Jack's lawyer jumped up and demanded: "How can you possibly *know* it was a *cricket bat?*"

The doctor said that her own pirate husband enjoyed playing cricket, and often left his cricket bats lying around, so that she was always tripping over them, or kicking her toes on them. This meant that she, the doctor, had become "desperately familiar" with the shape and size of a cricket bat.

"There is no doubt in my mind," the doctor finished firmly, "that the victim was murdered by a cricket bat."

Killer Jack's lawyer sat down again, dispirited.

Next, we heard from Plundering Pete's wife, a pirate named Sea Dog Tammy, who mostly sobbed and said how much she missed her husband. Her scruffy hair fell over her eyes and she kept shaking it away so we could see her tear-filled eyes. She had loved everything about Plundering Pete, she wept, even the rather haphazard way he careened their ship; even his ingrown toenails.

I didn't see how Sea Dog Tammy's sadness was relevant to whether Killer Jack was the murderer, but it made the jury look very sorry for the wife, and very annoyed with Killer Jack. He didn't even bother trying to smile glintingly at them. He just settled back into his seat and sighed. His lawyer also didn't bother jumping up and asking an angry question—she simply said, "Relevance?" from her table (as if she'd read my mind).

"Quite," said the judge. "Move along."

So Sea Dog Tammy came down from the witness stand and sat in the spectator seats, alongside Bilge-Guzzling Becky.

After that was a man who went by the name of Blunderbuss Bill when he was pirating, and who became Baker Bill whenever he resided in the pirate village. His bakery was next door to Pete and Tammy's cottage, apparently, and on the day of the murder, he'd seen Killer Jack rush into that cottage carrying a cricket bat and shouting, "I will kill you, Plundering Pete!"

Killer Jack's lawyer jumped up and asked, furiously: "Isn't

it possible that he was *actually* shouting, 'Would you like a game of cricket, Plundering Pete'?"

The baker considered this carefully and then he said that no, he did not think so at all. For one thing, "I will kill you!" sounds very different to "Would you like a game of cricket?" (he explained). For another thing, there would be no reason to rush into someone's house when you only wanted a game of cricket. You could just walk at an ordinary pace.

"Killer Jack is the best cricket player in the pirate village," the baker continued. "In fact, he made a fortune in the Pirates' Cricket League before it was disbanded. He played for the Handley Spiders—that is why he has that spider tattoo. He is a killer bowler and a killer batsman—that is how he got his nickname."

("Oh," Bronte whispered to me. "Killer Jack isn't even a pirating name. I'd advise him to use his regular name in any future murder trials."

I tried to smother my snickering.)

"He would never have trouble getting a game of cricket," the baker concluded, "what with his being so good at it. There is no *reason* for him to be running around shouting for people to play with him."

Killer Jack's lawyer sighed and sat down. The baker went and joined the sobbing wife and the doctor.

The last witness was a Splendid city police detective who had been called into the pirate village to investigate the murder. He said he had found Killer Jack's cricket bat in Pete and Tammy's garden.

Killer Jack's lawyer jumped up and demanded to know whether any of Killer Jack's fingerprints were on the cricket bat.

"Well no," the detective said, "but the bat was lying in a puddle in the garden so any fingerprints had been washed away."

"Then how could you possibly know it was *Killer Jack's* bat?" the lawyer crowed, very triumphantly.

"It had a label taped to it," the detective explained. "PROPERTY OF KILLER JACK."

The lawyer deflated. "So the murderer forgot to take his own *name* off the murder weapon?"

"Seems that way," the detective agreed.

The lawyer sent Killer Jack a dark look and sat down again. She put me in mind of a farmer in a drought who feels a drop of rain on her head and shouts, "HOORAY!" before realizing that it wasn't rain at all, but a passing bird that had decided, at that moment, to relieve itself.

It was certainly looking like an open and shut case.

For most of the trial, I was tapping my foot and thinking, *Oh for crying out loud, just send him to prison, Judge, and give us the key!* We had a lot to get on with.

Beside me, Bronte's eyebrows kept jumping up and down at the twists and turns in the trial. On my other side, Astrid seemed as absorbed as if she was at the cinema.

Along our row, Esther took turns gazing at the ceiling and at her fingernails. Alejandro hummed quietly—I think he was proud of himself about solving the judge's crossword clues, and deservedly so, and maybe he was also proud that he was no longer a pirate. We all kept whispering to him, "Do you know her?" and "How about that one?" until Alejandro whispered back, "I have not met any of these pirates—the sea is a large place, you know," so we stopped. Oscar, meanwhile, kept pulling out his own shoelaces and rethreading them. His shoes were battered and ripped—from the grip tape, I suppose, which he really ought to remove from his skateboard.

As for Gruffudd, he zipped about between us all, climbing onto our legs, shimmying up our shirtsleeves, muttering, over and over, that he was hungry.

I told him that we would get him food later, and that I couldn't see how he could still be hungry after the huge breakfast he'd eaten at the hotel.

I think it was at that point that a muffled chanting and thumping started up. It seemed to be coming from outside the courtroom, and it sounded like children.

The prosecutor had been in the middle of a grand speech about how there was no doubt in *anybody's* mind that Killer Jack was guilty, but he stopped midsentence and asked, "What *is* that noise?"

Everyone in the courtroom fell silent and turned around. However, the door was closed, and there was nothing to see up the back except for the reporters and the bearded photographer.

The chanting became clearer in the sudden silence. It went like this:

"You find it in the summer,

You find it in the spring,

You find it when you're humming,

You find it when you sing.

You find it by the moonlight,

You find it eating cake,

And if you don't find it

I'll toss you in the lake!"

Behind the chanting you could hear a rhythmic *thump, thump* and a quieter *whir, whir.*

"Are there children *skipping* in the corridor outside my court-room?" the judge demanded. His eyebrows seemed to grow bristly with disbelief.

"Seems like it," Oscar murmured, smile lines crinkling his eyes.

The woman with cat's-eye glasses hurried between the spectator seats to the back of the courtroom, opened the door, and cried: "*Children!* Court is in session!"

The chanting stopped abruptly.

The woman returned, closed the door tight, and said, "I do apologize, Your Honor."

After that, the lawyers summarized everything we'd heard. Killer Jack's lawyer tried her best to defend her client, but even she didn't sound especially convinced by her own arguments.

Killer Jack looked resigned and philosophical.

Once the lawyers were done, the judge sat up abruptly. I think he'd been having a short snooze. He told the jury they should now "retire" to consider the evidence and to make a decision about whether Killer Jack was guilty. One of the jurors said, "We shan't be long then," and there were snorts. The judge pretended not to hear that. The jurors rose, ready to leave.

That was the moment when Astrid spoke up in a clear, ringing voice: "Hold on," she said. "Don't you want to know who was lying?"

CHAPTER 60

OSCAR

ASTRID SEEMED SURPRISED nobody had asked her yet.

The whole courtroom, including the judge, the jury, the lawyers, and the witnesses, frowned at her.

Astrid stared around the room. "THE *DETECTIVE* WAS TELLING THE TRUTH," she bellowed, "AND *EVERYONE ELSE WAS LYING!*"

The frowns around the room got deeper, while Imogen and the rest of us did double takes. The witnesses were *all* lying? All except the police detective? Seriously?

The judge pounded both fists on his table. He didn't seem to have a hammer like they do on TV.

"That'll do, child," he said. "This is a court of law. Kindly refrain from shouting. A trial is a serious matter. Members of the jury, you will, of course, ignore what the child has said. The pirate honor system is a strong one, and pirates always speak the truth about each other. The witnesses today all struck me as very truthful people. Indeed—"

"But Killer Jack isn't guilty!" Astrid cried. She was really upset now. "There! Look at his face! Can't you *see* it?"

Killer Jack made an effort to look nonguilty by smiling a big silver-toothed smile. That didn't help.

The judge became cranky. "*Child*," he said.

"I'm not a *child*—I mean, I *am* a child, but I don't understand why nobody else can see it!" Astrid kicked her heel against the carpet. "Aren't you the *adults*? The *only* time Killer Jack looked guilty was when the doctor said that her husband left cricket bats lying around. I don't know why *that* made *him* feel guilty—"

"Well, I do not mean to leave the bats lying about," Killer Jack said. It was the first time he'd spoken in the trial. His pirate accent was melodious and friendly. "It is only that I get distracted. However, I feel *terrible* when Becky trips over my bats."

There was a moment of slow-motion confusion. Then the judge swiveled in his seat and stared at Killer Jack. "Are you saying," he demanded, "that *you* are Doctor Becky's husband?"

Killer Jack nodded.

"The doctor who just gave evidence in your own murder trial is your *wife*?" the judge checked.

Again, Killer Jack nodded. "This is another way of putting it," he agreed.

Killer Jack's lawyer leapt to her feet. "I move for a mistrial! A key witness has a close relationship with the accused!" To Killer Jack, she murmured: "You *might* have mentioned this before, Jack."

Jack looked surprised. "Becky and I keep our work and home lives strictly separate! Both at sea and in the village! Anyway, I am sure that she was honest when she gave her evidence."

Astrid shook her head—"Nope, she wasn't"—but nobody else heard this, as the prosecutor was shouting that there was *no* need for a mistrial because, if anything, Doctor Becky would have been biased in *favor* of her husband, so Killer Jack actually had an *advantage* in the—

The judge pounded his fists again. Everyone turned to him, and he sniffed. "Although I am sure that Doctor Becky *did* give her honest professional opinion," he said, "we require a doctor who is *not* related to the accused. Justice must not only be done, it must be *seen* to be done. All right, where is the victim at the moment? Could we bring a city doctor into the pirate village to examine him?"

Bilge-Guzzling Becky didn't answer.

"Doctor Becky?" the judge repeated.

Everyone was leaning forward or back, trying to see the doctor. Doctor Becky was still sitting in the audience, along with the other witnesses. There was some whispering going on between these witnesses. A loud *shhhh*, more fast whispering, and someone said, "Don't you *dare!*"

The doctor popped up in her place.

"Oh, there is no point," she said. "The game? It is up. You were asking where the victim is, Your Honor?"

The judge raised his eyebrows. "I was."

"He is down the back there." The doctor swung a thumb toward the back of the courtroom. There were horrified gasps throughout the room, and sudden squeals from the reporters up the back. Some of these reporters climbed onto chairs—as if there was a mouse there rather than a corpse.

The only one not scurrying around was the bearded photographer in the overcoat. He grinned. "Indeed, I am!" he said, and peeled off his beard. "Plundering Pete, alive and kicking! At your service!"

In the hullaballoo that followed this, I heard him say, in an aside, to one of the reporters: "I was supposed to be hiding out in the basement, was I not? Yes! I was! Yet how could I resist taking pictures of my own murder trial?"

CHAPTER 61

IMOGEN

IT TURNED OUT that the whole scheme had been concocted by Doctor Bilge-Guzzling Becky, Plundering Pete, Sea Dog Tammy, and Blunderbuss Bill. Here is why.

Becky and Pete, although both married to other people, had fallen in love with each other. This had happened when Pete went to see the doctor about his ingrown toenails.

Pete had confessed to his wife, Sea Dog Tammy, that he was in love with Bilge-Guzzling Becky, and Tammy had not been bothered. She herself had long ago begun to find him exasperating—always going on about those tiresome toenails—and had fallen in love with Bill the baker next door.

(Bill was single, so that was all right.)

Doctor Becky, however, had been very reluctant to tell her own husband, Killer Jack, that she wished to run away with Plundering Pete.

"I knew he would be heartbroken," she explained now. "It seemed so much kinder to frame him for murder."

The courtroom, particularly Killer Jack, stared at her. Plundering Pete gave her a loving pat.

"All we had to do was get one of Jack's cricket bats and plant it in Pete and Tammy's garden," the doctor continued. "Easy! He leaves them *everywhere*!"

"Then *I* ran screaming and sobbing to the Splendid city

police station," Sea Dog Tammy interjected excitedly, "and told them I had found my husband unconscious on the floor, and that I had called his doctor—Doctor Becky—who had pronounced him dead! Ever since, I have been sobbing to everyone about how I miss my husband. I ought to get an acting award! I have enjoyed myself, though. I feel I have done an excellent job."

The baker took her hand. "You *have*, my angel," he said.

"All I had to do was hide out in the basement," Plundering Pete put in. "Which, for the most part, I did."

"For the most part," Tammy echoed dryly. "Yet here you are. Do you not see why I grew exasperated by my husband?"

"Oh, stop," Doctor Becky cooed. "He is *adorable*."

Baker Bill spoke up modestly. "I pretended I had seen Jack running into the cottage next door," he said. "It was sensible to frame Killer Jack—he made a fortune in cricket, no? With him in prison, his wife would get all his money, yes? The four of us were planning to buy a new ship together and set out for some magnificent pirating."

"Killer Jack has never been properly interested in pirating," Tammy pointed out, giving the baker an encouraging hug. "For him? It was always about the Pirates' Cricket League. All us pirates knew this. Now that the league is disbanded, what else has he got to do except go to prison?"

The judge sort of fell back in his chair.

"I mean to say . . ." he began, leaning forward, but then he fell back again.

Eventually, he straightened his wig and addressed the detective: "For a start, you'd better arrest this lot, hadn't you?" He waved his hands in the general direction of Doctor Becky, Tammy and Pete, and Baker Bill.

All four seemed startled by this turn of events and protested noisily as they were led out of the courtroom about how kind and sensible they'd been, in keeping with the pirates' code of honor. The detective himself only muttered about how much of his time they'd wasted.

"Thank you for *your* time," the judge said next to the jury. "You have served your community well, and may go home."

The jurors gathered their bags and, chattering in low voices, filed out of the courtroom. I heard one of them, an elderly man, complain that he hadn't had a chance to say whether Killer Jack was guilty or not.

"Not fair!" he cried. "He was *definitely* guilty! Don't you think?"

The other jurors told him that no, they didn't think so at all. They promised to explain it all properly once they got outside.

At last, the judge turned to Killer Jack himself. All this time, Jack had been looking pale and thoughtful.

"What do you say to all this, Jack?" the judge asked him now.

Killer Jack glanced at the judge. "Well," he said heavily. "It's just not cricket, is it?"

At this, the audience laughed and gave him a round of applause.

"It certainly isn't," the judge agreed; then he told the audience and the reporters that the show was over and they ought to get out of his courtroom.

The audience didn't seem at all keen to go. They stayed in their places.

"Get!" said the judge, waving his hands at them. "Begone! Skedaddle! Melt away!"

They halfheartedly reached for their things, pretending they were on their way but staying in their seats, wanting to see what happened next.

"Melt away! Melt away! *Away!*" the judge roared.

The two lawyers repeated the shout: "Melt away! Melt away! *Away!*"

At last, the audience got the message and filed out of the courtroom.

We stayed where we were, in the front row.

"As for you two," the judge added, speaking to the lawyers at the bar table. "Come back to my chambers for morning tea, would you? These children are coming—I promised earlier they could join me—and we *all* need refreshments after a morning like that. Especially poor old Killer Jack! Chocolate éclair, Jack?

Got some from Bill's bakery in the pirate village this morning. Might be the last batch for a while, I suppose . . ."

The lawyers had already packed their papers up, and they appeared relaxed and friendly. Killer Jack's lawyer gave Jack a congratulatory handshake and thanked her for being "ace at her job."

"Oh, that's kind," the lawyer told him. "I was useless though. It's that little girl over there. She's the one to thank. Who *are* those children, anyway? Friends of yours, Your Honor?"

Both lawyers studied us curiously.

"Something about a key and an Elven city," the judge explained. "I've no idea what, but happy to listen, since they . . ." He was peering around the floor. "Lost my gavel, didn't I? Did I knock it off the bench earlier? . . . Since they helped me with my puzzle. And I'd like to talk to that child who knew which witnesses were lying. Ask her how she did it. There it is! No. That's not it." His voice grew muffled as he crawled under his bench.

"A key and an Elven city?" Killer Jack repeated, tilting his head. "Do not tell me you children are here about Dun-sorey-lo-vay-lo-hey."

"Indeed and indeed and indeed they are!" Gruffudd exclaimed, hoisting himself onto my shoulder. "I am the great Elf Gruffudd, and these children are here to serve me, on my quest to set my city free and become its king!"

Killer Jack grinned. "In that case, I am *more* than happy to give you my piece of the key," he declared. "This little girl just saved me from being locked away for life!"

He reached into his mouth, picked out his silver tooth, and tossed it to Astrid.

CHAPTER 62

OSCAR

GROSS.

That was my first thought.

Astrid, though, didn't seem fazed that an object from inside Killer Jack's mouth had just been tossed her way. Fast as lightning, she held out her skirt and caught it in the material.

We all leaned over to look. It was like the other key fragments—a strangely shaped chunk of metal.

"*Thank* you, Killer Jack!" Imogen exclaimed. "Other key keepers have kept theirs in pockets, or on shelves. One was taped to a movie camera, but you chose the most imaginative place of all! Your mouth! We'll give it a rinse and then we'll continue with our quest."

That's when the argument started.

While Imogen used the judge's water jug to wash the key fragment, Gruffudd squealed that he was "starving" and that we would "*not* continue with our quest until we had eaten morning tea with the judge!"

Imogen reckoned we should continue now and that Gruffudd could have an apple as we walked. Octavius had packed a food hamper for us at the hotel that morning, she said.

Astrid said she'd been looking forward to a chocolate éclair herself; Esther pointed out that Gruffudd might have trouble munching on an apple, what with being the *size* of an apple himself; and Imogen said, "Gruffudd, have you remembered your third song or do we need Oscar to take another memory out of the bottle? My three memories are all used up."

Alejandro said he'd tossed out the apple from the food hamper, as he'd noticed it was "more bruise than apple." Imogen said, "You should have told me that, Alejandro!" and Bronte asked why Alejandro "should be obliged to inform Imogen every time he threw away an apple."

That seemed a fair point to me, but Imogen had some angle on why it was *not* a fair point, and the argument grew more knotted from there. The lawyers leaned against the bar table, crossed their arms, and watched with interest. "Nicely expressed," one said. "Oh, she nailed that point," the other agreed. "Pithy," said the first.

Eventually, I couldn't hear the lawyers' commentary, because the girls and Alejandro were full-on shouting at each other. The judge—who was still crawling around on the floor—suddenly sat up, put his fingers in his mouth, and whistled.

Silence fell.

"*Cannot* find my gavel," the judge said, huffing a bit. "And I will *not* have this chaos in my courtroom. Are you having morning tea with me or not?"

"*Not*," Imogen said decisively, and the judge clapped his hands once, before anybody else could protest.

"On your way then," he said. "Thank you to the young fellow for help with my crossword, and thank you to the young girl for solving the murder case. Meanwhile, you can all come back and visit when you grow up and learn to treat each other with civility."

Then he stood and beckoned for the lawyers to follow him to his "chambers." The woman with the cat's-eye glasses followed, shutting the door without even a glance in our direction.

* * *

After that, nobody was in a friendly mood.

We stopped right away for me to get another memory— Gruffudd claimed to be too hungry to remember his own mother's name, let alone a song. This time the memory was only from the Friday before.

I was sitting in Mrs. Kugelhopf's office—in the middle chair of the three facing her desk—and she was lecturing me about snoring in class. The thing is, I'd made the class laugh during a death-defyingly boring lesson about compound interest, which was nice of me—but Mrs. Kugelhopf refused to take that into account.

While she was going on at me, there was a knock on the door. I turned around and a thin man in a three-piece suit came into the office. That hadn't happened in real life, so I knew I was up to the clue bit. The man was carrying a business card, which he handed to me. When he did, I noticed that his ears were so pointy they formed little triangles. I looked down at the card:

Moondazzle Jewelry of Clattering Street

Splendid City's Finest Trinkets & Gems

For some reason, reading that sent warning chimes down my spine and right through my body. When I looked up again the man smiled a small, mean smile.

The memory ended.

I shivered and outlined it to the others.

"No wonder you got warning chimes," Imogen said, sounding sharp. "Pointed ears? Jewelry? That man was a Sterling Silver Fox."

Then she led the way through the streets of Splendid, heading for the Moondazzle Jewelry store, and the argument started up again. They were all so cranky that I didn't ask for the lowdown on Sterling Silver Foxes. I didn't exactly know what they were all fighting about, to be honest, or why—they'd started the day in such a good mood. It was weird.

Gruffudd was screeching about how we had *destroyed* his once-in-a-lifetime chance of a morning éclair with a judge, Alejandro was telling Bronte that she had better take care on the icy path, Bronte was snapping that she knew perfectly well how to walk on an icy path, and the three sisters seemed to be caught up in an old fight from their childhood. One of them had moved the couch too close to the living room door, apparently, during a game of—there was a mini argument about what game it was—but whatever it was, the couch had been too close to the door, which meant that when their mother, carrying a tray of— Another argument about what was on the tray—

And so on.

The city was gray and slick, dirty snow in clumps here and there and lampposts so cold they burned your hand when you grabbed them to stop yourself slipping. The paths *were* super icy. They were also fairly crowded. People of all different types—size, color, race, fashion, style—were skidding and grabbing at the lampposts, some laughing, some swearing, some grimly carrying on. Big, old cars splashed cold water onto our shins as we walked, and horses stopped right beside us to relieve themselves on the road. That was funny at first, but then it became annoying and stinky. Esther went into a rant about how Astrid's pack kept swinging in front of her nose, claiming that the pack "stank as bad as the horse poop"—which seemed unlikely to me, and which offended Astrid, and another argument started up about personal hygiene in their family.

Bronte fell over and got gravel burns on her palms and knees. Alejandro was maybe a little too theatrical in how kindly he helped her up, which made Bronte furious.

"Just say *I told you so*," she demanded, and Alejandro pretended not to know what she meant—"No, no, Bronte! I am simply worried about you!"—which frustrated Bronte even more.

That's what it was like the whole way.

I was pretty busy trying not to breathe in the bad smells, and that's about it.

CHAPTER 63

IMOGEN

AS OSCAR HAS mentioned, we were reasonably cranky as we headed toward Moondazzle Jewelry that morning. This was the judge's fault. We felt embarrassed that he had scolded us. It seemed very unfair. We'd been battered and spun about by our quest the last few days, yet we had mostly got along very well and we'd collected six key fragments. And here he was treating us like naughty children?

So if we were hurrying through the streets behaving exactly like naughty children, this was, as I said, the judge's fault.

Oscar says he finds it "weird" that we went from being cheerful to fighting over nothing. I have boarding school friends who are "only children," like Oscar, and who grow visibly astonished by our sudden squabbles too. However, they are common among siblings and close cousins. Father often says that our passionate arguments are signs of our great love for one another and incidentally, could we cut it out at once.

If you want an additional reason for our short tempers, keep in mind that we had spent a frightening, frustrating few days together, that we still had to deal with the Doom Lantern Witches that afternoon—and that we were now on our way to see a Sterling Silver Fox.

This is probably my least favorite type of Shadow Mage. They're cunning and cruel, dress immaculately, love jewelry and gemstones, have pointed ears—and like to steal your laughter.

As we turned onto Clattering Street, I looked at Oscar. His face was set into a distant, blank expression as if he wasn't quite there. This happened to him now and then.

Across the street, facing the jewelers, was a confectionery shop, and I pointed this out to Oscar and asked if they had sweets in his world. He smiled without answering, and looked so haunted that I gave him a handful of coins and asked if he could please purchase some sweets for us while we were in the jewelers.

I don't know why I did this. It suddenly seemed like the right thing to do, like Oscar needed a break.

Oscar seemed surprised, but he darted across the street—between carriages and automobiles—and disappeared into the confectioners'.

The rest of us gathered on the corner to prepare. The fact that Oscar's memory clue had featured only *one* Sterling Silver Fox didn't mean that several others weren't hiding out the back of this shop, ready to pounce.

However, beneath the curling shop sign—

MOONDAZZLE JEWELRY: SPLENDID CITY'S FINEST TRINKETS & GEMS

—there was a second, printed notice:

MOONDAZZLE JEWELRY STORE

ALBERT C. CROFTS, PROPRIETOR (STERLING SILVER FOX)

GUARANTEE: NO SHADOW MAGIC OF ANY KIND IS PRACTICED INSIDE, OR IN THE ENVIRONS OF, THIS SHOP. ALL JEWELRY OF HIGHEST QUALITY. NO LAUGHTER STOLEN.

SPLENDID CITY CERTIFIED— SAFE STERLING SILVER FOX

Splendid had obviously set up some kind of scheme allow-ing Shadow Mages to establish commercial ventures here, as long as they guaranteed they would not practice shadow magic. This made sense from a business perspective too. Nobody would purchase jewelry from a shop where they might gain a pretty bracelet but would also lose their laughter. Not a fair trade.

I pushed open the door. It creaked.

The bespectacled, pointy-eared man behind the counter smiled and said, "Welcome. I am Albert C. Crofts, proprietor. How may I assist you, children?"

As arranged, Esther and Astrid pointed to some trinkets in the window and asked if they might examine them, while the rest of us milled around, pretending to be studying the various jewels but actually looking for a likely hiding spot for a key.

It was not hidden.

A silver key fragment, just like the others, was sitting on a pink satin cushion on a high shelf.

I stood on my tippy toes, reached for it, and slipped it in my pocket.

"Saw that," said a low, dry voice, and Albert C. Crofts straight-ened and peered at me over his spectacles.

I felt my face turning the same shade as the satin cushion and stammered: "Oh, sorry. Sorry. May we please—we are here to—"

Gruffudd, who was riding in my coat pocket, interrupted. "We are here on a *quest*," he piped up proudly, "to save the great city of—"

"Yes, yes, I know." Albert C. Crofts spoke in an elegant voice, like somebody reaching for a pipe and lighting it, although he did neither thing. He simply moved back around behind the counter. "Well done, children. You have distracted me and acquired my fragment of the key. Good day to you all. On your way."

And he nodded at the door.

So easy! I thought.

CHAPTER 64

OSCAR

WELL, AT LEAST I can do this.

That was my first thought when Imogen told me to go buy lollies. *Sweets,* she called them, which is what they call lollies in England. It's "candy" in America. "Dulce" in Spanish.

See? I thought. *I can handle buying lollies all over my own world. I'll be fine here too.*

Then I walked into the shop and changed my mind. The woman behind the counter wore an apron and a smiley expression as she talked to other customers. Then she glanced toward me and scowled. It was a bit like I'd walked into the school staff room and interrupted teachers having a nice cup of tea and a chat.

The other customers were a mother and two kids: a boy in a cap, jacket, collared shirt, and shiny shoes; a girl in a pinafore and ribbons. All three stared at me.

I looked down at myself. Pasta-sauce stain on my top, rip in my pants, dirty old, torn-up skate shoes. I'd never bothered to change into the clothes Alejandro had put in my backpack. I'd been wearing the same thing since Monday. My backpack itself was faded and sagging, skateboard razor-tailed with dirty old wheels. My hair was probably sticking up all over the place too, I realized. I ran my hand over it. Yep. It was.

Ah, well. Nothing I could do about all that.

The customers turned back to the shopkeeper, and I checked

out the lollies. They were lined up in jars behind the counter and I didn't recognize a single one. Multicolored and sugar-dusted like ours, sure, but with very unexpected shapes. Starfish, octagons, and rolled-up exercise books: those were the shapes I was seeing.

No prices anywhere either.

I looked at the coins that Imogen had poured into my palm. Dull bronze discs. No numbers or pictures printed on them. How was I supposed to know how many lollies I could get?

The family were already finishing up, both children holding brown paper bags, the mother paying, so I couldn't copy them. *Jangle* went the shop bell, and they left the store.

It was me and the shopkeeper.

"*Yes?*" she said, in the way you might hit a tennis ball sharp and hard at the net.

I showed her the coins in my hand. "What can I get for this?" I asked. (Although then I thought: *Wait, did Imogen mean me to spend all the coins?*)

The woman made her nose go long and thin by breathing into it.

"That depends." Her voice became long and thin, like her nose. "What do you *want* to get?"

"I don't know," I admitted. "What . . . I mean, what flavor are these?" I pointed to a random jar, filled with bright yellow trapezoids.

"What do you think?" she said, rolling her eyes. Actually rolling her eyes. Which didn't seem like ideal customer service.

"Um. Banana?" I guessed.

"*Banana?*" That word jarred, as if this time she'd got her tennis racket to the ball at the wrong angle. "Why would *sweets* be *banana* flavored?"

Then she swung around, grabbed a paper bag and a pair of tongs, started plucking lollies out of jars and dropping them in, crumpled up the top of the bag, thrust it at me, and grabbed two of the coins from my palm.

"Happy?" she demanded.

"I don't know," I replied, which was an honest answer.

"On your way!" She waved toward the door, seeming really exasperated by everything that had happened.

"Thanks?" I said and headed out of the shop.

At least I'd got some lollies.

Across the road, I could see the figures of the others moving around behind the jewelry shop window.

As I crossed over—getting tooted by an old-fashioned car, which is hard to take seriously—I realized there were numbers painted on the jewelry shop window. Prices, I figured. At least you were told how much jewelry cost here, even if you had to take wild guesses about lollies. Had I been ripped off just now? The paper bag was heavy and full, which was something, but what if the shopkeeper had chosen the nastiest-tasting lollies they had?

As I walked closer, I squinted and saw that the numbers on the window were actually fractions.

¾ ¾ ¾

The same fraction. Three quarters.

Three quarters of what?

Did it mean three quarters of a bronze coin? Imogen's left-over coins felt kind of sweaty in my hand now. I stopped outside the shop and stared at them. *There was so much I didn't know about this world.* Had Imogen sent me to the lolly shop to get me out of the way? Like, to stop me messing up the quest with all my ignorance?

What if I never got home?

That question blasted me out of nowhere. It sent a shudder from the base of my neck right down my spine and *wham!*—into my stomach. It actually made my body trip forward a little.

I straightened up, breathed in deep, and pushed open the door of the shop. The others were right there at the door and it was tricky to get in—and there he was. Behind the counter. The man from my memory. Same pointy ears, fancy suit.

I realized that the others were actually leaving the shop, so I went to follow them—they seemed jittery and excited—glancing behind me at the man as I did.

He was smiling to himself, looking down at the counter—and

then the smile washed away. He looked up, directly into my eyes, and bellowed, "STOP, THIEVES! STOP THOSE CHILDREN! NOW!"

Next thing, he was hurdling the counter and lunging at me. He nearly got me.

The others burst out of the shop and started running, while I was so shocked and confused I froze.

Bronte tripped back, grabbed my arm, and dragged me behind her shouting, "Run!"

My legs started moving.

People were everywhere on the street, and we were ducking around them, sliding between them, slamming into them, skidding on the icy cobblestones.

"STOP THEM!"

I glanced back and saw that he was closing in on us. He had a fast, smooth pace for an old guy. His elbows pumped, his long legs scissored, he swerved around people like a dancer. Face ice-cold with fury.

What had they stolen?

The guy swore and shouted at people to stop us. Nobody did. They sized up what was happening—and stepped aside for us. A woman with a cart loaded with fruit even wheeled it back to clear us a path—then shoved it forward to block the guy.

He leapt right over it.

Alejandro was leading, Imogen right behind him, and they kept darting around corners and down laneways. Laneways turned into other, narrower laneways. We skidded along a gutter behind row houses, had to climb over a metal staircase—I dropped the bag of lollies and the coins as I climbed, and they spilled and clattered and rolled away—ran face-first into sheets on a clothesline, sent them flying behind us.

He kept right on closing in on us.

Astrid was having trouble keeping up, got stuck behind a garbage heap. I picked her up and swung her over the top of it.

His footsteps pounded, his shouts blew cold air on my neck. He was right there—right behind us—

And then—

Whoosh.

A door swung open, two figures emerged—black capes, hoods over their heads—and blocked him.

As I swung around the next corner, hustling Astrid ahead of me, this is what I heard:

"Stop at once or be spellbound!"

"I'm not *doing* shadow magic. I don't *plan* to do shadow magic. Those children *stole* from me. I *gave* them the key, but they *also* stole a necklace! Why did they—"

Then the voices faded, lost behind car engines, the jangle of bottles falling somewhere, distant shouts. Just ahead of me, Bronte's brow was crinkled.

"Did he tell those Spellbinders that we stole a necklace?"

I nodded.

We had slowed to a jog.

"I thought he'd just changed his mind about letting us have the key so easily," she said. "Or was playing games with us. But somebody stole a necklace? Imogen!" She ran ahead and caught up with her cousin.

I slowed down then, thinking.

There was something about the pointy-eared guy's voice when he was defending himself—"not *doing* shadow magic . . . don't *plan* to do shadow magic . . ."—something familiar about it. Like he'd give it a shot, defending himself, even though he knew that there wasn't much point.

When I caught up with the others, they were crowded together on a street corner and Imogen was yelling.

"*Somebody* is *stealing* things!" That's what she was yelling. A man with a barrow full of cabbages turned and stared at her.

"*Crocheted doilies* from the inn!" she said. "A *ceramic frog* from the school steps! A *skullcap* belonging to the Radish Gnomes! A *silk snowflake* from the Crystal Faeries! A *shoelace* from the left boot of Edward T. Vashing! The judge this morning was missing his *gavel*! And *now* one of you has stolen—from a Sterling Silver Fox, of all people—a *necklace*!"

Each item that she listed got a stamp of her foot, the necklace receiving the most vigorous stamp of them all. She actually *shrieked* the word *necklace,* and a passing girl, who was carrying a carton on her shoulder, tripped sideways in fright.

We all stared at Imogen. Seemed to me that those were all the kinds of things that get forgotten or misplaced. It happens in life. Even the necklace—most likely the jewelry guy would arrive back at his store and go, "Whoops. It was here on the floor all along."

"*Who* is stealing things?" Imogen demanded. "Which of you thinks it is *amusing* or *acceptable* to take items from the key keepers? Perhaps you want to take home *souvenirs* from your trip? Well, know this! This is not how we do things—"

At that point, Gruffudd scrambled out of my pocket—how did he get *there?*—up onto my shoulder and spoke into my ear: "Why must she scream? I'm trying to sleep."

"Shhh," I told him. Something was occurring to me. I needed to concentrate. Gruffudd jumped from my shoulder onto Bronte's.

"—We do *not steal* in this world!" Imogen was finishing. She turned back and glared at each of us in turn—but she skipped over me.

That's when I knew for certain. She thought *I* was the thief.

"Before we go on," she said, "I'm going to ask each of you in turn if you are guilty, and Astrid will tell us who is lying."

"What if *Astrid* stole the necklace?" Alejandro joked—I could tell he didn't believe that any of us had taken anything, and was trying to lighten the mood, but Astrid was still scared after the chase. She burst into tears.

"I did *not* steal the necklace!" she sobbed.

Her sisters threw their arms around her and blazed at Alejandro: "How *dare* you accuse Astrid? You take that *back!*" while Alejandro backed away in confusion.

Bronte lost her temper then and started shouting at Imogen that it was *her* fault that Astrid was upset, not Alejandro's, and that *none* of us had taken a *thing!* And so on.

Imogen screamed right back at her, and it went on for a while, the screaming. It's not relevant what people said. Basically, Imogen's sisters supported her, and Alejandro tried to apologize to Astrid, to explain he'd only been joking, and to mediate. Only, he did that by saying, "Of *course* nobody here has stolen anything! It is impossible to believe!" which only infuriated Imogen.

I leaned against a brick wall and watched the passersby. They were all either staring openly or ducking their heads, embarrassed.

Eventually, Bronte said, "Ow!" Gruffudd was biting her shoulder.

"My dear and humble servant of the quest!" he cried. "Discontinue shrieking—and quest! You must *quest*! Quest! QUEST!"

Imogen noticed him, blinked, and took a deep breath.

"Yes," she said, in a calmer voice. "You're right, Gruffudd. Let's figure out the next key keeper *fast*, so that we can get to the coach stop by two o'clock—and whoever is stealing things? *Stop!*"

This time she looked directly at me.

I turned around and walked away from the lot of them.

CHAPTER 65

IMOGEN

I FELT SICK.

This terrible blankness fell over Oscar's face, like shutters being drawn, and he walked away. I watched his backpack with its battered old skateboard clinging to it, and his funny lopsided walk, and I felt sick.

Why had I decided it was him?

Just because he came from another world?

"Oscar!" I called. "Come back! I didn't mean it! Oscar!" I started running after him. He carried on walking, without looking back, and raised one hand in the air. Flat, like a stop sign. Meaning: *goodbye* and *don't follow*. It was such a strong and definite gesture, I stopped.

"OSCAR!" I called again. He started to jog then, the backpack bouncing, and turned a corner.

I looked back at the others. Their faces were grave. Astrid, though, seemed confused for a moment, then her face became horrified. "Don't tell me you think *Oscar* has been stealing?" she cried. "Is that why he walked away? Imogen, he *hasn't* been at all!"

The others murmured their agreement.

"I know, I know." I rubbed my face. "I don't know *why* I was suddenly convinced it was him. *None* of us would steal."

"He will come back," Alejandro promised. He pointed to a

café along an alleyway. "Let us go in there and wait for him. We still have time, no?"

So we went into the café and ordered cakes and tea and then pushed the cakes around our plates with our forks. Even Gruffudd moved at a more sluggish pace than usual as he sampled our cakes.

"We have lost the boy from another world," he said sorrowfully. "And I have remembered the third and final song."

Then he sat down, leaning against the sugar bowl, and strummed an imaginary guitar. He crooned so softly we squinted, leaning in to hear. There was a soulful expression on his little face as he sang, long pauses between lines:

> *"Essence . . .*
>
> *Quintessence . . .*
>
> *Chess set . . .*
>
> *Best bet . . .*
>
> *Zircon and zeallllll*
>
> *Thimble . . .*
>
> *Be nimble . . .*
>
> *Thirst must . . .*
>
> *Circus . . .*
>
> *Turncoat and teallllllll . . ."*

He sang it several times, each time seeming more anguished than the last.

"All right, we have probably heard enough," Alejandro suggested.

We were all watching the café window—we could see the corner where Oscar had walked away—and now and then we'd jump, thinking it was his dark head approaching. It always turned out to be somebody else.

At least trying to interpret Gruffudd's song was a good distraction.

"These school songs of yours get trickier and trickier," Astrid observed.

This was true. The first, about the Radish Gnomes, had given us their location; the second had provided Edward T. Vashing's name but had been tricksy about his occupation—and this one didn't make sense.

For a while we tried to decipher the words: It's somebody whose essence is their ability to play chess and their colorful personality (since zircon comes in many different colors); it's somebody whose coat needs mending (with a thimble); they live in a desert (thirsty) near a circus with performing . . . teals?

Our moods were growing tetchy again because Oscar was still not back. Occasionally one of us would run out into the street, look around, and then return. Whoever it was always shook their heads.

In the end, Alejandro leaned sideways and spoke to a man eating scones at the next table. "If I tell you the lyrics of a song, will you tell me if they mean anything to you?"

"Sod off," said the man.

Alejandro tried the two elderly women at the table on our other side instead. They agreed to listen, smiling fondly at Alejandro, and then, when he'd finished singing, one of them said: "Well, I don't know what the heck all those words mean, but Turncoat and Teal are crossroads in the wealthy northern part of the city."

I unfolded my map, found the inset of Splendid, and there they were, Turncoat Road and Teal Street, crossing one another in the north of the city, exactly as the woman had said. A children's playground was marked on the southwest corner of the crossroads.

"The key keeper must live in one of the houses on the other

corners," I suggested. "Once Oscar gets back, we'll have to knock on the—"

Esther was shaking her head, her eyes bright. "What if the *sounds* in the song count, more than the meaning?" she said. "Think about it. The *sss* and the *zzz*, the *b-t*, and the *thhh*!"

We all frowned, probably because this reminded us of school. Next, she would probably ask us to identify the *alliteration* and *assonance* and tell her what "effect" they had.

"The sounds make your mouth feel sort of tickly and shivery!" Esther added—like another student answering the teacher for us, which was a relief—"which is exactly like a Fizz! I think it means there's a Fizz there! Probably right *there*!"

And she jabbed her finger at the children's playground on the map.

"Or *is* there?" Bronte joked.

The reason that Bronte's question was a joke is this: many people do not believe that Fizzes exist.

A Fizz is a type of True Mage that nobody has ever seen. Thought to be as fine as dust, their presence is only sensed by a tingling sensation on your skin. If Fizzes wish to speak to you, they do so in the form of a tickling voice in your mind. They are found in patches of dandelion, sorrel, nettle, thistle, or crabgrass, where they perform quiet and powerful magic on items that get dropped or kicked into their patch.

Personally, I've always thought that people who hear Fizzes are just being fanciful—imagining tingling sensations and tickling voices—and that the magicked objects have most likely been left behind by other True Mages, up to mischief.

Esther, though, has always believed in Fizzes.

"When Oscar gets back, we can go there and find out," I said, and we all looked at the café window again.

Oscar was still not back.

CHAPTER 66

OSCAR

I HAD NO plan to go back.

It was cold. A strong wind was blowing in sudden gusts. Hats flew from people's heads and cloud shadows spun over us. I stopped at a lopsided lamppost and swung my backpack around to get my skateboard.

I hadn't been able to ride it at all lately, what with being in forests and boats, but now it was exactly what I needed. This was a great city for skating. Not too many people around, smooth wide pavement, stair sets and railings everywhere. They didn't have those bolts and brackets that are used as skate deterrents anywhere either, and I couldn't see a single No Skating sign. Made sense, since they didn't have skateboards.

Dropped my board to the road and a voice said, "Oscar."

"What?" I said, not looking.

Then I did look, because that was a man's voice and I didn't know any grown-ups in this world, only really annoying kids.

Oh, except this one.

Reuben, the Genie.

He was leaning against the lamppost, rubbing his hands together against the cold. He blew on them and smiled at me.

"You've gone off course," he told me.

"Nope." I didn't know what he was on about, except I had a strong feeling he meant I should be back with the others. No chance. "I'm not going back."

"Look her in the eye and tell her who you are," he said.

I knew he meant Imogen.

"She *knows* who I am," I argued, flipping my board up from the ground and grabbing it.

"But does she know?"

He made no sense.

"I'm not going back," I said again. I looked behind me. I'd walked a fair way. "Wouldn't even know *how* to get back. I'm fine on my own."

Reuben shrugged. "I'm sure you are," he said. "It's up to you. If you *do* go back, it's down there and to the right."

I looked where he was pointing, and when I turned around he'd gone.

Dropped my board again and did a substandard ollie.

CHAPTER 67

IMOGEN

IT WAS 1:00 P.M.

We needed to get to the north part of the city, ask (a possibly nonexistent) Fizz for a key piece, and get the 2:00 P.M. coach back to the Witches.

Gruffudd was growing impatient.

"It is a tragedy that Oscar is no longer with us," he announced. "A greater tragedy would be if we fail to bring the key and unlock my city. Remember, I am the only quester. Remember, I am their only hope."

Some of the others agreed. I stopped myself reminding Gruffudd he'd wanted to delay us by having morning tea with the judge.

"We find the final keys and set the Elves free and *then* we find Oscar," Alejandro suggested. "He will be all right."

Bronte was doubtful about that. "He has no money, he has no food, he's in another world. I think *I* should stay here and wait for him while you—"

"We're not doing *that* again." I was definite about that. No more splitting up the group. "We'll give him until twenty past one," I decided. "Then we'll have to . . . leave a note for him."

We paid for our coffee and cake.

We sat and stared at the door.

At 1:20 P.M., Gruffudd said, "Imogen?"

"Wait," I said. "One more minute."

At 1:25 P.M. I stood slowly.

"All right," I agreed. "We should go."

That's when the door opened and Oscar walked in.

"I didn't—" he began, and I threw my arms around him and said, "Of *course* you didn't!"

"I get into trouble a fair bit in my world," he explained. "So nobody believes me when I *haven't* done the wrong thing. The Sterling Silver Fox gave me a bad feeling because he . . . well, he reminded me of me. He can never convince anyone he's good."

"I'm so sorry, Oscar. Please forgive me and come and see a Fizz?"

I can't tell you how happy I was to see the dimple flash in his cheek.

* * *

As we approached the corner of Turncoat Road and Teal Street, Esther kept skipping ahead of me, giddy as the wind. She has always wanted to meet a Fizz.

We were in a neighborhood of wide, tree-lined streets, with grand homes boasting porches, gardens, and ornate gates. Polished automobiles stood in some driveways, and smoke whirled from every chimney. Elegant carriages rolled by, drawn by fine horses tossing their manes.

The sky had grown dark with cloud, and the wind flapped at our collars and the straps of our packs. As we reached the playground, the entry gate was opened by a smartly dressed woman in knee-high boots. She was leading two little girls, both in coats and mittens, who stared up at us.

"You'd better get home, children," the woman told us, as she and the little girls set off along the path. "There's going to be a thunderstorm."

Nodding our thanks for her advice, we walked into the park.

CHAPTER 68

OSCAR

 **AS SOON AS** we were inside the playground, the wind, which had been getting out of control, seemed to settle.

It turned more mysterious though—distant and low—and started making sudden pounces. Dead leaves would skim across the grass toward us in sudden, bristling rushes. The swings swayed on the swing set, and the merry-go-round creaked itself in slow circles.

Pretty spooky.

The sky had grown darker than dusk too, giving the air a kind of low-fi glow. Heavy grayness shot through with eerie light.

"Over there!" That was Esther's voice interrupting my thoughts. She was pointing to grass at the base of the slide. "Over there," she said. "Dandelions in the grass."

The moment I looked, I felt it. It's very tricky to describe, but it was a bit like I was about to sneeze. Or like someone was stroking the back of my neck with a feather. Or like static electricity.

I knew the others were feeling it too because they were twitching or scratching their wrists or the backs of their knees.

Then the voices started up in my head. It was as if several people had climbed into my skull and were speaking in very soft voices. All of them were whisper-wailing: "AEEEEEBA! AEEEEEBA! AEEEEEBA!"

I know how it's spelled because the words floated across my mind, in typewriter font.

AEEEEEBA! AEEEEEBA!

It started to get unpleasant.

AEEEEEBA! AEEEEEBA!

"All right, settle down," I said. I didn't mean to, it just came out. The wailing stopped instantly, and there was a fluttery giggling instead.

"Here," all the voices said in unison. "The key."

Those words also scrolled across my mind in print:

Here.

The key.

"Where?" I asked.

Another fluttery giggling, and then Alejandro spoke, sounding very surprised. "It is here!" he said. "In the cuff of my trousers!"

We all opened our eyes—I hadn't realized I'd closed mine—and he was straightening up and holding out his palm. A chunk of key lay there.

"Here," all the voices said next. "A gift."

From underneath the slide, a dark object emerged. At first, I thought it was a man in a black suit rolling along toward us and my heart nearly spat itself out of my mouth. But he trundled slowly across the grass, stopped at our feet—and turned into a picnic blanket.

Rolled up, with carry straps.

"For your journey," the voices said. "To the Elven city of Dun-sorey-lo-vay-lo-hey."

Imogen crouched down and picked up the picnic blanket. This was pretty awkward—the blanket was almost as long as she is tall, and you could tell by the way she stumbled that it was heavy. She was already wearing a big backpack, and now it looked like she'd got herself jammed between two pieces of furniture.

We waited a bit in case the Fizzes had anything else to say. The grass changed color as the wind washed across it, and the dandelions bent sideways, seeds blowing softly through the air.

Imogen cleared her throat. She tilted her head so she could be seen around the rolled-up blanket. "Thank you," she called.

"Thank you very much for the key. And for this picnic blanket."
She adjusted the blanket in her arms. "It is exactly what we need
to keep us warm on our train trip to Yellowspot tonight," she
tried. "Or to . . . have a picnic . . . while we wait for the train."

Another silence. The shivery feeling zapped into my fingernails and zipped around my wrists and my ankles. It was
weird because it was a sensation that seesawed back and forth
between lovely and intensely annoying.

"Well," Imogen called. "Thanks again! Must fly!"

"*Yes, yes, yes, you must, you must, you must*" came the voices and
then that terrible soft wailing again:

AEEEEEBA! AEEEEEBA! AEEEEEBA!

We glanced at each other, then scurried out of the park,
shivers and shudders and shakes in everyone's shoulders. I was
the last out, and I closed the gate behind me right as the first
drops of rain fell.

CHAPTER 69

IMOGEN

"*RUN!*" I CALLED to the others.
I hefted the picnic blanket under my arm, adjusted the straps on my pack, and broke into a stumbling, off-kilter run.

The rain began pelting down.

The others hunched their shoulders and followed me. I'd already figured out the fastest route to the coach stop. We could make it if we hurried.

Oscar, I noticed, swung his backpack around to his front, turning it so that his skateboard was clutched to his chest. Esther glanced at this, then swiped her hand in the air. At once, the rain falling on Oscar swooped upward, forming a kind of archway around him. His head swung back in confusion.

We'd almost reached the corner when a flash of light slithered down the sky and thunder grumbled in the distance.

"We should take cover!" Alejandro called. "Imogen, stop! Here! Let us shelter on this porch!"

Rain streamed between his words as he gestured at a house without a fence, its driveway running up to a large, covered porch.

"No!" I shouted back. "It's fine! The storm is far away! We have to go! Or we'll miss the coach!"

The others had all paused at the driveway—Oscar still bewildered by the dry air around him—and I beckoned them furiously.

"Come *on*! It's—"

There was a great crash of thunder like a sudden loss of temper. Jagged light streaked across the sky.

I pivoted and ran to the others, shouting: "Get to shelter! Get to shelter!"

We all ran up the driveway, clambered onto the porch, and crowded together in a shivering, dripping huddle. Gruffudd climbed out of Astrid's pocket, swung down onto the porch floor, and pulled off his tiny shoes. He emptied out *teeny* splashes of water.

Another *crack* of lightning. Another thunder *blast*! The sky was washed in vibrant purple, then plunged into dark gray again.

The rain fell in a steady, noisy stream.

"As soon as the lightning stops, we'll run," I said, speaking loudly over the sound of the rain. I rubbed my wristwatch on my sleeve, trying to dry it. "We don't have long."

Oscar, meanwhile, almost completely dry, kept comparing himself to us in a daze.

"Oh, sorry," Esther said to him. "I thought you needed to keep dry for some reason—the way you were trying to protect your, um . . . boardskate."

Oscar smiled. "Yeah, the rain rusts the bearings," he said. "Gets waterlogged. Loses its pop. But how . . . ?"

"I just asked the rain to avoid you," she explained.

"Cheers." Oscar raised one of his eyebrows, his smile broadening. "I knew you could make river water splash your sisters. Didn't know being a Rain Weaver meant you could actually stop *rain*. That was really nice of you."

"You could have kept *our things* dry too," Astrid complained, her teeth chattering.

It was true: our packs were set out around us, forming great puddles.

When I squeezed out the picnic blanket, a veritable deluge splashed onto the porch. The firecrackers that Octavius had given me to get the Witches out of their house were soaked through. Ruined.

"Sorry," Esther said. "It was sort of instinctive when I saw the way Oscar was holding his boardskate."

"Skateboard." Oscar smiled.

"We'll figure out another way to get the Witches out of their house," I said. "Now can you make the lightning stop so we can get to the coach in time?"

"I'm a Rain Weaver, not a Storm Weaver!" Esther protested.

A window creaked open behind us, and we all jumped. "Hello there, you lot!" a woman's voice called in a motherly way. "Sheltering from the storm, are you? Come on in and get dry!" The woman pushed out her head so we could see her curly hair and round glasses.

"Thank you," Bronte replied. "We won't trouble you though. We'd only drip all over your floor. We apologize for intruding— and dripping all over your porch. As soon as the storm stops, we'll be on our way."

"Suit yourself!" the woman said. "Give me a minute!"

A few moments later, she was back with a stack of towels and a plate of cookies, which she passed through to us.

"Enjoy!" she said and closed the window again.

For ten minutes or so, we stood on the porch, drying ourselves with a stranger's towels and eating her cookies. We'd hardly touched the cakes in the café, so this was just the thing. Nobody spoke except to admire the fluffiness of the towels and the warm, freshly baked taste of the cookies (slightly too salty, although nobody mentioned that until later).

Finally, the storm began to quieten. The thunder faded to a low, distant throat clearing. The lightning became more of a twitchiness.

The sky cleared, soft sunlight even eased back through the clouds.

When birds began chirping to each other—recounting their experiences of the storm, I suppose—we looked at each other uncertainly.

"Should we?" Alejandro began.

My eyes were on my watch. "Yes! Quick! We can still make it if we run!" And we grabbed our packs and pounded down the porch steps calling, "Thank you! Goodbye now! Fluffy towels! Delicious cookies!" hoping the friendly woman would hear.

* * *

We tried.

We gave it our absolute skidding, sliding, splashing best.

Around this corner, across this street, over this bridge, down these steps—oh, wrong steps, quick, back up the steps—down *these* steps, along this laneway.

Quick, it's there! It's down that hill! The coach stop! There's the coach! It's right—

And there went the coach, pulling away without us. *Clip-clop, clip-clop,* the four horses trotting along while all of us shouted, "Wait! Wait! Please wait!" and chased it, tripping and staggering, huffing and panting. "WAIT!"

The coach disappeared into the distance.

CHAPTER 70

OSCAR

IT SHOULDN'T REALLY be me describing the rest of that afternoon because I didn't participate.

I mean, I was *there*. But I was trailing along behind the others, not having any particular opinion and only vaguely aware of what was happening. A bit like a kid whose parents are doing an urgent shop for new bathroom tiles.

What I do know is this: we basically ran back and forth across the city for approximately one thousand hours.

The others asked at the coach station when the next coach would be, and learned that there was another coach, at a different coach station, five or six blocks away, and that if we *ran*, we might *just—*

So there we were, running again.

The roads were slippery and there were occasional potholes that had filled with muddy water. I stepped in one of these, right up to my thigh.

We missed that coach, of course, and then there was another one to try, and another after that.

If I could have a word with the city planners of Splendid, I'd tell them to gather all their coach stops together, please, and stick them in one place.

The only useful thing I did was notice that Imogen had left behind the picnic blanket—the gift from the Fizzes—by a coach station counter. I ran back and grabbed it for her. However, it turned out that she'd left it there on purpose.

"We don't actually need it," she explained apologetically. "The train tonight will be heated. And I don't expect we'll want to sit on the station platform having a picnic. There'll be benches. I was only saying all that to be polite to the Fizzes. But thanks for picking it up."

That caused an argument because the others overheard and told Imogen she'd had no right to abandon a gift that was meant for *all* of us, and Imogen replied that it was *heavy* and that if they wanted the gift so much they could have offered to carry it, which I guess made everyone feel guilty, which only made them even snappier.

So. Not so useful after all.

I ended up carrying it myself and was pretty impressed that Imogen had done all that sprinting with this thing under her arm, without complaining. Weighed about as much as a small whale.

Anyhow, I lost count of how many coach stations we visited, and how many coaches we *just* missed.

Once we'd run out of coach stations, there was a lot of using Faery dust in puddles to phone up family members and ask for advice. The parents were useless as they only wanted to use the conversations as extra opportunities to scold the kids for disappearing in the first place.

The kids seemed to have an excess of aunts, and they started phoning them—or Faery-dust-puddling them. It went like this:

Aunt Claire had once organized a conference in Splendid and she recommended a private carriage service down some back alley. Turned out that the owner had shut up shop for a holiday to the Northern Climes.

Aunt Sophy proposed sending dragons to give us all a ride— I assumed this was a joke, but nobody was laughing, so I started getting excited about a dragon ride. Turned out there were city ordinances forbidding dragons in or near the territory.

Aunts Emma, Sue, Alys, Franny, Lisbeth, and Maya had no

advice except to visit for tea and cakes at any time—and Aunt Carrie became very loud and adamant.

She was the only one who got the truth out of them about where exactly they wanted to go.

"The *Doom Lantern* Witches!" she boomed. "I *know* the Doom Lantern Witches! Bronte, while you are a very strong Spellbinder, you are *not strong enough*. Not to take on Doom Lantern Witches! Not even *one*! Do you hear me? Promise me. *Stay away from them*."

Gruffudd had a tantrum about all these aunts wanting to see his city crushed by silver just because they were scared of a few Witches.

We also tried contacting boat rental places on the river, thinking that if we could find our way back to the river—which would take hours—we could take a boat back *up* the river and reach the Witches that way. The boat rental places didn't answer the puddle or, if they did, they laughed their heads off at the idea.

Alejandro suggested asking Octavius for advice, but when we contacted him, he said: "To be honest, the hotel is enormously relieved you missed the coach. The hotel was tremendously worried about its guests returning to the vicinity of the Doom Lantern Witches. The hotel hopes you will stay again."

At this point, everyone was starting to get as worried as Imogen about timing. We kept checking our watches—even me, to be honest, although I don't have a watch. I looked at clocks on walls.

We still had to get back to the Witches' house, figure out how to distract them, track down their key (which was hiding in a "special place," I remembered one of the Witches saying), and then get back to Splendid railway station in time for the midnight train to Yellowspot.

Midnight had seemed like forever away when it was only 2:00 P.M., but now it was 8:00 P.M., and the calculations in my mind were getting tangled.

If it takes x minutes to get to the Witches' forest and y minutes to get to the Witches' house and z minutes to get the key and then . . . I ran out of letters of the alphabet and had to start again. If it takes *a* minutes to get to the Witches' forest . . .

Eventually, we were headed for a tourist information bureau, hoping to get advice on transport, and we happened to jog by a hospital. We skirted around paramedics unloading a family from an ambulance.

The family all seemed to have some kind of extreme fever. There was a father, mother, and two little boys, and all four were shaking uncontrollably. A couple of doctors ran out of the hospital and bent over the patients, barking questions at the paramedics. It was pretty distressing to see, and we were trying not to look, but then Bronte skidded to a stop.

"Esther?" she called. "I think that's shadow magic."

Esther, just ahead, turned back. "You're right," she said, and then—to one of the doctors—"Do you mind if I try curing them? I think it's shadow magic."

"It is," one of the paramedics replied, grim as a bushfire. "They were attacked by the Doom Lantern Witches."

* * *

The curing turned out to be pretty special to see.

Four people thrashing around on stretchers, foaming at the mouth, eyes wide and panicked, and here was Esther, more focused than I'd seen her all week.

She moved quickly and smoothly, starting with the little boys. Put one hand gently on a boy's shoulder, raised her other hand and waved it through the air like a ballerina.

It was like milk pouring into a glass—the calm pouring over that boy. All the kicking, the twitching, the trembling sort of *faded* out of him. He sighed the most relieved sigh, his small shoulders lifting high and sinking down again.

She did the exact same thing to his brother, and to both parents, so that, within a few moments, the family were turning to hug each other and cry.

The doctors and paramedics couldn't stop praising Esther. They told us that all *they* could have done was apply some Faery potion, which would have soothed the patients "to a moderate degree," but that the shadow spell would not have worn off for several days. The family, meanwhile, couldn't stop thanking her.

"We were on a boat on the river when the storm hit earlier," the mother explained. "We lost control and the boat got swept down the right branch and smashed to pieces by the rapids. The Witches got us when we crawled to shore."

"You've been under that fever spell since *this afternoon?*" Bronte asked.

All four nodded, their faces gray at the memory. "I don't know how we managed to get through the forest at all," the father said. "We flagged down a coach on the road and the driver brought us to the city and called the ambulance."

The doctors took the family into the hospital then, to treat them for their shock and aching muscles, and we carried on walking—slowly—down the road.

It was not long after this that, somewhere, a clock began to chime.

Bong,

Bong,

Bong,

Bong,

Bong,

Bong,

Bong,

Bong,

Bong,

Bong,

Bong.

Imogen stopped.

She turned and waited until we'd crowded around her. We were under a streetlight, which still dripped with old rain. The street itself was shadowed and empty. The moon was high, there were stars scattered amongst the clouds, and it was cold.

"It's eleven o'clock," Imogen announced.

"Yes! We must hurry!" That was Gruffudd, who was riding on Imogen's shoulder. "We have to get to the Witches! The tourist information center will—"

Imogen was shaking her head. "Gruffudd," she said. "I'm very sorry, but we cannot go back to the Witches."

Then, over the sounds of Gruffudd's cries and protests, she said gently: "The tourist information center will *not* have a solution. Most likely, they will be closed anyway. We have to be at your city by 10:00 A.M. tomorrow to use the key. If we are going to do that, we have to get the midnight train to Yellowspot and then a coach. We can't return the way we came—it seems impossible to get upriver. The train station is down this street here, and I think we should go there now."

Gruffudd howled.

The rest of us stared from him to Imogen and back again.

Imogen spoke over his howls. "We have *eight* of the *nine* pieces," she said. "Maybe that will be enough? I don't know. What I do know is this: it's too dangerous to travel anywhere near the Doom Lantern Witches and, even if it wasn't, we've run out of time."

One by one, the others murmured their agreement. I didn't say anything. There was no way this would work without all nine pieces of the key. For some reason I was sure about this.

I also knew she was right that we had to give up on the Witches. But I had a vicious heavy feeling in my stomach, like a big poisonous squid was sitting there.

Gruffudd screamed, "No! Keep trying! No!"

—And we turned in the direction of the train station.

CHAPTER 71

IMOGEN

AT THE TRAIN station, there was nobody about.

It was a grand city station with soaring ceilings, rows of ticket counters, and a café.

The café was closed, chairs stacked up on tables, cash register in darkness. The ticket counters were dark behind padlocked railings. Birds flapped around the cathedral ceiling.

Gruffudd's wails had quietened to hiccups and snuffles, and even these echoed in the cavernous space. It was disquieting.

I told the others to wait on a bench, and I marched across the tiled floor toward a distant door marked INQUIRIES. Gruffudd's cries kept up as I carried him along, but eventually they faded. The only sound was the *tap, tap, tap* of my footsteps, and then the *tock, tock, tock* as I knocked on the INQUIRIES door.

A few minutes later, I was back, Gruffudd curled into my neck asleep, his thumb in his mouth.

"Platform Seven," I said, and we gathered our packs again and dragged ourselves through a tunnel to Platform 7.

We had a long wait for the train to Yellowspot, and there were no benches—no seats of any kind—on the platform. Only a few rubbish bins. So Oscar had been right to bring the picnic blanket for us. We spread it on the concrete and sprawled out on it, along with our packs, tired, cold, hungry, and miserable.

I took out the little velvet pouch filled with fragments of key, loosened the drawstring, and tipped them onto the blanket. Each was about the size of a regular door key and each was a peculiar shape. They shone dully under the electric lighting.

"What I don't get," Oscar said, "is how we make them stick together."

"This, I have also wondered," Alejandro agreed. "Do we need some kind of adhesive? A glue?"

Esther said she had imagined that the bright magic would make them "sort of cling together" once we'd assembled them properly, and Astrid wondered if that would be effective without the ninth piece.

Gruffudd was still asleep on my shoulder—Bronte set up his hatbox bed and lifted him into it—so we couldn't ask him this question. I wondered why we hadn't asked before. Probably too distracted—or maybe too superstitious, wanting to gather the key pieces safely before taking the next step.

While the others watched, I began moving the pieces around on the blanket, trying to fit them together. The first thing that happened was that I realized we wouldn't need glue or magic—each piece had small cavities or holes, in addition to small protrusions or knobs—and when I fit one of these protrusions into the cavity of another piece, and turned it clockwise, it locked itself into place: *click!* That gave us all a brief moment of panic. What if I'd locked the wrong two pieces together? However, I remained calm, turned the pieces anticlockwise, and they sprang free of one another again.

Although I moved the pieces around for a while, they never seemed to form a key shape, so I suggested we take turns trying to solve it—I could feel them all itching to take over anyway—and pushed all the pieces toward Astrid to have the first turn.

For a while then, it was relaxing, watching the pieces slide around on the blanket. We began working together as if we were doing a jigsaw puzzle as a group. Of course, there was no picture on a box to compare, but we had all seen keys before. They have a standard shape. The blanket itself was soft, and was striped in pleasant colors—watermelon, lemon, and lime—and our hands reached across it, turning fragments of the key this way and that.

Quickly, though, we grew impatient. Our hands began to tangle as several of us reached for the same piece, and Esther worried that Astrid was forcing two pieces together and would break them. That made Astrid defensive. Pieces kept clashing noisily or they went skittering. There seemed too many curvy bits and not enough that were long and straight. At the same time, a weight seemed to press on our shoulders and necks and a voice seemed to breathe in our ears: *A vital piece is missing from this key, you know.*

Eventually, we heard a distant train whistle, and Esther cried, "It's almost midnight! Here's the train!" We scooped up the key pieces and returned them to the velvet pouch.

We rolled up the picnic blanket and gathered our packs.

The clattering and whistling, hiss and bluster of an approaching train grew louder and louder—and here it came, here it came—

Rushing toward another platform.

"Not our train," I said. "Let's stay standing though, because ours must be due any moment."

Three tracks away, the train had stopped. It huffed and steamed, chattering away over there. Nobody appeared to get off the train, and nobody was on the platform to board. We watched as a station guard stepped off the train, looked up and down, and then blew a shrill whistle.

"Train to Yellowspot!" he shouted. "All stations to Yellowspot now departing!"

He stepped smartly back aboard.

Yellowspot!

"THAT'S OUR TRAIN!" we shouted. "STOP! WAIT! STOP!"

And we rushed along the platform, wild-eyed, wide-eyed, astonished, breathless, through the tunnel and onto the next platform—

As the train to Yellowspot disappeared along the track.

FRIDAY

CHAPTER 72

OSCAR

YEP, WE'D MISSED the train. We'd also missed midnight—running between platforms—which meant that it was now Friday.

Everyone was furious with the guy in the Inquiries office who'd told Imogen to go to Platform 7.

All except Imogen. She was quiet during the ranting.

She then cleared her throat and admitted that the Inquiries door had been locked when she got there, and that nobody had answered when she knocked. A light had been on though, and by squinting through a window in the door, she'd been able to see half of a chalkboard. TONIGHT'S TRAINS, it had said.

Only she couldn't get her head at the right angle to see any more than that.

So Gruffudd had crawled under the gap at the bottom of the door. A moment later, he'd slid out, climbed back to her shoulder, and told her that the midnight train to Yellowspot departed from Platform 7.

"You're sure?" she'd asked him.

"I have never been so sure of anything in my short and wondrous life," he had replied, before curling up on her neck and falling asleep.

Ah, I thought to myself, as Imogen told this story. *The kid hasn't done his numbers yet. He did mention he'd missed a lot of school to play in a meadow.*

Next thing, though, Gruffudd popped up in his hatbox bed—which Imogen was holding under one arm—yawned, asked what was going on and, when we told him, *denied every word.*

"I did *not* say to go to Platform Seven!" he blasted. "Imogen! We missed the train? And you are blaming *me* for this? The injustice!"

Imogen tried to be kind. "Nobody blames you, Gruffudd. It was a mistake. You must have *thought* it said Platform Seven, only you were—"

But Gruffudd jumped up and down in his box shrieking his tiny head off. "I did *not* tell you it was Platform Seven! I did not! I did not! I did not!"

Imogen set the hatbox on the ground—I guess it was wobbling in her hands—and repeated: "Well, you did, Gruffudd. You did. You *did. YOU DID, GRUFFUDD! YOU TOLD ME IT WAS PLATFORM SEVEN!*"

Losing it, see, as she went along.

Astrid, looking from the shouting Imogen to the shrieking Gruffudd, shrugged and said: "They're both telling the truth. Imogen, he must have said a different number and you *thought* he said Platform Seven. Gruffudd, what did you actually say?"

Gruffudd was too busy screaming and Imogen was pretty loud herself about the fact that she didn't *blame* him but that he absolutely, positively *did* say that it was—

And so on.

Eventually, Bronte told them both to "hush up," that this was "not a productive argument," and that we needed to find out if there was another train to Yellowspot tonight.

She and Alejandro ran off to see if they could find any more information, taking Gruffudd with them—Alejandro kind of plucked him out of his box, I guess to break up the fight.

While they were gone, Imogen carried on trying to persuade the rest of us that Gruffudd *had* said Platform 7—and then became *furious* because we all went quiet. Looking around and humming to ourselves.

Bronte and Alejandro came back saying that there'd been a man in the Inquiries room this time. His name was Ronaldo, apparently. ("Cristiano?" I joked. "The soccer player?" The others blinked at me and turned back to Bronte.)

"He told us he was having his supper earlier," she continued. "He seemed to find it *hilarious* that we went to the wrong platform and missed the train."

This caused another delay as we all had to restrain Imogen from hurtling out to the Inquiries office to strangle Ronaldo.

Bronte calmed her down and said, "All we can do now is wait for the next train. It leaves from this very platform in an hour. It's true we'll miss the coach, but I'm sure we'll find another way to get to Dun-sorey-lo-vay-lo-hey. Let's set up the picnic blanket and try to solve the key puzzle again."

Doing this gave us about thirty seconds of peace before the arguing started up again.

I don't know. It's not worth recounting. The key was in pieces and so were all the tempers.

The shorthand version: Someone was thirsty. Someone else drank from a water canister then set it down without screwing the lid on properly, thinking the first thirsty person would pick it up. It got knocked over. Water everywhere. Someone leapt over to set the water bottle straight again and accidentally sent a piece of the key flying.

This skimmed right over the platform and *ding!* landed on the train track below.

Alejandro jumped onto the track, retrieved it, and scrambled back up. A train blasted through the platform—an express, it didn't stop—*just* after he'd pulled himself up.

That gave everyone a scare, which caused more yelling. "Look! Alejandro could have been *killed* because you knocked that key piece onto the track!"

"I only knocked it because *you* knocked over the water!"

"I only knocked over the water because the lid wasn't on properly!"

"I only left the lid off because *you* said you wanted some!"

"You could have *killed* Alejandro!"

"Well, Alejandro shouldn't have jumped onto the track right then!"

For the first time all week, Alejandro looked angry. He's always so happy, I didn't think he was *capable* of being as fierce as this. "Do not make *me* a part of your argument!" he yelled. "I had *plenty* of time!"

Okay, I thought. *That's it.*

Put two fingers in my mouth and whistled. Doesn't always work when I do that, but this time it was good, piercing and loud.

They all stopped shouting and turned to me.

CHAPTER 73

IMOGEN

EVERYONE WENT VERY still except Esther, who was still mopping up the spilled water, and Gruffudd, who had once again curled up in the hatbox and fallen asleep. (Therefore, he was already still.)

Oscar cleared his throat and blinked, as if suddenly nervous about having our attention. "What I don't get," he said, "is why you fight all the time when you actually adore each other."

That startled us. It also seemed unlikely at that particular moment, but Oscar held up his hands.

"Trust me, you do." He began counting items off on his fingers: "In the last few days, Alejandro has told me that Astrid has a nature like sunshine. Esther has said that Alejandro is a marvel. Bronte told me that Esther is amazing and strong. Esther and Astrid both told me that Bronte is brilliant and kind. You were *all* going on about how Imogen basically has killer determination. I mean, the whole lot of you are OP—"

We were glowing at this unexpected praise—and smiling at the people who had praised us—but we frowned in unison at this.

"OP?"

"OP," Oscar repeated, as if he was making sense. "Overpowered. Like in video games. You've got way too many skills, I mean. My point is, you like each other for *more* than just your skills." He thought for a moment. "When people who like each other fight, it's usually because they're sad about something else. So here's what I suggest."

The wind blew along the platform then, rustling rubbish in the bin. We huddled closer together.

"A group therapy session," Oscar said.

A pause. We glanced at each other, then chorused: "What's a group—"

"I don't actually know for sure," Oscar interrupted (surprising us). "Based on TV, we should be sitting in a circle of chairs. I guess a picnic blanket will do. What happens is, everyone takes turns saying why they're sad. The rest of us listen and look sympathetic. Ideally, the person speaking breaks down and cries and then the person in charge—me—says something wise. I'll skip that bit as I haven't got anything wise to say, but let's see how it goes. Okay?"

We must have looked extremely doubtful because Oscar said, "Nah, it's not optional. It's compulsory." He turned to Bronte, who was beside him, and said, "You go first."

What Bronte said was very unexpected yet somehow made sense.

She started by saying that she was perfectly happy, actually, with nothing to be sad about, as she was with her cousins and Alejandro—her favorite people in all the Kingdoms and Empires—and that it had been a pleasure to meet Oscar, a boy from another world, and Gruffudd, an Elf, so that—

Then she gave a kind of shudder as if a jolt had run through her body and said, "If I'm honest, I *am* desperately sad."

Then she explained why.

Alejandro, who had become like her brother in the last two years, would soon be returning to his newly found royal parents. He would be far across the Kingdoms and Empires; they would scarcely ever see each other, and he *did not seem to care.*

She said this very politely and then she burst into tears.

Alejandro exclaimed that he would please take his turn, which seemed unfair as Bronte had only just started. He took his turn anyway. He spoke with piratical passion.

"My royal parents are very fine people," he said. "Kind? Yes! And fascinating! So? I must get to know them. They were sad to lose me as a baby and are happy to have me back. And yet? Well, I grew up with the pirates as my family. When they found out I did not wish to be a pirate? They beat me. Is this how a loving family behaves?"

"No," Oscar replied wisely.

"It is not! Then I met Bronte and she became like a sister to me! And her aunt Isabelle and the Butler and her parents? Like parents to me! Loving parents who would not care if I did not wish to become a pirate! I went to the cinema with Aunt Isabelle, I did crosswords with the Butler, but most of all I liked to be with you, Bronte!"

He placed a gentle palm on the top of her head—which was bent, as she was trying to hide her tears—and said: "I pretend not to mind, Bronte, so that I will not be swallowed by a huge and dangerous shark—the shark that is my sadness at leaving you and your family."

Tears ran down Alejandro's cheeks. He didn't seem at all embarrassed by this. Bronte looked up, saw his tears, and reached out to hug him. Then they both cried and said how much they would miss each other.

When they sat back up, they said, "Oh, this *is* very good, Oscar! You're right! Thank you!"

Oscar's dimple appeared and he shook his head. "You're the ones doing it right. Okay, Esther, your turn."

Esther took some time starting—she kept beginning sentences then changing her mind and discarding them. She was distracted by a flutter of wind or split hairs at the end of one of her braids. We remained patient as there was nothing else to do.

Eventually, she began to speak and what she said surprised me even more—but also made such sense I'm surprised it hadn't occurred to me.

"All my life," Esther murmured, "I've been obsessed with magic. I thought that I was useless because there was nothing magical about me—all I could do was write stories—and that if only I knew magic, I'd be all right. Now it turns out that I'm a Rain Weaver. I can manipulate water! I can sense magic, and spellbind! I can cure people of shadow magic illness!"

"See?" Oscar put in. "OP."

We hushed him, nodding along with Esther.

"Anyway, it's wonderful!" Esther said.

Again, we nodded, privately wondering if she might have misunderstood the game.

"It means that all of my dreams have come true and more!" she added.

We frowned at each other. "Mmm."

"But I'm *terrible!*" she exclaimed (finally getting to the point). "When I try to spellbind, I get *so* tired! I've been practicing whenever I can and I'm *exhausted*! I can't think straight! I'm so absentminded! When the Witches were chasing us? I could hardly get my thoughts straight to make a Spellbinding. I have no idea if it was an effective Spellbinding ring or not in that tree! It's just lucky the Witches went back to their house."

We all began to say soothing and sympathetic things (although I shot Bronte an alarmed look)—only Esther hadn't finished.

"And I have such weak magical senses! I don't have a clue if something has magic or not. I didn't realize that the silver wave was bright magic! We were *inside* the Witches' log cabin and it was *Astrid* who realized it was a coven. And then I nearly let Astrid . . . I thought it was a puddle! I nearly let Astrid . . . I nearly let Astrid . . ."

Her voice trembled and disappeared, and it seemed as if she might have reached the part of group therapy session where you burst into tears, but she gathered herself together to say one final thing.

"This is the worst thing," she whispered. "I love curing people. I really do. Yet sometimes I think I'm going to have to spend every moment for the rest of my life doing it—because I'm the only one who can—and this is terrible to say, but I don't want . . . not always . . . I just . . . I *really miss writing stories.*"

Then, in keeping with the rules of the game, she burst into tears.

It was easy to comfort her. You could tell she'd been thinking we'd be horrified and call her ungrateful, whereas in fact we saw exactly what she meant.

Astrid and I told her that we *love* her stories, and never imagined she'd stop writing them. That seemed to please her. Bronte told her that it was very common to feel exhausted by Spellbinding.

"Really?" she said, blinking away her tears.

"Most people think that children shouldn't spellbind at all," Bronte reminded her. "And you've hardly even started training. If you're trying to practice all the time, it's not surprising you're absentminded. You should eat regularly when you train, too, which you haven't exactly been doing."

The relief on Esther's face was lovely, like a cure.

"So you need practice with rest and nutrition," I said, "and eventually it will be as easy as ice-skating!"

"That's not easy," Oscar pointed out.

"Because you haven't practiced," everyone reminded him, which proved my point.

We also told her we understood the dilemma of a dream not matching expectations.

Oscar said: "One time, I saw a movie star talking on a YouTube video about how he always thought he'd be happy once his Hollywood dream came true and he won an Academy Award, and how shocked he was to realize he still got annoyed when his Wi-Fi was acting up or the Uber ran late."

That was just garbled nonsense to us, but we smiled at him politely.

"Yes, a dream coming true is a complicated thing," Alejandro said, heavily—and we realized he meant that he had dreamed of meeting his parents, and that had now happened.

Oscar chimed up again to say that there are plenty of doctors in his world who enjoy curing people, "and make sure they have downtime and, like, go on holiday to Queensland with their families."

I was interested to hear that there was a land of queens in his world, but he brushed over this, and asked Esther if she was feeling better yet.

"*Much* better!" she said. "Astrid, it's your turn! You are going to *love* it!"

"Will I?" Astrid asked doubtfully.

Then she sat up straight and, in a very practical voice, told us the most surprising thing of all.

CHAPTER 74

OSCAR

 **WHEN I FIRST** met the three sisters—only a few days before this—I'd thought of them as basically one girl in different sizes. Imogen, Esther, Astrid: large, medium, small. All three had braids, and all three had noses with cute tilts.

As time went by, though, I'd started to see differences. Imogen's eyes are narrower, her forehead is higher, and her ears stick out a bit more. Esther has faint freckles that you can see when the sun's on her face. Astrid's face is softer and rounder.

She's only ten years old. No wonder her face is soft and round. I'd been forgetting how young she was because she was confident and spoke with good grammar.

It was the same now: self-assured and all the punctuation in exactly the right place—but, actually, just a kid.

"As you know," she said, "I can always tell when people are lying, which is very helpful in poker."

Everyone agreed that this was true. She paused to think, then carried on.

"The reverse side of my skill, the side that people always forget about, is equally as important in poker. Nobody knows when *I'm* lying."

Her sisters nodded. "True, but, Astrid . . ."

She waved them into silence. "On Tuesday morning, when we

were packing up to leave the Apple Blossom Bed and Breakfast, I saw these scraps of material on the sideboard in our room. They had rosebuds stitched into them. I thought they must be part of Gruffudd's bed—his little sheets, I mean—and so I packed them into my bag for him. I had no idea they were doilies. I'd never even heard of a doily. Then Marion-Louise started shouting about her stolen doilies, and I realized my mistake. I *almost* explained and gave them back. But she was so angry! It scared me. I decided to use my talent for pretending and keep my face innocent. I don't like getting in trouble, so I decided I'd *always* use that talent. I pushed the doilies deeper in my bag."

We stared at her. She reached for the water canister, remembered it was empty, and set it back down.

"At Mrs. Chakrabarti's school, I picked up the frog from the staircase—to look at it, and to wonder why it was named Ferdinand—and then I put it in my pocket when the game began—as somewhere to keep it. I meant to put it back but got distracted. By the time I realized I still had it, we'd already left the school. It was such a small frog I thought nobody would mind. I decided I'd keep it and would collect souvenirs from *all* the key keepers—small things nobody would miss. The skullcap? The Radish Gnome threw it on the ground and stamped on it! I thought that meant she was finished with it! The snowflake? That was just scuffing along the floor at the Crystal Faery palace! The shoelace was lying on the ground near the riverbank—very threadbare and ratty—and the judge's gavel looked like a scratched old tool that a carpenter had left behind. I was *sure* nobody would miss that!"

All of us were shaking our heads in that slow, amazed way, like when you can't believe you left the water running and it's overflowed the bathtub and flooded the bathroom.

"It's lucky I already apologized to Oscar for thinking it was him," Imogen said. She turned to me: "Sorry again, Oscar."

To be honest, I was starting to find the situation pretty funny.

"And the necklace from the Sterling Silver Fox?" Esther asked her sister. "*That* wasn't a small thing that nobody would miss!"

"I honestly didn't take that," she said. "I took an old screw that I found on the shop floor as my souvenir."

Everyone started to giggle. "*Astrid,*" Bronte said thoughtfully. "You know that just because you have a particular talent—like the ability to pretend—doesn't mean you should use it to become a criminal?"

"Edward T. Vashing is a very fine actor," Alejandro contributed. "I am sure *he* could also trick people into believing anything he wanted. Most fine actors could. Yet? They do not. I hope they do not, anyway."

"I never thought of that," Astrid said.

"Yeah, I think you have to choose right over wrong even if you can get away with wrong," I told her, "otherwise it makes you a psychopath."

The giggling started up again.

"At least she didn't take anything from the Witches." Imogen sighed. "Imagine if she had."

"Oh, wait! I forgot about that!" Astrid spoke brightly. "I took a dirty sock from their laundry hamper."

That's when everyone lost it.

It was probably tiredness, but we laughed so hard I got stomach cramps.

Astrid joined in, became more hysterical than all of us, fell back, and bumped her head on the platform. We settled down then, and Imogen comforted her little sister's bumped head.

"You're supposed to cry," Imogen reminded Astrid. "Not laugh. That's the rules of the game."

"No, it's all right. I cried earlier, remember? When Alejandro said that nobody would be able to tell if *I* had stolen the necklace? It gave me a shock when he said it and I realized how guilty I was feeling. That's why I didn't take anything from the Fizzes— not that there was anything to take in a park. So my turn has been split into two parts—the earlier part when I cried, and this part when I spoke. I feel much better, thank you, Oscar."

Her sisters fixed her with iron gazes, and Astrid assured them, "Don't worry. I'll tell the truth from now on." And she sat back looking happy.

After that it was Imogen's turn, but she just said she was sad about not having all nine pieces of the key and that she didn't want to think about that.

"Say more," I said, getting into the swing of my character.

"There's nothing more," she said, "except that I find bright magic absurd. The Elves cast a bright magic spell to bury themselves under silver, which put us in extreme danger from Radish Gnomes, Witches, and a Sterling Silver Fox, not to mention several other irritating people, and now the entire Elven city is on the verge of getting"—she checked that Gruffudd was still sleeping and whispered—"crushed. It's preposterous."

I tended to agree, although Esther, who'd been stretched out on the blanket, sat up quickly. "I see what you mean, Imogen, but it helps if you think of it like this. Bright magic works through game play, and the best games are those with challenges and twists. You know how awful a game is if it's boring? Or if people are mucking about, not taking it seriously? For a game to be successful, it has to have surprises, and it has to have high stakes—the more dangerous, the better."

Imogen did not look convinced. "Anyway, it's Oscar's turn," she said.

"No, I'm the person in charge," I explained. "I listen and say the wise things. Besides, it's all good with me. No secret sadness."

"I don't believe you," Bronte said, and then when I carried on assuring them that I was totally fine, she added, very gently: "Oscar, we know your mother is trapped in a place called Byron Bay."

That made me laugh out loud—one of those yelps of laughter—but they kept right on gazing at me with tragic faces.

"We read your letter from her," Esther explained. "Sorry. It was back when you were dead. Is it Shadow Mages who have your mother trapped?"

The others chimed in: "Have you tried to rescue her? Perhaps we could help you? We'd be glad to help."

"Or is she in prison there? Has she been wrongfully convicted of a crime? Astrid could work out who's lying and clear her name?"

"Is the Kingdom of Byron Bay very far from where you live?"

"Is there a dragon you might fly to reach her, perhaps? Bronte speaks the language of dragons."

And on they went, being such nice people, and so caring, and yet so completely wrong, that for a moment I thought I might even start crying myself.

I didn't.

I remembered that I'm fine. I set out the situation for them.

My mother moved to Byron Bay a few years back and she has a new boyfriend there. It's only about an eight-hour drive north of Sydney, where I live with my stepdad, or around a one-hour flight. I've been to see her a couple of times, and to check out their vegetable patch and their chooks. ("Chickens," I explained. "They lay eggs.") My mother hasn't been able to come visit me much as she's too busy—as well as the chooks, she's started her own jewelry design business and she sells earrings made from seashells on Etsy. (More explaining.)

So she can't make it down for my birthday. It's all good, though—she's really sad about not being able to make it, so it's not like she doesn't care. And I'll probably FaceTime her.

"You must miss her very much," they all told me, but I said, "Nah, it's all good. I live with my stepdad and things are fine. It's pretty chill. He goes to his girlfriend's place a lot and I can do my own thing." I thought about all their parents' faces shouting at them from the river water. "He never even gets annoyed with me unless I leave junk all over the living room. It's fine."

Astrid sighed. "He's lying, you know. It's *not* fine."

"We don't need you to tell us that this time, Astrid," Bronte put in. "He's used the phrase *it's all good* more times than I thought possible in the last five minutes."

The others all murmured, "Exactly," and I felt a bit exasperated. How could I convince them that it *was* all good if I couldn't use the phrase?

CHAPTER 75

IMOGEN

"IT'S LIKE THIS," Oscar said, and he reached over to his backpack and pulled out the Genie bottle. He held it up.

"See this? The memories in here were obviously meant to teach me a lesson. I didn't really want to learn a lesson, but whatever. You want to know what my memories were?"

We waited, staring at him. Of course we wanted to know. He was such a mystery to us, this boy from another world. Although we suspected his memories would be as unfathomable as he himself was, generally speaking. They'd only intensify the mystery.

"The first one was my stepdad teaching me to surf, the second was me mucking up in class, and the third was me getting busted for mucking up in class. The message couldn't be clearer: I'm lucky 'cause I've got a good stepdad, and all I do is mess around and ride my skateboard. Look how great you lot are in comparison. I'm the most useless person here. That's the real message. So if I'm sad?" He paused and shrugged. "I deserve it. It's all good."

I can't explain why, but the lion in my throat leapt to its feet at Oscar's words.

"You think *you're* the most useless person here?" I demanded. I was really angry. Oscar flinched. "Do you know what *my* memories were? The first was my mother giving me a silver coin, the second was me bossing my little sisters around, and in the third I was shouting at a woman buying flowers! She'd made a mistake, that woman, sure, but everyone makes mistakes. What does all this tell you? That I was a spoiled child and now I've grown into a bossy, bad-tempered person. You think *you're* the most useless person here, well *I'm* as useless as toothpaste to a fish!"

"Nah," he began, except it was too late; the lion was out of my throat. The lion was me, or I was the lion, and both of us were roaring.

"I have *failed* every single moment since this whole thing began! I should *never* have brought these children on that morning coach. All I've done all week is *lose* them! First Esther, then Esther and Bronte, then Esther, Astrid, and Oscar, then Oscar. Because I basically accused him of stealing!"

I was vaguely aware of Alejandro murmuring, "Ah, but you never lost *me*, Imogen, so that counts for—" and Astrid muttering, "Oops, well, the *stealing* thing was—" and I stormed right over them.

"When I'm not losing you people, I'm losing my temper! Look! It's happening *right now*. I'm shouting my head off! And I've failed. I've *failed* at this entire quest! We only got eight pieces of the key. We should have gone back to the Witches while we were *there*! And we've missed the train! That must have been my fault, not Gruffudd's. All those Elves are going to be killed and it's *my* fault! I had all you talented, clever people on my team; I had *the help of a GENIE*, for crying out loud! I failed even though we had a *GENIE BOTTLE!*"

And I grabbed the bottle from Oscar's hand, raised it high in the air, and smashed it on the platform.

CHAPTER 76

OSCAR

IMOGEN'S EYES POPPED open in disbelief at what she'd done.

She looked at her hand—still holding the neck of the bottle, cork in place, edges jagged, then she looked at the fragments and splinters of blue glass scattered right across the platform.

Her eyes found mine, still wide with shock at herself.

I looked into those panicked eyes of hers: light blue, with lime-green flecks, and that's when I realized—*those* were the eyes I'd seen in the mirror, the mirror that had brought me to this world.

IMOGEN

I LOOKED INTO Oscar's eyes, deep brown with circles of gold, and realized: those were the eyes I'd seen reflected in the silver, right before Oscar appeared in our world.

A rainfall of memories poured over me then, and they were memories that were not my own.

I saw a little boy pushing a board through waves. He looked up shyly at a broad-shouldered man, who was talking to him, offering advice.

I saw a small boy in class, all his attention focused on a single piece of paper, getting the angle *just* right to tear it.

In a school office, he was studying a framed photo on the desk between himself and the deputy principal, pretending not to mind what she was saying.

It was more than simply seeing him.

I could also feel the chill and swirl of currents at my knees, hear the pleasing *zzzip!* of paper tearing and the *scritch, scritch* of other children writing around me. I could smell stale coffee in the mug on the deputy's desk.

OSCAR

I TUMBLED INTO memories too.

A little girl reaching for a big red strawberry, checking out her own shiny shoes, holding out her hand for the cold weight of a silver coin.

Same girl worrying about her sister's grazed knees, trying to figure out if her other sister knows how to count, looking around an empty town square.

Blasting a woman who was holding a bunch of flowers.

IMOGEN

THE SPACES *AROUND* the boy's memories stretched and expanded so I could see those too.

Before he'd pushed the board into the surf, the boy had waited, impatient with excitement, while the man named Joel—his mother's new boyfriend—waxed and polished his own surfboard. At last they were in the water.

"As soon as you feel the wave start to take you," Joel said, "you paddle like your arms are turbo-charged."

The boy held the board with both hands and twisted it toward the shore, watching over his shoulder, waiting for his first wave.

"That's it, buddy," Joel called to him. "You know what do. Stay in the shallow water, won't you? I'll see you soon."

And the man strode out of the water to the sand, picked up his own surfboard, and headed out to the break to catch some waves of his own.

OSCAR

BEFORE THE MOTHER handed the girl the silver coin, she crouched down and explained: "See that building over there? I have to run in there for a meeting. Spend this money on treats for the three of you. Watch your sisters closely, all right?"

After, the girl used the silver to buy strawberries. When she turned back around from the stall, her sisters had wandered away.

The panic swelled up from her throat. "ESTHER! ASTRID! COME BACK HERE *AT ONCE!*" she bellowed, chasing them down.

IMOGEN

BEFORE THE BOY tore strips from the page of his school-work, he had colored in a map, completed an arithmetic work-sheet, and listened to other children do speeches on "The Person I Admire." He was all used up.

Now they were doing comprehension. The sentences turned into tea leaves when he read them—broke into small pieces and swirled around. He tried it again. He read the first line, only it refused to hook up with the second. He tapped his fingertips quickly on the desk, forcing the sentences back together. "*Stop it,*" the boy beside him complained. But when he stopped tap-ping, the sentences tapped instead. They tapped on thoughts in his head. His mother and stepfather talking late at night. They had decided to separate. His mother was going to Byron Bay to start a design business. "It's meant to be," his mother had said. It was best for Oscar to stay here with the stepdad, and keep going to the same school, if that was all right? The stepdad agreed it was all right so long as he got the government payments and the mother sent money for the boy's food and clothes.

The boy read the first question: *Why do marine turtles migrate between feeding grounds and nesting sites?* Nests. Birds collected twigs and stones, mud and grass for their nests. They could use paper in their nests too. He could tear up this paper for a bird's nest.

Zzzzip. A good, neat tear. His mind settled down; his chest felt good. He lined up his hands, carefully, carefully, ready for the next tear.

OSCAR

THE GIRL AND her sisters had taken the coach back from boarding school.

Their father was away for work. Their mother was meant to meet them and hadn't turned up. They waited at the fountain in the square with their suitcases. The shops were shut. Nobody was around.

Her sister Esther pulled off her shoes and climbed into the fountain to paddle. When she tried to climb back out she slipped on the edge, fell, grazed her knees, and twisted her ankle. The sun was sinking.

The girl needed to find her mother, but Esther was limping. How could she make her little sisters stay where they were while she ran to get help? *Count to one hundred,* she ordered them.

IMOGEN

THE NIGHT BEFORE, the boy had been alone in his home. His stepdad was staying at his girlfriend's place for the night.

The boy had made himself dinner and then fallen asleep in his clothes.

CRASH!

He woke and leapt up from his bed in one swift motion. Grabbed the baseball bat he always kept in the corner of the room. Crept slowly, slowly, heart-poundingly down the dark hall.

Reached for the light switch.

A blaze of light.

Ah. He laughed. It was a framed print from the wall. It had slipped down and crashed to the floor.

He went back to bed. Lay there with his heart hammering.

The next day, in class, his teacher was explaining compound interest. When he looked at the teacher, the man's words made no sense. Focusing on his face took up all the space in the boy's brain. He pulled out the laces of his shoes instead. Compound interest started to make sense while he did that.

"Oscar, stop fidgeting and *look* at me when I speak!"

He sat up again and tried to watch the teacher's face. The words slipped away again. He was pretty tired. Imagine if he fell asleep. Imagine if he snored. What would it sound like?

SNORE. He did it without planning to. A loud, rattling, snoring sound. It was pretty good. The kids around him burst out laughing. So he did it again.

The teacher sent him to the deputy principal's office.

Mrs. Kugelhopf made him sit in the middle seat.

"You see my little boy Eddie there?" She pointed to a framed photo of a small child standing on a lawn, a bucket of water in his hand. "Look. He's carrying that bucket to help his father water our herb garden."

"Why didn't they use the hose?" the boy suggested.

"That's not the point, Oscar! The point is that my child, who is only *four,* is already adding more value to the world than you ever have! I don't like to say this to a student, Oscar, but you are shaping up to be a waste of space."

OSCAR

THE GIRL HAD taken her little sister Astrid to the doctor for her ear infection.

The girl had said very clearly to the doctor that Astrid was allergic to sulfonamides. "So if you are giving her antibiotics, only those without sulfonamides."

"Yes, Imogen." The doctor smirked.

Half an hour later, Imogen was at the pharmacy, reading the medicine bottle she'd collected. *Contains sulfonamides.*

If her little sister took this medicine, she could go into anaphylactic shock. Terror rose in the girl's throat. When she stepped out of the pharmacy, there was the doctor buying tulips at the flower stall.

"I *told* you!" Imogen shouted. "I was *very clear*! This is ridiculous! *You could have killed my little sister!*"

IMOGEN

FOR A MOMENT, I knew everything. Not just the events unfolding in Oscar's memories but the places, the names, the reasons behind it all.

OSCAR

I KNEW EVERYTHING about Imogen for that moment too. I never get angry, but that's exactly what I was.

"Listen to me, Imogen," I said, the memories dissolving, and my angry voice sounding strange to me. It was deeper than my usual voice, which I liked—although then it kind of squeaked on some syllables, which I didn't like. "Imogen, your parents have let you do all the work of looking after your little sisters. Even if they've started paying attention *now*, you've always had way too much responsibility. And you still have! You're still taking

Astrid to the doctor! It's been overwhelming for you. You don't have a temper, Imogen, you have *anxiety*! And no *wonder*. I mean, Imogen, who's been looking after *you*?"

IMOGEN

"OSCAR," I SAID, falling back into the present with an ice-cold calm. "You're not *useless* or a *waste of space*. How dare a teacher say that to you! Who cares that her little boy can carry a bucket of water across a lawn? He probably enjoys it. Four-year-olds are easily amused.

"More to the point, you're not *useless*, Oscar, you have concentration issues. My friend Djuna at school has that too. She's worse when she hasn't had enough sleep or isn't eating properly, you know. But the people who should be helping you, and making sure you get enough sleep and proper food? They're not even there. Your mother's gone off to the Kingdom of Byron, and your stepfather goes surfing and visiting his girlfriend. He leaves you alone all night, Oscar, and you're only twelve years old. You should *not* be alone all night. You're making your own food. Packaged noodles in boiling water. *Not nutritious.* Your stepfather doesn't take you to *school.* You get yourself there. And when the school contacts him about you missing school, he sends messages pretending he dropped you there. He *pretends* he's being a good father, and the school believes him. So, who's looking after *you*, Oscar?"

Oscar was shaking his head. "Nah," he began. "It's all good . . ."

And he was away again, being "chill" and "all good." I looked across at the others, still on the blanket, utterly silent. Their heads had been swinging back and forth between us as if they were watching a table tennis match. The whole thing must have been pretty confusing to them, as they weren't seeing the memories.

"What I want to know is this," I said, turning back to Oscar. "Why is your mother, in her letter, so upset about not being with you for your birthday? Isn't it *your* birthday and not hers? Shouldn't *you* be the one who's upset?"

He burst into tears then. It really caught him by surprise. Proper, angry, hurting sobs that made my heart hurt.

I forced him to let me hug him.

Even between sobs, though, he was still trying to tell me that it wasn't fair on me, that I had too much responsibility.

"Well," I said, holding him tight. "It would be nice if the adults said *thank you* now and then." I noticed there were tears on my face too, but mostly they were for Oscar.

What a thing.

CHAPTER 77

OSCAR

 **A LOUDSPEAKER CRACKLED,** making us jump, and a voice announced: "All passengers, attention please. The one A.M. train to Yellowspot has been canceled. I repeat, the one A.M. to Yellowspot is *canceled*."

There was total silence. Imogen and I wiped our eyes and looked at the others.

"I'm going to see Ronaldo again and find out what's happening," Bronte announced. Alejandro joined her.

They were back a few minutes later with the news that there were no more trains to Yellowspot that night.

Imogen was very calm, considering.

She opened her map on the picnic blanket. Everyone fell quiet, studying it. Gruffudd woke, sat up in his hatbox bed, and asked why his "questing servants" were so silent.

"It's disturbing my sleep," he said, "all this quiet. Please commence another argument at once."

Imogen explained that the train had been canceled, assuring him that we were not giving up—we would find another way—and we all braced for his temper tantrum.

That was the moment when I knew for certain we weren't going to make it.

It was the features on Gruffudd's little face. They seemed to sink slowly, like a sandcastle close to the shore washed away one wave at a time. He didn't cry or scream, complain or protest, he just sat there, slowly sinking.

I mean, I'd already been privately thinking that a key with a missing piece would never work, but I'd assumed we'd at least *get* there in time.

You must fly, said a voice in my head. *You must fly to the Elven city.*

"Yes, this I know," Alejandro said. "And I *would* fly to the Elven city if only there were a train to take us there."

That was confusing.

Alejandro had answered the voice in my head.

You must fly! You must fly! You must fly! Fly to the Elven city.

Now the voice in my head was *bzzzzz*ing, and *fzzzzz*ing. Vibrating like an old roller-coaster carriage climbing the rails. *You must fly! You must fly!* A gentle, almost pleasant tremble one moment, a wild shudder the next. It reminded me a lot of—

"The Fizzes!" Bronte said.

I realized the others were all wriggling and squirming while muttering, "I *know* we must fly!"

All of us were hearing the same thing.

Then Esther exclaimed: "It's the picnic blanket! It's full of bright magic! It's talking to us!"

It still looked like a regular blanket to me, so I guess that was her super sensitive vision kicking in.

"How did I not see that before?" she cried.

It was hidden, said the voice in my head—and I guess in everyone else's heads. *Hidden until you were in harmony.*

"You mean until we stopped arguing?"

Exactly. Yes. Fly to the Elven city! Fly!

"But . . ." Esther shook her head. "*How?*" And then, her voice coming out like a gasp: "Wait, do you mean this is a *flying* blanket?"

Yes! Yes! Shall we fly?

Then there was a sound like *pffffft,* and the blanket, along with all of us and our luggage—well, it shot up into the air.

CHAPTER 78

IMOGEN

I NEARLY FELL off.

I was close to the edge, and I tumbled sideways in shock, several packs sliding with me. The edges of the blanket curled themselves up sharply with another sucking sound—*pffft*—and caught me

We all tipped about for a bit, crashing into each other, grabbing at bags, and at Gruffudd's hatbox, and generally shrieking. We were rocketing along just above the platform, the wind tearing at our hair, into the tunnel, out into the vast station hall, where the blanket, possibly excited to have more height, zoomed up into the rafters and frightened some pigeons.

It darted sideways, as if the pigeons had frightened *it*, and paused, hovering alongside a stained-glass window. I think it was admiring the pattern.

"OI?" called a voice.

I peeked over the edge and then scuffled back toward the center of the blanket in terror. We were extremely high.

"OI! WHAT'S GOING ON UP THERE?"

It was Ronaldo, standing outside his Inquiries office. He looked like a doll.

Nobody answered. Most of us were still untangling ourselves and catching our breath.

Fly? Fly to the Elven city of Dun-sorey-lo-vay-lo-hey?

The blanket was talking in our heads again. A sort of sizzling sound, it made.

"That would be lovely, thank you," Bronte replied aloud.

"It *would*," I added quickly. "*Enormously* helpful. However, I wonder if we could drop by the Doom Lantern Witches on the way, and pick up a piece of a key?"

The blanket wobbled back and forth, as if it was shaking its head.

To the Elven city of Dun-sorey-lo-vay-lo-hey, it said. *I am embedded with directions to the Elven city of Dun-sorey-lo-vay-lo-hey.*

"I have a map," I offered. "I could tell you how to—"

Another wobble from the blanket.

I am spelled to bring you to the Elven city of Dun-sorey-lo-vay-lo-hey, it said. *To clarify.*

"Yes, that's great, but perhaps we could—"

Take it or leave it.

"Take it!" Gruffudd shouted. "TAKE IT! TAKE IT! LET US GO TO MY HOME! LET US FLY THERE! OH, BLANKET! THANK YOU! TAKE IT, IMOGEN!"

His little face was vibrant with color again.

"Ah well," I said. "Hopefully the key will still work with eight pieces. That's *most* of a key, after all. All right, blanket. Thank you ever so much. We'd love to go to the Elven city of Dun-sorey-lo-vay-lo-hey."

And we plummeted—shrieking again—down, down, down to the station entrance, tilted at an extremely precarious angle— all of us sliding down in a rush and being caught by a firm curl of blanket—out into the lamplit street and—

SWOOOOOOOOOOOOOOP . . . up, up into the clouds.

CHAPTER 79

OSCAR

ONCE THE BLANKET had its flight path sorted, it settled into a smooth cruising altitude. The edges stayed curved up enough to make you feel like you wouldn't forget where you were and roll right off, yet still flat enough that you could see the landscape below.

The wind had a bite to it, and Imogen found the sleeping-bags and handed them around. We were cozy, warm, smiling around at each other—and *flying on a blanket*.

I admit, I spent most of that flight thinking this: *I'm flying on a blanket*. Over and over. *I'm flying on a blanket*. Grinning my head off, leaning over the edge to watch the city lights below, and then the forests, the countryside, the winding roads and rivers—sometimes laughing out loud. You could feel the occasional breeze ruffle your hair like it was a friendly uncle. You could stretch out and gaze up at the stars and it was like they were scattered, not over the sky, but over *you*.

I felt strangely light after breaking down with Imogen too—I mean, it wasn't just that I'd cried. It was that she'd seen all my memories clearly. It didn't feel like an invasion. It felt like she'd taken ahold of the memories for me so it was less for me to carry on my own.

I also felt *stronger* than I had because I was holding some of *her* memories, if you see what I mean. On my own issues, I'm usually pretty chill, but thinking about her, and how much she'd always had to do, I felt this surge of something *real* and *concrete* in my veins. It was good.

The others seemed pretty happy too, and we floated along with the faintest ripples of turbulence. Imogen, Alejandro, and Bronte spread out the pieces of the key between them and worked quietly in the moonlight, trying to fix them together into a key shape. Gruffudd sat up in his hatbox, his arms wrapped around his knees, watching them and calling out now and then, "Yes! Yes! That looks right!" And then, "Hmm, no. Maybe not. Try again, servants of the quest!"

Esther and Astrid talked softly. Esther was suggesting that Astrid should post back all the objects she'd taken, along with apology notes, and Astrid was agreeing.

"Although would the Sterling Silver Fox really need that old screw I found on the floor of his shop?" she wondered.

Esther said that you never knew, it might be the screw that holds his favorite glasses together. He might be delighted to see it again.

Still, she added, he'd probably prefer his necklace back. It was a shame Astrid hadn't stolen that.

Then they got into a quiet discussion about whether they should send back the Witches' sweaty sock.

"It's quite a nice sock," Astrid admitted. "It's fluffy and has a crisscrossed pink and purple pattern."

"So it might be a favorite of one of the Witches," Esther reasoned. "Does a Doom Lantern Witch deserve to have a favorite sock returned?"

"Not at all!" Gruffudd piped up. "The terror I felt when they chased us through the forest *far* surpassed anything I have felt when encountering rats twice my size in meadows! Remember how they shouted about the sharpness of their brooms?" He gave a little shudder. "No, don't return it. Ah, brilliant work, Imogen, you've composed a perfect key—that's exactly the— Oh. No. Doesn't work at all. You try, Bronte."

Esther and Astrid's conversation resumed. Back and forth they went—not arguing or getting impatient, just turning over the ethics of Witches' old socks.

Generally, everyone seemed happy not to be sitting on a train platform waiting for a nonexistent train, and it might have been a perfect trip, except for one thing: a piece of the key was still missing.

I couldn't get this out of my head. Based on my knowledge of quests—taken from video games, movies, and books—it's never any use to *almost* get it right. Quests are like tests where it's 100 percent or fail.

Also, based on my understanding of how keys work, they need all their parts.

Alejandro must have been thinking the same thing because he suddenly announced that he was going to *make* the missing key piece. He found his little travel toolbox, clunked it open, and started riffling through it. I offered him my skate tool, and he said, "This looks perfect! I believe it will help!" That might just have been politeness.

Great that he was trying, but how could he know what the piece looked like? And what exactly was he going to find in the toolbox that he could turn into a key? He didn't have a welding torch, did he?

Imogen and Bronte kept clinking bits of keys together and changing their minds, Gruffudd kept calling out encouragement, and Esther and Astrid were still on about the Witches' sock. Astrid seemed to have settled on returning the sock, mainly because she was worried that the sock's owner would be so cranky without it, they'd go on a shadow spell rampage.

"Of course, those Doom Lantern Witches seem to do that anyway," Esther pointed out. "If only there was a way . . ."

She stopped suddenly. The moonlight glinted in her eyes.

"I wonder if I could . . ." she said. "If I . . . But only if . . . Still, it could . . ."

"Finish a sentence, Esther," Imogen advised—fairly kindly.

"I don't know if this will work or not, but I have an idea," Esther said in a rush. "What if I could put one of my healing spells *into* the sock? And *then* return it? So that, if the Witch was wearing the sock when they cast a shadow spell there'd be an inbuilt cure right there."

OSCAR *from* ELSEWHERE

"Could you *do* that?" Bronte wondered.

"I don't know. I could *try?*"

"Could you put a curing spell in it that somehow spread to the *other* Witches' socks?" Imogen suggested. "One that infected *all* of the Witches' clothes in the laundry hamper even? So their shadow magic *always* had inbuilt cures when they wore those clothes?"

"I don't know!" Esther repeated. "I could *try!*"

Everyone exclaimed that she *should* try, and Astrid was keen for her to try *at once!*

"Let me get the sock for you!" she offered, crawling around, making the blanket bump slightly, searching for her pack.

"This idea? It is genius," Alejandro told Esther, still rummaging around in his toolbox. "You are genius, Esther. Ah, what about this?" He had found a little tube in the toolbox. "This, it is a kind of putty that I use to repair holes and leaks and so on. If I could *mold* it into the right shape, maybe it would slot into place?"

"Yes, yes! That's *genius!*" everyone enthused, and it was like everything was suddenly working out—falling into place.

And then:

"Oh, that won't work," Gruffudd said, distractedly. "That tube, Alejandro? Putty or whatever it is? No use at all. The key to save the Elven city must be made up of all nine true pieces. Otherwise it won't work. Keep at it, Imogen and Bronte, those two bits seemed just right together! Yes, that's it— Wait, why are you stopping?"

A silence fell over the blanket. Imogen and Bronte turned to Gruffudd. Alejandro let the putty slide back into the toolbox.

I knew it, I thought.

Without the usual cheerful feeling you get when you're right.

"The key only works with all nine pieces?" Imogen said slowly.

"Yes, yes." Gruffudd nodded, still distracted. "Keep going, Imogen, I'm sure those two bits fit! But yes, of *course* the key only works with nine pieces! It's a magical quest. You can't just *fashion* things out of bits of mud and bark! You need every original part from the nine key keepers! Anyway, on you go."

The only person not staring at him was Astrid, who was still rummaging in her pack, and who now cried: "Oh, here it is! I found the sock! Ooh. It's sweaty!"

"Hush, Astrid," Imogen murmured. "Something important is—"

Astrid was still talking. "Perhaps you should use your Rain Weaving to *wash* it before you try to spell it, Esther? It's so dirty it's actually *heavy*! Look, feel it—oh, wait there's something—"

She tipped the sock upside down, shook it—

—and out fell the ninth piece of key.

CHAPTER 80

IMOGEN

IT WAS EXACTLY like a surprise party.

A sudden roar of cheers and shouts. Astonished disbelief. Intense delight.

That knobbly little silver stick shining in the moonlight on Astrid's outstretched palm!

We shouted with laughter until we cried. It was all a bit hysterical, to be honest. I think it was how startled we were, and how relieved and how the key was inside a smelly sock.

"Of *course!*" Esther sobbed, wrung out with laughter. "Remember, Oscar and Astrid? Remember we overheard that Witch saying there was no way we could have found the key? Because it was in a "special place"? In a dirty sock, they meant! In their laundry hamper!"

We hooted and yowled until the blanket murmured, *Hush now. Hush now, you'll wake the sleeping children in the cottages below.*

The blanket flew higher, I suppose to avoid that.

We settled down, but we kept yelping accidentally.

"I suppose the lesson here," Bronte said, "is that stealing is actually a really sensible thing to do."

The others shouted with laughter again and the blanket quietly sighed. (To Astrid, I murmured, "That's *not* the lesson. To be clear.")

It was late though, and the screaming and laughing wore us

out. We sat in a circle and passed the ninth piece around, staring at it in wonder, turning it over and over on our palms. Gruffudd asked for us to place it in his hatbox so he could also gaze at it. It reached up past his knees. He leaned over and stroked it lovingly.

"Who wants first turn putting the key together?" I asked, and Astrid raised her hand.

After that, we all grew quiet. There was the *chink-clunk, chink-clunk* as Astrid pressed pieces together then changed her mind and pulled them apart. ("It's still too curvy," she said, "even with this new little straight piece!" But she carried on happily.) Esther, meanwhile, was weaving her hands in slow loops and circles over the Witch's sock. Alejandro, watching her, murmured that the tricky thing would be returning the sock to the Witches without their getting suspicious about *why* we had returned it. That was a good point.

I myself relaxed on the blanket and enjoyed the flight. I have flown on a dragon before—Bronte has dragon friends and invited us—and I loved the heat and strength of its body, the surge of its wingspan, and the bursts of steam from its mouth. I missed that a bit now. On the other hand, this was more relaxing—there was no risk at all that the blanket would grow hungry and eat us.

The blanket was softer too, and had room for us all to stretch out, as well as our luggage. It whooshed along at a steady speed, occasionally slowing to catch an updraft. Stars were sprinkled around us, and sometimes birds soared by in formation. It was a clear night, although sometimes we flew through the soft dampness of a cloud. The skin on my hands and face felt dewy when that happened.

We were following the river, a rich black road that glinted, seeming to turn itself over with sparkles. The moon glowed softly on fields, and the landscape was pillowy beneath us, squat little houses resting on crests and in valleys. We drifted low, and I saw a man in a nightcap and pajamas crossing his lawn in bare feet. Most windows were dark, but behind some we saw golden lamplight, or silhouettes gazing into the night.

(If I'm getting too descriptive, that is the fault of flight by blanket. It's very good.)

I lay back and stared up at the stars. Everything was going to be all right now. We had all nine pieces of the key. We would arrive in time. Esther would weave a spell into the sock, and that would ripple out to the Witches' other socks, curing any of the Witches' victims. That made me especially glad. I thought of that little family, gripped by fever, shaking and foaming at the mouth. I thought of Astrid and the fear in her eyes as she described the Witches chasing her and the others with sharpened broomsticks. The Witches had boasted about their sharp brooms, Gruffudd had just—

"Gruffudd," I said, sitting up abruptly. "You weren't *with* the others when they ran from the Witches. You were with us."

Gruffudd scrambled to his feet and put his teeny hands on his hips. "I *was so* there when the Witches were chasing us!"

"Actually, we were glad that you *weren't* with us," Astrid put in, studying the edge of a key piece. "We got thrown out into the river and almost drowned."

"I know!" Gruffudd spluttered. "I was *there*! *I* almost drowned too! I was deep inside your jacket pocket, Astrid, and I clung on and clung on as you were tossed this way and that, and water poured in and—"

I laughed. "None of that happened, Gruffudd! You were in the boat with us talking to the Water Sprite. Remember?"

An expression zipped across Gruffudd's face then, something like panic and guilt both at once. He blinked rapidly, rubbed his face with his hands.

"Ah, yes," he said. "I'm tired, you see. I must have imagined—"

"Gruffudd," I said, staring at him—and I don't know how I suddenly knew this, but it fell into my mind all at once like an apple falling from a tree into an outstretched hand. "Gruffudd, are there *two* of you?"

Gruffudd grinned at me. "Game's up!" he said. "You got us, Imogen! Well done! Come on out, Brother! It's time!"

And another little Elf boy, identical to Gruffudd, scrambled out from underneath a sleeping bag.

CHAPTER 81

OSCAR

I DON'T KNOW about you, but I've always found that *two* of anything has a strange effect.

Like one baby rolling by in a pram is cute, sure. You might glance sideways and think, *Cute,* or you might keep walking and ignore it.

But *two* babies, side by side, in matching little overalls, holding matching purple monkeys? Cutest thing ever. More than twice as cute. It's like *Oh, look at the pair of them!*

One snake on the path up ahead? You might get a bit of a fright, step back, and take a photo to show your friends. *Two* snakes though? That's like *Snakes everywhere!* More than twice as scary. *Run for your life!*

When Gruffudd turned into a pair, right before our eyes, it was kind of a combination of babies and snakes.

Super cute to have two tiny people jumping up and down on a flying picnic blanket, yet super creepy somehow—how many more Gruffudds could be hiding under backpacks, about to come squirming out and overrun the blanket?

"Gruffudd with a *u!*" said one and bowed.

"Gruffydd with a *y!*" said the other, also bowing.

They grinned at each other, then started bouncing on the spot again.

"We're twins! We tricked you! You didn't know, did you?"

None of us replied. We were all in too much shock. Of course we hadn't known.

"One of us always hid!"

"When the other was out!"

"We were *both* playing in the meadows when the Witches attacked our city!"

"Neither of us likes to go to school!"

"We *both* hid in Oscar's backpack!"

"I distracted Astrid so she fell off her bike!"

"I ran ahead and scattered thorns from the trees onto the road!"

"What did we do at the Radish Gnomes' cave?"

"Nothing—too scared. We ran away."

"Oh, that's right, and it was funny when we both had to sing about beauty at the Crystal Faeries' palace so we could get in!"

"Without them noticing!"

"And *I'm* the one who hid the food pack after we visited the Crystal Faeries' palace! It was so heavy! Took me hours to drag behind a rock!"

"*I'm* the one who deliberately stayed behind on the riverbank when you rowed away from Edward T. Vashing's film set!"

"Oh yes, that was a good one! Esther *did* pick me up! Exactly as she promised! And then *I* hid in Astrid's jacket pocket while my brother shouted from the shore and Bronte had to run back for him and you all blamed Esther! Brilliant!"

"And *I* took the map from Imogen's pocket so she wouldn't know which branch of the river to take! And dropped it on the floor of the boat so she'd see it *a moment* too late!"

Both Elves stopped bouncing to join hands and swing in a gleeful circle.

We were still staring, open-mouthed.

"I stayed hidden in Astrid's pocket the whole time you were with the Witches! I forgot just now that I'd done that! I've given it away!"

"Don't blame yourself!"

"Thanks!"

"No trouble!"

"We *both* stole the necklace from the Sterling Silver Fox! We knew that he would notice and chase you!"

"And he did!"

"He did!"

"I suppose we should send it back."

"I already did—zipped back and dropped it in his pocket when the Spellbinders stopped him!"

"Genius. *I* told Imogen that the train left from Platform Seven! It did *not* leave from Platform Seven!"

"No, it didn't!"

"Which meant they missed the train!"

More squeals and swinging in circles.

"And then *I* could say—quite honestly—that I *never said the train left from Platform Seven!* So Astrid believed me! Because I didn't!"

"No, you didn't! I did!"

More swinging in circles.

They paused and frowned at each other.

"Is that all?"

"I think it's all."

"We were so hungry though! Weren't we, Gruffudd? You lot seemed to think you only needed to feed one of us!"

"Well, we can't blame them for that, I suppose, Gruffydd."

"No."

"They thought there *was* only one of us!"

"Yes. True."

Both sat down, suddenly tired.

At this point, I have to say they struck me more as snakes than as babies.

Imogen was the first to speak. She kept her voice quite calm, considering.

"But . . . why?" she said. Excellent question. "Why would you do this? Pretend to be one person and make our quest so much more difficult?" She took a deep breath and held it together enough to say: "Don't you *want* your city to be saved?"

Right away they both popped up again. They nodded wildly.

"Of *course* we do!"

"You *must* set our city free!"

"You're our only hope! There are no other questers! The Witches put them all to sleep, remember?"

"Our *parents* are under that silver!"

"Our *grandparents*! Our *aunts*! Our *uncles*! Our *cousins*! Our *friends*!"

"Our *schoolteachers*!"

"Oh, well, that's less important."

"Yes, less important. True. But we don't want *a single Elf* getting crushed by the final silver wave!"

"You *must* save our city."

"We've been so worried!"

"Thinking you might fail!"

Imogen tried to speak and kept choking on her words.

Alejandro spoke up instead. "And yet . . ." he said significantly.

"Oh yes, and yet we have thwarted you at every turn on your quest!"

"Do you think at *every* turn, Gruffudd?"

"Perhaps not, Gruffydd. We could have done more."

"Still, we did our best!"

"We did!"

Another long pause.

"I think they want to know why."

"Yes. Let's tell them. It's like this."

"It was our *job*."

"We were given the special job—"

"—of zipping about between questers—"

"—thwarting them at every turn we could."

"Causing mischief—"

"—and discord!"

"We were so proud—"

"—to have that job."

"We got it on our first day of school."

"Because the teacher found us *impossible*."

"She told the King she'd found thwarters for the quest. The King came to see us and agreed. We were perfect."

"That's what we're called. *Thwarters.*"

"Lucky we were out in the meadows when the Witches came!"

"It meant we could do our job!"

"Our job was to thwart the questers—"

"But *we* were the only questers!"

"And you lot! Questing on our behalf! So we zipped between you."

"And thwarted, made mischief, and sowed discord."

"Exactly. Well put."

"Thank you."

They shook hands.

Imogen sighed. "This is about bright magic and its games, isn't it?"

"Yes." Both Elves turned to her and chanted together: "The more challenging a game, the better."

"What's the point in a quest if it's too easy?" one asked.

"No point," replied the other. "None at all."

Then they both climbed into the hatbox bed and lay down side by side.

"Anyhow, thwarting is hard work," said one, his eyes closed.

"We're very tired."

"And hungry."

"You've got the nine pieces now."

"All you have to do is . . . *yawn* . . . put them together."

"And get to the entrance of the city by ten A.M."

"The city entrance is exactly where you all were . . ."

"When you first came to the city . . ."

"On Monday morning . . ."

"On that laneway . . ."

"By the cow field . . ."

"Near where Oscar smashed into the fence . . ."

They both giggled.

"Yes . . ."

"Be there . . ."

"Ready to open the city . . ."

"With the key . . ."

Those last words faded and faded, and then both Elves were snoring.

"For crying out loud," said Astrid.

Nothing more to say.

CHAPTER 82

STILL OSCAR

WE SAT THERE looking at each other.

"I don't know whether to laugh or cry," Imogen admitted, and we all laughed, for some reason—grimly. Also softly, not wanting to wake the two Gruffudds and have them bouncing up and down again.

Astrid had given up trying to piece the key together and handed the job to Alejandro. He tried for a while, then passed the pieces to Bronte, who gave up and passed them to me.

The blanket wove through clouds, and I'll tell you what, uneasiness began weaving between us.

We were on our way to the city. We had all the pieces of the key.

And we couldn't fit them together.

Not so they made a key shape anyway, no matter how much we tried.

Nobody spoke this aloud, but I'm pretty sure it's what we were all thinking. *Clink, clink, clink.* I couldn't get anything close to a key and I'm generally pretty good with Lego and Ikea furniture.

Soon the clouds thickened, the moon disappeared, and the night was almost black.

"I cannot see the pieces," Alejandro said—it was his turn again. "And I am very tired."

Those five words seemed to set off a round of yawning. We realized we were *all* exhausted. Esther said she'd finished putting cures into the sock.

"Any Witch who wears this sock, or who wears an article of clothing that has come into contact with the sock, will cast shadow spells that are self-curing," she confirmed.

Everyone told her she was brilliant. "We have to be sure that the Witches accept it back without getting suspicious," Imogen said. "Let's sort that out later." She suggested we sleep and put the key together in the morning when the sun came out.

"Is that all right with you, picnic blanket?" she checked. "If we all fall asleep?"

That's how polite these kids were.

Yessss. Of course. I will bring you to the Elven city of Dunsorey-lo-vay-lo-hey before ten. I will keep my edges curved so nobody falls. Sweet dreams.

So the picnic blanket was even politer.

I think I fell asleep before I'd even closed my eyes, if that's possible.

I can't remember lying down, I can only remember drifting in and out of the darkness. Opening my eyes, seeing stars, and smiling. *I'm sleeping in the stars.* Wisps of cloud running across my fingertips.

Then the deepest sleep hit me. Or maybe I hit it. We slammed into each other, anyway, me and this deep, deep sleep.

It was like a snap of the fingers and *bam!* I was gone.

* * *

A long time later, I half-woke, but didn't open my eyes.

I could feel sunshine on my face, and sense light speckling my eyelids. Some of the others were awake, and I could hear them murmuring. A faint and rhythmic *clink-clunk, clink-clunk* as somebody tried to make a key. I dozed in the distant sounds of morning rising from below. A crackling like someone breaking toffee. A creaking like an old rocking chair. Wind rustling trees. A train horn. Birdsong.

Clink-clunk, clink-clunk, clink-clunk.

The rhythm was lulling me to sleep again. Pieces of thoughts floated with me.

The strangest days. The trickiest trip. One Elf splits into two Elves. One river splits into two branches. A single red hair on a path. *Not* the redheaded teacher, but a girl with a skipping rope. Clues in letters on a sign. Waverley East Nature School. West East North South. A twitchy map. A cryptic crossword.

A murder trial where the victim stands up the back taking photographs.

You find it when you're happy, you find it when you're sad.

A Sterling Silver Fox selling jewelry. A blanket that flies, hidden until—

The wind blew like a flute through my thoughts. The girls' voices rose and fell like tunes.

My thoughts sang along with the birds.

This tricky, tricksy trip. Nothing is what it seems.

Fragments of ideas. Fragments of keys. Fragments of skipping songs.

You find it in the morning, you find it in the night.

A key in pieces.

Distant songs.

And if you don't find it . . .

A lost key. A broken key.

A blanket that flies, hidden until—

Hidden until you find harmony.

And if you don't find it—

Nothing is what it seems.

You find it in the summer, you find it in the spring.

It's everywhere.

You find it everywhere.

The key to—

I sat up so fast everything spun.

"Music!" I said. "What if it's a *musical* key?"

CHAPTER 83

IMOGEN

I THOUGHT HE was sleep-talking and ignored him.

In the distance, a silver mountain was surging up out of the green.

"What mountain is that?" I wondered.

"Not a mountain," Bronte replied, sorting through key pieces—*clink-clunk, clink-clunk.*

Not a mountain? What else could—

"It's *not*," I breathed.

Alejandro was staring too. "It is," he said, nodding slowly.

The silver waves had accumulated, piling up and up and up. The Elven city of Dun-sorey-lo-vay-lo-hey was buried beneath a mountain.

"Music!" Oscar repeated. "It could be a *musical* key!"

He sounded so emphatic that I felt shot through by excitement. Even though he made no sense.

"You mean it's a key that plays music?" Esther seemed doubtful.

"No, I mean the answer might *be* music." Oscar was grinning and rubbing his eyes. "Music is played in a certain key. Can we make the key into a letter?"

"Any letter of the alphabet?" Alejandro asked.

Bronte shook her head. "Not any letter," she said. "If Oscar is right, it would be from A to G. Those are the only musical keys and . . . And these are all so curvy, so maybe . . . C?"

A rapid *ca-clink, ca-clink, ca-clink,* and she held up a perfect letter *C.*

"You've missed a piece," Astrid told her. "The ninth piece—the little straight one. Here."

She added the final piece and there it was:

G.

"It looks right," Bronte said, studying it. "But a musical key is more than a letter, isn't it? It has to be major or minor?"

"Of course." My own piano lessons were coming back to me. "A piece could be in the key of E flat minor, say. How would we know?"

"You already do know!" a voice exclaimed.

"The clues were on the quest!" another agreed.

The Elf twins were awake. They were standing at the side of their hatbox, grinning at us.

"You've done it!" one said.

"Or almost!" said the other.

"So it *is* supposed to be a musical key?" we asked, and the twins nodded. "Of course!"

"Only you had to work that out for yourselves. We couldn't tell you."

It seemed as if I could hear *all* our hearts begin to beat at high speed.

"So we also have to work out if it's major or minor? And whether there's a sharp or flat—or neither?" I checked. "And the clues were on the quest?"

Again, the twins inclined their heads.

"The clue magic is triggered whenever a quester comes within range of a key keeper. Sometimes the key keeper—or people around the key keeper—find themselves speaking the clue aloud! They don't even realize they're doing it! The questers are meant to watch out for clues while they're with or near each key keeper."

Very well. We studied one another. *We already know. The clues were on the quest.*

At exactly the same time, two things happened.

Alejandro murmured: "Remember the Radish Gnomes? As

soon as we mentioned the key, they started talking about the *minor* issue of getting into their cave without suffering *minor* damage. I remember I thought: *I did not know Radish Gnomes were sarcastic!* Could that be a clue that it is a minor key?"

At the same time, Astrid said: "When we were hiding in the tree, the Witches suddenly started shouting about how *sharp* their brooms were. As sharp as razors, as sharp as the venom of a death adder, as sharp as the teeth of the tiger shark. They did that the moment they realized we might be looking for the key. Does that mean it's a sharp key?"

It took a few moments for us to untangle Alejandro's and Astrid's words from each other, but eventually we did.

"So the answer is G-sharp minor?" I asked, in a wondering sort of voice.

We looked at the Elf twins, who bounced up and down on the spot, grinning, and then we looked at the G in Bronte's hand.

"G-sharp minor?" she said—and the G glowed brightly, gave a sort of descending shiver, and became perfectly smooth.

All the cracks where the joins were had gone.

It was a solid G.

We gasped and began cheering and applauding. This was it! Oscar had been right! We all slapped his back or ruffled his hair, to express our congratulations. It was the key of G-sharp minor!

That would unlock the city!

Only . . .

"How will you use it, Gruffudd?" I asked. "And Gruffydd? I mean, do you just go to the entrance to the city and hold up this G at ten o'clock? And shout *G-sharp minor*? Which of you will do it? Or both of you? The Elf that does it becomes king, right? So which of you . . . and will you be able to *carry* it?"

Bronte handed it to me, and I hefted the weight of the G. It was over twice as big as an Elf.

The twins chuckled at my questions, and then, when they realized I'd been serious, one asked: "Do you really not know?"

"Well," Esther said, her voice a little acidic, "we've never helped save an Elven city before."

"You already figured out that the answer is music!" one Elf crowed.

"So you *know* the answer!"

We all looked at them. "You mean, you'll need to . . . sing a song?" I tried. "A song in G-sharp minor?"

The Elves applauded. "Exactly!"

All six of us sighed with relief and leaned back on the blanket. It was 9:44 A.M. and all we had to do was deliver the Elves to the city so they could sing their song in G-sharp minor. They hadn't replied to my question about which of them would do it, and become king—both were surely too young for that anyway—but I supposed that was up to them to sort out.

We had done our job.

The blanket sailed through the morning blue at a steady pace. The silver mountain gleamed and glinted in the sunlight, its texture becoming clearer. It was not like a structure that had been smoothed down, that's for sure. Instead, it was an accumulation of waves, one after the other, crisscrossing at various angles. As a result, there were ridges, some thick like cement blocks, others long and fine like sheer vertical rails. There were clefts, curves, and indentations. In places there even appeared to be short staircases etched into the surface, and elsewhere holes had been gouged out as if by an ice cream scoop.

"Of course," one of the Elves piped up, "we'll need to know the tune."

"And the lyrics," said the other. "We'll need the lyrics."

"And the time signature."

"Oh, for crying out loud." Astrid sighed once again.

CHAPTER 84

STILL IMOGEN

"WHAT DO YOU mean, you need to know the tune and the lyrics and the time signature?" I asked, as patiently as I could.

"*We* don't know what they are," the Elves said in unison. "But you do!"

Alejandro rubbed his palm over his face. "This? These are *more* puzzles for us to solve?"

The twins smiled at him. "The final test. The clues were on the quest."

"You should have told us at the start of the quest there'd be a test at the end," Esther observed. "We would have paid closer attention."

"And taken notes," Astrid suggested.

The twins giggled. "Hurry," they said. "There's not much time."

I frowned at my watch. "Thirteen minutes."

Automatically, we all turned to check the silver mountain again. It drew inexorably closer, seeming to grow more immense and foreboding as it did. That was just a question of perspective, of course. Still.

"All right, everyone," I said. "A melody. Did we hear any tunes on our quest?"

"It might not have been the tune itself," Gruffudd—or Gruffydd—said quickly.

"It could have been the *notes*," his twin added.

"A string of random letters," the first Gruffudd suggested. "Perhaps it looked or sounded like a curious word? Or even a curious set of words?"

"That might have been too generous a clue," they both muttered.

"Ah, well. Time is—"

"—running out."

"They'd better hurry."

"Or our city—"

"—will be crushed."

Both Elves were peering at the mountain themselves now, their voices growing softer and more anxious.

Esther's eyes widened. "The Crystal Faery palace!" she cried. "There was a strange word hung up on the wall there! Was that a string of random letters? Wait, I remember it! AFEEBA!"

Bronte tugged at her ears. "The Water Sprite," she murmured. "Remember how she said something like *be a cad, be a cad*? Over and over? Could that have been the letters? Like B-E-A-C-A-D?"

Astrid giggled suddenly. "What about the Fizzes?" she said. "Remember that strange wailing they did and the letters strung themselves up inside our minds? AEEEEEBA."

I pulled out a notebook and pencil from my pack and wrote down the letters:

AFEEBA

BEACAD

AEEEEEBA

"Those *could* all be notes," I mused, "but we might have missed—"

"They could! They could! They *are*! That's them!" the Elves were shouting over their shoulders as they watched the mountain. "Quick, figure out the lyrics!" They were scuttling close to the blanket's edge, where they threw themselves onto their stomachs and carried on watching intently.

Words?

What song lyrics had we heard on our journey?

There had been the skipping chants, of course. Was that it? Or too obvious?

"Just a few words," an Elf called back.

"Three lines," his twin added.

"That's all you need."

"Think of three lines! Hurry!"

"Ten minutes," Alejandro interjected.

A long pause. My eyes caught Oscar's. We both shrugged helplessly.

"Perhaps a line that rhymed!" a twin urged.

"Some internal repetition!" the other added.

"That silver mountain is so *high*," Astrid breathed. "It practically touches the sky."

Alejandro grinned suddenly. "At the school," he said. "The little girl—Sharmilla. When I was on the roof fetching the ball for her, she said, *You're so high! Touch the sky!* And the other children laughed and copied her. I remember it seemed strange at the time."

"That's the way," the Elves called. "That's it! Write that down!"

I did.

"Anything else like that?" the Elves demanded.

"When we were on the film set," I recalled. "Edward T. Vashing kept telling the actors something before each take. What was it?"

"*Make me sigh! Make me cry!*" Alejandro recited. "And the actors? They laughed and copied it."

"Write it down!" the twins ordered.

"The third one must be the judge," Bronte remembered. "He told the audience: *Melt away! Melt away! Away!* And the lawyers repeated *that*. Is that it, Gruffudd and Gruffydd?"

"Of course it is! Write it *down*!"

I was scribbling furiously.

"Nine minutes," Alejandro said. "What's the other thing we need?"

The mountain was looming, its surface etched with whirls, bumps, jagged lines, and shapes. At its base, crowds stretched out into the fields, scattered across the ground like spring blossoms after a storm.

We could hear them now—the buzz of conversation, tinny little snatches of music, sudden roars, and bursts of applause, like a radio playing in another room.

"Time signature," an Elf said briskly.

"Like a fraction," his twin agreed.

"Four over four, say. Two over four."

"Come on. Come on." Tiny fingers clicked at us.

"Think. Think. Come on."

"On the window of the Sterling Silver Fox's jewelry shop," Oscar suggested, "it said ¾ over and over. I thought it was to do with the price of—"

"Who cares what you thought?" the Elves cried. "That's perfect! That's the answer! Write it down!"

"Write it down!"

"Have you written it?"

"Good! Give it here!"

"Seven minutes," Bronte breathed.

Gently, we bumped against the side of the mountain. I handed the torn sheet to the Elf twins.

A F E E B A

You're so high! Touch the sky!

B E A C A D

Make me sigh! Make me cry!

A E E E E E B A

Melt away! Melt away! Away!

The Elves studied the paper together.

"G-sharp minor?" one checked.

The other nodded.

They both began to sing.

"They know how the tune works just from seeing it on paper?" Astrid asked, surprised.

"How do they know if it's bass or treble clef?" Imogen whispered.

"We've *Elves*," the Elves snapped. "Music in our *fingers* and *toes*!"

Then they sang it again.

They sang it three times, very sweetly and crisply. It had a rhythm like a waltz and a strange, mournful tune, but it stuck in your head—in all our heads.

Three more times they sang it.

"You've got it?" one asked.

"Yes. You?"

"You bet."

They crumpled the paper.

"Right," they said. "The quest is complete."

The blanket bumped against the side of the mountain again, and then, very surprisingly, it swooped *up* higher, higher and higher still, to the crest, where it hovered over the flat surface and—gently and gracefully—landed.

CHAPTER 85

OSCAR

THERE WAS A fairly lengthy silence. The mountain didn't have a pointy peak, by the way. Its top seemed to have been patted down, leaving a flat surface the size of a small living room.

The sun was warm, the sky blue, and we were about five stories high on a giant splat of silver. Behind us, the silver ended abruptly in one long, sharp line, like a cliff edge. That gave way to a sheer drop—I backed away from that, after checking it out, onto the blanket again.

In front of us, the silver sloped gently for a bit then turned into a mess: some parts fell straight down, almost vertical; others were littered with ridges, ledges, sharp protrusions, indentations, curvy bumps, all the way down to the base—where another smooth slope eventually flattened off.

People were lined up all along the laneway, in both directions, sitting or climbing along the fence, and swarming the fields behind it. Acrobats, dancers, jugglers, clowns, and musicians performed. Children sat on the shoulders of adults to see. Adults poured glasses of wine for one another.

Cows had retreated to far corners.

The only clear space down below was a wooden podium, or lectern I guess, which stood in the laneway facing the silver. It had a slanted desk at the top, like it was ready for someone to read out a speech. Red velvet ropes cordoned this off from the crowd.

"Do you know what that's for, Gruffudd and Gruffydd?" Imogen asked curiously.

"It's where the song must be sung," both Elves told her. "That's right at the entrance to the city. Someone with knowledge has kindly set it up. Singing the song from up here would never work," they added.

Gradually, people below began noticing us and calling to each other to "hush up and look." The acrobats and dancers paused. Jugglers caught hold of their whizzing batons. Music stopped abruptly, and the crowd noise fell to a low murmur and then to a silence. Faces tilted toward us.

I felt pretty awkward. It was like a huge audience was waiting for us to perform and all we were doing was sitting around having a picnic.

"How should we get down there?" one Elf asked politely. The pair stood at the edge of the blanket, holding hands.

"Ah, excuse me? Picnic blanket?" Imogen cleared her throat. "Would you be so kind as to fly us down to the base of the mountain?"

The quest is complete, the blanket replied.

"Well, not really." Astrid tried to keep her voice on the right side of impatient. "The Elves need to be down there, and it looks dangerous to climb."

Impossible to climb, the rest of us agreed, all talking at once. Too sheer, too slippery, too steep.

"You would need climbing equipment," Alejandro added.

Elves can fly. My task is done, my magic gone—as the voice spoke that final word—*gone*—there was a shivery rush across my mind and then a sudden emptiness.

"It *is* gone," Esther said. "It's a regular picnic blanket now. Sad! But the blanket was right! Elves *can* fly. They just need to cast the spell for flight. It's a difficult one though, and it's usually only experienced Elves who cast it. You don't happen to know how to do the spell, twins?"

"Of course!" both Elves replied, a bit huffily.

"Six minutes until ten," Imogen murmured. "Could you do it fast?"

Their teeny hands rose, their teeny tiny fingers wiggled. It was like they were sewing *teeny teeny* stitches in the air.

Thirty seconds went by.

"Done!" they both exclaimed.

"I was faster," one said.

"No, me," said the other.

"You finished at the same time!" Imogen wailed. "Get down there and set your city free!"

The Elves floated into the air and hovered about eye height.

"You know," began one.

"I agree," said the other.

And you know what they did?

They swooped up and flew over our heads, *away* from the crowd, *away* from the podium, *in the completely wrong direction.*

"We miss the meadows!" one called, flying backward.

"That was hard work sewing that spell!" the other noted.

"Time for us to play!" the first declared. "We will fly to distant meadows!"

"COME BACK HERE THIS INSTANT!" Imogen bellowed. "YOUR CITY *NEEDS* YOU!"

The further they flew from us, the more their voices faded.

"Be sure and free our city!"

"Yes! That's vital!"

"Don't let our city be crushed!"

"Doesn't have to be an Elf!"

We were all still shouting, "HEY! COME *BACK!*" and "Are they *kidding*?" but they had shrunk to little specks in the distance.

That's when a close and furious howl pierced the air from the left: "YOU FOUND OUR PIECE OF THE KEY!"

And five Witches of the Doom Lantern Coven, each riding a sharpened broomstick, came rocketing toward us.

CHAPTER 86

IMOGEN

THEY LANDED WITH a crash, dismounted, and lined up, facing us. Their backs were to the cliff edge behind them. Fixing us with furious gazes, they held their brooms steady, the sharpened ends pointing down.

There were two men and three women, all middle-aged, and all dressed in loose slacks and linen shirts, strings of beads around their necks, socks and sandals on their feet. One carried a black cat on her shoulder, and this cat slithered down, stalked to the furthest corner of the silver, lay down, and fell asleep.

"You found our piece of the key," a bald Witch hissed, repeating the howl. "Now you will *pay*."

And all five raised their hands in sync, ready to perform broomstick crochet.

Instantly, Astrid burst into tears.

"Don't let them take the sock! Don't let them take it back!" she howled, grabbing wildly at the stolen Witch's sock and clutching it to her chest.

For a moment, this confused me. When had Astrid grown so attached to the smelly sock?

That's how convincing she was. It truly seemed as if the sock had become her most treasured possession.

Then two of the Witches lunged toward her and I realized

what she was doing—*oh, of course, you genius, Astrid*—at the same time I noticed that Bronte had lifted her hands into Spellbinding position. Beside her, Esther was doing the same.

Everything happened at dizzying speed then.

As one Witch lunged toward Astrid, my foot flew into the air and kicked the broom from his hand. Alejandro caught it and swung it sideways at the back of the Witch's knees, sending him sprawling.

The second Witch grasped at the sock and Astrid spun in place, tossing the sock to Oscar as she did. He caught it and ducked sideways. The Witch changed direction, lunging for him instead.

The three remaining Witches raised their brooms and, sure and steady, began the motions of broomstick crochet. Their eyes were fixed on Bronte, their mouths curved into sneers.

A Witch leapt toward Oscar, reaching for the sock, and I intercepted: *Jab, round kick.*

The Witch recovered fast, but I could see I had surprised him.

Out of the corner of my eye, I saw Bronte's hands move rapidly in the air. Beside her, Esther's hands moved too, more slowly and uncertainly than Bronte's.

Cross, hook, round kick.

Cross, hook, round kick.

"Oof," said a Witch, glaring at me. I squeezed my eyes tight, trying to remember my kickboxing routines.

The crocheting Witches held their brooms in their left hands and made a *loop, loop, up-and-over* motion with their right. I saw Esther falter, Bronte pick up speed.

A cry from Oscar.

He had curled over, shaking violently. A Witch danced around him, grabbing at the sock. He twisted, avoiding her, while his shaking intensified.

The shadow spell had escaped Bronte's and Esther's Spellbinding. It was taking effect.

Esther saw it too, and she turned in place, gesturing toward Oscar, her palms open, spinning in slow circles, curing him—his shivering stopped. He stumbled to his feet, relief flooding his face, curled his fist, and pounded the Witch hard in the man's solar plexus.

Esther turned back, rocking slightly.

It was too much for her—to heal and spellbind at the same time.

The crocheting Witches smiled grimly. I saw Bronte's foot stamping on the silver as her pace quickened, her eyes closing again.

Left foot, jab, jab, right hook, kick.

A sock-chasing Witch yowled with rage as my foot made contact with his knee.

Alejandro swiped the broom at his other knee. *Thud, thwack. Cross, switch kick.*

My foot connected with a Witch's nose.

Astrid and Oscar darted around, tossing the sock back and forth between them.

I heard Esther groan in frustration, drop her hands a moment, then raise them and bind again.

That's when I heard it.

A low and ominous roar.

Distant but growing—familiar.

The Witches also paused briefly—frowning.

And then, another sound, the sound of a crowd shouting as one:

"THIRTY!"

A pause.

The roaring grew.

Oscar and I glanced at each other.

"TWENTY-NINE!"

The crowd were counting.

Counting backward.

Twenty-nine seconds until—

Still the sound swelled, like a wind that stirs up drifts of dead leaves, or carries a rainstorm with it. A roar that seemed formed of thousands of individual pins of sound.

"Twenty-eight!"

"Twenty-seven!"

The last silver wave.

Behind the shoulders of the Witches, there it was. A distant haze, steadily growing.

"Twenty-six!"

"Twenty-five!"

The Witches saw it too.

One paused in her broomstick crochet and shouted: "Get that sock! Come on! We have to go!"

"*Shadow* them!" the other Witch bellowed back, in a fury. His nose was bleeding. "And we *will!*"

As one, the other three Witches resumed broomstick crochet at a dizzying speed. Their arms, their brooms, became a blur.

Bronte and Esther worked quicker and quicker, but the Witches were even faster.

A violent spasm grasped my stomach. How? I'd avoided all their strikes. I fell to the ground, clutching my sides, screaming. It was as if axes were hacking at me.

"GOOD!" shouted a Witch behind me, wrenching back his stolen broom from Alejandro. "It's working! Now shadow the others! Shadow them all!"

The shadow spell had worked on me.

Esther swung around, almost tripped, waved her arms in my direction—and I was free, back on my feet and

Jab, right hook, right crescent kick, right spinning back kick.

THUD, THUD, THUD, the power from my hips, the power from my belly, my fists guarding my cheekbones.

The Witches howled.

"Twenty-two!"

"Twenty-one!"

The crowd chant had grown even louder, competing with the monstrous racket of the wave.

Oscar and Astrid danced around, dodging the Witches, dodging my kicks and Alejandro's right hooks, tossing the sock back and forth.

Eventually a Witch would succeed. They'd intercept and grab the sock. The distraction would end. They'd join their friends in the broomstick crochet.

Bronte and Esther were barely holding off three Witches—but five of them?

From the corner of my eye I saw Bronte take Esther's hand and raise it in the air. Esther's eyes flew open and I saw horror on her face—how could they spellbind with one hand!—then I saw her comprehend.

Their hands began to move at precisely the same time.

They were binding as one.

I could feel their power surging through the air.

"Seventeen!"

"Sixteen!"

It was merging, interlinking; the crocheting Witches were slowing, glancing at one another in disbelief.

Alejandro saw it too. He glanced my way.

We took the chance, ducked around the sock-chasing Witches and—

Uppercut, right foot, jab, spinning back kick—

Knocked the broom from one Witch's hands; the other Witches gasped; Bronte and Esther pressed closer together, their hands still working as one—and the three Witches froze.

I caught Astrid's eye, and she *flung* the sock at just the right angle for a Witch to swipe it from the air.

"NO!!!!" Astrid's mouth opened in a long and extremely convincing wail—but the sound was swept away by the furious roar.

A wall of silver was closing in on us.

The Witch with the sock grinned gloatingly. "COME ON! I'VE GOT THE SOCK! SHADOW THEM ALL!" he bellowed.

The three Witches shook their heads at him, grim.

"Don't tell me they've *spellbound* you! *Two little girls!*"

Esther and Bronte still clutched hands, fixing the Witches in place, their power zipping back and forth between them.

"LET'S GET OUT OF HERE!" the Witch with the bleeding nose shouted. "THAT SILVER IS COMING!"

"YES! LEAVE THEM HERE TO BE CRUSHED!"

"ALONG WITH THE ELVES!"

And the three spellbound Witches nodded, cheering up, climbing onto their brooms—

With great bursts of laughter all five Witches rose and soared away, the sock safe in their clutches—
"Fifteen!"
"Fourteen!"
"Thirteen . . ."

CHAPTER 87

OSCAR

"TWELVE!"

"Eleven!"

Behind us, a wall of silver was hurtling in our direction.

In front of us, a crowd was shouting numbers.

I looked down at the surface of the mountain. Ridges and ledges, steep bits, raised bits, crooked bits.

First bit would be easy, I thought.

Ollie the 6-stair.

Quarterpipe.

Bluntslide.

Boardslide.

5-stair.

Lip grind.

Slide.

Halfpipe.

Wallride.

Crooked grind.

Stair set.

Transition.

Another stair set.

Carve—pole jam—quarterpipe—

—finish with a wheelslide.

The pipes would slow you *just* enough not to spin out of control.

Or would they?

Maybe?

Of course, one mistake and you'd be dead. Or most of your bones shattered.

I glanced behind me again.

That silver wave was like a giant unfolding roll of tinfoil.

Even in all that noise, the chanting of the crowd was clear and strong:

"Ten!"

"Nine!"

Grabbed my board and went for it.

CHAPTER 88

IMOGEN

THE WHEELS OF Oscar's board sounded like thunder. The shock of it dimmed the volume of the crowd's countdown below.

"Eight!"

He hit a ridge and *flew* through the air—he would surely crash! He'd be smashed to—*THWACK*—

"Seven!"

Wheels hit the surface and rolled again, Oscar with knees bent, steady—but again he was in the air, even higher! And higher! Soaring! This time there was no way he could safely—

"Six!"

The crowd's *six* rode on a gasp of relief as the wheels hit again, rolling onward—Oscar's feet controlling the board so that it darted side to side, side to side, *crack, crack, crack, crack,* at astonishing speed, and—

"Five!"

He was plunging deep into a scooped-out crevice, disappeared almost, then *whoosh,* up and out the other side, landing with a clatter, straightening again and—impossibly—up onto a long railing, scraping along it noisily and *thwack*—onto the surface—

"Four!"

The count now hushed with suspense, disbelief—another leap, crouched low, clutching the edges of the board with both hands—and *clunk*—landed again, wobbled, wobbled! His hands windmilled—he was going to fall! He would—

"Three . . ."

—the *three* was a horrified whisper——he righted himself, restored his balance, he was almost at the base, but hurtling along at such speed! How would he—

"*Two* . . ."

Pffffft, he had spun sideways, skidding and scraping, leaning almost to the ground, holding himself just so, until the board had slowed enough for him to leap off, run a few steps—propelled by momentum—then he touched a foot to the edge of the board, flipped it into the air, and caught it—all this in one gliding motion—and with a leap, he was up on the podium, board under his arm, as the crowd roared:

"*ONE!*"

—and Oscar faced the mountain and sang.

CHAPTER 89

OSCAR

YOU'RE SO HIGH! *Touch the sky!*
Make me sigh! Make me cry!
Melt away! Melt away! Away!
Hadn't even realized until that moment, facing the silver mountain, trying to get my breath back—legs still shaking—voice a bit shaky too—that, in the circumstances, the song made perfect sense.

CHAPTER 90

IMOGEN

 **OSCAR HAD MENTIONED** earlier that his mother used to praise his singing, and then he added that we should ignore her praise because she exaggerated.

Well, Oscar's mother might be unreliable on some issues, but on the issue of Oscar's voice, she was correct.

As he sang, my heart shone.

Smiles of wonder rippled across the crowd below too—and Bronte breathed, "My goodness."

The song's final word—*away*—faded into a deep, deep silence. The silence continued.

We all swung around to face that giant silver wave—a waterfall of silver—hanging in the air.

Had it worked?

We all held our breath, watching it.

It gathered itself.

It leaned toward us—

It hadn't worked!

And then it collapsed, fell like a curtain, forming a fine line of silver across the landscape that glinted once and then vanished.

When we turned back, breathing out long sighs of relief, shadows were crossing the face of the mountain like wind forming patterns in a wheat field.

From beneath us came a sound like a long, low sigh, and the silver began to melt.

It was a slow, slow tumbling into itself. It sagged and slid, like drizzle frosting, folding and twisting in place. Our picnic blanket slid down, down, down along with it, sometimes smoothly, sometimes bumping and tipping side to side, as if we were riding the back of a huge creature that was settling itself down for a sleep.

Our blanket stopped alongside the podium where Oscar still stood, looking uncertain.

Now the silver had sunk to the same shimmering cover it had been when we first arrived.

As we watched, the silver melted, pooling itself into a lake, then a pond, then dissolving into a fine silver powder—which floated away on the breeze.

Spread out before us was the city of Dun-sorey-lo-vay-lo-hey. Little houses, little schools, little banks, little shops, little roads, little parks, little gardens.

All of it empty.

All of it perfectly still.

The Elves?

Where were the Elves?

The entire crowd was silent.

Then I realized: "Esther," I hissed. "The Witches' spell! The Elves are probably still sleeping!"

Esther gave a soft gasp, then nodded and looked out over the city. Once again, she raised her hands—slowly; she was exhausted—and her movements were the gentle, graceful sweeps she uses when she cures.

"That should do it," she said after a moment and sat back down.

Another silence.

A *creaking* sound.

A pause.

Then doors began to fly open, and here they came, the Elves, each in pajamas or a nightgown, from every house and building, pouring into the streets in a smiling, waving stream. The crowd burst into riotous applause.

CHAPTER 91

OSCAR

THOUSANDS OF ELVES.
Scurrying along, chattering in teeny Elf voices, some springing up and down as they walked, some even carrying *baby Elves*!

Seriously. Baby Elves. Smaller than my pinkie fingernail.

I was grinning my head off—partly because the Elves were alive and free, and partly because they were Elves.

They all lined up in rows on their little Elven streets, one row forming behind another. When they'd stopped streaming out of their houses, one of them, a little guy in striped pajamas and a beret, came flying up to the podium, a bit like a large dragonfly. He settled down on the ledge where you might set a paper to read out.

"What's your name?" he asked me.

"Oscar."

"You quested alone?"

I was confused a moment, then realized what he meant. "No, no," I said. "Imogen and the others—right there. It was their quest. And the Elf twins—Gruffudd and Gruffydd."

The Elf nodded, tapped his throat with two fingers, and when he next spoke I almost toppled over in fright. His voice was suddenly amplified, see, as if he was speaking into a microphone at top volume.

"MY FELLOW ELVES!" he boomed. "THE AUDIENCE OF

OVERSIZE STRANGERS IN THE FIELDS AND LANE-
WAYS! I, KING MADDOX OF THE CITY OF DUN-SOREY-
LO-VAY-LO-HEY, *WELCOME* YOU!"

The Elves cheered. The crowds cheered. Even Imogen and
the others cheered.

"WE ARE SO— Hey, where are you going?"

He was talking to me. I had decided to slip down from the
lectern to join the others on the blanket.

"I just—" I began.

He frowned. "Get back here!"

I had to go stand on the podium again. This was awkward.
Beret guy had turned out to be an Elf king: it seemed to me he
deserved a podium to himself.

"WE ARE SO GLAD TO BE ALIVE!" the Elf king
continued—another cheer. He turned down the volume a fraction. Still amplified, but less thunderous. "Between us," he told
his audience, "I thought we were done for!"

Now the crowd laughed, which was an unexpected reaction.

"No, seriously," he told them. "The Doom Lantern Witches
cast a sleeping spell on us right before the silver waves were
due! I tried to summon the Rain Weaver, Esther, in time, only the
first silver wave came half an hour early—typical bright magic
being tricksy. *None* of the Elves who'd trained for the quest
were outside when the silver waves arrived! They were all
asleep!"

"Oh, my!" the crowd murmured, and all the little Elves in
their rows nodded solemnly: "Yes."

"We had *planned* to spend a pleasant few days doing jigsaw
puzzles and baking, confident that fifty of our strongest, brav-
est Elves would be questing. Instead, we have slept the days
away! We are well rested, of course—"

"Ah, yes. Of course," went whirring through the crowd.

"—Still, what a *state* I was in when I sent that letter to Esther!
Oh, the horror! The terror! However, I have awoken to relief
and joy! Thanks, it seems, to this boy named Oscar!"

More cheering. Some people shouted, "Oscar! Hoorah for
Oscar!" which was embarrassing.

"Oscar has earned the right to become our king," the Elf announced next. "The question remains: is he *worthy* to be king?"

I laughed then. "Nah," I said. "All I did was skate down a hill. It's Imogen and that lot who—"

"YOU ARE NOT AN EXPERT ON YOURSELF, OSCAR!" The booming microphone was back. "I WAS ASKING THAT QUESTION TO THE ELVEN TWINS! GRUFFUDD? GRUFF-YDD? I SUMMON YOU!"

And soaring down from the sky came the little Elf twins.

CHAPTER 92

IMOGEN

THE TWINS LANDED alongside the Elven king.

"Hello, sleepyhead!" said one.

"Your drowsy majesty!" added the other.

They giggled.

"Boys," the King replied, testily. "Amplify your voices and answer my question!"

The twins nodded. Their little fingers stitched rapid spells in the air, then both tapped their throats.

Now they spoke as if with a microphone, tone abruptly serious.

"We have quested with a fine group of children," began one.

"Those you see on the picnic blanket beside us," the other said with a nod.

"While the bright magic did its best to thwart them, trip them, skedaddle them, puzzle them, confuse and labyrinthine them . . ." began one twin.

". . . and while my brother and I did our best to frustrate them further—" put in the other.

"Well done, boys," the Elven king interjected.

". . . these children nevertheless carried on!"

A mighty cheer from the crowd.

"Hush," commanded a twin. "We are not finished."

"No," agreed the other. "Exhausted, hungry, and bewildered, they nevertheless gathered the nine pieces of key!"

Another cheer.

"As for this boy, this Oscar? You ask if he is worthy to be king?"

The King nodded.

"Here is what we observed of Oscar," the twins proclaimed, in unison.

"He is a boy from another world—"

"So he must have been more confused than any—"

"Yet, he kept his calm, he kept his humor—"

"Never lost his temper—"

"Never became cranky—"

"Even when his shin was badly gashed by a nail on the film set of Edward T. Vashing."

"Even when his forehead bled profusely after the river flung him from a boat."

"He saw to Astrid, who was ill with cold, before he saw to himself and that wound."

"He is a boy of much hidden sadness—"

"—yet does not allow his sadness to become violent or cruel."

"In fact, he listened to the others with compassion—"

"—and remembered the words the others spoke to him."

"He used those memories to distribute kindness—"

"—exactly when kindness was required—"

"—in a ritual he called a 'group therapy session.'"

"He brought harmony—"

"—when it was needed . . ."

"It was he who solved the puzzle of the musical key—"

"The greatest puzzle of all."

"*Moreover,* we have all just witnessed his considerable skill on this plank of wood with wheels—"

"—and we've all heard the beauty of his voice when he sings."

"But we have known from the first day of questing . . ."

"—from the very first piece of key . . ."

"—that Oscar was destined to be King of the Elves—"

"—for his approach to the game devised by the teacher Mrs. Chakrabarti."

"He played so well! To the north! To the south! And so on."

"And he—along with Esther, the Rain Weaver—deciphered the code in the game."

"Such that he could have *won* the game."

"Only he had also caught a trick. The clue in the teacher's words. That only *one* quester could win!"

"And thus he sacrificed himself—"

"—allowing Esther to win—"

"—thus saving the day—"

"And not *once* revealing that this was his intent all along."

"We saw it though."

"He smiled while the children in that playground laughed at him—"

"—without anger—"

"—without trying to explain—"

"He is the finest player of games."

"And thus he deserves to be king."

There was a pause.

"That's why we flew away," they both added. "And left it to Oscar to set the city free. No idea how he'd do it! But he did!"

The King raised his eyebrows. "You took a risk there, boys."

The twins shrugged. "It paid off."

"It did. And it seems you have done an excellent job as thwarters and observers, Gruffudd and Gruffydd. I thank you. Your city thanks you. Go see your parents—they'll be proud and want to hug you. Oscar?"

Oscar had been standing there all this time, turning different shades of crimson, embarrassed by the praise. His mouth had also twitched into smiles he could not help.

Now he answered, "Yes?"

"Will you be King of the Elves?"

Oscar smiled more broadly. "Thanks," he said, "but I've gotta get back to my own world. I wouldn't know how to be a king. Plus, I doubt I'd fit in your . . . city."

"Do not blame yourself for your size," the King told him kindly. "Another thing: kings do not *rule* our city. We have weekly votes for elected directors to do that. I happen to be on the board of directors along with three grandmothers and two aunts.

Kings have zero responsibility. They don't even necessarily *live* here, although they may visit whenever they like. You see, every hundred years, we seek out somebody with the *qualities* of a king so that we may crown them. It's usually an Elf, of course; however, it's technically open to anyone. Will you be King of the Elves?"

Oscar blinked, confused.

"As a bonus," the King said persuasively, "you will be endowed with one Elven power. When an *Elf* becomes king, their Elven powers are enhanced. That's what happened to me. However, a non-Elf may choose a single Elven power—and can use it without having to cast the spell for it. Options include things like occasional invisibility, curing minor ailments, enhanced leg muscles, the ability to understand the language of birds—they're terrible gossips, birds, I don't recommend that one—and several others. We'll give you a list."

Oscar looked tempted.

"At any rate," the King continued, "I'm not allowed to carry on being king. I've already had my hundred years. So somebody must take it. Final offer. Will you be King of the Elves?"

A long pause.

The crowd leaned forward, eager to hear his answer. The Elves waited patiently. I accidentally shouted: "Oscar! Say yes!"

"My issue," Oscar began—there was disgruntled muttering all around—"no, seriously, wait. My issue is that we all got the key together. Imogen, Esther, Astrid, Bronte, Alejandro, and Gruffudd—the twins, I guess—they did most of it. If I get to be king, they *all* deserve it too."

The twins flew back to the lectern.

"Isn't he kingly?" one of the Gruffudds whispered loudly.

"Indeed he is," the King himself agreed. "What do you say about this, twins?"

They considered.

"He's right," one said, "only those children are mostly already OP."

"Eh?"

"It means *overpowered*—we learned it from Oscar. Most of them don't need the gift of an extra Elven skill as they already have gifts of their own. We *should* give them all Elvish Medals for Bravery."

The King nodded. "These shall be conferred. We'll arrange a ceremony."

"Imogen, though . . ." The twins looked at each other.

"She was the leader," one said. "And a very good one. And no offense to her, but she's *not* OP like the others. Certainly, she's quite a good kickboxer, and I hear she can swim. Still, all she really has is determination."

The King nodded. "Sounds just like a queen. Come over here, Imogen."

While I was feeling embarrassed—and reasonably offended—the others laughed and pushed me toward the podium. I found myself standing next to Oscar.

"This is *truly* the final offer," the King said, frowning up at Oscar and me. "Will you, Oscar, and you, Imogen, be King and Queen of the Elves?"

Oscar looked at me. I looked back. His dimple appeared.

We both shrugged. "All right," we said.

The King beamed and switched to the loudest amplification: "THEY SAY *YES!*"

A huge burst of applause.

The King removed the crown protector from his own head—although Oscar had referred to it as a "beret" earlier, it's a cloth crown protector—revealing the golden crown beneath. He split it neatly into two halves—the top and the bottom—and handed one to Oscar and the other to me.

We looked at the little circles on our palms.

"I wouldn't put these on your heads," the King advised. "They will just get lost in your hair. Perhaps . . . perhaps wear them . . . there?"

He pointed at our hands.

Oscar slid the crown onto the pointer finger of his right

hand, and I did the same. The crowns slid into place like rings. We accidentally smiled.

And that is how a boy named Oscar from another world, and a girl named Imogen from our world (me), were crowned King and Queen of the Elven city of Dun-sorey-lo-vay-lo-hey.

CHAPTER 93

OSCAR

THE CROWD WHOOPED and hollered. Imogen and I couldn't help grinning at each other and over at the others—who didn't seem bothered that they'd missed out. Blushes kept washing over Imogen's face and I'm sure the same was happening to mine.

People rushed forward then—being careful not to stamp on Elves—scooped us both up onto their shoulders, and paraded around shouting: "The King of the Elves! The Queen of the Elves! Three cheers for the King and Queen of the Elves!"

The former king sat cross-legged on the podium smiling at all this. He seemed not to mind no longer being king.

There was a party then with crowds of both regular- and tiny-size people playing music, dancing, performing tricks and acrobatics, and setting off fireworks. The Elven music and dancing were especially impressive—they all ran back into their cute little houses, changed from their pajamas into party clothes, and came out with musical instruments.

A lot of treats were handed around—red-velvet chewy chocolate brownies, toffee cream cheese pies, butterscotch sticky buns—and everyone wanted to shake our hands and hear our stories.

Eventually, Imogen realized that it was almost time for her and the others to get the afternoon coach home—which meant I ought to try to go home myself.

We couldn't find the others in the crowd, so Imogen promised she'd say goodbye for me, and she and I walked across the city together. There was one main street, the width of a narrow footpath that ran right through. Even though it was pretty slow going, because of stepping over Elves, and because there were so many cute teeny things to look at—teeny swings and slides in parks, *teeny* flowerpots on window ledges, and so on—we got to the far end pretty fast. I couldn't tell exactly where I'd been when I first came through—it had been covered in silver then—but we stopped right at the edge of the city in an Elf's back garden and it seemed about right.

I was keen to get back to my own home, do some proper skating, see some buddies, watch some TV, play some Xbox, sleep in my own bed, get food from my own fridge—only I also felt pretty strange.

Once I was home, would I ever be able to come here again?

Come to think of it, how was I meant to get back?

"How do we return you to your world?" Imogen asked suddenly, speaking my thought aloud.

"Well, how did he come to be here in the first place?" said a voice—and there was Reuben the Genie.

His beard looked like it had been combed and trimmed. His skin looked a darker brown, like he'd been getting some sun.

Imogen's face, though, turned all kinds of colors—like a sunset really—as she blinked at him. "Reuben," she said. "I'm very sorry, ah—"

"Oh, the Genie bottle?" he interrupted. "Breaking it was exactly what I intended you do. How else would you get all those memories out? No regrets; let's move on. How did Oscar come here originally?"

"Mirrors," Imogen answered, her voice turning faint with relief. I guess she'd thought she was about to get severely busted for breaking the bottle. I'd forgotten about that.

"You looked at yourselves and you saw each other," Reuben corrected. "For Oscar to return, the reverse of that is necessary."

The reverse of that?

Tricky.

"Look at *each other*," Imogen said slowly, "and see . . . ourselves?"

"Exactly. That'll do the trick. It simply means to look into each other's eyes. Because you're so alike, the pair of you. So different, from different worlds, and yet so connected. I'll let you carry on." He swiveled around, but then swiveled back.

"One final thing," he said. "This issue you two have with magic. Oscar, you say there is none in your world; Imogen, you say you don't like it. Children, listen: magic is life. Life is twisty-turny, topsy-turvy, and breaks as many rules as bright magic. Life can be as dark and cruel as shadow magic. And life can zigzag between them both. You'll meet good people who are vain, self-absorbed, and careless, like the Crystal Faeries. You'll meet bad people who reform and start jewelry shops in cities. Wise old innkeepers will infuriate you with their absentmindedness yet surprise you with their generosity; distinguished judges will be mulish and cantankerous yet ultimately fair. Those meant to care for you will fail you, or fade from your life; strangers will offer shelter, or step in and become family. Find the thread of love and beauty in it all—beauty like occasional descriptive language, Imogen. Beauty like a kickflip for no reason, Oscar." He fell silent, gazing across the Elven city to the celebration. The sound of the party was fading, his words taking its place.

"Right, you'd best get home, Oscar," he said. "You can come back anytime, by the way. By moving through a crack between worlds in both directions, you open up a path that's just for you."

CHAPTER 94

IMOGEN

❦

 **OSCAR SMILED AT** that. He slung his backpack over his shoulder and propped his skateboard under his arm.

"Take a small step back, Imogen," Reuben said. "Take a small step forward, Oscar."

We both obeyed.

"I meant that metaphorically," he murmured, and he vanished.

Oscar chuckled. "Well," he said, "it's been real"—then he looked me in the eye and, like the Genie, he was gone.

As usual, I was confused by Oscar's turn of phrase for a moment. Still, it was true that it *had* been real. Those five days we spent together had been neither imagination nor fancy.

There were tears in my eyes then, which blurred my vision, so I thought I imagined it when I saw two familiar figures approaching carefully down the Elves' main street.

Then one of them called, "Imogen!" and I knew it was true. My parents had come to fetch us all home, and that's what made me properly cry—the fact that I didn't have to track down my sisters and cousins and our things, find our way to the coach stop, buy tickets, and get the coach home.

But that is incidental.

And now, Mrs. Kugelhopf, here it is.

A complete account of Monday through Friday of last week.

THURSDAY (THREE WEEKS LATER)

EPILOGUE

OSCAR

 **IMOGEN AND I** decided that our story needed a short postscript.

I'll start and say this: Reuben was right about me being able to get back to this world. All I have to do is return to the skate park where I first came through, and skate back. It's like a choice. People never notice me disappear. (Since then I've run into the two boys who first told me about "the other skate park." They seemed pretty embarrassed to have believed in it. They said an old guy with a beard had turned up and told them about it. He'd been so convincing they'd gone off to buy themselves a mirror.)

Anyhow, so I came back here to the Kingdoms and Empires the very next day, Saturday, and the Elves were welcoming and called me "Your Majesty." That was pretty funny.

They told me that Imogen and the others were still around and hadn't taken the coach back to the mountains yet.

Imogen's parents had decided to spend the rest of the school holiday at the Apple Blossom Bed and Breakfast with the kids. So I've been coming through each day after school ever since, and hanging out with them. It's good to get to know them without having to hunt down key keepers. We do more relaxed things, like go horse riding across the countryside, ride bikes, swim in a water hole, meet baby ducklings, chill with the Elves.

Also, of course, Imogen and I have been writing our account for Mrs. Kugelhopf.

When I gave it to her, though, Mrs. Kugelhopf flicked through the pages, then chucked it in her wastepaper basket. She gave me a lecture about how I had "clearly stolen somebody else's school assignment."

I should have guessed she wouldn't read it. She never wants the truth—I've told her so many times that I was mucking up because I was bored out of my mind, and that only ever makes her angrier. All she *actually* wants is for me to say that I'm a terrible human being who's been wasting time in a skate park and that I'm sorry and will never do it again.

Ah, well. I'm still glad we wrote it. It's good to have a record. You forget things otherwise. I fished it out of her wastepaper basket, shook it clean, and left.

The other thing we've been doing is looking through the list of Elven powers. It needed a big magnifying glass to read. Funnily enough, Imogen and I both chose the exact same power. I'll leave it to Imogen to tell you what we chose.

IMOGEN

YES. IT WAS a good choice.

In other news, we heard the other day that the Doom Lantern Witches had tried to attack Mrs. Chakrabarti's school. Only, they found that their broomstick crochet had absolutely no effect. The schoolchildren were able to overcome them and lock them in the school supply closet, and Mrs. Chakrabarti then forced them do a number of cleaning chores.

We were all having ice cream sodas to celebrate this news, and laughing with delight that Esther's spell had been successful, when Alejandro spoke up. "Esther, if you can weave cures into a sock, what if you could weave them into stories?"

As I've mentioned, Alejandro is very good at gadgets and repairs, using whatever object is at hand, and I think he was applying that lateral thinking here. Esther is extremely excited by the idea and she has made her first attempt on our account of Monday-to-Friday (retrieved from Mrs. Kugelhopf's waste-paper bin).

She says that it has now been spelled so that anyone who reads its words will be immediately cured if they are affected by shadow magic. If they are *not* affected by shadow magic, Esther says, the spell will transmute so that the next time the reader feels cranky, sad, lonely, or confused, that emotion will fall away, replaced by a swelling of joy in the heart.

It's been wonderful having Oscar visit each afternoon after his day at school. (He says that he does have homework, only he finds it "unnecessary.") As well as having fun using our new power, Oscar has been teaching us all to ride his skateboard—it's much trickier than it looks, and Bronte is the best at it so far.

Another thing I've done is to make telephone calls to the principal of Nicholas Valley Boarding School for Boys. This is in the next valley along from our own boarding school, the Katherine Valley Boarding School for Girls. The school has a division especially for students with concentration issues—they do most of their learning outside in the form of games—and they have agreed to offer a scholarship to Oscar. My parents were helpful with this as my father is an esteemed history professor, and my mother does something important to do with committees. Not sure what. My parents spoke to the principal of Nicholas Valley Boarding School for me, and they were very persuasive, pointing out that a boy who had been crowned an Elven king and who came from another world would be an asset to their school.

Therefore, when we go back to school next week, Oscar will be at the school that is close by. He will be well fed there, and well taken care of, and will not need to sleep with a baseball bat by his bed. We will be able to meet up with him in Pillar Box Town and keep an eye on him.

Also, we have invited him to spend school holidays with our family whenever he likes. *We* can be his family. (Although, I've told him he should have a serious talk with his mother about how his life has looked lately, and how that makes him feel. And what about his father's family in the Kingdoms of California and Chile? He should ask about contacting them. Maybe they are better family than his mother and stepfather? He has promised to try. He mentioned that I have not exactly "taken a step back," despite Reuben's advice. He was smiling as he said that though.)

Finally, I don't think I'll tell you the Elven power we chose. Instead, I'll finish with this newspaper article. Oscar tells me it was "posted online" yesterday and that he "printed it out" to show me. I don't know what any of that means, but read it, if you like: it contains a strong clue about our choice.

DRAMATIC RESCUE CAUGHT ON FILM:

HOAX OR THE REAL DEAL?

www.news.com.au

REMARKABLE FOOTAGE IS currently circulating on social media, apparently taken at a school in Sydney's Lower North Shore.

In the brief clip, a very young child, around four years old, is seen climbing along the roof of a school building that is two stories high. The child was precariously close to the edge, so this is heart-stopping footage, distressing to watch.

In the next shot, a boy of twelve literally "soars" through the air. After "hovering" by the toddler for a few moments, he reaches out his hands, gathers up the child, and "flies" back to safety on the ground below.

While the clip is obviously a hoax, we contacted the school for comment and were able to speak with the deputy principal, Clara Kugelhopf. That's where our story takes an unexpected turn.

"It all happened exactly as you see in the video," Mrs. Kugelhopf insisted. "My little boy Eddie was at school with me that day, as he had a cold and couldn't go to preschool. Well, one moment he was playing with his coloring-in books on my office floor, the next I heard screams from the school playground.

"When I ran outside I saw Eddie climbing up the scaffolding that had been placed there by window cleaners. He loves to climb. He'd already reached the roof and must have decided to explore. Honestly, I have never been so terrified in my life. My heart was in my throat. A moment later, though, one of our students flew through the air, lifted Eddie from the roof, and carried him safely to the ground."

When pressed to explain how the school had edited the footage to make both the danger to Eddie and the boy's flight appear so convincing, Mrs. Kugelhopf doubled down on her story. "I'm not joking! The footage is the real deal!" she exclaimed. "Eddie was in *life-threatening* danger and it turns out that that child—truly a gem of a child, oh, what a lovely boy—can *literally* fly. He is apparently leaving our school next week though, which just absolutely breaks my heart."

We tracked down the boy himself in a local skate park. "No comment," he said with a crooked smile—and he skated out of sight.

ACKNOWLEDGMENTS

Thank you so much to the superb people at Levine Querido, especially the truly wonderful Arthur Levine and Madelyn McZeal: you are insightful, brilliant, funny and very, very patient.

To Antonio Gonzalez Cerna and Irene Vazquez, thank you for your marketing and publicity prowess and kindness. Thank you to Susan M. S. Brown for copy-editing, Liberty Martin for proofreading, and Paul Kepple for interiors.

I am speechless with delight over Jim Tierney's cover for this book, and very, very grateful to him.

Special thanks also to my Australian and UK publishers (Allen & Unwin, and Guppy Books, respectively), to my fantastic agents, Tara Wynne and Jill Grinberg; to Laura Bloom, Jared Thomas and Michael McCabe, who all answered text requests for help like lightning (comprehensive, very helpful lightning); to Rachel Cohn and Corrie Stepan; to my nieces and nephews; to the Menasse family; to my sister Liane, without whose kind and considerable support this book would have dissolved into a puddle; to my other sisters, Kati, Fiona and Nicola, who each deserve individualized praise of their own but I'm already going on too long; to Mum, who is so lovely and funny; to Dad, who I know is still right here with us, as exuberant as ever; to my Charlie (and his skater friends) for the inspiration and expertise—and for being your own hilarious, thoughtful and original self; and to Nod, who knows how to make life an adventure.

Some Notes on This Book's Production

The art for the jacket and the title lettering were hand-drawn by Jim Tierney using a Cintiq tablet and Adobe Photoshop. The text was set by Westchester Publishing Services in Danbury, CT. The body text is set in Gazette, designed in 1977 at D. Stempel AG, a type foundry in Frankfurt founded by David Stempel in 1895. The Gazette font family was designed to with newspaper print in mind; to withstand high-speed presses and coarse newsprint, and to guarantee legibility despite long press runs. The chapter headings are set in Rough Cut, a sturdy, gothic font designed by Simon Walker, and the illustrated framings for each initial cap were created by Jim Tierney. The book is printed on 78 gsm Yunshidai Ivory woodfree FSC-certified paper and bound at R R Donnelly in China.

Production was supervised by Freesia Blizard

Jacket design by Jim Tierney

Interior design by Paul Kepple at Headcase Design

Editor: Arthur A. Levine

Editorial Assistant: Madelyn McZeal

LEVINE QUERIDO